CREEDoR

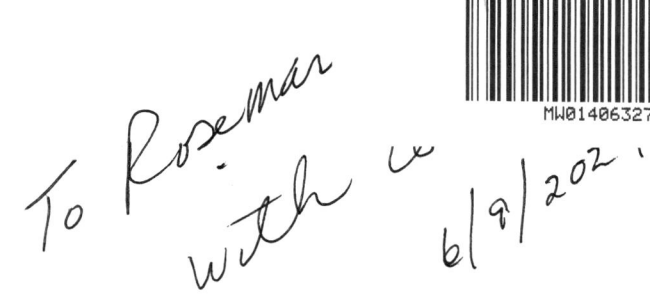

by

Gail Morgan McRae

REVISED 2020

CREEDOR

Gail Morgan McRae

REVISED 2020

Creedor is a work of fiction. Any resemblance to any person, living or dead, with the exception of historical figures, is purely coincidental.

Creedor

Copyright © 2013 by Gail Morgan McRae Published by Hickory Grove Press (NC) 2015 – **Revised 2020**

All rights reserved. No part of this book may be reproduced or transmitted in any form or by any means without written permission of the publisher who may be contacted via email at hickorygrovepressnc@gmail.com.

ISBN: 9781670422903

Other books by Gail Morgan McRae include Hellritch, Part 2 of the Reglon Empire Series, and Dunmyrr, Part 3 of the Reglon Empire Series.

Dedication

This book is dedicated to the fans of Creedor and rest of
the Reglon Empire Series who've supported
my efforts all these years.
Thank you!

THE RIDER

He leaned against the skiabar tree; shadows hid his watching. How long would he have before he was summoned again? Brushing the remnants of his meal from his tunic, the Rider turned back to his world. How odd, to live between times, among the infinity of the universe.

It's just my luck to be assigned to these people who ruined their own planet and then came here with no plan and hardly any of their technology. And now they're ruining these worlds, too. What can I do? Nothing.

He sighed. His young son slid clumsily from the tree across the clearing. He'd been trying desperately to ride as his father did, effortlessly and undetected. At his age, the boy should be riding by now, but it was a parent's duty to teach his child, and Rax had not been there.

Oh, well. He's still young. He walked over, picked up the disappointed boy and wrapped his arms around him.

With a pop, they disappeared into the nothingness that took them home.

THE CAMDUS FAMILY

Camdus sat with his mom and dad, Rose and Willem, on their patio. He shared his mom's good cooking and his dad's wisdom laced with humor. Soon young Michael Camdus would be off to the military academy, leaving his home to follow his dream. But his parents were okay with that; at least Willem was. Willem had served, so he expected his son would want to serve as well.

As the day waned and the conversation became serious, Rose went inside to clean the kitchen – and maybe shed a tear or two. Willem took this opportunity to give his son a gift – a tredon leather pouch on a chain.

"Uh, what's this, Dad?"

"Well, Michael, I can't tell you right now. And you have to promise to keep it with you always and not to open it until you've run out of options."

"I'm confused, but I trust you, Dad, so I promise."

He put the pouch around his neck and dropped it inside his shirt.

Willem smiled.

They watched the sun set behind the trees, marking more than the end of the day. This sunset marked a new beginning for the Camdus family.

THE CHANGING OF THE GUARD

Horatio Borm, Emperor of the Reglon Empire, sat staring at the plate of food his wife set down in front of him. He lifted a forkful of the succulent roast pig to his mouth and gagged.

"Blast it all," the normally reverent man swore under his breath. Food had lost its flavor and so had his life.

His wife, Andria, got up from her seat, walked from the other end of the long table. She placed her arms around his shoulders.

"Horatio, you should eat. Please try. Do it for me."

"It'll do no good even if I do. It's down and up these days, you know."

His words pierced her heart. She handed him a glass of thick green liquid.

"Well, at least drink this," she said hopefully.

He tried sipping it first. "Yecchh," he said before he could stop himself, but he gulped it down anyway. Though he could feel it churning in his gut, the hopeful look on Andria's face gave him the determination to keep it down.

"I need to rest now, Andy," he said, wiping his mouth with the freshly pressed cotton napkin. "Please tell Vandalen to handle the meeting for me this evening. I'll try to join them later."

Horatio hoisted his frail body up and tentatively shuffled through the side door to their bed chamber. She helped him lie down on their four-poster bed. His polished tredon leather shoes clattered to the floor.

Andria slumped in the plush wingback chair beside his bed and watched him drift off to sleep. After a few minutes of giving in, she roughly wiped away her tears as if wiping away the illness that was consuming her husband.

She closed her eyes and allowed herself to remember the days when they had been so young and carefree. Horatio had been so handsome, with his wavy hair and piercing green eyes. He had taken her breath away. She laughed softly remembering how she'd pretended not to notice him. And just as she planned, he hadn't been able to stand it. Pretty soon it was clear to everyone but him that he'd chased her until she caught him.

"Rats," she whispered as she remembered what he'd asked her to do. She leaned over and gave him a gentle kiss. Then she tiptoed to the door, quietly closed it behind her, and went to find Vandalen. She had long since stopped trusting any other form of communication.

Down the long, dimly lit hall, through the arched stone passageways, and down yet again she went to the mysterious quarters of the resident wizard. Andria stopped outside the roughly hewn oak door, took a breath, and knocked. She heard the familiar, firm steps approach. The door opened to reveal Vandalen, wizard extraordinaire and her husband's most trusted advisor.

"Again?"

"I'm afraid so. He's resting now, but he won't be able to attend his Council meeting tonight. He's asked if you…,"

"It's okay, Andria, please tell him I'll handle it. He shouldn't be worrying about anything, especially not right now, not while he's so sick."

"Yes, I know he's sick, but what are we going to do about someone trying to kill him?!"

"Andria, the rumors of an assassination plot are just that – rumors. We have no proof, none."

If she'd been looking, Andria would have seen the doubt in his eyes as he spoke those words. But she was intently studying the large book that lay open on the long bench sitting in the middle of his low-ceilinged room. Well-worn, yellowed pages hinted at the book's advanced age.

"What are these symbols?"

She traced the fingers of her right hand over the oddly shaped characters, felt a tingling sensation that was both exciting and a little scary. She pulled her hand away, subconsciously rubbing her fingertips.

"I'm not sure yet. I've been studying them for over a week. Every time I think I've figured it out, pretty soon it's clear that I haven't. It's quite maddening, you know."

He carefully closed the book. Then he looked down at Andria. He didn't see the care-worn face that everyone else saw. No, he still saw the graceful, strong woman who had become as much a friend to him and his wife as Horatio had. Yet he knew she did not need to be in his chamber right now. Even though he trusted her completely, he didn't know if she'd approve of what he was working on.

"Maybe you should go back and sit with Horatio. You don't want him to wake up alone, do you?"

"No, of course not. You're right."

With one last look toward the bench, Andria headed back to her ailing husband's side.

Vandalen sent for the Rider, whose soft pop alerted the wizard to his arrival.

"Umm, Rax. Woke you again, I see. Pop back home, change your clothes, and then come back, okay?"

Vandalen had to bite his lip to keep a straight face.

Rax rubbed his sleepy eyes with his fists and looked down. He blushed brightly when he realized he was wearing his old, red flannel pajamas. An equally worn red gingham night cap completed his comical look.

"At once."

Rax popped out as quickly as he'd come.

Vandalen shook his head and opened the book again. The passage he'd been studying was beginning to make sense – at least in part. What it revealed was troubling and would surely set Horatio off if he knew. Too much was at stake. And as much as he admired Horatio, Vandalen knew that he was no longer able to handle anything major.

No, I gotta take care of this one myself.

He cleared off the top of the old trunk that sat at the end of his work bench. He closed his eyes and carefully opened it. Blinding light flooded the room. Rolling up his sleeves, Vandalen plunged his hands into the trunk and pulled out a brilliantly glowing skull.

"Why have you disturbed me, Wizard?" the skull asked in a raspy voice.

"I need your help, Oscar."

"What sort of help?"

"I need to brew a potion to heal the Emperor, for starters."

The skull went dark for a moment then glowed blue.

"There is no potion that will heal him for his time is upon him. Do not try to interfere. If you do, it will only bring you grief."

Oscar went dark again.

Vandalen waited for it to speak again. When it didn't, he asked another question.

"What should I be doing, then?"

"Watch out for the peacock."

"What? Watch out for the peacock? That's it? That's all you've got? At least tell me *which* peacock."

But Oscar had gone completely dark this time, and Vandalen knew he was wasting his breath. *A peacock, really, a peacock?*

"Damn it all to hell, Oscar!"

He jammed the skull back into the trunk, slamming the lid out of frustration.

Just at that moment Rax returned, appearing so close to Vandalen that the startled wizard abruptly whirled around.

Rax took one long step back just in time to miss the small red fireball that whizzed past his chin.

"Sorry," Vandalen said after he regained his composure. Then he gave Rax a new task.

"There's something ugly afoot tonight, Rax. Find who's responsible and bring whoever it is to me. But not until after midnight; I'll be gone until then."

The sleepy but properly attired Rider nodded and popped out again.

Vandalen took a deep breath and brushed the dust from his robe. Then he picked up the notes he'd taken the last time Horatio had briefed him. After securing his quarters, he climbed the staircase to the upper level where the meeting would soon begin.

The room was already filled with Council members, some seated, patiently waiting for Emperor Borm. Others milled around, talking. Only two stood by the massive hearth warming their hands by the fire. Elder Spetch and Jarlod, Supreme Commander of the Reglon Empire Guard, were in a deep, whispered conversation.

Vandalen made note of this and then took Emperor Borm's seat.

No one was surprised; they'd gotten used to the Elder's absences in recent months.

"Gentlemen – and Lady," Vandalen said by way of address to the Council, "I'm afraid Emperor Borm is indisposed."

"Well, big surprise there," Elder Kiza sneered, flipping her long, dull gray hair which fell like cur-grass on her bony shoulders.

Vandalen ignored her. He was fed up with her snarky attitude and figured most of the Council members were as well.

Kiza was the only woman on the Council, having been a member for just five years. Before that, she had been an academic aspiring to become the Superintendent of Education for the entire Reglon Empire. However, each time the position had come open, she'd been passed over. She told anyone who'd listen that Emperor Borm was retaliating because she'd rejected his advances. But they knew she was lying. No, she'd been passed over because she had made some irresponsible decisions as Sociology Department Chair. Deciding to dispense with seats in the classrooms was one of them. When complaints started coming in, she was brought before the Superintendent. She explained that she'd been running a sociological experiment. The fact was she hadn't asked approval from her superiors. She also couldn't explain the scientific value of such an experiment. But the worst part was she didn't tell her students that they were being used as human guinea pigs. However, she had persevered by apologizing and vowing never to do it again.

When the opportunity presented itself fifteen years later with any record of her problems long gone, she landed this seat on the Council. She'd never questioned how she got the position, but the truth was the Superintendent wanted her out of the classroom and away from the students; he was just glad to see her go. He couldn't have known that Emperor Borm would not remember what she'd done and would give her even more authority over the education of the Reglon children.

Vandalen wanted to get this meeting over with as quickly as possible so he could get back to the cryptic text in his chambers.

"Reports first. Elder Kiza, please give us an update on what's going on in the EdTech Department," Vandalen said, trying to maintain a respectful tone.

"Well, as you know, Emperor Borm has cut our budget severely this year, but we have managed. Our Level Ones are doing quite well now that we've removed their social interaction time and are enforcing silence throughout the facilities, except for the classrooms, of course. The Level Twos are not performing quite as well, but we've taken care of the problem with alternative programs." She held up her scarf, a sad affair poorly constructed of kittle yarn and cheap bells.

"They are learning trades – quite nicely, I think," she added. "This is one of the items they made in Fabrication 101."

Some of the Elders groaned.

"And the Level Threes?" Vandalen asked.

"Well, they're a work in progress you might say because so many of them are just too uncooperative. We're regrouping to discover a way to keep them inside the unit. Apparently, the lure of the woods behind it is quite tempting. But we've only lost three this semester," Kiza replied, still somewhat miffed at the reaction to her scarf.

"Have you made Emperor Borm aware of this situation?"

"Borm doesn't need to know," she flung back.

"Really? I beg to differ. Have you done anything to find them?"

"Well, sure, we sent the custodians out to look for them, but they were able to get just so far before the brambles blocked their way. But then you, of all people, should know that."

Vandalen ignored the implied insult. "We'll bring them home, Elder Kiza, which is what you should've done."

He felt his anger rising but knew he couldn't give in to it. That was the surest way to hand over control of the situation to the jackals on the Council. Instead, he looked at the secretary making a holographic record of the meeting and said, "Miss, please take a moment and contact the authorities."

Then he said to Jarlod, "Just to be on the safe side, I want you to personally lead a search and rescue unit. I'll need a full report for Emperor Borm when the lost students have been rescued."

Vandalen could see that Jarlod wasn't pleased, but he didn't care. He didn't trust him and wanted to get him away from the palace.

The secretary stepped out, while Jarlod sent a message to the captain of the local search and rescue unit to get ready.

Vandalen gave the Council a break until the secretary returned. He noticed Spetch seemed restless and approached him.

"What's on your mind?" he asked the startled elder.

"Well, since you asked, I'm getting tired of these senseless meetings. There are more important uses of my time."

Vandalen understood his frustration because he felt it, too, though no doubt his frustration differed from the Elder's.

The secretary returned before he could pursue this conversation. As soon as she resumed her perch on the stool in the corner, Vandalen said, "Now, please take your seats. Let's move on, shall we? Elder Spetch?"

Spetch was a thin, middle-aged man with sharp features and eyes too close together to inspire trust.

Vandalen had never liked Spetch, who to him was nothing more than a sycophant fawning over the Emperor, flattering him at every turn as he tried to gain his favor. After their interrupted conversation, Vandalen liked him even less.

Spetch pushed back his chair and stood before he answered. "The plans for the new trizactl mine are coming along just a little slow. We've had a glitch with the drill. Apparently, Creedor has a very hard substratum for all its damnable sand swirling around." Spetch was hoping Vandalen would not ask for more information. He was disappointed.

"What kind of problem?" Vandalen asked.

"The bits cut through the crust like it's made of woely pudding for about a thousand feet, and then they get stuck. We can't go in any deeper and we can't get the bits out. We have to saw them off and start at a new location. But the good news is we think we've found a softer place near one of the valleys. We're scheduled to begin work there within the next three weeks."

"Three weeks? Why the delay?" Vandalen knew that they needed the trizactl now more than ever. This mineral was crucial for their power plants and for their military.

"Our men are tired. They've been going nonstop for weeks. They have to rest, or you'll get nothing from them." Spetch was tired, too, tired of waiting. He checked himself before he said too much.

"That's about it for mining. Hopefully, I'll be able to report a breakthrough at our next meeting," he said. Some of them smiled at the unintended pun.

"Thank you, Elder Spetch. Now, Elder Arking," Vandalen looked at the balding man who authorized the troop deployments.

Tomer Arking was one of the humblest people Vandalen had ever known. And he always made time for this elder whenever he stopped by.

Elder Arking stood up slowly, his joints sounding off like the popping of a rusty Rider. "Sorry," he apologized. "It seems my poor old bones want to be heard today, too." Some of the other elders knew exactly what he was talking about and laughed out loud.

He continued, "I'm pleased to report that construction of the Base Camp Entellés on Reglon Minor is now finished and fully staffed. We've begun exploring the uncharted planets nearby. We're also conducting some domestic crop production experiments to enhance our food supply," Elder Arking said and sat down, glad to be off his feet again. His knees were throbbing like a toothache.

"Thank you. Commander Jarlod, let's hear your report."

Jarlod stood, swept to the center of the room, and gestured grandly.

"This, all of it, is possible because my military are the finest to be found," he boasted as he began to pace.

Oh, my Lord, spare us another session of self-adoration from this jackass. Vandalen clenched his jaw as he prepared for the dung that was about to be piled too high.

"I believe you mean *our* military but go on."

"Yes, of course. My, I mean *our* soldiers have been vigilantly protecting Elsnith Oasis. Dozens of peasants and their filthy brats have been removed." Jarlod paused, expecting applause which only came from Spetch and Kiza.

"Jarlod, to the point please," Vandalen prompted.

"Yes, well then. We have completed our latest covert operation on Q'Arrel. Unfortunately, Hellritch got away again, but we were able to collect data on their weaponry. We also managed to place spies in the palace itself but had to abort. So, we didn't get what we wanted, but what we got elsewhere is very valuable, very valuable, indeed," Jarlod glossed over the truth, hoping for no further questions.

Vandalen raised an eyebrow but continued, "Elder Weilz, please give us a report on Domestic Affairs."

Weilz, a rather round family man with five children, was pleased to report.

"My sons have both finished their courses at University, and my daughters hopefully are all following in their mother's footsteps. The two older girls already have established a couture house together, specializing in the finest tredon leather creations. And Lulu, our bonus baby, is …."

Vandalen interrupted, "I meant the Domestic Affairs of the Empire."

"Oh, yes, well, of course. Our factories are running at about three quarters capacity, employment is down. The value of our currency has dropped, and we've fallen behind in our infrastructure repairs. Other than that, we're doing fine. Thank you," he said and sat down. He was somewhat offended that his personal domestic affairs would not be heard yet again.

"It sounds like a dire situation, indeed. Do you have any suggestions?" Vandalen asked.

Weilz had thought about that a great deal, but Emperor Borm had not seemed interested during Council meetings, and Weilz had not been able to get an appointment with him to discuss his ideas.

"Well, for one thing, we can establish trading partners with other empires for commodities not available here. But, in my opinion, we should stop farming out our work to the colonies. The labor's cheap, but we need to keep more jobs here. I'd like to see us reward companies that use Empire citizens to repair the infrastructure. If we did that, we'd have jobs and better roads and communications and ...."

When he paused for a breath, Vandalen interrupted again. "These all sound like good ideas. Do you have them written down? I'd like to run them by the Emperor."

Weilz pulled a sheaf of papers from beneath his robe and passed it to Vandalen.

"Thank you. We'll get back to you after the Emperor has had time to study them."

Vandalen glanced at the detailed recommendations on the papers Weilz had presented and was genuinely surprised at the depth of thought he had given these issues. He was pleased that Weilz had researched and analyzed potential solutions. *Impressive.*

"Does anyone else have anything?" Vandalen asked the group, some of whom had nodded off.

Kiza looked as if she wanted to add something, but hostile looks caused her to reconsider.

"Then meeting adjourned," Vandalen said and walked over to the most ancient of the Elders to wake him, surprised that the jangling bells of Kiza's scarf hadn't already.

"Elder Addler, Sir, please wake up. The meeting's over; everyone's gone," he said as he gently tapped the old man's shoulder.

"What? What's that you say? Over? But I just got here. Was there anything new?" the befuddled Elder sputtered, his bushy white eyebrows twitching like two granddaddy longlegs spiders caught in a brisk wind.

"Well, not new exactly, but interesting. I'll make sure you get a holocopy of the meeting," he said as he helped Addler to his feet.

Just as he got to the door, Addler turned back to face Vandalen, his eyes suddenly clear. He stood up straight and said in a remarkably strong voice, "Watch Jarlod, Commander. Watch him. There is a darkness in him that I do not trust." With that, he resumed his befuddled demeanor, doddered out, and disappeared down the long hallway.

Somewhat surprised by what was shared in the meeting and not a little troubled by Elder Addler's comments, Vandalen went back to his quarters. He checked to see that no one was lurking about before he removed the security enchantment and went inside. He was relieved to find the book as he had left it. He went back to it and read the passage again. Addler had just reinforced what it said and most surely revealed the identity of the would-be perpetrator.

Vandalen stood up straight, stretched his back and in that instant, he had the answer.

Jarlod! He's the peacock.

He shook his head again at the strange turns this day had taken. He had to tell Horatio, but he knew that getting the Emperor to believe any of it was a long shot. Vandalen figured he'd start by telling him about Entellés Base Camp's completion. He also wanted to share Elder Weilz' suggestions. He hoped that would make talking to him about Jarlod and the threats on his life a little easier.

Though it was getting late, the wizard left the room, secured it, and climbed the many stairs to Horatio's sitting room. He knocked on the door and waited.

In a few moments, Andria opened the door. He could see that she had been crying again. She stepped aside and let him enter.

"How is he?" he gently asked the distraught woman.

"He's sleeping now. I slipped a potion into his milk to give him at least a bit of peace," she said, weeping openly now.

Vandalen stepped close to comfort her. She leaned into his arms and gratefully accepted the hug. Just for a moment, she let herself find comfort there. She laid her head on his chest and wept softly.

He could feel her strength returning as she tensed against him, but he didn't say anything. He just held her until she felt like stepping away. Though he'd known Andria and Horatio for many years, this was still awkward for him. But he endured because he felt the need to do something to offer her comfort, even if all it meant was holding her long enough for her to get a grip.

When she let go and stepped away, he said, "If you'll allow her to, I know Nell would like to come stay with you awhile, maybe sit with Horatio, so you can get a little rest. Would you like that?"

"Oh, yes. Yes, I would. I haven't had a visitor in such a long time. You know, Nell and I used to have such lovely chats. Please tell her for me," she said, then added, "and thank you, Van, for being there for us. It means so much to him – and to me."

This conversation was making him a bit uncomfortable, so he changed the subject. "When do you think he'll be up for a briefing? We need to discuss some issues, and I really think he should be the one to make the decisions."

Just then the door opened, and Horatio stood there smiling. Andria and Vandalen thought they were seeing a ghost.

"Oh posh, you two. I don't know what was in that last concoction you gave me, Andy, but I feel so much better – and stronger." He flexed his muscles, drawing surprised laughter from Andria and Vandalen. "Tasted worse than anything I've ever put in my mouth, but I'll take it again if it makes me feel this good. Now tell me, Van. How did the meeting go?"

Andria grabbed her husband and gave him a big hug and a kiss.

"Ewww! Go brush your teeth, Horatio, your breath is awful!"

Vandalen chuckled at this exchange, but Horatio disappeared into their chamber only to appear a few minutes later blowing air from his now clean mouth.

"Ahh, fresh as can be. Now how about another kiss, my bride?"

Andria gave him a tender kiss and left the two men to discuss the Empire's business.

Once he was sure she was gone, Borm invited Vandalen to sit.

"It wasn't the elixir. I asked the doctor for something strong to kill the pain. I don't think I have much time left, and I want to make sure that Andy and the Empire will be safe when I'm gone."

Vandalen was quiet. Oscar said Horatio's time was nearing the end. But the wizard wasn't going to tell him that. No, but he needed to tell him about the plot on his life. If the man had to die, it should be of natural causes. He didn't know how to explain all he'd learned and absolutely didn't intend to tell him how he'd learned it.

Horatio could see that Vandalen was struggling with something, so like always he took charge.

"Just say whatever's sticking in your craw. We've been friends way too long for you to hold back now."

Relieved, Vandalen reviewed everything he'd learned from translating the passage in the book and what Addler had told him afterwards.

"I'm not surprised. Jarlod was always ambitious. Too bad he can't wait for an old man to die. But he cannot rule after I'm gone; he must not. If he takes control, no good will come of it. He'll destroy the Empire with his lust for things and power. You know, Van, before Jarlod, I thought I was a pretty good judge of character. He had me fooled. And if he murders me, it'll be as much my fault as his," Horatio said sadly. But then he added, "Still, I don't want him to know how sick I really am. And I don't want him to quench his thirst for power with my blood. But he knows; he knows. If he doesn't kill me first, he'll never get his hands on the Empire – at least as long as you're alive. Be careful, Van. He lets nothing get in the way of his desires. I imagine he'll enjoy taking both our lives to become emperor."

Vandalen figured Jarlod was going to try to do that anyway but decided it would be cruel to say so.

"Van, when I'm gone, I want you to look out for Andy. You know we never had children and her family's all gone now. You and Nell will be all she has left," he said somberly.

Vandalen could see the pain in his old friend's eyes.

"You don't have to ask me that, Horatio. You know we'll look out for her. But you shouldn't be talking like this. You should be trying to find a cure, not planning for ... well, for after ... you know," he said, reluctant to talk about this particular inevitability.

"Now's not the time for tiptoeing around the facts. Jarlod will take over if you don't stop him. I trust you and know that you'd lead the Reglon Empire fairly and successfully.

Will you take it?"

"That's a huge responsibility, Horatio, and some of your Elders would just as soon I didn't exist. How's that going to work?"

"It'll work if I decree it," Horatio declared. "Think it over for a day or two, and then we'll talk again. Now I'm going to find my sweet wife and take her to the kitchen for a tredon steak that I intend to cook for her myself."

As he walked with him to the stairs, he noticed that Horatio had a smile on his face and a spring in his step. It had been a long time since he'd seen this in Emperor Borm, and he welcomed it – drug-induced or not.

Vandalen's mind was flooded with troubling thoughts as he made his way back down to his chambers more slowly this time; his body seemed as heavy as his heart.

When he got to his door, he checked the alcove to be he sure was alone, then he removed the enchantments. He stepped inside just as the clock struck twelve midnight. He sat down, still thinking about the events of the day.

The soft pop that signaled the Rider's return brought him to his feet. A tall, dark-haired witch stood smiling blissfully beside Rax, who was clearly trying to remove himself from her presence.

"Well, who do we have here?" Vandalen asked, unsure of why Rax had brought her to him.

"Elga, me lord," the witch answered, somewhat sobered at the realization that she was in the presence of none other than the greatest wizard in the Empire.

Vandalen looked at the Rider for explanation, but Rax said nothing.

Not to be deterred, he asked, "Rax, why did you bring Elga to me? That wasn't your assignment."

Rax reached for the witch's robe, but she slapped his hand away.

"Dere now, don't you get fresh wi' me, you overgrown beanpole. I came wi' you 'cause I thought you 'uz a wantin' some feminine company, if you know whad I mean. But I draws the line at sharing the table with some un else, even the great Wizard Vandalen," Elga said indignantly.

"No, Madam, I'm sorry you misunderstood. I most certainly do not wish to share your company, nor did I say that when I asked you to come with me. However, I would appreciate it if you'd lift your robe just above your ankles, please," Rax replied.

Elga reached for something inside her robe. Vandalen stopped her.

"Please, Elga. I promise no harm is intended."

Elga shrugged. She had always thought that Vandalen was the most handsome as well as the most powerful of all the wizards and had secretly been jealous when he'd married the Ordinary. And now as she stood in his presence, she was keenly aware of how inadequate her powers were. She grabbed the dusty, green robe with her grimy hands and lifted it just a bit to reveal a perfectly formed right foot covered discretely with a purple satin slipper.

"Rax, please explain."

Rax frowned at Elga. "Madam, show us your left."

The wizard drew a sharp breath when she stuck out her other foot. Grossly deformed and covered in coarse black hair, this foot looked like a mangy wharf rat. Its crusty, yellow-gray toenails gave the unforgettable impression of gnarly teeth. Vandalen shuddered.

Elga mistook his reaction and sidled up to him. He quickly walked to the other side of his table, giving him a buffer.

"I'm sorry for your inconvenience, Elga, but I see that there's been a serious misunderstanding," he said, trying hard to keep a straight face.

"Please return Elga to her home, Rax. Then you are relieved for the evening."

"But I...," she sputtered as the Rider reluctantly wrapped his arms around her and popped them out.

Vandalen laughed out loud when he realized that like most Riders, Rax more often than not took things literally.

Gotta give it to Rax. That was one ugly foot. I'll have to be more careful with what I tell him from now on.

Just as he was regaining his composure, the thought of Elga and Rax hit him again, making him laugh so hard he cried. But then he took a breath and looked around the room, the threats and worries flooded his mind, instantly sucking away all of his joy.

He closed the ancient book of prophesies, then took off his robe, and stretched his back again. He opened a hidden door at the back of the main chamber revealing a small room with a long cot. He used it when he worked too late to keep from disturbing Nell, who was quite the bear when awakened before morning. As he sat down on the side of the cot to remove his shoes, he smiled.

Wonder if Rax managed to get away from his 'feminine company' this evening.

He lay back on the bed and, still smiling, drifted off to sleep.

***

Two days later, Horatio was back in his office. His first order of business was to prepare a decree appointing Vandalen as his successor. He placed it in his middle desk drawer then met with some Elders and visiting dignitaries. When they were gone, he sat thinking about the decree. As dusk fell, he knew what he had to do. He pulled out the card with the micro-holo on it, carefully copied it and placed his seal on both. He hid the original between the canvas and brown paper seal on the back of the portrait of his wife. Then he put the copy in the original hiding place. Satisfied now that the decree was safe, he decided to review the holocopy of the meeting.

Afterwards he was tired, but instead of resting he picked up a stack of papers that needed his attention. In about a half-hour, he came to Weilz' proposals.

Remarkable. I never knew Weilz had such....

His concentration was broken by a rustling sound coming from the antechamber where he kept his files.

"Emmitt, is that you?" he called out, thinking it must be his assistant. No answer. He shrugged and picked up Kiza's written report from EdTech. Then he heard the sound again, this time louder.

Horatio got up and stepped into the antechamber. The last thing he saw was the hideous grin spread across Jarlod's face as he flung a trizactalyn-powered shuriken into Horatio's chest where it dug its way into his heart so swiftly and precisely that Borm didn't have time to utter a cry. He was dead when he hit the floor.

Jarlod retrieved the shuriken, stepped over the body, and ransacked the office. When he found the decree, he was furious. One nucleo blast and the micro-holo caught fire; he dropped it on the floor and left by the secret passage he'd used to enter the antechamber.

Most men would try to hide their crime but not Jarlod. He had already spread his soldiers throughout the Empire, assuring there'd be no reprisal once the news got out. No, his only worry had been the wizard. But Jarlod had taken care of him, too.

During the night, while Vandalen slept, Jarlod's men broke into his home. They crept into the bedroom where the wizard and his wife lay peacefully sleeping. Nell lay on her side with her back to her husband.

The marauders injected Vandalen with a sedative and tried to take him quietly so as not to wake his wife, who by all accounts was capable of putting up one hell of a fight herself. To make sure she wouldn't wake up, one of the men drugged her by covering her nose and mouth with a cloth soaked in sleeping potion. Meanwhile, the men trying to move Vandalen had their hands full as the drug was taking longer than expected to work. Apparently, they had miscalculated his size and constitution when they filled the syringe. Groggy and confused, the wizard began to struggle with his abductors. He grabbed at his ring that lay on the chest of drawers by the door. He almost had it when the drug finally took effect. His eyes rolled back in his head and he went down hard onto the stone floor. A sharp-eyed assailant saw what Vandalen was reaching for. He snatched the ring and tucked it into his pocket. The well-orchestrated attack had taken less than five minutes. Nell slept on, floating through fitful dreams.

When Vandalen awoke, he realized he was in a holding cell far below the first official level of the Emperor's castle.

Jarlod, flanked by armed guards, smirked through the bars at his prisoner.

"Well, well. It's about time you woke up. I'm afraid you've slept through your trial," he gloated.

"What trial? What charges? What in the hell have you done?" Vandalen asked though he already knew the answer.

"I've claimed what is mine, nothing more," Jarlod said triumphantly. "And from now on, I am to be addressed as Your Majesty or Your Highness as is fitting the Emperor of the Reglon Empire."

"You will never be the Emperor!" Vandalen shouted, trying to use his power to free himself only to realize that he didn't have his ring.

Jarlod held up his right index finger. "Is this what you're looking for? Perhaps you could tell me how to use it," he goaded.

"When Elsnith freezes over!" Vandalen felt stupid for having taken off his ring, especially knowing the threats to Horatio. He'd done it out of habit. But he would have slept with it if he thought the attack was coming this soon. He himself had told Jarlod to go find the missing students.

What was I thinking? I should've known better. He thought he'd have at least another couple of weeks, but he'd underestimated Jarlod. Now he was powerless to overcome the self-proclaimed Emperor. His rival, the wizard Elsnor, stepped into view.

Vandalen knew there must be an enchantment on the cell to prevent his escape. *If only I had my ring.* Then the reality of what had happened hit him.

"Jarlod! You will never pull this off. You don't have what it takes to lead a kittle to a milk bowl, much less to run an empire," Vandalen roared, allowing his temper to best him.

"Now, now. Disrespect is not tolerated. It will not go well for those who do. And just so you understand me, Wizard, I know where your wife and daughter are, and I find the girl most appealing."

Before Vandalen could say another word, Jarlod nodded to Elsnor and said, "If you please."

In the next moment, Vandalen had the sensation of his body stinging all over causing him to lose his breath.

As quickly as it started, the sensation stopped, though spasms racked him violently for several more minutes.

When he was breathing normally and his body still again, he knew he'd been transported to Dartal. Escape from here was virtually impossible if Elsnor had placed an enchantment on his cell – and Vandalen knew he had. But Elsnor was a sloppy wizard whose enchantments were known to fail when something else got his attention.

I know it won't be easy, but I have to escape to protect my family. I will not give in to that murderous traitor.

He summoned Rax to help him. With a soft pop, Rax appeared outside the cell.

"Get me out of here!" Vandalen cried desperately.

"Sir, I'm afraid I can't do that. The enchantment is too strong."

Vandalen felt the anger rising within him again as he looked at the stone-faced Rider. *No use being ticked off. He's right. The enchantment is too strong for him.*

"Will that be all, Sir?" the Rider asked.

"No, Rax. Now's a good time for you to go see your family. Take a little time off, then report to General Michael Camdus, understood?"

"Thank you, Sir. How much time?"

"A few weeks. Return to duty before the lull."

"Yes, Sir. I'll report to General Camdus at the end of summer."

Rax popped out, leaving the despondent wizard alone with his thoughts.

Vandalen looked at the tiny cot in the dingy cell and vowed that he would not lose his mind like so many other prisoners had. Their rambling words of sheer submission and utter hopelessness were jaggedly etched into the stone walls. Deep seated anger was recorded there as well.

"I get it. But I can't give in to it. I'm not like them," he said to no one. "By God's grace, I will be free."

He flopped down hard on the filthy cot wondering, for all his bravado, how he would survive with his wits intact enough to remember why he wanted to escape in the first place. The hum of what he thought must be an ancient furnace located somewhere beyond his cell coupled with the occasional yelp from another prisoner became the music he set his plans to.

***

Nell awoke to loud banging on her door. She tried to get up, but her head felt as if it would split every time. She grabbed her temples in her hands and squeezed as hard as she could to stop the spinning. Slowly, she pushed herself up and sat on the side of the bed, the sound of her heart pounding loudly in her ears. She knew something was wrong, but she didn't know what. The door knocker banged again, sending a sharp pain zigzagging through her brain. She hopped off the bed and stumbled to the door, opening it a crack when she got there. Andria stood there disheveled, her deep sobs causing her to tremble violently.

"Andy, good heavens! Come in," Nell said as she gently took her arm and led her into the sitting room.

Once they were both seated, Andria asked, "Where is Van? He was supposed to protect Horatio and now he's …," she resumed sobbing uncontrollably.

Nell's head still throbbed so much she was having trouble comprehending. She got up without a word, went to the kitchen, opened a cabinet, and pulled a bottle of pills from the top shelf. Then she poured three pills into her hand, tossed them into her mouth, and swallowed. She chugged a glass of water to keep from choking and waited. Within seconds, her headache began to ease off. Then she poured Andria a glass and took it to her.

"Here, drink this."

Andria took a sip, set the glass down and asked, "Do you have anything stronger?"

"I think we have some brandy," Nell said. She reached over and opened a cabinet sitting beside her, grabbed the liquor, and poured her a small glass.

"Better," Andria said after she'd downed it.

"Now, tell me what's going on? I've never seen you so upset," Nell said, still trying to shake the cobwebs from her brain.

"Where's Van?"

"I'm not sure. He was gone when I woke up this morning. Why?"

"Because Jarlod has murdered Horatio. He may have gotten to Van, too," Andria said through her sobs.

Nell jumped up and raced to their bedroom. Signs of a struggle were evident. Everything on her husband's chest of drawers had been raked carelessly to the floor. His cloak still hung on the peg behind the door. *But how could this have happened without waking me?* In that instant she knew she'd been drugged.

She ran to her daughter's room. Nell was relieved to see her precious girl curled up in her bed sleeping soundly. Then she checked on her son. He too was safe. They were home now from university and would sleep for some time as they had stayed out late with friends celebrating their graduation. She closed the door to their wing of the house. Even though she desperately wanted to go find her husband, she knew that he was probably locked up somewhere – if not dead. That, and she needed to help bury Horatio.

When Nell and Andria stepped outside her home later that morning, evidence of the new order was all around. Armed soldiers stood guard throughout the city. No one greeted either of the women as they made their way to the palace. Once there, they were allowed to go in. Though Andria had to bite the inside of her cheek to keep from crying, she and Nell managed to hold their emotions in check while they met with Jarlod.

"Ah, ladies. So good to see you, though I wish it were under different circumstances," Jarlod said, unable to hide the glee he truly felt.

They couldn't help noticing that he had placed Andria's portrait in a pile of her husband's things.

"I wish to claim my belongings and my husband's body," Andria said.

Then she reached for the portrait. "I'll take this with me, Your Majesty, if you'll allow it," she said humbly.

"Of course, dear lady. Where would you like me to have the rest of your things delivered?"

"Send them to, to …." She realized that she had no home.

"Send My Lady's things to my home," Nell said.

"Thank you," Andria said softly to Nell.

Then to Jarlod she said, "Yes, send my personal belongings to the Vandalen residence. And the Emperor's body should go to the mortuary at Arbor Station. Tell them I shall be around later to make the arrangements," she said bitterly and turned to go. But Nell didn't move.

"And how may I help you, madam?" the cocky Jarlod asked.

"You can tell me what you've done with my husband, Jarlod."

"You will address me as *Your Majesty*, madam. As to Vandalen, well, I deemed him guilty of treason and sentenced him to life in prison. He is currently incarcerated in Dartal."

"Dartal! The children and I will never see him again. So, yesterday, he was Chief Advisor to the Emperor, and today he's a prisoner serving a life sentence. Jarlod," she threw his name in his face, refusing to give him obeisance, "you will answer for this." She turned on her heel to leave.

He grabbed her roughly by her elbow and pulled her close to him.

"That's *Your Majesty*! You will do well to control that sharp tongue of yours, madam. There are still some empty cells there. Unless you want your son to be enlisted in the military and your daughter to become my concubine, you need to adjust your attitude."

Nell knew he had no qualms at doing just that, so she calmed down and said, "Your Majesty, good day."

The anger rising in her chest was hard to control, but she forced herself to stay calm and to appear at least somewhat respectful. The women left the palace with heavy hearts.

As they headed back home, Nell asked, "Why the portrait, Andy? Why not one of Horatio's robes or his pipe?"

"Horatio loved this picture. That and I just don't want that devil ogling it – or using it for target practice."

They walked the rest of the way in silence. When they got there, Nell took the picture from Andria and placed it on the wall of the long corridor that led to the dining room. Andria didn't even look at it. What she wanted was no longer in this world, but she was determined not to dwell on it.

Ironically, what had happened to their lives affected Nell worse than Andria. She felt she was as much a widow as her friend, even though Vandalen was alive. The thought of life without him was overwhelming. Even worse was telling the children. Nell knew that he must have fought, that it wasn't his fault, but she still felt a little angry with him for leaving her. *Why didn't he use his powers? What's wrong with him?*

This was not a time when rational thought could prevail. It was a dark time of raw emotion for them all. But the Empire had yet to feel the full impact of what had transpired in this one night of greed-driven violence.

Nell kept her word and helped Andria see to the burial of her husband. They lived in Vandalen's home, both fighting to live each day. Though Andria had lost her husband, she became stronger while Nell sank deeper and deeper into depression, finally deciding she just didn't want to wake up again. One morning, she didn't.

Andria contacted Nell's daughter who had moved to a nearby county, but they'd been unable to locate her son. After the funeral, Andria was once again alone, this time in the rambling home that Vandalen had built for his family. She could have gone elsewhere, but something inside her made her stay. Hope, perhaps, that one day he would come home. If that day came, she wanted to be here to fill him in on his wife and children's lives while he was away. It was the least she could do for the friend who had comforted her so many times. Then it would be her turn.

***

THE NEW ORDER

True to the nature of a peacock, Emperor Jarlod preened in front of his newly appointed Council. He'd kept the old advisors, except for Vandalen, of course, and added more Elders from the military branches. He fully intended to conquer every world in his path, effectively rendering him ruler of the universe.

"Welcome, welcome. Please be seated," he said as he stood grandly before his newly constructed throne of chestnut oak from Earth's northern hemisphere. It was accented with precious metals. The seat's purple overstuffed cushions were edged with the finest, tredon suede leather.

To most of the Council, the gaudy throne was a painful reminder that their leader had been assassinated and they were left with this imposter. But to a handful, it was the prize Jarlod had earned by outsmarting Born and his overly confident wizard to get what he wanted. To those elders, all that mattered was they'd won. Once the Council members were seated, Jarlod sat down, obviously enjoying all the perks of his freshly stolen position.

The new Reglon Empire Guard Commander Michael Camdus sat across from Kiza at the far end of the table. General Harom Bulfez of the Army's Third Division was seated to his right. These seasoned soldiers, the youngest members, sat ramrod straight, listening, watching and hoping Jarlod wouldn't call on them for anything as their only instruction had been to show up.

Jarlod began excitedly pacing the floor. He looked at his Council and soaked up the feeling of absolute power.

He stopped pacing, planted his feet, spread a bit apart, and crossed his arms over his chest. The huge gold necklace that bore the Reglon Empire symbol of seven overlapping circles gouged him painfully.

"Ahem," he cleared his throat as he adjusted the pendant and adopted the speech patterns he thought were appropriate coming from such a powerful leader as he now was.

"We can see how honored you all are to have been selected to share in the protection of our Royal personage's protection," he began, faltering with the awkwardness of his own words. "Well, let us begin," he tried again.

The Council waited. With no agenda, no prep, no hint of what he wanted from them, not even his supporters knew what to expect. Those who were familiar with him either loved him or hated him. There was no place for lukewarm. The ones who professed to love him were just like him in many ways – just trying to work an angle to their own benefit. But the others knew that they were looking at a pile of fresh dung. They also knew that if they stirred it, it would stink. No, they had to wait for Jarlod's new coin to lose its shine. Then they'd reassess the situation. Hopefully, there'd still be an empire when that happened.

"Would anyone care to tell us what you're doing these days? Anything? Your thoughts?" Jarlod asked.

No one spoke, as no one wished to tell him their thoughts – some because they didn't have any and some because they knew that'd be a sure way to end up dead.

Jarlod began to pace again, this time in frustration. He'd been warned by one of his Elders that it was too soon, but it was not his way to take advice from underlings, so he hadn't listened.

"Haarruuummpphhh," he cleared his throat. The lack of enthusiasm from his Council had somewhat dulled his victory. Meeting with them had suddenly lost its appeal.

"Well then, we're adjourned. Carry on."

He turned and stomped to his private quarters, changed out of his bodacious royal garments and went to see his wives. Perhaps the new girl would provide him with some relief from the indecipherable feeling that had begun to nag at him. While he changed clothes, he looked out the street-side window in time to see Weilz and his eldest daughter walking by the palace. The wind caught her long blond tresses. Then it whipped open her skirt revealing her shapely legs.

My, my, my! What a delectable treat! Jarlod smiled wickedly at the thoughts running through his twisted mind.

Meanwhile, Camdus and Bulfez left the palace without a backward glance.

"Don't forget our staff meeting tomorrow, Bully," Camdus said to his colleague.

"Right. See you then," Bulfez replied.

They parted ways, Bulfez to the nearest grill to grab a bite and Camdus to see if he could find Rayalla Enright.

Camdus had done as she'd asked and backed off to give her time to think about their relationship. He'd been surprised and a little hurt when she told him that the way things were going, she didn't see a future for them. He'd asked her to please give it some more time, but she'd held her ground. Now he needed to know if there was any hope for them.

When he got to her house, the windows were all dark, the curtains were gone.

"Odd," Camdus thought as he peered through the glass. The room was empty. He ran to the next and the next until he'd looked into all the first-floor windows. The place was empty. He ran to the neighbor's house and pounded on the door.

"Who's there?" a quavery voice asked.

"It's me, Michael Camdus."

The old lady opened the door. "Well then, dear, please come in."

"Have you seen the Enrights lately? There's no one home. Have they moved?" His anxiety was fighting with his desire to stay calm.

"Oh, my, yes. They left right after our new Emperor installed himself. Her father received a new posting to … well, I'm sure I knew once, but I just can't remember. Sorry, dear. Would you like some tea?" she offered.

"No, thank you, ma'am. I have to get back."

Camdus could have kicked himself. He'd let her get away. Every time he'd had the chance to tell her, he'd chickened out and changed the subject. *No wonder she gave up on us. And now....* He couldn't finish the thought; it hurt too much.

He threw himself into his work, hoping to ease the pain of his stupid mistake. And to some degree it did. Except in the wee hours of the morning, when he had little control of his thoughts, they always seemed to wander to Rayalla.

***

Far away from the politics of Reglon Major and the treachery among the Empire's leaders, Simon Slogar had grown up in an affluent family who lived quite comfortably on the planet Ashtar. He'd never had to worry about where his next meal was coming from and always had the most desirable electronic gadgets. His rather rotund parents enjoyed their size as they felt it reflected their great wealth. While his dad was busy in his role of Director of the Monetary Exchange, Mrs. Slogar, the epitome of the stay-at-home mom, turned her focus almost entirely to her only child, Simon. She home-schooled him for fear of his coming into contact with the Less-Thans, the class of people she was certain filled the seats in the Empire-run schools. So, she taught him his lessons, took him to museums, public buildings, cultural exhibits, and frequently took him for outings with others of their social standing. Despite their wealth, Mrs. Slogar chose to do her own cooking. And to keep her family nice and round, she'd learned to cook ribs and steak, rolls slathered in butter with few vegetables or fresh fruit in the mix. But most of all, she loved to bake. Pies, cakes, scones, cookies, all luscious and oozing with calories, graced the plates she left on tables throughout the vast downstairs of their house. Needless to say, her son had grown fat, much to the delight of his proud, equally round parents.

As the years passed, though, Simon became a typical bored teen. He began to read things that his mother would never have approved. For one thing, he discovered that many of the people his mother looked down her nose at were not poor by choice. A serious lack of forethought by their leaders for the economic growth of all Empire residents had hurt the ordinary people. Through these forbidden readings, a seed was planted in his tender mind. The seed of doubt that he was living the perfect life his parents had told him he was privileged to have, began to grow and grow. As he matured, he became more uncomfortable with his status. He didn't know how to broach the subject with his mother and father, so he continued to study in secret – and eat, eat, eat.

At last the day came when he was old enough to go to University. His mother had to admit it was time to let her baby boy go. Through tears and hugs, and with a large chest of sweets in tow, Simon Slogar told them *good-bye,* and waddled off to the transport pod that took him to his new life.

Once he settled into the routine of independent college life, he began pursuing a degree in medical history. He'd come quite far toward that end, too, when genetic engineering erased all major diseases – or so the Emperor decreed. He had always been more of a bookworm than a do-er, so studying medical history had seemed the path for him. Medicine, as in becoming a doctor, would have required sure-enough work and dedication, two things Slogar had no interest in.

To support his claim of a disease-free empire, Jarlod discontinued all medical programs, including classes in its history. Medical students were sent into other fields or sent home. Physicians were rounded up and forced into new professions. Those who resisted were not heard from again.

Lazy though he was, Slogar was hacked by the Emperor's thoughtless actions. He could not accept the notion that there would never again be a need for physicians because he couldn't believe that tampering with genetics wouldn't create other problems – and diseases – in the long run.

With no way to complete his studies and determined not to return home, Slogar left Ashtar and went to Andalla. For three years he quietly continued his study of ancient medicine without being noticed – or so he thought. Yet he *was* noticed, and not favorably.

The Andallans were a simple people for the most part. The majority of them were content to live in mediocrity, never challenging edicts sent out by the Emperor, no matter how ludicrous. Some of them didn't challenge the writs because they didn't know what Jarlod had deprived them of. For others their obedience wasn't blind at all but was in response to Jarlod's narcissistic nature, which framed his leadership style. He was used to persecuting and bullying to get what he wanted. He disrespected everyone around him, including his Council of Elders to whom he owed so much. Without the support of three or four key members, his coup would have failed. Even though he had kissed their backsides to get where he was, now he deceived and outright lied to all of them as he sank deeper into his own delusions.

But the Andallans Slogar dealt with just smiled, complacently believing their Emperor was God, or a very good facsimile.

Despite his great size, Slogar had on more than one occasion taken a pounding for daring to disagree with something the Emperor had said or done. And this business of no doctors, well, he was just plain furious.

The angrier he became, the greater Slogar's thirst for knowledge grew. His anger was replaced by a fire burning within him that kept him awake at night.

As the days passed, he felt a sense of urgency he couldn't explain. Now he knew he had to do more than learn about the history of medicine. He had to master the techniques involved in treating the sick. *How can I possibly do any of this without getting the life beaten out of me?* The only way was to watch out for the Emperor's spies and for the Andallans who thought it their duty to trounce anyone who disagreed with Jarlod. Undeterred, Slogar continued his midnight break-ins every chance he got.

He wandered the streets of Llanndan, the Andallan city he'd decided to settle in. Affluent neighborhoods were within his financial grasp because his parents still treated him like their little boy and made sure he always had more than enough money in his bank account. But he didn't want to live there. No, he'd thought it out. The only way to learn about the dreaded Less-Thans was to live among them. So, he found an apartment in a seedy side of town. The skinny landlord stood up from his gamer, looked the stranger over, correctly assuming the man had money, and said, "Cash only."

Slogar pulled the required amount from his wallet and handed it over to the landlord. The man gladly took it and tucked it into his grimy pocket.

"I'd like a receipt, please," Slogar told the man, who gave him a dirty look, scribbled a makeshift receipt on the back of a used napkin and handed it to him. Slogar gingerly took the receipt between his thumb and index finger only and dropped it into a side pocket of his luggage.

With a laugh at the persnickety new tenant, the landlord turned to a filthy board lined with rows of nails laden with a multitude of objects – bottle openers, baby flashlights, and of course, keys. The man reached up and rattled through the mess of keys, finally picking one out and handing it to Simon.

"Room 1313, 13th floor, 13th door on the left; rent is due on...,"

Slogar interrupted, "Let me guess, the 13th?"

The landlord gave him a "bless his heart look" and continued, "No, by the first of each month. If it's late, then it doubles."

He started to sit back down, but Slogar stopped him.

"Don't I need to register or something?" he asked.

"Register? Ha, that's a good one! Hahaha," the man nearly choked on his laughter.

"Well, how will you know who I am? What if I stop paying the rent? What if something happens to me?" Slogar asked.

"Well then either way, I 'spect I'll have me a room to rent, now won't I?" With that the landlord sat down before the gamer and once again resumed his gambling, which he apparently was no good at, judging by the money he fed into the machine.

Slogar took the key, picked up his bags and walked down the hall looking for the lift. Seeing none, he went back to the desk and asked the man, "Where's the elevator?"

"Hahahahahaha," the man slapped the counter, tears now running down his face he was laughing so hard. "Now that's a good one."

Slogar ignored his rude landlord and waited for an answer. "There ain't no elevator. The stairs is at th' end o' th' hall there," the man said dismissively.

Slogar couldn't believe his bad luck. But he'd wanted to see how the other half lived, so he headed down the hall.

When he opened the stairwell door, the heat and a strong smell of urine made him gag. But he was determined, so he began his trek up the dark stairwell.

After he'd been climbing and dragging his bag for what seemed like an hour, he came to a landing and tossed his bag ahead of him so he could sit on it just like he had at all the ones before it.

"Ooof! Watch whatcher doin, now." The gruff voice startled him.

"Who's there?" Slogar asked, still unable to see on the dimly lit landing, suddenly far too close to an old woman.

"Carona Lishton, if you please, not that it's any of your bidness. And who are you, I might ask?" Her breath was rank, making him feel queasy again.

He ignored her question and asked another one of his own. "Well, what are you doing out here? Are you too sick to go to your apartment?"

"This *is* my apartment, as you call it, thank you very much," she said, clearly irritated by his questions.

"Never mind then," he said, grabbing his bag and going on his way.

Thankfully, in only two more flights of stairs, he was on the 13th floor. When he found his room, he stuck the key into the lock and tried to turn it. It wouldn't budge. He jiggled the key inside the lock, thinking maybe it was just rusty. It still didn't work. About halfway down the hall he found a phone barely attached to the dingy wall. He looked at it, started to reach for it, but decided he'd rather not risk contracting an infectious disease by picking up a receiver on a phone that was clearly out of order.

He pulled back his hand, involuntarily wiping it on his cloak, and started down the stairs again.

When he reached Carona, she growled, "Well, back so soon?"

"My key doesn't work," he said defensively.

"Whyn't you call Old Moldy?"

"Old Moldy? You mean the landlord?"

"Who else would I mean?" she replied before adding, "There's a phone on every floor, you know."

"Yes, I saw it, but it's out of order," he replied exasperated.

"Did you try it?" she asked.

"No, but it's falling off the wall. How could it work?" he snapped.

"You shoulda tried it," she said knowingly.

"You mean it works?" he asked, thinking she was just fooling him.

"You'd a knowed that if you'd a tried it 'fore you come back down, wouldn't cha? Now that's just pitiful, it is," she said snidely.

He thought about it only a little; two floors down and two floors back up versus all 13 down and 13 back up. He went back, picked up the phone, which worked just fine, though a little crackly.

After Slogar had waited more than an hour, the landlord came up with all the keys, trying first one then another until he found the right one.

Slogar gladly exchanged keys with the aggravating man and entered his room. He'd been dreading what he'd find even though he needed to get off his feet. When the door swung open, his jaw dropped. The room was not the dank hole he'd been expecting at all. It was clean and beautifully appointed, with multiple doors leading from the living room. Thinking he must be hallucinating from the strain of his journey, he walked out, closed the door, and opened it again.

"Wait. What? This is crazy."

He dropped his bag in the living room and began to explore. The place had three bedrooms, three bathrooms, a kitchen and a pantry. There was also a huge sitting area and a balcony off the master bedroom. He put his clothes in the exquisitely handcrafted chest of drawers. Then he walked back to the sitting room, still in shock at how nice it was. There was a bank of windows that started about a third of the way from the floor and ran almost to the ceiling. When he pulled back the drapes, he was greeted by a breathtaking view of the city. *How can this be?*

He investigated the kitchen. It was quite nice, and the pantry was fully stocked. However, the empty refrigerator had been turned off. He was not up for eating just staples – soup, bread, and hoop cheese – though that was one of his favorite meals. What he really wanted was a platter of ribs and some ale. He'd become quite fond of both when he was at University, and now that he was on his own, he partook every chance he got. He remembered seeing a restaurant on the corner across from his building. It'd looked inviting, so he decided to give it a try.

"Damn stairs," he muttered as he locked his door and made the trek back to the killer stairwell. When he'd arrived at the 11th floor landing, he was relieved the smelly old woman wasn't there. *Well, at least I don't have to deal with that Carolona Lifton or Ligthen or whatever she said her name is.* His stomach rumbled and he picked up his pace. Going down without his luggage was a relief.

Once outside, Slogar made a right turn and walked to the pedestrian crossing. South bound pods of all sizes whizzed by in their designated lane about two feet from the surface of the street, while north bound pods occupied their lanes twenty feet above them. A few folks peddled by in the bike lane. When traffic in all lower lanes stopped, he crossed and entered the Red Bud café.

His mouth watered at the smell of meat grilling, *Ahhh! Roast or ribs, maybe both.* He was hopeful now and even hungrier. A sign just inside the door invited visitors to "Seat yourself. A waiter will be with you shortly." He looked around for a vacant table in the nearly packed house. Not seeing one right off, he walked down the row of high-backed booths toward the kitchen.

When he finally spied an empty booth, it was against the back wall giving him a view of the rest of the dining room. Slogar moved as quickly as he could toward it and lowered his hulk onto the seat. He was surprised to find that sitting across from him was none other than the homeless woman who'd taken up residence in the stairwell in his apartment building. He immediately stood up to leave, but she caught his arm.

"Now, now, no need to rush off, is there? You's welcome to stay if you wantta," she said with no trace of the gruffness he remembered.

Slogar looked around the restaurant again and was disappointed to see that this was the only seat left in the place. If he hadn't been so famished, he'd have told her good-day and gone to find a different establishment. But he was famished and decided to take her up on her offer.

"Thank you, Coralana," he said, mauling her name.

"The name's Carona Lishton. What's your name, mister?"

"Slogar. Simon Slogar."

"Nice to meetcha, Slogar Simon Slogar. Don't mean no harm, but why's your name like a sammich?" she asked.

Slogar thought that was about the dumbest thing he'd ever been asked, until he realized how he'd said it.

"No, it's just Simon Slogar, that's all."

The waiter, barely five feet tall, saw the big man who'd just sat down and fairly flew to him, guessing him to be a big tipper as well.

"Welcome, welcome to the Red Bud. I'm Justice and I'll be taking care of you this evening," he gushed.

"Really?" Carona asked. "Then could I git my feet rubbed? They's aching like nobody's business, I swanny they is."

The waiter didn't know how to answer that, so Slogar spoke up.

"Carona, he didn't mean that literally. What he means is he'll tell us about the menu, take our order, bring us our food, and keep our glasses filled. Now, young man, what's good tonight?" he asked.

"Why everything, Sir. But the dry rubbed ribs and pork tenderloin are just to die for," he schmoozed.

"Well, I don't want ter die fer a meal, but I think I get whatcha saying. I wants me some riiuubs. And some taters, and lots o' bread an' butter and tea. You got that sweetie tea like the place over in Shotown has?" Carona asked excitedly.

"Yes, Ma'am, we do," he said as he keyed her order into his electronic pad. Then he turned to Slogar and said, "For you, Sir?"

Slogar was fascinated by Carona's speech patterns, but it was her order that really caught his attention.

"I'll have what she's having, except I want a pitcher of ale instead of tea," he answered.

"Thank you," Justice said and finished sending their order. Then he fetched their drinks, flashed that cheesy grin, and hurried off to help other patrons.

"So, Carona, how did you come to live in the stairwell?" Slogar asked, feeling no need to cushion his question with pleasantries.

"The same way you came to live in that dull apartment. It's my choice," she answered.

"You mean you don't have to live there?" he asked incredulously.

Carona's clear, ice blue eyes flashed. "You don't know nothin' about me, Sonny Boy, so don't go judgin'."

Slogar and Carona ate to the sounds of forks and bones clattering on plates, and the greedy gulping of their drinks, each too hungry to stop once their platters had been delivered.

From time to time, the waiter stopped by, refilled their glasses, asked if they needed anything – except a foot rub – and darted away. He thought the old lady must be the gentleman's granny, but if that was so, he should be ashamed for not taking better care of her. He kept these thoughts to himself because he wanted a big tip and prying was a sure way to get none.

When Slogar and Carona were full as ticks on a fuzzy krike's ear, they sat back and looked at each other.

Slogar's conscience kicked in. *Oh, what the hell.* Before he could stop himself, he opened his big mouth and said, "Carona, my apartment is actually quite nice and has three bedrooms. You are welcome to stay in one until you find a place you like better." He waited for her answer.

"Why, that's mighty nice of you, Simon Slogar. But I've been thinking 'bout moving on from here. I think I've done learnt about as much as I need to in this town. 'Sides, who knows what's over in th' next town? I like adventure, don't you?" she said.

"Well, I guess I like it about as well as the next fellow, but I think I need to stay here a while longer. I've got some research I want to do," he answered.

"Is that a fact? Well, I shore hopes you finds out whatcha's tryin' to find out," Carona said simply.

When the waiter brought their checks, Slogar reached for Carona's, but she stopped him from picking it up.

"Nope, I pays ma own way, I does, Simon Slogar. But it wuz nice o' you to offer." With that the old lady stood, dragged her rucksack from beneath the table, fished out a pouch, and left a generous tip for the waiter.

She turned back to Slogar and said, "I hope to see you again someday, Simon Slogar. Until then, may God hold you in his hands."

Slogar was confused. The old woman's dialect had lost its rough edge and was instead quite polished. *Well, I don't have time to worry about her. She seems to be quite able to take care of herself anyway.*

He too left a nice tip for their server, who was overjoyed at his good fortune.

"Thank you, thank you, Sir. Please come back and do ask for Justice. I'd be pleased to serve you again. Have a good day."

"I'll do that. See you next time," Slogar answered as he squeezed past the diminutive waiter on his way to pay his check.

By the time Slogar got back to his apartment, he was ready for a much-needed shower and even more needed rest. But he tripped over the empty luggage he'd forgotten to put away. Rubbing his sore knee, he grabbed the bags and stomped to the living room and snatched open the door of what he'd thought was a closet. He was stunned to find a folding grate. *An elevator? But the landlord said this building doesn't have one.*

He stood there, debating the prudence of getting on, but his natural curiosity got the better of him.

He stepped inside, closed the grate and pulled the lever marked "Down." After he got over his brief near-panic attack, he realized that the ride was actually quite smooth.

He'd expected the door to open to a back lobby, but instead found that it opened to an alley that led to a street he hadn't seen before. He stepped out and began to explore, with the possibilities tantalizing his insatiable quest for knowledge.

After plundering through several grot shops, he stumbled upon an antique bookstore. Inside he discovered a treasure trove of medical books. Here he purchased as many of the tomes as he felt he could easily carry and returned to his apartment. He was relieved that the elevator worked equally well on the trip up.

He spent the next several months studying, going back and buying more, until he'd bought one of each of the medical books the shopkeeper had to sell. But after a while, he realized he still had too many gaps in his knowledge.

Slogar then began exploring the seedy side of town where he had intended to start in the first place. He found that the Less-Thans were for the most part just like him, only they hadn't had the opportunities he'd been given. He squirrelled away that insight for the time being. He had set a task for himself and he intended to finish it. So he began to take huge risks to get access to the forbidden knowledge of medicine that had so far eluded him.

Sneaking into abandoned libraries under the cloak of night gave up little information that he didn't already have. But as he continued his search, he began to wonder what had happened to the physicians who practiced before the ban but were never heard of again.

There was a legend of one who used to live on Andalla. He searched carefully for information to lead him to this doctor with the hope she was still alive. While almost every Andallan had heard of the Elder Woman who lived a solitary life away from civilization, few knew anything about her. Some people thought she was an oracle. Others thought she was just a crazy old lady. Slogar didn't know which one she was, but he knew he had to find out.

In one of his frequent nightly forays, he entered a seldom-used museum through its rickety backdoor. Inside he found a dust-laden room way in the back. After easing his bulk into the narrow room, he discovered that it housed a small archive of articles from an old medical journal. In one of them, he found a piece that spoke of this same lady as having been not only a physician but also a researcher until she was *purified*. Slogar was not sure what that meant, and the article didn't spell it out, but he was pretty sure that it had been a messy business. He wondered if she survived. And if she had, could she possibly have her right mind after the purification?

With these questions nagging him more and more incessantly, he realized he no longer could take not knowing. So, he set out across Andalla's sparsely populated plain to find the Elder Woman of Silden.

After several days of slow travel over the bleak terrain, he came upon a lonely farm. He had been walking for some time that day and decided to take a rest inside the old shanty house about a hundred yard off the rutted road. He trudged, ankle deep in extremely warm sand, up the path littered with tangles of weeds the whole way. By the time he got there, the hem of his dusty robe was covered with what the ancients called *beggar lice*, which were nothing more than prickly seeds.

Carefully, Slogar navigated his bulk up the rickety steps onto the uneven porch. There was a wooden chair, but its legs were so rotted it sat at a forty-five-degree angle. He thought maybe the inside would prove to be more solid, so he entered the door which hung raggedly from its hinges.

At first all he saw was a dirty wooden table surrounded by broken chairs. A straw mat lay on the floor near a fireplace that looked as if it had not been used for many years. He gingerly, well as gingerly as he was able, made his way to the hearth. A round of tree trunk about two and a half feet high sat beside it. He lowered himself onto the rough seat and emptied the sand from his shoes on the scarred, wooden floor.

Slogar reckoned he was close to the Elder Woman's home, so he decided to stop for the evening. After resting a bit, he got up and began to investigate the small shelter. He was pleasantly surprised to find two tredon oil lamps and a striker. He lit one of them, set it on the table in the center of the room, and then turned up the wick to cast a brighter light.

A pair of glowing eyes among a pile of rags on the straw mat startled him. He jumped back, shaking the floor so violently that one of the chairs fell over. His heart raced. *Okay, now what?* He'd been so careful to carry all that he needed to continue his studies that he didn't even think about a weapon.

Well, I still have my wits, he reasoned with himself.

The eyes glowed yellow.

Taking a deep breath, Slogar said, "Umm, ah, hello. Uh, I, ah, just thought I'd stop for a minute to rest. So, um, now I have. I'll be on my way."

The rags rose from the floor so fast that Slogar had no time to escape. Before he could even blink, they turned into fine, emerald green robes and the yellow eyes became a translucent, pale blue.

He stood there, speechless.

"So, Simon Slogar, you finally found me. I've waited for this day."

Slogar stammered, "You know me? How? But I ...."

The stately woman who now stood before him waved him to silence. "Don't you recognize me?"

The blank look on his face answered for him.

"Well, then, fair enough. We have met before, but perhaps you don't remember the homeless woman in Llanndan. When I'm away from here, I travel as Carona Lishton, but I am Seelah, the Elder Woman of Silden. You should know that your search for me was by my design. We have much to discuss, and I must teach you what you'll need to know if you are to fulfill your destiny."

"But, why? Why didn't you just tell me who you were back then and save me all those months of frustration and work?" he asked.

"You had more to learn before you were ready," she answered quietly.

This new turn of events was infinitely disquieting to Slogar, who tended to babble when scared, so he began.

"Uh, no, I mean wait just a minute! My destiny? I don't have a destiny, other than to do my best to dodge the Emperor's henchmen. I'm just a renegade student of ancient cures and not very well taught at that. My curiosity has caused more trouble than you can know, but I haven't been able to curb it. So, you know, I've had to move from place to place, planet to planet to keep from becoming a guest at Helgrad. But, how did you...? I mean, what are you talking about? I came looking for you because *I* want to ask *you* about medicine. Why would you think you brought me here?" He was a little indignant that this woman, elder or not, thought she could control him, could make him do something without his knowing it. Besides, she had tricked him once. He couldn't trust her.

Seelah laughed softly. She hadn't meant to laugh at him, but she couldn't help herself.

"I'm sorry, Simon. Oh my, I've forgotten to ask if you mind my calling you by your given name. May I?"

He nodded. "Why not? You seem to know me pretty well."

"I suppose I do. But I brought you here for a reason. You are here because the whole Empire is in danger. There's still time to prepare, in large part because you've spent much of your life studying every medical document you could find. Now you're ready to let me teach you how to use your knowledge and innate talents to figure out a solution."

Slogar looked at Seelah for a moment before he spoke.

"Why don't you solve the problem yourself, whatever it is? I mean, after all, you did will me here, right? If you can do that, you ought to be able to figure out how to overcome any problem.

Seeing the look on Seelah's face, he quickly added, "No disrespect intended, Elder Woman."

Seelah sighed. She had expected this. "I am the Elder Woman *of Silden*. If I leave these plains, I lose my most powerful abilities, my gifts, if you will. You've seen how I travel. I had to bring you here to take on this task. Though you see yourself as, well, a lost cause, I don't. I know that the intellectual gifts God has given you are not bound to any one place. Like it or not, you are our best hope. Will you stay with me a while? I promise you that much of the knowledge you have so futilely sought will be made known to you. Are you willing?"

"Do I have to give you my answer right now?" Slogar asked, deeply regretting his decision to take a rest in this cottage. No, worse than that – he regretted setting out in the first place.

The Elder Woman responded evenly. "I'm afraid so, Simon." Slogar was overcome by an intense craving for ale. He reached into his pack, desperately looking through the bottles until he found one that wasn't empty, but it was awfully close.

Oh, great, just my luck.

He lifted his head and gave Seelah the only viable answer. "All right. I'll stay, but I have limitations."

Seelah looked at him as a mother looks at her petulant child. "Yes, I am aware of your limitations. I'm also aware that most of them are of your own making. We will work on getting rid of them as we go." She reached out and took the pack from him, taking the bottles one by one and placing them on the table. "You won't need these where we're going."

Without any more questions, Simon Slogar became a reluctant student of the Elder Woman of Silden on the desolate plains of Andalla, far away from civilization.

Seelah walked to the hearth and with her left hand touched the dusty mantel. "Take my hand," she said quietly.

Slogar looked tentatively at the extended right hand, wondering what he was getting into. With a deep sigh, he took the hand. The room as he knew it faded away. He had the distinct feeling of free falling through a fog. When he could catch his breath again, he saw that they were standing in a pristine, blindingly white room. Bottles and vials glinted under the bright light whose source he could not determine. The air bore an acrid smell so sharp that Slogar's eyes began to water.

"My eyes! Seelah, what's happening to me?" Slogar instinctively rubbed his burning eyes.

The Elder Woman placed a cool hand over his eyelids. He felt instant relief.

"Disinfectant. You'll get used to it," she said.

He wondered what else he'd have to get used to, but he was in it now and saw no way out.

She gave him a small jar of the cooling salve she had just used to calm his burning eyes.

"Use this until your eyes adjust to the stringent effects of the disinfectant. I keep this room germ free. As we fell, we passed through a mist that killed any bacteria we may have picked up on the surface."

"The surface?" he asked, "So that means we're underground?" He was beginning to understand.

She nodded and changed the lighting to a setting kinder to his eyes.

"We'll get started soon, but first let me show you to your room so you can settle in."

She led him through a passageway he hadn't noticed before. All along the way were doors, each bearing a symbol that was totally unknown to him. At last they stopped before one of them. He was surprised to see his own name there. Seelah opened the door and invited him to enter. This room was an exact replica of the room he had occupied at his home on Ashtar.

"I hope you are pleased, Simon."

At a loss for words, he could only blink at her. This was beyond anything he could comprehend. *How could she have known?* He walked over to his bureau and opened the top drawer, half expecting to find the clothes he had worn all those years ago. He was relieved to find cloaks and uniforms that were distinctly more practical as his girth had more than doubled.

"Simon, dinner is at six. I'll send Elani to escort you to the dining chamber." Seelah left him still clearly confused.

He took some time to put his things away and then found a bath chamber adjacent to a large closet. It had been several days since he had actually disrobed and bathed, but he felt the need to do so in this pristine facility. He stepped into the ample shower stall and was instantly soaked with jets of foam spraying him from all directions.

After a few minutes of this, the foam was replaced by clear water. The disinfectant smell that had permeated his senses ever since he got here was replaced by a fresh scent that reminded him of a sunshine-drenched meadow where he'd played as a child on Ashtar. The water stopped and he stepped out into a small alcove just to the left of the bath. There he found a large, warm towel which he gratefully clutched as he walked back into his room to dress.

A knock at the door sometime later let him know it was time for dinner.

Elani was a tall, thin woman of indeterminate age and ancestry. Her soft voice had a soothing quality to it that he found immensely appealing.

"Dr. Slogar, please come with me."

"Gladly, my dear," he said as he offered her his arm. Not really understanding this custom, she smiled and preceded him to the elevator. After a brief moment, the elevator paused then opened its doors onto yet another chamber. This one was softly lit and filled with the smell of roasted meat and savory spices. His mouth began to water.

The Elder Woman was standing by a huge brick hearth. She seemed lost in thought, so he quietly followed Elani to a sturdy sofa. Elani did not speak but nodded her farewell and quietly glided from the chamber. Slogar waited for Seelah to join him.

A few moments later, she turned and smiled at him.

"Good evening, Simon. Are you hungry? Elani has prepared a roast for us with pickled eggs and some greens she grew in the hydro garden."

Slogar was ravenous and indicated this by rising and offering her his arm to escort her to the table, which stood in an alcove to the rear of the sitting area. Seelah gracefully laid her hand on his arm. It had been quite a long time since a gentleman had made this gallant gesture. Though he was not as old as she, he did observe the old rules of courtesy that she found pleasing.

After seating her at one end of the wooden table, he seated himself at the other. The meal before him was more a feast than anything else. He placed his napkin in his lap and took up his fork and knife.

"Simon, would you please ask the blessing for the meal?"

Slogar had not returned thanks since he was a child, but he felt he had to do as Seelah asked.

"God is great, God is good. Let us thank him for this food. Ah-men."

Seelah smiled. She knew a child's prayer when she heard one, but at least somewhere in his childhood he had been exposed to faith in something greater than himself. So maybe he wasn't hopeless in that regard either. Slogar looked up, a sheepish smile on his face.

After they had eaten in silence for a while, he asked, "How long have you lived here, Seelah?"

The Elder Woman finished the morsel in her mouth before she answered him.

"I've been here since my purification about twenty years ago. The Emperor's henchmen loaded me and seventeen others into a podtrans and then dumped us out on the edge of the plain without even a bottle of water or crust of bread. Some went into hysterics and ran after them only to be vaporized right in front of us. The rest of us, twelve there were, huddled among the tumblers and scroots that grow wild along the roadsides. As soon as we were alone, we struck out across the plain, with no one talking, no one leading, just walking. Fairly soon I realized that most of them would not make it because they now had the minds of small children. They followed us, but often strayed to look at a pretty flower or strange design in the sand. Only three of us managed to survive purification without any real damage to our minds by pretending to be like the others."

Slogar listened to Seelah's story as he reached for more bread and meat. The wine, a mild red, was nowhere near as strong as he would have liked, but it went well with the meal. He refilled his glass. Seelah drank the last of her wine and delicately wiped her mouth with her linen napkin. She sat quietly. Slogar wanted to hear more but felt it best to wait for her to pick up the story again.

He was disappointed when she said, "I think that's enough for now. I'm going to retire for the evening. Please feel free to stay up as long as you like, but I must caution you to stay in this wing. And do not try to return to the surface."

Slogar said nothing but was thinking, *I'd rather eat scroots than go back through that hateful mist.*

He had to make himself focus on what Seelah was saying.

"Jarlod's men patrol this area frequently. I think it best they don't know about this place. I have no desire to be captured again. Once in a lifetime is one time too many. Well, good night then. Elani will know when you are ready and will come to escort you back to your room. We'll begin in the morning."

Slogar had one question that wouldn't wait. "Seelah, who were the other two?"

She looked at him for a moment trying to think what *two* he could be asking about. *Oh yes, the purification survivors.*

"You've met one of them already – Elani of Trilvar. The other, Alesander of Vartuch, left us after five seasons to return to his home planet. He was armed with plans and knowledge for revitalizing his ecosphere, determined to bring his dead planet back to life. He was well disguised and sent a coded confirmation of his arrival. I haven't heard from him since."

Slogar was stunned, not by Alesander – he had never heard of him and knew no one from his planet. But Elani – Elani of Trilvar? He had gone to university with two Trilvarians: Vandalen and Elsnor. Both of them were older than he was. They had returned to study the latest theories in metallurgy. Vandalen had gone on to become quite prominent under Emperor Borm's rule but had met with unfortunate circumstances after the coup. What became of Elsnor, he had no idea. Could Elani be related to either of these men? Perhaps she was kin to Vandalen as she was tall like he was. Slogar knew the wizard well and in truth had much more recent knowledge of him, but for his own safety, he told no one – not even the Elder Woman, though he was fairly sure she knew anyway.

For the next six months, Seelah worked with Slogar to produce remedies for a multitude of illnesses, most of which no one had even thought of in centuries. They were convinced that the disease-free era was rapidly ending.

Some of their medicines were wrought from formulas found in old books, but others they designed as new treatments for old diseases.

True to her promise, Seelah also addressed Slogar's weight-related health issues. Each day after the evening meal, Seelah and Slogar took a walkabout through Elani's spectacular gardens.

He marveled at the intricate design of this facility that made gardening possible. Abundant water and sunshine down here seemed impossible. And yet here they were.

One area was reminiscent of the beaches of old. There were coconut and banana trees and plenty of shells, which led Slogar to surmise that sea creatures including fish were abundant in the clear blue-green waters that rhythmically lapped the shore.

How I would love to have fresh flounder prepared with some of Elani's herbs. Just the thought of it made him hungry, but Seelah kept him so busy he let the idea pass for the time being.

But then one day after their lunch when he and Seelah went for their usual stroll, he thought about it again.

"Seelah," he began, "does Elani ever catch fish for dinner? I'm not complaining, mind you, but we eat mostly tredon and fowl, or vegetables with bread and cheese. Fish would be a nice change, don't you think?"

The Elder Woman wasn't offended. "Yes, it probably would, though I've never asked Elani to prepare any fish. But I will ask her for you."

"Thank you. Uhm, do you think she might like help in catching them?" Slogar's eyes lit up at the thought of fishing again, something he'd not done since he was a child on Ashtar.

Gracious as always, Seelah replied, "I'm sure she will be most appreciative for any help you care to give. Just remember that we have bigger fish to fry, pardon the pun."

Slogar found that extremely funny and laughed out loud for the first time since he'd been here. He would never have guessed the Elder Woman of Silden had a sense of humor. The look she gave him let him know she wasn't joking. Seelah went on ahead, but Slogar sat down on a rocky protrusion by the shore to take in the sunset. That there was a sunset down here amazed him. *How could that be?* He could only guess that this was one of the Elder Woman's innovations.

There was something infinitely peaceful about this chamber, with its gentle breezes and warm sand. The smell of the salty air invigorated him. He marveled at how much he'd grown to like these walks that he'd dreaded so much at first. the chambers were so interesting that he hadn't really thought of it as exercise, but it was, and he had lost most of his excess bulk in the process. Seeing that Seelah was a tiny speck moving up the beach, he got up, dusted his backside, and walked briskly to catch up. He knew soon it would be time for supper and then off to bed for the evening. Even so, he still had a stack of papers to read leaving him fairly certain he wouldn't get much sleep.

As he reached Seelah, she turned and motioned him to a small boat with a sail. They walked over to it, and Seelah called out to Elani who was on the opposite side, tugging it onto the shore. When she came around to the bow, he noticed she wasn't wearing her long flowing robe as usual but instead wore what looked like a waterproof uni to him.

"Dr. Slogar would like to go fishing with you, Elani. Do you have the requisite paraphernalia for him?"

Elani and Slogar exchanged a glance, instantly knowing though the Elder Woman was wise, she knew little of fishing. The tiniest hint of a smile crossed Elani's lips as she replied, "Yes, ma'am. I believe I do. When would you like to go, Doctor?"

Slogar replied quickly. "Tomorrow, if we could. I haven't fished in years. I think it might be relaxing. We have been working awfully hard. What do you say, Seelah? Do you want to come with us?"

Seelah could think of nothing she would dread more.

"I have many more formulas to work out before we can test the new remedies. You two can go in the morning. If you have good fortune, perhaps we'll have some of your catch for lunch."

Slogar helped Elani to bring the boat in, and the three of them made their way to the far end of the beach. The camouflaged door led them back into the main enclave.

As they walked, the Elder Woman asked, "Elani, would you like to join us this evening for dinner?"

"Yes, ma'am, thank you." Elani was a little surprised. She was seldom asked to join Seelah and her guests. But that was fine with her as she preferred to eat in the quiet kitchen. *Hmmm. Might be nice for a change*, she thought.

A little later as they sat enjoying the sumptuous meal, Slogar found himself debating the merits of using this rare time together to ask the questions that were nagging at him but decided to wait. The three of them chatted lightly of tomorrow's fishing adventure. Slogar wondered aloud if the fish were as delicious as the ones he'd eaten as a child.

Elani responded, somewhat more coolly than usual, "I do not know what kind of fish you had as a child. These are native to Andalla, so they are probably not the same. However, fish, no matter where they are from, are still fish. They share similar characteristics but distinctive flavors. Some of our fish are so flavorful you may never want Ashtarian fish again."

Slogar was immediately sorry. He was afraid he'd spoiled his chance to go fishing, so he said, "I'm sure the Andallan fish are every bit as tasty as those of Ashtar, probably better. I can't wait to try them."

Elani was mollified a little and graced him with a fleeting smile. Slogar breathed a sigh of relief. He had to be more sensitive. He could see that Elani had dedicated herself to nurturing all the plants, animals, and yes, fish, here to make sure they were healthy and nutritious. He knew he had to gain her trust if he was to ever learn of her connection, if one existed, to Elsnor and Vandalen.

Seelah could tell that his thoughts had left the present and were going in directions sure to lead him to some of the answers he had been so desperately seeking. With a final *good evening,* she left him still seated at the table.

Elani stood and said, "I will be back for you in half an hour, Doctor."

Alone at the table, Slogar gazed at the great portion of roast that lay before him. Though still full of questions and yearning for answers, he lived by *waste not, want not.* He reached for yet another serving of the succulent meat.

After he had eaten himself into a stupor, Elani reappeared without a sound.

"As you know, the Elder Woman has retired for the evening and will not be joining you for your nightly walkabout. Would you like me to go with you?"

Elani asked this as she surveyed the heap of tredon bones on his plate. She could tell he didn't want to go, but she knew that he'd overeaten and really needed the exercise.

She sighed as she looked again at the messy table. She'd have to clean the dining room later. She had grown fond of this rather odd doctor and wanted him to regain his health. She smiled shyly and offered him her arm.

Though amused, he took it and let her lead him from the room. They walked, this time through her hydro garden. When they were about halfway in, the misters engaged, catching them off guard. Elani danced in the mist like a child in the rain. Slogar liked this carefree side of her. He didn't care that he was getting soaked.

They left the garden and continued their walk on the trail that led them back to the main enclave. Elani, once again somber, accompanied him to his room. With a quiet *good night,* she left him for the evening.

Slogar found her utterly intriguing. He wanted to ask about her father, but instinctively knew the time still was not right. Maybe he'd get the chance on their fishing expedition tomorrow.

The next morning, earlier than he would have liked, he heard the gentle tap on his door and knew that Elani was ready to go. Quickly putting on his robe, he ushered her into his sitting area while he stepped back into his bedroom to dress for the day. After a few minutes he returned to find her sitting perfectly still, looking at one of his books.

"Ah, you've found my book of ancient surgical techniques. You interested in that?"

Elani replied, looking up from the book, "Very much. I once was a surgeon."

He noticed the long, slender fingers and guessed she must have been good at it. When he also considered her intelligence and calm demeanor, he could see clearly that she had all the attributes to be quite successful.

Slogar seized on this opening. "Where did you practice, my dear?"

"On Trilvar. I was a pediatric surgeon. So many of our children had deformities residual from the days of excessive drug use among our people. I knew that's where I could make a difference. My father encouraged me in my profession, though my mother was worried that I was too tender-hearted."

Tender-hearted would not have been a descriptor Slogar would use for her, but then he didn't really know her – yet.

He mused aloud, "Trilvar. I went to school with some Trilvarians. What is your father's name?"

Elani, who'd been speaking easily before, stopped to look at Slogar. She considered how much to tell him.

"My father is Vandalen. He practiced a different type of medicine. I'm sure you know who he was and what happened to him. But I do not wish to dwell on that right now. Are you ready to catch our lunch?"

He had learned all he needed to know for now and was eager to get back to the extraordinary beach chamber. Someday he would get the Elder Woman to tell him how she had created this incredibly complex, yet beautiful, world. But today, the fish were waiting, and Simon Slogar intended to catch them.

***

SLOGAR LEAVES SILDEN

Ten months and many experiments later, Simon Slogar left Seelah and Elani. Together they had helped him overcome his craving for ale and had helped him lose much of the excess weight he had carried for so long. He was still a large man, but he was determined to continue to live as they had taught him.

When he took his leave of the Elder Woman, he felt a tug at his heart. She had become something of a mother-figure for him, which he found simultaneously comforting and troubling as she was nothing like his mother. He promised to return to see her when it was safe. Leaving Elani was harder. He had become genuinely fond of her.

During their fishing trips, they had gotten to know each other's strengths and flaws. Only Elani's flaws weren't flaws to Slogar; they were endearing quirks that made her infinitely appealing on so many levels. Their brief farewell embrace was the only physical contact they had ever had, but they knew they were forever connected. They had not expected these feelings, and both knew that he must leave.

With a deep breath of determination, he left these extraordinary women from whom he had learned so much. But the one thing he had not learned was the thing that had brought him here in the first place. Seelah had not revealed his destiny to him, saying that only God could do that, and only in His time. Slogar knew better than to question her on this point.

Once away from the plains of Silden, he was eager to test some of the remedies he had gotten from the Elder Woman. And so Slogar traveled into the City of Llanhana to find the sick child he'd heard lived there. When he found the family, he realized that the boy had an inflamed respiratory system. Using some of the albuterol that he and Seelah had formulated in her secret lab beneath the shanty, he was able to ease the little one's breathing.

He stayed with the family a few days, convinced the frazzled mother that having furry kittles and cubbers around the boy was triggering his ailment. After a thorough cleaning of the home and relocating the fuzzy little critters outdoors, the child recovered. Slogar gave the mother a bottle of albuterol syrup with strict instructions to use the medicine sparingly, not to tell anyone what had happened, and above all, to keep his involvement secret.

It was not too long, however, before he was on the run, as the mother could not contain herself in the telling and retelling of her child's miraculous recovery and the wonderful Dr. Slogar who had made it happen.

Inevitably, word of this event reached Emperor Jarlod. He was not at all pleased that the truth was being revealed. He was so enamored of himself that he had actually bought into his own hype, at least superficially. Jarlod had made sure that no one questioned his claim of a disease-free empire. That's why he'd gotten rid of the physicians and professors of medicine. But now, he had to deal with this threat to his legacy. Because of Slogar, Jarlod was now forced to face the fact that diseases still existed. But he would never admit it, and he knew he had to make sure this information didn't go any further. Jarlod thought that if it did, his subjects would probably panic. And that could lead to another coup, this time against him. He reasoned that if the doctor and the family he helped disappeared, then there could be no one to dispute his word. So, with the exception of the Empire's couriers, all inter-world travel was stopped to and from Andalla until this crisis passed. The family whose little boy had been helped was whisked away and placed in the locked turret, much to Jarlod's displeasure. He had ordered them eliminated, but his advisors had intervened, convincing him to spare their lives, if not their freedom.

HELGRAD

Slogar was deep into a most pleasant dream that involved Elani and the quiet beach under Silden when he was awakened by the sound of his door being blasted. The Emperor's Troopers crashed into his quarters and dragged him out in the middle of the night. They thrust him unceremoniously onto a ship to transport him to Helgrad – the prison he had so carefully tried to avoid. But before they took off, he convinced them to let him take one bag, nothing else. In the lining of this somewhat large bag, he hid the tiny computer that housed his medical research on its drives. He also hid among his shaving cream and other necessities, the antidotes and other ancient medicines he and Seelah had formulated.

He asked to be allowed to contact his father, but his captor only laughed. "You are on extended holiday, or so your family thinks. Don't expect them to help you. And don't get any ideas about trying to slip a message to them. We monitor every communication where you're going."

And where he was going turned out to be another one of several truly unpleasant events in Slogar's life. His saving grace was patience. By now, he had enough years and experience on him to know to wait this out. But for him, the worst part would be withdrawal. *I've done it before, and I can do it now. Who knows? Maybe this time I'll kick this habit for good.*

The prisoner transport pod landed outside his new home. As Slogar exited, he looked at the massive edifice before him. Helgrad stood starkly white against the black mountains it was carved from. He wondered how they managed to do that. Its outer walls stood forty feet high and were fifteen feet thick. The tiny round windows that let in what little light the prisoners were allowed, made the prison look like a giant sieve. Guard towers had been built into the ledge atop the outer walls that enclosed the prison. Heavily armed guards walked from tower to tower, taking in every movement inside and outside the prison.

Slogar was herded through the massive entrance by one of the guards who had captured him. The man was shorter than Slogar, but his muscles and wiry frame revealed his incredible strength. He poked Slogar to move him along a bit faster.

Slogar stopped dead still and looked down at the guard, careful to present himself as respectful but stern. "Young man, I am going as fast as I can. Please give me a moment to rest."

The guard, hearing the awful wheezing, looked into the eyes of his charge. He read no threat, so he backed off, but with a warning. "You will do well to do as you are told when you are told to do it. If you do, you may shorten your sentence. If you don't . . . well, let's just say, your issues will be resolved." Even so, in a rare show of compassion and quite without giving it any thought, he decided to help Slogar in the only way he could.

The armed guard at Processing barked, "Who do you have this time, Officer Olsen?"

He replied, "This is Simon Slogar, political prisoner of the Emperor. He is to be kept healthy and to be allowed to have his things, but he is to have no visitors."

The Emperor had given no such stipulations for Slogar's treatment. In fact, he had hoped that the man who'd become a thorn in his side wound up dead at the hands of some other prisoner. The only reason he hadn't ordered his execution was purely political. The Slogar family was still well-respected on Ashtar and on occasion socialized with King Eldreth. Slogar's imprisonment could be covered-up but his death, probably not.

The two officers laughed and joked as they finished the necessary paperwork. Once Slogar was processed, he was taken to his cell. On the way, he noticed that the tiny windows to the outside widened as they sloped downward on the inside allowing the light to illuminate the cells during the day.

However, as night was rapidly falling, he realized there was no lighting other than a dim glow skirting the edges of the ceiling and floor. He also noticed that most of the cells were quite small, only six feet by eight feet would have been his guess. He was relieved to find that he had been put in a special wing of the prison where he had a larger cell isolated from the main prisoner population.

Thank you, Olsen, he thought. He just hoped he really would have reason to thank him, but only time would tell.

The thought of having limited human contact saddened Slogar, who enjoyed talking to anyone who'd listen to his ramblings.

At least I'll have plenty of time to do my research.

Slogar laughed bitterly. He had never been charged, tried, or convicted. Yet here he sat in this despicable place. He didn't even know how long his sentence was, but guessed he'd be blessed to ever enjoy freedom again. He spent his days studying, eating the food that was pushed into his cell through the feeding slot, and relishing his daily walk. The thought of that made him laugh roundly from time to time, solidifying his guards' notion that he was quite mad.

The weeks turned into months and the months into nearly a year. By then, he'd gotten used to his routine and looked forward to his one hour in the yard, the only exercise he ever got. Every day the same routine, until one day as he was getting ready to go for his exercise, a different guard rushed up to his cell, waving a handful of papers in his fist.

"I don't know how you managed it, old man, but I have your release papers. Get your belongings. You're free to go."

The guard's words weren't registering fast enough on Slogar's brain. He was just about to ask about his daily walkabout, when the fog lifted, and he understood.

I'm free! How and why he didn't know, or care for that matter, though he would have bet everything he had Seelah had something to do with it. He grabbed his belongings, crammed them into his trunk, and followed the guard out of the cell.

FREEDOM

Once Slogar was certain no one was coming after him to correct a mistaken release, he hurried to the closest village and found a pub. There he proceeded to swill as much as he could hold without passing out. Everything that Seelah had warned him about concerning his health was forgotten, hopelessly drowned in the bitter ale that at the moment was nectar. He wondered if this was the destiny Seelah had alluded to, but he doubted it.

Well, I guess now I'll never know.

After he had drunk and eaten his fill that first night of freedom, he caught the earliest freighter he could find and headed to Boldoon, a planet known for its easy life and laid-back pace. There were beautiful women and plenty of cheap ale. This was his idea of the perfect place to fly below the radar. If he felt like continuing his research, he could do it in private. If he felt like drinking all day, he could drink all day. As long as he paid his tab, nobody cared. But he didn't know how much longer he would be able to survive on the funds he had with him. He wished he could access his wealth back on Ashtar, but the Empire had frozen his account. Well, frozen wasn't exactly what they did. His bank account and the belongings he left behind had been confiscated by the Reglon Empire Guard when he was sent to Helgrad. By Reglon law, felons were stripped of everything of value the authorities could find as part of their punishment. This was just another way the Emperor fed his greed under the guise of justice. Jarlod had not yet realized that an oppressed, unappreciated people will inevitably become a rebellious people. And that was far more dangerous than any other threat to the Empire.

Slogar thought the worst was behind him when he left Helgrad under the cover of darkness for Boldoon. But it didn't take long for him to realize his life on this planet was the worst yet. The locals thought he was just a useless old man who did nothing except eat, drink, and sleep. He had come to Boldoon seeking a place where he might be able to live unnoticed, maybe even regain some sense of the old Slogar. Instead, he found this world was without need of his knowledge and experience. The allure of the food and drink was more than he could resist.

In the beginning he had tried to fit into one of the preferred

Boldoonian professions but was unable to master law, mineral technology, or politics. He gave in to his addictions to food and drink: the only activities he'd ever excelled in. Each day he drank himself into a peaceful oblivion, starting when he woke up just as the day was breaking and not stopping until he collapsed in his own sweaty, drunken stench at the Boor's Nad Inn. This was the last of many sleazy establishments Slogar chose to patronize, mainly because all the others had stopped his credit and not so politely ejected his stinking hulk from their premises.

It was in this comfortable sty that Commander Michael Camdus of the Reglon Empire Guard found him slumped over a platter of tredon bones. Though Camdus had communicated with him recently, it had been many years since he had actually seen Slogar. Except for his increased bulk, the doctor hadn't changed.

"Slogar. Wake up, you old buzzard. You were supposed to meet me at the dock at nine o'clock this morning"

Slogar grunted.

"We checked all of the supply houses to see if maybe you were there stocking up. But no one had seen you. For that matter, most of them had never heard of you. You chickened out, didn't you, you spineless old fart? Hey, are you listening to me or what?"

"What." Slogar burped the word with a snort.

Camdus could feel his anger rising but knew that it was important to get through to him without antagonizing him.

Slogar's self-pity was disgusting, but according to the Emperor, he was the only known medical doctor on any of the Reglon Empire's worlds or its asteroid colonies.

Slogar didn't appreciate Camdus tracking him down, prodding old memories, memories Slogar had tried to drown, though they had turned out to be pretty good swimmers.

Even through his ale-fogged brain, he thought yet again about his erstwhile journey to where he was now. It was only by pure stubbornness that Slogar had become a doctor, with Seelah's help, of course.

"Look, Commanner," a completely snockered Slogar groused, "I nefer wanted to be a dockor. I'uz gonna be a perfessor at one a 'em biggg univershaties, not shome podung school where I wud be jus' anofer dried up old teasher. Ya know, back then, it wuz all about money an' tresp... preswege... Ah hell, you know whad I mean."

Camdus offered a guess. "It was about money and prestige?"

"Yeah, thash whad I said. Bu' I din nee' th' money; it wuz th' power I want'd. More power, more money, plain and shimple. Bud shomewhere along the way I musta los' my mind 'cause I wuz more attracted to he'ping ever'body, not jush th' priverleged few. I wuz one of 'em priverleged few, ya know. So why wu'd I care 'bout th' lesh forshunut? And look where tha' go' me?"

His words were really slurring now, "I can't efen ge' drung anymore wifout being harashed by one o' the Empersh's flungies."

Camdus was sick of Slogar's bellyaching; and when Slogar was drinking, it seemed like that's all he wanted to do. He silently sent for Rax.

"Don't blame me for your choices, Slogar. You're the one who wanted to become a doctor, licensed or not, so just look in the mirror next time you want to complain. On one point, you're almost right. I am one of the Emperor's soldiers, but I'm nobody's flungy – er, flunky. But let's just get this crap out here and now so we can move on. Tell me the rest of your sorry story." Rax popped in at that moment with a small bottle in his hand. Camdus took it, thanked the Rider, and dismissed him.

"I'm listening, Slogar, but take one of these transcaps so I can understand you."

Camdus handed him the pills.

Slogar, though offended, took the transcaps, swallowed one, and poured the others onto the filthy table. In a few seconds, he had sobered up enough to share this part of his life with someone. If Camdus was willing to listen, then Slogar was eager to talk.

After a while, Camdus became aware that he wasn't paying attention. He tuned back in as Slogar was saying, "….of medicine without financial worry. That's how I became a doctor without benefit of formal education and practical experience."

Camdus interrupted, "But surely you knew you'd be breaking Empire law, so you could never have a medical practice, right?"

Slogar nodded affirmatively.

"So why do it?"

Slogar had asked himself that a thousand times.

"I decided there must be some part of the vast Reglon Empire that was not as advanced as the political leaders would have everyone believe. My research pointed me to the tiny world of Andalla or so I thought until I realized that Seelah had willed me there, but that's another story. I practiced ancient medicine briefly until Helgrad and now the same

Emperor who threw me in prison wants my help. Well," Slogar said with particular venom, "Jarlod can just kiss my big, fat ..."

Just as Slogar was ready to verbally skewer the Emperor, Camdus interrupted him. He was fed up and was not inclined to listen to any more of his complaining.

"Okay, okay. We don't have time for your unabridged autobiography or your opinion of the Emperor. As you know from the Emperor's last communication with you – don't roll your eyes at me – Creedor is in serious trouble. This epidemic has baffled even the wisest of Jarlod's advisors. None of them has ever seen an epidemic. For that matter, none of them has ever seen even a simple twentieth century disease like muselees."

"That's *measles*," Slogar corrected.

"Muselees, measles, whatever. The bottom line is that you're the only person we know of in the Empire who has any experience with disease of any kind, and now we have this epidemic destroying what's left of the population of Creedor."

Camdus paused before going on. "We have all this data from our ancient history archives and it's meaningless to everyone. Everyone except you, that is. Now, will you come on your own or do I have to drag your sorry behind out of this dump and have you escorted to the ship?"

Slogar was getting tired of people putting the fate of the Empire on his shoulders. "If this is my destiny, I want no part of it. Who do they think I am, anyway? And how do they expect me, of all people, to be of any help?"

Camdus didn't respond.

One transcap had not been enough to stop the headache Slogar felt coming on. He pushed aside the greasy ale mug and reached for another pill, swallowing it without benefit of water.

Camdus began counting. At fifteen, Slogar looked up with piercing, brown eyes that were no longer glazed over with the onset of stabbing pain. When he spoke, there was a leaden quality to his voice.

"The Creedorians are better off without a doctor at all than one who doesn't seem to know what he's doing anymore. Most of what I haven't drowned in ale is just theory and that won't do them any good. The last thing they need is a broken-down, besotted has-been telling them what to do to get well. I'm not even sure that I would recognize the ailment once I get there – if I get there. I just think that you're banking on a loser. If I do go along with it, the Creedorians will be the real losers. They'll be risking their lives when maybe the disease will run its course and they'll recover without interference. Why don't you just go on without me? My life here is just fine anyway, just the way it is." He wiped his greasy hands on his ale-soaked outer shirt.

"Spare me, Slogar. Sure, your life looks great. I mean just look around you. You haven't had a decent meal in months. You don't have any friends. Some of the most beautiful women in the Empire are all around you and you stay too drunk to notice. Not that any of them would have anything to do with you. Come on, Slo, look at you. You haven't had a bath in so long they aren't making the same kind of soap anymore. And your clothes are so filthy they could probably stand alone, if you'd ever take them off. Not to mention your belly. When's the last time you saw your feet? Do you even remember what kind of shoes you're wearing?"

"Hey, all right. Enough. I get it. And I do know what kind of shoes I'm wearing, wise guy," Slogar huffed.

Camdus couldn't resist. "What kind?"

Until this moment Slogar had no clue how obese he had become. "Damn it, Cam. I *don't* know; I can't see them. There you go, you've made my point for me. How do you expect a man who can't even see his own feet to save a planet?"

Camdus hadn't expected this turn in the argument, but he was not to be dissuaded. "All right, you know, truth is truth, but I didn't mean to be quite so blunt. But if you come with me, I think we can help you get in better shape in no time, especially once we get moving. And we have got to get moving; no more arguments. What do you say?"

Slogar had begun to tremble violently, not from emotion but from withdrawal. Camdus retrieved another transcap from among the tredon bones and gave it to Slogar, who took it without acknowledging he needed it. He had trouble admitting that he was hooked on ale – again. But hooked he was and at this moment Camdus was tempted to take Slogar up on his invitation to leave him alone. But instead he said, "Come off it, Slo. You know, you used to have a pretty sharp mind. All that knowledge can't have been washed away, no matter how much ale you've swilled. As to the epidemic going away on its own, give me a break. Since last month, more than two thousand Creedorians have died from it. We've got a cruiser to catch at eleven tonight. That doesn't give us much time. So how about it? Are you coming with us, or do I have to let the Emperor know you refuse to obey his orders? I'm sure your old cell in Helgrad is still available if you don't come with us."

Slogar wanted to tell Camdus and the rest of these you-can-save-the-Empire fanatics where to go and how to get there. But that wasn't an option.

"All right, all right, I'll be there. Now don't you have somewhere to go?" Slogar asked sarcastically.

Camdus knew that dealing with an alcoholic was a gamble, but it was the only one he had. Just as the door to the inn closed, Camdus heard Slogar shout, "Barkeep, another here."

THE SHIP

Camdus stood beside the ship, the REG Ursidae. He let out a deep sigh. *Slogar isn't the only one who looks like a tredon bull that's seen too many seasons.* Then he remembered the Ursidae's secret and smiled.

Though the cruiser looked like it too had seen better days, he knew that her engines, electronics, and weaponry had been updated. Still, Camdus was used to flying the finest the fleet had to offer, and this ship looked nothing like them, not even the old trainers he'd flown as a cadet looked this bad. No, the Ursidae's once flawless glaze was now scratched and pocked, her call letters barely visible. In truth, she looked like she was ready for the scrap heap. He could still see the worn image of a gorgeous two-headed wench some pilot in years past had painted on the side. *Obviously a Talean beauty. Oh well, to each his own, I suppose.*

Camdus was brought out of his mental ramblings by a gruff grunt and a shove from one of the Boldoonian laborers straining under the loaded crate of supplies.

"Damn it, watch where you're going!" Camdus swore in frustration at the sweating laborer. "Are you blind, or just dumb? And be careful with that crate. Those supplies had better be intact or you won't be. You got that?"

The worker carefully placed the crate to the side, turned to face Camdus, and spoke in a controlled voice.

"My name is Jacar Grunden. I will carry your crates, but I will not be talked to as if I were one of your sluggard dogs. Is *that* understood, Sir?"

Camdus considered this man – Grunden – for the first time. *How did I overlook this one when I searched for men of mettle for the mission on Creedor? Obviously, this is a man with integrity.*

Camdus couldn't overlook the man's sheer strength that was evident even beneath the bulky laborers over shirt. *I guess that's why he's been relegated to the position of common laborer. But most of them are too ignorant to be insulted.* Studying his face, Camdus tried to place Grunden in his mind. His features and name were familiar, but he just could not remember. *He can't be related to the military Grunden family. The Admiral would never allow his kin to serve in such a lowly capacity. But still, he does look familiar. Well, it'll come to me sooner or later, I suppose.*

He then addressed Grunden in a more respectful tone. "Tell me, Grunden, why aren't you one of our fighters or builders? What brought you here, of all places?"

Grunden looked away. The western sol was riding low just before dusk, giving the sky an aura of blue and purple, tinged with feathers of green. The beauty of dusk never disappointed when he sought peace in it. He attributed his appreciation of nature to his mother, who had passed away five years ago.

He spoke quietly, yet there was an undertone to his voice that put Camdus on his guard. "Commander, not all grunts are mindless fools. Some of us chose to come into this service. And those of us who did have reasons for keeping a low profile."

"What reasons? Who are you loyal to, Grunden?"

Camdus had his hand on his side arm.

Grunden studied him. He had already said too much and hoped that his research had been correct.

"We, uh, that is, I am loyal to the Empire. But since Jarlod came into power, I have had to struggle to stay loyal. I keep reminding myself that he's just one …."

Camdus interrupted, "One what? He's our Emperor; loyalty to him is mandatory."

A group of recruits came into view tramping up the boarding ramp. Both men fell silent, waiting for them to pass.

"Look, Commander," Grunden said in a low voice. "Take me with you and I'll tell you everything you want to know, only not out here – it's not safe."

"All right, Grunden. I'm conscripting you into the Reglon Empire Guard Creedorian Task Force, effective immediately. After we launch, we'll talk. Understood?"

"Aye, Sir."

After he took Grunden to a holding area, Camdus made his way to his quarters, thinking about the coming mission. He hated to return to the stench of Creedor; its mass graves were filling by the hour. Death was everywhere; it seemed to permeate one's body, leaving nothing but a hollow cavern of dread and despair. But Emperor Jarlod had personally given Camdus the order.

Slogar was a no-show, and they couldn't afford to wait for him.

There's other business we need to take care of in Clandil, anyway. Enough worrying about the old has-been. I should have known he wouldn't come. He's too far gone. Who knows? Maybe it's for the best.

He picked up his battle helmet and dusted it off with his sleeve. The ship was loaded. All he needed now was to contact the pilot to make sure the preflight check had been successfully completed. *Only God knows what we'll find this time. Whoever or whatever's behind the Creedorian epidemic has gotta be dangerous.*

With these thoughts in mind, he headed for the bridge. When he stopped to make sure the crew port was locked, he thought he heard someone wheezing. Peering out into the growing darkness, he saw Slogar lumbering up the boarding ramp. Suddenly, the ramp started to move away from the ship.

Camdus slammed the interrupt switch with his open hand, stopping the ramp's movement and returning it to the ship, nearly knocking the doctor off his feet in the process. Slogar was carrying a small black case in one hand and with the other tugging at a rope tethered to a large trunk. Camdus opened the door to let him in.

"You wouldn't leave without me, would you, Commander? It takes a while to get a rusty old relic like me moving. You know, you really should be more patient and have a little consideration for the infirmities of your elders," he huffed at Camdus, who'd stepped out onto the ramp and was nearly knocked off his feet as Slogar struggled with his luggage.

"Slogar, sometimes you are such an ass. You could have let me know you were on the way. Too bad you're under the Emperor's protection," Camdus said aloud. Then he mused, *Amazing how fast a man's worth can change in this Empire.*

Still, Camdus felt the urge to slug him but thought better of it. After all, the Emperor had ordered Camdus to get him on that cruiser one way or another. This way he would not have to explain to Emperor Jarlod why he'd disobeyed. But after his meeting with Slogar, he thought that the old drunk was more trouble than he was worth. And up until this moment, Camdus had been prepared to leave him behind if he didn't show up. He'd take whatever Jarlod dished out. But if that happened, Camdus was determined to drag the old sot right along with him. Slogar wouldn't know where he was anyway – he was so used to dismal ale holes. And when he sobered up enough to know that there wouldn't be any more …. *Oh well, I don't have to worry about that now.*

Camdus finally managed to align the large trunk properly to get it through the door. He swore silently, sweat pouring down his back, stood up again, pulled the doctor's belongings inside, and barked, "Haul your worthless ass in here now, Slogar. I've had just about all of you I can take for one day."

Just then, Grunden stepped out of the holding area to see what all the ruckus was about. He hurried over, stood beside Camdus, and glowered at Slogar.

Grunden spoke directly to Camdus, "Sir, do you want me to take care of this riffraff for you?"

"This riffraff, as you so aptly put it, is Dr. Simon Slogar of Ashtar, more recently of the Boor's Nad Inn on Boldoon. Despite his unseemly appearance, Dr. Slogar is here on orders from Emperor Jarlod himself. He has been assigned the task of ending the epidemic on Creedor." Camdus paused a moment as he watched Grunden's expression go from hostility to total disbelief.

Grunden, for his part, knew where he had seen this man before. *But a physician? How can that be possible?*

"Slogar, we'll get you to your quarters in a bit. You will be in OQ2, right beside me – just in case. You'll have an assistant to work directly with you and to provide you with whatever you need for your scientific or medical pursuits. But if there is anything else that you may require, Slogar, you must see me directly. Do you understand?" This last statement was delivered as Camdus sent a penetrating stare that seemed to bore into Slogar's brain.

Slogar responded, somewhat pettishly, "I understand all too well what you mean. No ale. That won't be a problem. I'm sure I can do it. Now, if you'll show me to my quarters." He turned to walk down the corridor, but Camdus clutched his elbow. He'd noticed several bulges in Slogar's filthy cloak.

He reached in and removed the hidden ale bottles, which he handed to Grunden. "Mr. Grunden, please dispose of these."

"You can't take my belongings! Who do you think you are? Give me those!" Slogar made a lunge for the bottles that Grunden held tightly in his hands high above his head. The doctor tripped over his large case, landing with a loud thud on his well-padded backside. He knew defeat when it stared him in the face. "I hope you have enough transcaps on board, Commander," Slogar said, as he took Camdus' arm and with great effort, pulled himself up.

Camdus waited for him to get an even footing, and then reminded him, "You want to know who I am? I am the Commander of the Reglon Empire Guard, and I decide who brings what on board. And you, Sir, will not bring any unauthorized spirits on this ship. Am I making myself clear?"

By this time, Slogar had regained his composure and responded, "Yes, Commander. And as to the assistant, I will welcome one, if that's what you really mean." Then he huffed, "But I don't much like the idea of a babysitter. I need my privacy."

"Then grow up, Slogar," Camdus said sharply. He led the doctor and Grunden to the holding area.

"Stay here, Doctor. Mr. Grunden, come with me," Camdus ordered.

Grunden went with the Commander, not knowing what to expect.

Camdus led the way to the bridge. Before entering, he said to Grunden, "Wait here."

Inside, he found Captain Victor Slag studying a panel with odd charts on it. He stood and saluted.

"At ease, Captain," Camdus ordered. "I have a new recruit I'd like to place under your supervision. I want you to keep a close eye on him, no sensitive assignments just yet. He was a laborer on Boldoon, so he can continue in that role here until I know more about him. You can use him to load the shuttles for starters," Camdus said.

"Aye, sir, I can use all the help I can get. But who is he and why did you bring him aboard?" Slag asked the obvious.

"He's part of a group of displaced soldiers. He has information I want, but until I know more about him and what he's up to, I'm keeping him with us. Let me know what you think. Any threat, even a hint of a threat, and I'll make sure he spends the next ten years in prison."

Slag looked puzzled but knew better than to ask any more questions. Camdus opened the door and asked his new recruit to join them.

Slag and Grunden stood staring at each other for only a moment. Instant
recognition registered plainly on each man's face. Slag, normally reserved, broke into a grin and exclaimed, "Well, I'll be damned! Jack, what the hell are you doing here?"

All the tension Grunden had felt rising from the stress of this new situation melted away when he saw Slag.

"Yes, you probably will, you old dog!" Grunden said and grabbed Slag in a bear hug. "What're *you* doing here?"

"I'm here because Commander Camdus drafted me to help with this mission."

Camdus took this in.

"How do you know this man, Captain?"

"We grew up in the same town, went to the same school, and fell in love with the same girl," Slag explained.

"Yes, and as I recall, I won the baseball trophy, but you got the girl. How is Janara?" Grunden asked.

"Fine, as far as I know," Slag said, the smile gone from his face.

"But I thought...," Grunden started, but Camdus broke in.

"Save the reunion, gentlemen. We have work to do."

"Aye, Sir," both replied.

Camdus left the bridge and returned to his quarters to pick up some of his papers. But, by the time he got there, his head felt like it was about to explode, throbbing intensely. He hadn't endured one of these headaches in years. Lying down on his bed, he closed his eyes and tried to rest, but he couldn't turn off his thoughts and the pounding in his head got progressively worse. Finally, he gave up. There was a stack of old solar powered e-tablets on his table. Some of them contained news clippings along with photos of military leaders and their stories. He picked one of them up, touched it on, and began re-reading the articles, studying each picture. He scrolled a page and felt a jolt of recognition. Staring up at him was the face of Grunden, Admiral Maximus Grunden. At his knee was a young boy, listed as Jacar, the Admiral's son.

Camdus was amazed at how much he looked like his father, even as a youngster. *But how can this be? Why would the son of an Admiral be nothing more than a common laborer? I don't get it.*

He hadn't even thought of the Admiral for many years. But now he had reason to learn more. Maybe once he did, it would explain at least some of the mystery surrounding what was going on in the Empire now. He knew that after Emperor Borm was overthrown, the Admiral and many other Counselors had dropped out of the public eye. Everyone assumed they'd been encouraged to retire and that they'd chosen to live out their days as quietly as possible. What if that was not the case? Camdus knew he'd have to contact his father, but not now, not until he was sure his head wouldn't split wide open.

Camdus stood up, went to his sleep chamber and found his rucksack. He rummaged through it until he found a bottle of pain medicine that had been given for him the last time he'd been wounded. Though they were way out of date, he took two of them with a glass of water.

"Oh, what the hell," he said aloud. "What doesn't kill me will make me stronger, or so I'm told. We'll see."

He sat down with the article and plowed through it in spite of the pain still thumping in his temples. It looked like there was nothing in it other than the party line for the Admiral's achievements. There was no mention of his reassignment, if that's what had happened to him.

Camdus wanted to try some of the other e-tablets, but after about half an hour the pills kicked in. The absence of pain was such a relief he thought he could sleep. He crawled back into his bed, but within another hour, he was full-on hallucinating. He jumped out of bed and grabbed his weapon.

"Better run, boys!" he shouted to the imaginary soldiers under his new command. "Take cover, take cover!" A giant electrified, purple snake was after them, striking left and right, lunging closer and closer as it shot lightning bolts at them. He continued to give commands, all the while firing his nucleo at the monster.

Slag and Grunden were headed back to their quarters when they heard the commotion. They rushed to Camdus' door and called out to him. They heard shouting followed by loud crashing, and then all was quiet.

"Commander! Commander! Let us in! Camdus, please let us in!" Slag shouted as he and Grunden tried to get his door to open.

"Stand back," Slag ordered. Grunden stepped aside.

Slag pulled his nucleo and jolted the lock until they heard it give way.

Shouldering their way through the door, they found their leader lying on the floor. His cheek leaked plasma where it had been seared with a ricocheted shot.

"Help me, Jack," Slag said as he bent down to check for a pulse. They stood him up, but his knees buckled. His eyes were open, but he didn't seem to be awake.

Grunden hoisted Camdus over his shoulder and said, "Lead the way."

Slag took off running with Grunden close on his heels. Once they got to the infirmary, Slag called in a medi-droid to take over and sent the ensign to bring Dr. Slogar from the holding area.

Maybe he can help, too.

"What's going on with him?" Grunden asked.

"I don't know, but I'm going back to see if I can find any clues in his quarters. It shouldn't take long, but if anything changes before I get back, call me." With that Slag took off back down the corridor, now crowded with curious crew members.

When he got back to OQ1, Slag surveyed the damaged quarters. *What in the hell happened here?* He shook his head and began methodically processing the sitting area where they found him. E-tablets, some still smoldering, littered the floor near the sofa. Gray horok feather stuffing from the throw pillows were everywhere, some even sticking out between books on the shelves that were built into one wall. Just when Slag was ready to wrap it up, he spied the pill bottle. He picked it up, read the label, and took off to the infirmary.

Once there, he saw Slogar with Camdus. He handed the bottle to the droid, who immediately placed one of the tiny white pills in the ChemId processor.

Slag found Grunden sitting in the waiting area outside the patient exam rooms. They could see Camdus through the observation window. He was sleeping soundly.

"What'd you find in the Commander's quarters, Victor?"

"Well, besides the wreckage, nothing but a bottle of pills. It was sitting beside a half empty glass of water. So my best guess is he took something for that headache he's been complaining about and it had some weird effect on him."

The medi-droid and Slogar entered the waiting area at the same time, nearly getting stuck in the doorway. Slogar, fairly aggravated with the bot now, started to speak but was cut off by the droid who gave them the report.

"Diagnosis: Psychotic break induced by ingesting outdated oxymethalyn." The droid turned to go.

"Wait," Grunden said. "I thought outdated meds lost their potency. Why did he react this way?"

The droid's eyes flickered off, then on again.

"Unknown." Then it glided away before they could ask any more questions.

Slogar answered the question, pleased to one-up the smart-aleck droid.

"The potency of this particular medicine was multiplied. He ingested enough to kill most men."

"Well, he's not most men. When will he be ready to return to duty?" Slag asked. "Tomorrow, if his vital signs are normal. The Commander has a strong constitution," Slogar said and returned to Camdus' side to check him once more.

The following day, Camdus was deemed fit for duty and released. He returned to his rooms and spent the morning putting his belongings back in order. He was disappointed that he'd blasted the e-tablets. But he hoped once he got back to Command HQ on Reglon Major, one of the historical device techs could retrieve at least some of the data. By afternoon, he was pleased that his day had calmed down with no further surprises.

The next few days passed fairly uneventfully with only a minor glitch in the docking system giving them trouble. Once Camdus was sure there were no more technical issues, he turned his attention again to Grunden. He summoned Slag to report to his quarters.

"Anything I need to be worried about from Mr. Grunden?" he asked in his typical blunt style.

"Nothing, Sir. He's the same man he always was, genuine and hardworking. He never complains, no matter how menial or difficult the job is. There is no threat there, Sir," Slag said earnestly, the asked, "How're you feeling, Commander? You gave us one hell of a scare."

"Yeah, I know. But I'm fine now. Thanks for asking. It'll be a cold day before I ever do that again. That was bizarre."

"Commander, what exactly did you see when you were out of it?"

"Victor, it was so jumbled up, I don't really remember. I guess you could say my deepest fears manifested in that hallucination." He stopped at the memory of the big snake – he was petrified of snakes. He also remembered having to order retreat, which was truly his greatest fear as Commander.

Seeing the concern on Slag's face, he tried to reassure him. "But the good news is it was just some crazy figment of my imagination," he said. Then he changed the subject. "So you think Grunden's solid?"

"Yes Sir. Solid as they come. He'll be an asset to the mission," Slag said without hesitation.

"I figured as much. The son of Admiral Maximus Grunden could hardly be expected to be anything less, but I had to double-check. It helps that you've known him pretty much all your life, Victor. I trust your opinion," Camdus said with a slap on Slag's shoulder.

Slag took the praise without looking Camdus in the eye, which Camdus took as humility.

"Send Mr. Grunden to my quarters after supper," Camdus said.

GRUNDEN'S STORY

The purple iris sky had already begun to darken as the ship got under way on its journey to Creedor. Normally, the beginning of a new mission spawned excitement among the crew. This time it was different. The shadow of Creedor's unknown dangers loomed in each mind as they hurtled through space. Even the stars seemed to pull away as they flew, shimmering cowards of the night.

When Grunden saw his quarters, he was pleased to find them quite spacious which was almost unheard of for a noncom. His room, OQ3, adjoined Slogar's. Grunden appreciated this strategy. After all, it made sense to keep the doctor surrounded by men proven in battle. *But how could he know?* he wondered.

Captain Slag had ordered him to meet with Camdus as soon as he finished his shift. He hoped he'd find out more then. On his way, he tried to remember all the details of the events that had led him to form his opposition group. He knew if he left anything out Commander Camdus would suspect his loyalty.

Wait a minute. He did an about-face, returned to his quarters, and retrieved something he was certain he'd need. He stopped just before he got to the Commander's door. Though he was a brave man, Grunden knew that what he had to tell him was risky. He pulled his handkerchief out of his pocket and wiped the sweat from his face and neck.

The door swooshed shut behind him. He noticed that the Commander had managed to return his living space to normal. If he hadn't been with Slag after Camdus' violent episode, he would not have known there'd ever been a problem. *Well, except for the stray horok feathers still sticking out of the most unexpected places, but still....*

Camdus interrupted his thoughts, motioned him to sit in one of the simple leather chair s near him. On a table in front of him were small plates of fruit, vegetables, and some kind of dried meat. Two tall mugs of a dark, golden liquid were on either side of the table.

"Let's eat while we talk. You're probably as hungry as I am after the work we've put in today."

Grunden settled in with a plate of food, which was surprisingly good. Either that, or it had been a long time since he'd had anything other than canned military rations; pretty much anything else would taste good. He sipped the beverage. Ale wasn't his favorite, but it was tolerable. Yet as it slid down his throat, he felt an easy warmth spreading over him. Until that moment, he hadn't realized just how to-the-bone cold he'd gotten working in the poorly heated space suit. Ever since the evening Slogar had boarded, the docking mechanism had been giving them trouble. They'd tried to make the repairs from the inside with no luck. So he and some of the others had spent the day floating outside the ship trying to repair it. They'd hit the right combination just before they were ready to call it quits, much to everyone's relief.

Now sitting here, he leaned back in his chair and began to relax. For some time neither man spoke. Then Camdus stood up, pushed a button and sweet strains of classical music filled the room. He developed this habit when he ran a covert op on Ashtar.

"All right, then, Grunden. Why did you risk your position by talking to me? You have to be aware that more than a few commanders would have you thrown in the brig for your insolence."

Grunden took a deep breath and said, "Yes, Sir. I'm aware of that. But things have changed over the past few months. We've been trying to find ways to get to Creedor. As to why I chose you – let's just say we did our research. I had to trust our intel, even though you might have been one of them." Grunden could tell that Camdus still didn't understand. "You see, our mission is even more urgent now. I had to risk getting thrown in the brig for insubordination. I decided bumping you with the crate was one sure way to get your attention. By the way, thank you for *not* throwing me in the brig. Look, Commander, I can't afford to get locked up, even for a little while, not now anyway."

Camdus was struggling to make sense of what Grunden was saying, wondering who exactly he was talking about.

"For future reference, Mr. Grunden, you can be straight-forward with me. There's no need to give me another bruise. I have enough already."

Grunden sat in silence, not knowing what to say to that, so Camdus made it easy for him.

"Look, Grunden, there's a world on the path to total extinction if we don't get there and stop it. Now, what I don't understand is while most sane people are trying to leave Creedor, you and your group are trying to go there. I don't have time to play guessing games. Cut the bull and tell me what you're up to – now."

Grunden realized that Camdus was focused on the epidemic. He wondered if the Commander was unaware of what else was going on.

"Commander, the epidemic is only one of your problems on Creedor. I don't know everything, but our intelligence reports indicate that there are outsiders deep within the planet."

Camdus felt his heart sink. "Outsiders? Outside Creedor or the Empire? What do you think they're doing?" Camdus asked.

Grunden tried to answer his questions. "I'm not sure where they're from, but most likely they're stealing trizactl. We don't know who they are, so we don't know if they're Reglon or not. But we have reason to believe that they're behind the disease that's killing the Creedorians."

He stopped talking and waited for Camdus to respond.

"But why?" Camdus asked. "Why kill innocent people? That doesn't make any sense. What else do you know, Grunden?"

"I don't know anything else, I swear. I've given you the only answer I've got," he paused, "but I have this disk with data on it," he said and reached into his pocket. It wasn't there. He patted the rest of his pockets but couldn't feel anything. *Oh hell, I must have lost it between my room and here,* he thought.

"I'll find it, Commander. I must have missed when I went to put it in my pocket, or maybe it's out in the hall. I don't know, but I'll find it."

Then he said, "I trusted you, Commander. Now I'm asking you to trust me."

Camdus sat motionless, trying to digest this new information. Intruders stealing trizactl would more than likely delay their fight to save the Creedorians from the plague. If what Grunden suspected were true, then the game just changed.

And what if this disease has been genetically engineered to have no antidote? He could not entertain these thoughts for they meant almost certain defeat. Camdus knew he could trust him. If Grunden had risked everything for the Empire, then he welcomed his help.

"That's enough for this evening. Find the disk and we'll meet here again tomorrow, same time. Dismissed," Camdus said, his attention already on one of his reports.

Grunden left, grateful for a chance to look for the missing item. Along the way he scoured every inch of the corridor, but no luck. Frustrated and sick on his stomach from his fruitless search, he went to his quarters.

"You lookin' for this?" The voice was coming from his sofa.

Grunden couldn't see anyone, only a tiny square suspended above the table in front of the sofa.

He instinctively pulled his weapon. "Who's here? Show yourself," he ordered.

"No need for that, Jack." The voice suddenly had a body attached to it.

Grunden, not sure what was happening, recognized his old friend Zander. But Zander had been killed during the last Great War. *Now I must be hallucinating,* he thought.

"What the hell, Zander? What's going on?"

Zander laughed and tossed the small disk to Grunden. "Don't ask me, Jack. One minute I was peacefully spending eternity in Soldiers Field and the next I was here picking up the disk that fell out of your pocket when you reached for your handkerchief. What's going on here, old buddy? Looks like you've got your hands full."

Grunden didn't know if this was Zander or a result of stuffing himself earlier. Either way, he was glad to have the disk back.

He returned the item he'd picked up to its place on his desk.

Deciding to go with it, Grunden sat down in the side chair opposite Zander. "Yeah, we've got a mess, all right. You see...," he began and didn't stop until he told him everything he knew about what was going on.

Zander listened, and then looked away as if hearing someone else speaking.

"I have to go now, Jack. Good luck, old buddy."

"Zander, wait! When are you coming back?"

The now-disembodied voice drifted back, "Beats me."

Grunden was left with the disk he'd lost and an experience he could never tell anyone about if he didn't want to go to the psych ward. *Just as well. Most of the time, it's harder to deal with the living anyway.* Exhausted, he fell on his bed without bothering to change out of his work clothes. He spent a restless night filled with indecipherable dreams.

The next day was tiring, though not nearly as labor intensive as the day before. At the appointed time, Grunden reported to the Commander's quarters to continue his interview. With permission to enter granted, the Commander's door slid open. Camdus motioned Grunden again to the same chair, with an even better meal laid out before him.

Maybe I should become like Scheherazade, the ancient storyteller. The Commander spreads a decent table. I wouldn't mind eating here every day.

Grunden roused himself from these thoughts to see Commander Camdus watching him intently. He did not flinch under the steady gaze, yet he was not comfortable either. He sighed. *May as well get this over with.*

"Now, Mr. Grunden, I'm still trying to make sense out of what you told me last night. But for now, tell me what you're trying to accomplish and who you're working with."

Grunden hardly knew where to start, but he knew he'd better try.

"Commander, Creedor isn't the only planet with unregistered visitors. About six months ago, I was serving on the Emperor's Orbital Patrol on Reglon Major. My unit was charged with ensuring that the Elsnith Oasis was used only by the Royals and their guests, no one else. Late one evening, after an especially boring watch, I started to pack it in and report back to my quarters. Just as I was about to enter my pod, I heard something beyond the trees to the west. I froze and listened to see if I could hear it again. The officer on watch with me didn't hear anything and wanted to go. I told him we needed to go see if we could find what made that noise. He didn't want to, but we were under orders to investigate anything suspicious. We went on foot about a quarter mile, careful to stay in the darkest shadows. We saw maybe a dozen hooded figures with odd looking shields. Just behind them was a sheer cliff that seemed to be solid rock. But the intruders lifted the shields and disappeared one by one through an opening that closed up after the last one was inside. We crept up to the cliff for a closer look. There was no sign of an entry way. I have no idea how they got in."

Camdus interrupted Grunden's story by asking, "What did Command say when you reported it?"

"We, uh, talked about making the report and even began initial contact with Command," Grunden said reluctantly.

Camdus was getting irritated again. "Did you make the report? A simple *yes* or *no* will do."

Grunden answered, "No, Sir."

"All right. Explain yourself, Mr. Grunden." Camdus was a stickler for procedure. "This had better be good."

Grunden started again. "You'd think with all we've gone through and all the other emperors Jarlod has ticked off, he'd be more receptive to any report of unauthorized activity, no matter how bizarre. But it seems our Emperor is more interested in preventing peasants from visiting Elsnith than in protecting the Empire. At any rate, we both knew other soldiers who'd made similar reports and were subsequently removed from duty. So, we didn't. Right or wrong – we didn't."

Camdus took a long drink of his ale, and then he asked, "Let me get this straight. You and your patrol partner decided to save your own hide rather than follow procedure? That seems inconsistent with the kind of soldier I took you for and the kind of man I know your father is."

Though the words stung, Grunden replied, "Commander, think about it – if we disappeared like some of them did, who would be left to fight, if a fight was needed?"

"I understand your reasons, Mr. Grunden, but what I want to know is how does what you're doing tie into this mission to Creedor? It does, doesn't it?"

"Yes, Commander, it definitely does. From that night on I knew something was out of place. More than that, I guess you could say I had a gut feeling that we were in danger. How much and what kind of danger, I didn't know then and don't know now. But to get back to how this ties in. I managed to get busted down to grunt so I could put together a hand-picked group of men, who like me, love all our worlds and want them to be safe so that we can live in peace. Most of the men are soldiers who were relieved of duty after reporting suspicious activity. It wasn't too hard to convince them to join me."

Camdus sat quietly for a moment before he spoke. "You deliberately lost your rank, got reassigned to this detail as a laborer, and somehow formed a rebel band to fight clandestinely to save the Reglon Empire. Would that sum it up?"

"Yes, Sir, pretty much. There aren't many of us, but we're not afraid to fight, and we are fiercely loyal to the people – not Jarlod. If Reglon Major and now Creedor are under attack, Boldoon will probably be next. We don't know how much time we have. We don't know exactly what we're facing. But we do know whoever they are, they have extraordinary powers. If they meant no harm, they'd have registered and would not come and go under cover of darkness. We need your help, Commander. You have contacts among very gifted and loyal people. It'll take all the talent, courage, and skill we can muster. Please think about it. I know your mission is important, but somehow, I think this is just as urgent."

Camdus considered what Grunden had told him, and then he asked, "Did you bring the proof with you tonight?"

Grunden nodded affirmatively and passed the tiny disk to him.

"Everything we have is on here."

Camdus held the tiny revelation in his hand. Then he said, "There's just one more thing I want to know. Who did the soldiers make the reports to?"

Without hesitation, Grunden said, "They all reported to Elder Tomer Arking."

"Elder Arking? Mr. Grunden, are you sure it wasn't Elder Spetch?" Camdus would put nothing past Spetch, but Tomer Arking?

"Yes, Sir, I'm sure it was Elder Arking."

Camdus had always thought highly of him as the Elder had been a close friend of his father. Now he needed to find out more. He said, "I want you to take the position of assistant to Dr. Slogar. His safety is extremely important to the fate of Creedor, maybe ours, too. At least as far as the plague is concerned."

Grunden considered this without comment, as Camdus sank back in his chair and let the ale take hold, easing him into thoughts so deep Grunden sensed it best not to disturb him.

He thought it over a moment and said, "Thank you for the assignment, Commander. Something about him intrigues me." Besides, he figured he could learn something from this pseudo-relic. He knew that Dr. Slogar was nobody's fool, even though it was obvious he often chose to play a fool's role.

"You know, Commander, I've seen Dr. Slogar on several occasions at the Boor's Nad Inn. Once in a while the regulars used to set him up with rounds of ale so they could watch his drunken antics. But one evening, I saw him huddled in the corner booth with a heavily robed figure. I tried to eavesdrop but only heard bits and pieces of the conversation, not enough to know exactly what the two were discussing. But I gathered they were talking about the Emperor and his thugs. The man was covered up so much that the only thing I could see was his rather large right hand. There was an odd-shaped indention on his right index finger, sure sign that the man had worn a large ring at some time. The man's size was consistent with Vandalen. I know Jarlod stole his ring when he was arrested. If this was the Wizard, then he still doesn't have his ring."

Camdus listened intently for he knew that Grunden most likely had seen Vandalen. *But how can that be? He's exiled in Dartal on Killund,* Camdus thought.

"You're sure of this?" Camdus asked.

"I sent scouts out at once to discover the identity of the man. No luck. Commander, I am well-versed in Reglon history and know for a fact that the Trilvarian wizard Vandalen had great powers. But I thought he only had them when he was wearing the ring, so how could he be on Boldoon? It makes no sense to me." He stopped as if pondering something, then he continued his story. "When the reports came back to us, they indicated Vandalen was still locked up on Dartal. The stranger had to be one of the other wizards. But I still don't know which one or why he was on Boldoon or what he could possibly want with the village drunk. And if he was one of the others, where was his ring?"

Camdus took this bit of information in stride. At least now he knew that some vestige of the old Slogar was still beneath his ale-soaked exterior. He was a physician, and if they could sober him up long enough, he just might be able to tackle the problem on Creedor. *But that doesn't explain the Trilvarian wizard, unless ....*

They sat in the dim light, each so deep in thought the music no longer registered. In their semi-relaxed state, they struggled with what they knew and even more, what they needed to know for survival as they sped ever closer to Creedor and whatever challenges it would bring.

"If there's nothing else, Sir, I'll go check on Dr. Slogar."

"Thank you, Mr. Grunden. That's all for this evening. We'll talk again when I know more."

Relieved, Grunden headed to see Slogar, leaving Camdus with his thoughts.

Elder Arking. I don't get it. He's always been an advocate for the people. What's he hiding? Think I'll have to give Dad a call.

Camdus touched his computer, which sprang to life. He popped the disk into the port and sat back to see what was on it, but not before he poured himself another drink. He listened to the whirring machine as it read the contents. Soon he'd know what Grunden was talking about. And after he did, he'd find out what the Empire buzz said about Elder Arking. Then he'd call his dad to see what he could learn about Tomer Arking, the man. As he sat back down with his glass in hand, he continued to think about the unsettling conversation he'd just had with Grunden. But right now, he needed to understand the threat that caused these men to band together. What did they think they could do? Maybe the new data would provide some of the answers. Unless Slogar could unlock the secret of the disease and find its cure, their chances of getting off Creedor alive were pretty slim anyway. In that case, Grunden's group wouldn't matter.

The disk contained a collection of secret documents and video clips of suspicious activity on several planets, but mostly on Creedor, with one from an abandoned airship landing site on Boldoon. Camdus could see why Grunden had begun his own counter-offensive. The people on the clips were armed with powerful weapons, some of which he'd never seen before. The invaders seemed to appear and disappear at will, something that, as far as he knew, even the most powerful Reglon wizards had yet to master.

He secured his computer, and locked Grunden's disk in his safe. He knew the disease on Creedor had to be stopped, and now he had a fight on his hands, but he could only guess with whom. He'd recognized the Q'Aron uniforms but that didn't mean that's who it was. Anyone could dress up like them to throw them off the trail. *I can only hope it isn't those Q'Aron devils. If it is, we're in for it.*

After leaving Camdus, Grunden checked in with Dr. Slogar before returning to his quarters. Slogar had shooed him away every time he'd gone to check on him before. Determined not to let that happen again, Grunden intended to go in this time no matter what. Besides, he needed to let him know that he had been assigned as his assistant, whether he liked it or not. He also wanted to make sure the old fellow knew how to access all the features found in his room. He touched the door. It didn't open. Then he knocked loudly and called out, "Doctor. Dr. Slogar, are you there? I'm not leaving until you let me in to talk to you." He listened carefully and then heard the familiar wheezing. The door slid open.

"Good evening, Mr. Grunden. How can I help you?"

"May I come in?"

Slogar gestured to a small seating area.

Grunden waited for Slogar to sit down before taking a seat.

"Doctor, Commander Camdus has assigned me to be your assistant. My quarters are right next door, if you need me. This is the com center; just push OQ3. See, right here. Even if I'm not in my quarters, I'll still be paged with this remote communicator I carry at all times. I'll be available whenever you need me. And you don't have to get up to answer the door. Once we voice train the computer, just say *enter* from anywhere in the room. The door will open. But always check this monitor before you let anyone in."

Slogar scratched his head. *Voice train? Well, at least that explains why every time I've tried to use that command, the confounded door refused to obey.*

For some moments Slogar studied the soldier, for that seemed to be the best description of Grunden. It looked as if he would have a bodyguard, whether he wanted one or not. He sighed. If he were honest with himself, he knew he needed one because he had long since lost the ability to fight or run.

May as well be gracious. Slogar mentally conceded defeat. "Well, Mr. Grunden, I welcome your help. I just hope that you won't find this assignment too boring."

Grunden doubted anything that happened on board the ship, or on Creedor, would be boring. That would be wishful thinking.

"Thank you, Dr. Slogar. Now, let me help familiarize you with your new home. To have full access to the features you'll find here, you need to train the voice-activated computer which controls the door, intercom, nutrition center, as well as its entertainment features and library archives. If you'll be so kind, please speak to your computerized control center so that it will recognize your voice and will be able to respond to you."

"Wait a minute. You mean I don't have to go to the mess hall to eat?" Slogar marveled.

"That's right. If you please, Doctor, can we continue?"

"Oh, yes, of course. Hello. Hello. Dr. Simon Slogar here," he said to no one in particular. He waited. "How do I know it worked?"

"The indicator light right here is blue," Grunden said. Then he continued. "Now, if you'll allow me demonstrate your launch chair."

"That won't be necessary. I figured it out after the first time I got knocked off my feet." Slogar rubbed his bruised knee at the memory. Then he asked, "Mr. Grunden, who else on the ship is authorized to enter these quarters?"

Grunden studied him for a brief moment. "Since you have taken over the voice control of this unit, only you, the Commander, Captain Slag, and me. And unless you give us permission, we can only enter when the control senses you are either in need of assistance or are no longer viable."

Slogar thought about this for a moment. "You mean if I'm sick or dead, you can enter. No other time, without an invitation. Right?"

"That's correct, Sir. Now if you'll excuse me, I have to report to my station. Good evening, Doctor. Please remember to secure yourself in your launch chair whenever an alert is sounded. Just call me if you need me. When it's time to transport to Creedor, I'll come help you with your equipment."

With that, Grunden left Slogar, who was busy punching buttons on the nutrition center control panel.

Grunden shook his head. *Maybe I should have skipped that part.* As he walked down the corridor to his station, he remembered that the doctor had not let the little bag out of his reach the entire time he'd been there. *It doesn't look like much, but whatever's in it must be pretty important,* he thought as he reached his destination. He knew he better make sure that he helped the doctor keep it safe, just in case.

CAMDUS SEEKS INFORMATION

After Camdus had gotten as much as he could from the disk Grunden gave him, he called his father. He always welcomed any opportunity to hear his dad's voice. It bore that deep baritone that demanded respect. Though for Camdus, respecting his father was out of love, not obligation.

Willem Camdus had been a humble shopkeeper to everyone but Camdus. When he was growing up, he thought no one was smarter or stronger than his dad. Sometimes when the young Camdus had pretended to be a soldier, his father had found it hard to keep from laughing at his little boy's antics.

It was only after he had entered the Academy that he began to hear stories of his dad's bravery, when Willem had served in the military under Emperor Borm's rule. He and Tomer Arking had both served for a time under Admiral Grunden. He hoped his father's experience with the Admiral would prove helpful.

As to Camdus entering the military, his father couldn't have been happier when he was accepted into the Academy. His mother was another story. She was not at all happy about it. She couldn't bear the thought of her son going into harm's way. She had hated the separations that stretched throughout her husband's years in the military and absolutely did not want her son walking in those shoes. Inevitably, though, he was in the military and shipped out.

His father later told him the story of their first night after he left. Evidently, his mother had managed to keep a brave face until he was out of sight.

"I just wish you'd taken the time to counsel him, Will," she'd pouted.

"Come on, Rose. Don't worry. The package I gave him before he left will help him more than any advice I could have given him."

"Package? What sort of package?"

"Oh, just a few little things left over from my military days. But don't worry. I told him not to open it until he had run out of ideas."

Rose nearly shouted, "That makes no sense at all, Willem. He may be dead before he knows he needs whatever it is."

Willem hadn't dared point out that she was being illogical. He knew better.

Rose had cried herself to sleep that night and several more before coming to terms with her son's enlistment.

Camdus snapped out of his daydream and initiated the call to his father.

The communicator alerted Willem Camdus to an incoming call. He touched the display button and was delighted to see his son's face pop up on the screen.

"Hi, Dad, you got a minute? I need to talk to you."

Willem detected an urgent undertone in his son's voice. "I do. What's on your mind, Son?"

Camdus had struggled with how to ask what he needed to know without putting his father at risk.

"Dad, I'd like to ask you some questions about a couple of your old friends, Elder Tomer Arking and Admiral Maximus Grunden. You knew them both pretty well when you were in the military, didn't you?"

Willem thought this a strange question but answered as best he could.

"Yes, I knew them both. The Admiral was the kind of leader that men don't mind following. He ordered his troops into battle, but he was right there among them. He never asked a soldier to do anything he couldn't or wouldn't do himself. I'd follow him again, if he needed me."

That was a relief to Camdus. It removed the doubt that had lingered at the back of his mind about the younger Grunden.

His dad continued. "Now Tomer, he's a different story. He's as good as gold. But even though he was an adequate soldier, he was more scholarly, if you know what I mean. He could recite the details of any battle from any war, but fighting was not his strong suit. No, it was his grasp of strategic warfare and logistics that made him a good officer. His forte was giving effective orders to the soldiers under his command. For him, having physical military skill was not as important as using his extensive knowledge of military procedure and tactical warfare. But I think he didn't find his true calling until he got into the intelligence community. I'm pretty sure that's what helped him rise to the rank of admiral and later to become an Elder."

Willem was unsure what Tomer Arking had to do with his son, but he intended to find out. "Is he all right? I haven't seen him much since Jarlod became Emperor. Okay now it's your turn, Michael. What's going on?"

"Well, Dad, it looks like Elder Arking is connected to the disappearance of some soldiers and for some others being mustered out of the service. Why do you think he'd do that?"

Willem considered the information his son had provided in his questions and decided he didn't have enough to answer.

"Son, I guess it'd depend on what the soldiers did or failed to do that would have prompted Tomer to take such drastic action. But first, let me tell you I've known Tomer Arking for most of my life, and as sure as I am he would relieve a malingerer of duty, I'm equally sure he would *not* make a soldier disappear. He's an honorable man, Michael."

Camdus was afraid that he'd offended his father, who was known for his fierce loyalty to friends as well as family.

"Dad, I'm not accusing Elder Arking of any wrongdoing. I'm just trying to get to the bottom of why the scouts who've reported unauthorized activity to him have either lost their posts or have never been heard of again."

Willem paused, then he asked, "Are you sure these reports were made directly to Tomer? You know he has an assistant who screens most of the communications to him."

In fact, Camdus had not known that and doubted Grunden knew it. But it made perfect sense, when he thought of it. *What high ranking official in the Empire doesn't have an assistant?*

He answered his father. "I don't know if they reported directly to him or not, but I'll try to find out. Do you still have friends on the Emperor's Council?"

Willem found this conversation troubling but wanted to help his son.

"Well, as you know, Tomer and I grew up together, so maybe a call on him during a visit to Capitol City in the next few weeks wouldn't raise any suspicions. Once I've talked to him, maybe I'll be able to answer your questions."

"Dad, we may not have a few weeks to get to the bottom of this problem. I need you to try to get this information for me now. But please be careful. Soldiers being relieved of duty or sent away could be the least of our worries."

Willem appreciated the gravity of his son's warning but said, "Now Michael, thanks for the heads-up, but please remember your old man was a pretty accomplished soldier in his day."

"I know, Dad. I just don't want you to take this too lightly. Please make sure you speak only to Tomer and watch how much you tell him – at least until you're satisfied that he has no part in what's going on. Take care, Dad. Get back to me on this secure channel. Tell Mom I love her and that I'll see you all as soon as I can. Thanks."

"Don't thank me just yet, Son. Let's wait and see what I find out."

Camdus wished his father good luck and signed off.

THE WARNING

Camdus was awakened by a beeping beside his bed. He wiped the sleep away and saw that a message was waiting for him on his communicator. He didn't remember nodding off but knew he must have done just that. He'd have to do something about that, but right now he didn't have time to sleep.

The message was a mass communication from the Deputy Director of Intergalactic Warfare. He noted that it was encrypted. Camdus hated encryption, though he knew that there must be a good reason for using it, especially over secure lines. The message was a warning: *Be vigilant, intruders have been reported.*

"Humph," he grumbled out loud, "tell me something I don't know." What he wanted to know was of a more practical nature, like how many intruders and what weapons they have. *It would be nice to know if there are any other Empire cruisers in the area,* he thought. More bungling by this preening Emperor seemed to be the rule of the day. Camdus could think these things, but would never, under any circumstances, say them. He might not like some of Jarlod's decisions, but he was still their leader, and they had to respect the office if not the man. Camdus thought it was about time he visited his erstwhile charge, Dr. Simon Slogar. He'd not spent any time with him, other than when Camdus was in the infirmary and that didn't count. Now was as good a time as any to find out what Slogar knew. He touched the door panel that alerted the occupant a visitor was waiting for permission to enter. Slogar was still having trouble with all the modern technology. "Come in." The door didn't open. He said it again, still nothing. Exasperated, he got up and touched the *open* button. After the door closed behind Camdus, he greeted the doctor with a serious look.

"Cut me some slack, will you? I'm not as young as I used to be. I can't remember the code word to get the door to open."

"Enter," Camdus said. "The very complicated code word is *enter*." He looked around to see if Slogar had any contraband. *Nothing I can see. That's good news – I hope.*

Slogar misunderstood and became defensive again.

"Hey, don't look at me that way. I just haven't had time to tidy up. But they're a sight better than the greasy table at the Boor's Nad Inn."

"Your housekeeping isn't what concerns me. What have you been doing? I haven't heard a peep from you since you checked on me in the infirmary the other night. But that's been a while. I was beginning to think I missed some of the ale you tried to smuggle on board."

Slogar feigned insult. "Who me? Why, I would never stoop that low. Only because I didn't think of it, mind you. The truth, I'm sad to say, is that I am as sober as an Elder."

Camdus suspected that the only reason this was true was the old reprobate couldn't figure out how to get into the ship's store and filch a bottle.

"I'm glad to hear that, Slogar. Now tell me what you've been doing."

Slogar waved his arm toward the L-shaped table in the corner of his study, which was merely the far side of the sitting room.

"I've been researching the symptoms that are particular to the epidemic on Creedor. Any one of several ancient diseases could be behind them. But my money's on a neuroinvasive virus, probably rabies."

Exasperated, Camdus asked, "Rabbis? I thought rabbis were ancient holy men. How can they be the source of this awful epidemic?"

"Not rabbis, *rabies*. You know, Commander, for a smart man, your knowledge of history is pathetic."

Camdus indignantly replied, "I know all the *military* history there is to know. Can I help it if ancient diseases weren't covered?"

"Well, they should've been. Didn't you study Adolph Hitler or Saddam Hussein from 20th century Earth? Both of those despots used biological warfare to control their own and to try to destroy their enemies."

"Yes, I studied them, but bio warfare was mentioned, not expounded upon. But it doesn't matter what I do or don't know about ancient maladies. It does, however, matter what you know. So, what have you got?"

Slogar sat down, placed his readers on his nose and motioned Camdus to sit. He had rejected the notion of corrective surgery for his vision. There was something soothing about the familiar old vision aid.

Taking the chair beside Slogar at the table, Camdus waited.

"As you know, the Emperor tasked his scientific researchers with finding a way to eliminate all diseases among the Empire's citizens. They set about a long and laborious journey that led them to genetically engineering antidotes that eventually wiped out all major diseases – among the people. But what the Emperor and his researchers failed to consider was that some of the most horrendous ailments spring not from man, but from animals. Diseases like rabies, Eastern equine encephalitis, and Lyme disease were totally overlooked. Over time, all of the pharmaceutical companies stopped producing medicines and treatments other than those that had been designed through the disease eradication project. As cities grew, wild animal habitats dwindled, driving the poor beasts farther and farther from man into areas too small to support them. They should have been driven into the cities to find food, but they weren't. Why do you think that is, Cam?"

Camdus had been listening intently to what Slogar was saying. "I never really thought about it. Where are they now? Has anyone tried to assess their condition there?"

"As a matter of fact," Slogar explained, "some covert animal studies have been done. Covert, mind you, because the Emperor doesn't think that the lower animals, other than tredon herds, have a place in our worlds. What they didn't find was more interesting than what was there. It stands to reason that with these animals having been pushed into the woodlands to the east some of them would get sick and naturally some would die. But they found that all the animals were healthy, which is not possible unless …."

"Unless someone was harvesting the sick ones. But why would anyone harvest the sick and leave the healthy? Did they leave any of the carcasses unburied?"

"That's the other thing," Slogar said. "There were no carcasses, no sign that any had been buried. They were just gone – vanished."

Camdus processed this information, and then asked, "Do you think that the intruders harvested the sick animals to generate bio-weapons?"

"That's exactly what I think. I only hope that once we've identified the cause, we can get what we need to treat it. If it's rabies, a post-exposure prophylaxis can be administered to save the patients. But we have to collect some of the virus to formulate a vaccine like the one they used in the 20th century on the Earth. Seelah helped me to make a lot of antidotes and treatments, and she gave me formulas for a lot more. But we didn't think of rabies. If that's what it is, then I'll need to go back to her facility at Silden. I can't do this without her."

Camdus wasn't about to let Slogar make this journey and said so.

"But if we bring the Elder Woman here, she loses her powers. Besides, you can't transport her entire lab here. It's quite extensive," Slogar argued.

Camdus sighed. "Well, we'll just have to deal with that when or if it becomes necessary. Right now, I have to go. It's time to check in on the bridge. Don't worry, I'll make sure you have a lab once we get to Creedor."

He was well down the corridor when he heard Slogar's door swoosh shut behind him.

OLD FRIENDS

When Willem arrived in Capitol City, he checked into the local hostel known for its discretion. He decided to keep a low profile, just in case. In case of what, he didn't know. He registered under his real name but was given his old identity. The Emperor hated hostels like this one because their security was so sophisticated his Empire Guardsmen couldn't identify which ones were part of the network. Willem had learned of their existence as a young soldier in the covert ops corps under Admiral Grunden. One of the few benefits from the years of separation from Rose was his discovery of this hostel network that allowed him to disappear while remaining in plain sight.

After a few moments in the identity protection chamber, which doubled as a closet, Willem emerged a new man – literally. Instead of being a wrinkled, middle aged man with thinning hair, he now appeared to be a robust gentleman of about thirty years.

He looked at himself in the full-length mirror. *Hmmm. I wish Rose could see me now. But I don't know what's going on here, so it's best to keep her in the dark awhile longer.*

Willem nodded appreciatively to the inn keeper and stepped out into the briskly paced pedestrian traffic flowing both ways along the moving sidewalk.

He passed several of the men he had served with. None of them recognized him. He knew his next challenge would be to get in to see Tomer Arking. He was aware of the risk he was taking by using his old identity, but he had to give Tomer a chance to prove he was innocent of what Michael thought he was doing. He quickly arrived at the vast office building where Tomer worked. He checked the directory and saw that Tomer was still in the same office. Then he approached the receptionist and signed in.

The young girl was so struck by this handsome man standing before her that she simply smiled and handed him a visitor's pass. The lift stopped on the eighteenth floor.

Willem walked purposefully to Tomer's office suite. He was greeted by a much older receptionist. Her name plate read *Miss Stewling*.

"I'd like to see Elder Arking, if that's possible. I'm in town on business and need to speak to him privately while I'm here."

"Do you have an appointment, Sir?" the receptionist asked.

"I'm sorry, I don't, but it's important that I see him," Willem said.

"Your name, Sir?" she asked, tapping her pencil on the appointment book.

"Zachary Radfield."

The name he had given her was his code name from the days he and Tomer were in covert ops together. He knew using it was risky, but he was convinced Tomer was still an honest man.

Ms. Stewling touched a button and spoke into the air. "Elder Arking, a Mr. Zachary Radfield is here to see you. He doesn't have an appointment. Would you like me to schedule him one?"

Tomer's unmistakable voice floated back, again seemingly from nowhere.

"Of course, I'll see him, Ms. Stewling. Please show him in."

She ushered Willem into Tomer's office. With a prudish look, she closed the door on her way out, leaving a small crack.

Willem could see the nosy woman lurking just beyond the door trying to eavesdrop. He casually walked to the door and closed it with a loud snap.

Tomer chuckled at his old friend. Now that he was sure it was safe to speak, he said in a low voice, "Will, my friend. It's been too long. Have a seat. How is Rose? Pretty as ever I imagine."

"She is that, Tomer. We're fine, enjoying retirement. We're putterers, you know."

Both men laughed at that.

The tone became somber when Tomer asked, "Then why the disguise, Will? What's going on?"

"I was hoping you could tell me. Surely you have an assistant other than Ms. Stewling?"

"Yes, of course I do. I couldn't possibly perform all my duties without one, especially now that I have been placed over Diplomatic Affairs as well as certain classified military missions."

Willem looked at his old friend sensing no deception in him. Still he wondered how much he could tell him without putting his old friend in danger. Willem decided to give it a go.

"Tomer, some very disturbing rumors are being spread about you in certain circles. I need to know the truth."

Annoyed at the thought of being fodder for the gossip mill, Tomer sat down and studied Willem. He found it difficult to believe that this thirty-something man sitting across from him was, in fact, his own contemporary. If he hadn't recognized the code name, he wouldn't have let him in.

"What kind of rumors?"

Willem quickly filled him in, speaking very softly.

"But that's absurd! I've had no such reports. And I am quite confident that Matt Enright would have told me if there were any."

Willem detected an unpleasant mix of emotions Tomer's voice. But that was to be expected.

"Tomer, how long has Enright worked for you?"

"He's been with me two years now. He came to me from the Empire Intelligence Agency on the best of recommendations."

Willem could see that even though Tomer was defending Enright, questions were already forming.

He decided that talking here was too dangerous and invited Tomer to the hostel later in the evening. He thanked Ms. Stewling for her courtesy and rode the lift down. He returned the visitor's badge to the young receptionist in the lobby. She nearly fell out of her chair watching him go. Willem smiled as he caught a glimpse of her out of the corner of his eye. *If she only knew. Ah, sweet Rose. I miss you already.*

Just after dark, someone knocked on Willem's door.

"Who is it?"

"Lynwood Styles."

Willem put away his book and let Tomer in.

"You transformed yourself quite nicely, old man. How does it feel to have a full head of hair again?"

"About as well for me as you, I would imagine."

Willem offered him a seat and a glass of whiskey. Tomer couldn't believe it – Irish whiskey that must have been hundreds of years old.

"Where on Earth did you get this? It's the nectar of the gods."

"You guessed it. Earth. My ancestors had a distillery in Ireland for centuries. Rose and I have cases of it in the basement beneath our house, though we only open a bottle for special occasions. I'm afraid today is only the first of many special occasions, and we'll probably regret most of them." Tomer and Willem sipped their whiskey with the perfectly prepared tredon steaks that Will had ordered before Tomer arrived. After savoring the whiskey and their meal, they talked into the night. By morning, they knew what they had to do. Willem would go back home and contact

Michael to let him know what he'd learned. Tomer had to find a way to use Enright, if it turned out he was in league with an unknown enemy.

Willem knew that the way ahead was dangerous but necessary. He longed for the time he could lay his weary head on his pillow and no longer worry about the Empire he loved.

***

Captain Slag was at the helm of the Ursidae. His story was unusual, to say the least. He'd been somewhat of a maverick as captains in the service went. But he'd been busted from admiral to captain after losing the Empire's number one fighter ship in what should have been a routine flight. They were near a supposedly uninhabited planet in the Troglite solar system. The young captain piloting the ship panicked when they started taking fire from the planet. Admiral Slag took the helm and managed to evacuate the crew in the transpods but refused to go down with the ship. He used the mini-pod for his own escape when he realized that nothing he could do would salvage the ship. He saw nothing heroic in giving his life for a piece of equipment.

But no matter how many times he reviewed the events of that day, he was convinced that he had done about as well as anyone could have under the circumstances, but the Reglon Empire Guard Command was not pleased. He'd endured the Inquiry to appease them. But his punishment didn't stop there. He was reassigned to the nearest thing to a garbage scow in the fleet. The ship was in such bad shape that it had been on the list to be scrapped. But Jarlod's wicked sense of humor kicked in. They pulled it out of the scrap heap and gave it to Slag.

When he had first come aboard, the ship was so rusty and outdated it barely responded to any commands. And its weapons systems were obsolete. But Slag had sat back and studied his situation. *I will not let them whip me on this,* he silently vowed.

He had rallied some of his former crewmen who managed to get assigned to his quadrant. They began furtively working on the ship to update its weapons and give it a power booster. In retrospect, Slag realized that what he had now was the perfect warship. She looked like a rust bucket ready to be scrapped, but she ran like the well-tuned, heavily armed precision machine she had become. The best part was that nowhere in Reglon Empire Guard records was any trace of her modifications. Nothing could be leaked to any of the Emperor's moles. What he had was a secret weapon just waiting for a call to service. It was Commander Michael Camdus who had made that call.

Now he swiveled around to face Camdus, "We have orbit, Sir. We're ready to load the shuttlecraft on your order," Captain Slag reported.

Camdus looked at the endless blanket of black sky studded with stars and space debris. Looking down he saw the brown ball with tiny green specks that was Creedor. It looked hazy from this altitude because of the hellish winds whipping its natural sand surface. If one looked long enough, it seemed to change shape, almost as if it were breathing.

Camdus shuddered at the thought of returning to its surface. Prolonging the mission would only make it worse, he knew, yet his sense of dread grew minute by minute.

He responded to Slag, "Order the shuttles loaded with all the supplies they'll hold. We will make as many trips as necessary to complete the transfer. Contact Base C Leader. Secure permission to transport all cargo. Let me know when you're done so that we can begin boarding the landing party. I'll be in my quarters. Captain."

Out of the Frying Pan

The southern moon floated high above the Creedorian Mountains. Fierce wind whipped the dark sand across the yard. Mara Tonlin busied herself in the kitchen. She was waiting for her husband to finish taking care of the animals and come home.

The years since Jarlod had stolen the Empire had been harsh. He'd removed virtually all environmental protections and dismissed human rights as a bad idea. This, this hell she was living in could be directly attributed to Jarlod's inept, greed-driven leadership.

Mara felt a shiver run down her spine as the wind howled around their rustic home. It was dangerous to be out when the southern moon was full, especially now that the epidemic was ravaging their village.

She jumped as the back door slammed into the wall. Ram hurried in, bringing swirls of sand with him. Mara raced to secure the door as he collapsed at the table.

"We can't hold out much longer, Mara. Most of the herd's strayed so far away from the ranch I don't think I can round them up until after demon wind season. And that'll be too late," Ram said glumly.

Mara set a mug of steaming thistle tea down in front of him. He held it a moment to warm his freezing hands.

"The ones left are starving. I'm sure that's why the cows have stopped giving milk; and the bull's all yellow-eyed now like Abalon."

Mara winced at the mention of her beloved mare. Her father had given the horse to her when she was a teenager. Wherever Mara had gone, Abalon had been brought along, too. Even so, the knowledge that Abalon was dying was the smallest of her pain. She had shed too many tears already. Now she needed to look after Ram.

Mara sat down beside him and leaned her head on his shoulder; the grit on his shirt stuck to her cheek. How could she comfort him when she felt no comfort herself? Ram had been her rock, her source of strength since they lost their only child to the disease. Watching their tiny daughter change from a beautiful, happy toddler into a sallow, growling animal had been sheer agony for them both. As much as he loved his child, he knew that she was so out of control he had to protect himself from her, so he'd put on his old battle uniform before he sedated her.

Once she was asleep, Ram had cradled her tenderly in his arms, praying for God to take him instead. Astril regained consciousness only once before she died. In that moment, Ram was graced with his child, finally at peace, smiling up at him.

With Astril gone, Mara felt as if her heart had been ripped from her chest, leaving a gaping hole in her soul. She'd managed to pull herself together, but there were days her entire being was sucked into that abyss, leaving no room for joy. And Mara knew Ram's misery reflected his pain. Astril had been the bright spot in his life and he had doted on her, as many a father before him had doted on an only daughter.

Mara's grief had been spent holding onto Ram as she cried herself to sleep each night for what felt like forever. He'd had no time to grieve, for Mara had needed him to be strong.

But now, with the onset of the demon winds, it seemed that Ram just could not hold up anymore. Every time she was tempted to break into the store of emergency food, Ram stopped her with, "Not yet, Mara."

All of these worries distanced Ram even further from her. It was as if the very heart and life had abandoned him, and that nearly broke her spirit completely. She placed her arms around his neck and stroked his thick black hair. A sprinkle of reddish-brown sand fell, salting the table.

Ram was the bravest, kindest man Mara had ever known. When they first met, his vivid blue eyes seemed to sparkle from his rugged, tanned face. His smile made her happy. But now there was no light in his eyes, no smile on his face. He seemed to have aged twenty years in less than one. She remembered how Ram used to play with her corn silk hair, teasing that she must have had elvish ancestors. That had all changed. They lived in the same house, but the wall between them just kept growing.

How long can we survive like this? There must be something we can do. Somewhere, somehow, somebody has got to help us, she thought, her fragile spirit heavy with despair. Even in the depth of her sorrow, an ardent prayer for help ran once again through her mind.

"Ram, come on," Mara said, "you need to get some rest. I'll run your bath so you can clean up and then turn in. There's nothing else you can do this evening anyway."

He looked at her with lifeless eyes and got up from the chair. Sand was embedded in his skin, hair, and clothes. His anger was so great that he felt like shouting in God's face.

Ram followed his wife to their bathroom where he mechanically undressed. Though the warmth of the bath water seeped into his body, misery clung to his spirit like a squished slug to a bare foot.

Mara quietly closed the door as she left him. She was drawn as always to the window that faced the walking yard. The endless patterns of shifting sand fascinated her, though the demon wind season was one to be feared during the best of times.

She stared out the window, her heart heavy. Soon she realized the sound of the wind had changed.

What's that noise? A ship landing, maybe. No, that can't be. No one is foolish enough to try to land on Creedor during demon wind season.

She squinted into the growing darkness and saw something on the horizon. Mara thought her prayers were being answered.

"Ram! Come here. Hurry! Something's happening outside. Looks like we have company. Maybe the Emperor finally sent us some help."

Ram didn't answer, so she called again louder this time, "Ram, Ram!"

He had heard her the first time, but her words had taken a moment to register. He sprang from the tub, swiftly drying off and deftly covering his too lean, yet still strong body with his battle uniform.

"Mara, get away from that window!" he shouted as he raced to the living room.

He reached for her and shouted, "Put out the lights. It could be one of them. Mara, we've got to keep our wits. We don't know who it is."

She stood transfixed peering into the gloomy night.

"Mara, please help me secure the house," he said and tugged her elbow.

Alert now, she swiftly made sure windows and shutters were locked down tight.

"Go to your station and stay there until I come for you," Ram said as he buckled on his side arm. He gave her a quick hug and kiss. "Now, go, okay?"

Mara nodded. She realized how careless she'd been. She raced to the secret room behind the panel in the closet of their bedroom. The room lit up, instantly bathed in pale blue gray light. Her heart was pounding so loudly she was afraid whoever was outside would hear it and find her. She began taking deep, steady breaths to calm herself. "Ram, please be careful," she whispered into the night, though she knew he could not hear her. The two-foot thick wall Ram had built was soundproof. Thankfully, he also had made sure the room was ventilated and had a filtration system to let in fresh air without the stifling sand. During demon wind season, she had to remember to push the button marked *Purge* at least twice a day to keep the filter clean. He had located a natural spring in the rock wall, a perfect source of cool, fresh water. Then he'd stored their meager survival supplies under the handmade cot. He also had hewn a tiny water closet into the far end of the space and plumbed it to run well away from their home, determined to provide for the essentials.

She remembered the excitement and pride when he had finished their secret room. Her memories of their celebration at his triumph usually made her smile. But now, Mara could only hope that he would come for her soon. She lay on the cot, her heart aching, and prayed herself into a fitful sleep.

The silence around her was unbearable. She had been in hiding for what seemed like an eternity, and still Ram had not returned. She listened so intently she could hear her own heart beating loudly in her ears. He'd sent her into hiding days ago, she was not sure how many. *Why hasn't he come for me?*

On the verge of panic now, Mara carefully opened the panel as quietly as she could. When she had an opening wide enough for her to hear, she held her breath so she could detect the slightest sound.

She called out, "Ram, Ram. Are you here? Ram?" No answer. All she heard was the bitter wind whipping; it sounded as if it were raging through her house. He would never have opened the door during demon wind season unless he had to check on the livestock, especially when on guard against intruders. But he had just come from the barn before he sent her into hiding.

Now more afraid for Ram than herself, Mara left her hiding place, careful to replace the panel. She looked at their bedroom. Everything was topsy turvy, their clothes strewn, shutters torn from windows, and Astril's picture was smashed against the wall. Mara's heart sank. Ram would have to be dead for anyone to be able to touch Astril's picture.

She ran to the kitchen, fearing what she felt sure she would find. The door was open, sand swirling in tiny dunes across her floor. Ram was not there.

Covering her face with an old wool scarf, Mara ran to the barn. All the animals had been slaughtered and left to rot. Mara forced herself to look past Abalon; she needed to search the shelter and the feed room.

Ram's nucleo-laser was lying on the floor in the corner. Blood was on the handle – yellow blood. *He wounded one of them. But where is he?*

They've taken him, I know it. How could they have taken the only person I have left on Creedor?

Anxiety gripped her chest. She was afraid she would never see him again. In addition to losing their daughter, she and Ram had also lost all their friends to either the intruders or the epidemic. *Why couldn't they have taken me, too?* She threw sand on the handle of the weapon to cover the blood and picked it up.

The roaring argument that she and Ram had about their plan if they were attacked by the intruders crossed her mind. He had refused to go into hiding with her, convinced that he would be able to stop them. He had laid an elaborate set of traps on the perimeter of the walking yard and at strategic places in the outer arcas as well. Any who managed to get through would be eliminated with his nucleo-laser. She had scorned this as paltry in the face of such powerful enemies. Now she wished she'd been wrong.

Once back inside the cottage, she closed the door and barred it. She put Ram's weapon in the cupboard. Then, overcome by what had happened, Mara slid to the floor and sobbed until there were no tears left. Yet she felt no relief from the ache in her chest. She sat amid the sand dunes in her kitchen and began to feel angry.

What do they think gives them the right to destroy everything and everyone in my world?! And just who in the hell are they anyway? Mara fumed to herself.

She and Ram had settled on Creedor when their home planet of Vartuch had been so irreversibly polluted that the environment became unbearable. The beautiful green pastures and forests had become wastelands. The once clear sky was now so hazy from toxic fumes, it disintegrated the fabric of pedestrians' outer clothing. Children were going blind from exposure to the hazardous chemicals found in their drinking water. All mobile craft were banned and there was no energy to fuel even the lights, much less the appliances. In the forced blackouts, crime thrived.

Living on Vartuch had become such a nightmare that they had looked for jobs on other planets that were environmentally tolerable.

After several months, Mara had gotten a job as a mineral technician on Creedor, a planet rich with iron ore as well as gold and, even more valuable, trizactl. Her new employer had provided transportation for her and her family.

Ram still hadn't found a job, so Mara encouraged him to take this opportunity to raise a herd of tredons like he had always wanted to do.

Tredons were hardy stock that had a market Empire-wide. All he had to do was get a herd established, build a good reputation, and he would never have to work for anyone else again. Mara had been so proud of him when he bought his first cow and bull.

Astril was two then and loved to follow her father around the stockyard as he tended the animals. She had given pet names to them, even though Ram told her they could not keep them.

Ram tasted success when he sold the first calf for enough to buy another cow and feed for all the animals for the winter. Bossy and Maude, as Astril dubbed the cows, were very fertile and each produced a calf the following spring. With some of the proceeds from the sale of one of the calves, he had bought Mara a carriage for her horse.

Mobile craft that burned fossil fuel had been banned on Creedor years ago, so having Abalon and a carriage made her life much easier.

Though the environment had in some respects rejuvenated itself, the awful legacy left by their forefathers was so great no one dared to suggest reinstating mobile craft for public use. The only vehicles allowed on Creedor were the Reglon Empire Guard cruisers and pods that emitted no noxious fumes. This restricted transportation was good for the environment but made it hard for folks to get around. No one could legally operate personal vehicles, not even Emperor Jarlod, though he and his cronies regularly broke this law.

Mara finally got up and looked out the window again; it was already dark outside. Though she had only eaten tiny portions of the emergency rations while in hiding, she wasn't hungry. The house was getting cold and the howling had started again. She built a small fire for warmth and heated water for tea.

As she nailed the broken shutters back over the windows, she thought how stupid it all was. She didn't understand what was happening to her world, but more than that, what had happened to her family.

Her thoughts took a more personal turn. *If the intruders don't get me, then the epidemic or some crazed epidemic victim will – that is, if I don't starve to death first. But it's too dangerous to try to save any of that meat from the dead animals. Who knows what contaminants they've been exposed to Only God knows how long I might have before somebody finds me. And they will. I just pray it won't be some of those twisted relics of humanity left by the epidemic.*

When Mara finished her task, she was physically exhausted and emotionally wrung. Collapsing on her bed, she could smell Ram's special scent on his pillow. To her, he had always smelled like sunshine. Holding his pillow, she fell once again into a fitful sleep.

Demon Winds

"There, Captain, I see a house next to the edge of that plateau. It looks as if it's abandoned. There are no lights and no, wait! I think I see a wisp of smoke coming from the chimney. See there? Either someone is home or hasn't been gone long. Permission to land on that sheltered plateau over there."

The shuttle pilot had reservations about the Captain and Commander's orders to steer clear of Clandil, the capital city of Creedor. He knew that was where the epidemic was at its worst, so why didn't his commanding officers want to go there first? They'd been told their mission was to discover some way to at least control the epidemic even if they couldn't stop it.

Captain Slag gave Cronwell permission to land.

"Steady. We don't want to get caught in the wind. Land behind those rocks. They should protect us from the wind currents enough to land safely. Nice and easy, now."

Cronwell nervously maneuvered the shuttle to that location. As he was lowering the landing stilts, a brutal wind gust caught the craft and bounced it as if it were a kite.

"Damn it, Cronwell, step aside!" Slag took the helm and righted the craft just in time to prevent its crashing. Cronwell looked on, amazed at the sure-handed way the Captain regained stability, and in the process, saved the ship and their skins. He had just witnessed what had become legend among the Fleet.

As a cadet he'd heard about the daring and skill of Captain Slag, but none of the cadets believed that Slag was anything more than an egotistical blowhard who had lucked out on some mission or other and impressed the brass. That he was busted convinced them they'd been right. After all, it took a real screw-up to lose an admiralty.

Captain Slag completed the landing maneuver without a word. When everyone else had left the craft, he called Cronwell to him. "You didn't have the auxiliary stabilizers engaged. That was stupid. I don't like stupid mistakes. Do you understand, Mr. Cronwell, or do I have to quote Fleet Code to you?"

Cronwell knew Fleet Code very well. And he did not want to face a Command Inquiry into the question of his competence.

"Captain Slag, Sir. I'm sorry. I made an error in judgment. I didn't consider the pattern of the wind current and the strength of the wind shear. I acknowledge my negligence and am fully prepared to be relieved of duty until further notice."

"Cronwell, sorry doesn't cut it in the real world. Lucky for you we can't spare you right now. But mark me well. You need to give serious thought to what you should have done, what you didn't do, and what the consequences would have been if I hadn't been here. When this is over, Commander Camdus may well want to implement disciplinary measures that your infraction merits. But know this – if you ever make a mistake like this again, I will personally recommend the Inquiry for you. Do you understand me, Mister?"

"Very clearly, Sir." Cronwell swallowed hard.

"Good. Take your place with the landing party and begin the search of the plateau for any, I repeat, any, humans. Dismissed."

Cronwell and other REG soldiers fanned out to search the plateau, while Slogar and Grunden headed straight for the cottage.

Captain Slag didn't use the threat of the Inquiry lightly; he still remembered his own vividly. Yes, he had lived through it, but it had left its indelible mark seared into his psyche. That he was still sane was amazing after the torturous interrogation he'd been subjected to. No one in the Fleet spoke of the event anymore. Even when the ordeal was underway, it was only mentioned by those inexperienced pilots and cadets who had never known anyone who'd been through it.

The Inquiry was held behind barred doors with only authorized personnel present, but there were inevitable leaks of the inhumane treatment and torture of Slag and the threats to his family, which caused him a deeper, more permanent pain. He would never forget – ever.

Most who underwent the ordeal broke after only a few hours, signing an admission of guilt or negligence, as the case may be, and accepting their term in the military prison Vuthral with something akin to joy. Victor Slag had not broken. Not when they brought in his wife and son and forced him to watch as they brutally interrogated them as if they were criminals. Not even when his wife Janara begged their tormentors to have pity on the boy and spare him. Victor's heart felt like it was being squeezed in a huge fist, yet he made not one sound. Their marriage had not survived because

Janara didn't understand how he could just sit there and watch. To her, it was evidence that he didn't care enough to fight for them.

To Slag, the insanity of this farce of an inquiry was not nearly as insane as the premise that he'd conspired with the enemy, whoever the hell they were, to systematically sabotage all the Fleet super cruisers. In time, he had been exonerated, but his life had been forever changed. The silent oath of vengeance he'd taken that day kept him going.

Once the landing party had left the shuttle, they knew they had to find cover before dark. But after trying to move them through the shifting sands, rapidly falling temperature, and howling winds, Grunden started to return to the ship. But on second thought, he knew he had to get Slogar to the cottage no matter what. Still, he sent Cronwell and the others back to the ship. He'd send for them if he needed their help, but right now it was just too dangerous. Handling Slogar was about all he could manage.

The sound of voices woke Mara from her troubled sleep. It was dark out now, so she couldn't tell if it was the intruders returning or villagers getting ready to put some poor demented soul out of his misery. Either way, she needed to be cautious. Slipping from the bed to the floor without making a sound, Mara edged her way to the window that faced the walking yard. Through the slats of the shutters, she could see the light coming from the direction of the animal stalls. She held her breath hoping to hear better, but it didn't help.

"Dr. Slogar, be careful. There are traps around the edge of this property. Whoever lives here or used to live here must have been expecting trouble. I can help you with that, Doctor," Grunden said as he reached for Slogar's bag, which seemed to be throwing the doctor off balance. Slogar snatched it from his grasp.

"That won't be necessary, Mr. Grunden. I am quite capable of – ooof!" Slogar stepped into a soft drift of sand, lost his balance entirely, and fell smack-dab on his round belly.

Grunden, much taller and stronger, floundered after him and dragged him roughly to his feet.

"Listen. If we've got to work together, then you gotta trust me. You may as well start now, or we may both find ourselves chin-deep in sand. Now, give me that bag and take my arm so I can get us out of here. Let's head for the back of the cottage. Maybe we can get inside and out of this dismal wind."

"Good point, Mr. Grunden, but you must give me your word on your honorable mother's head that you will protect it with your life if need be."

Grunden heaved Slogar to a halt. "Wait just a minute. I want to know what's in that bag if I may have to die for it. So, tell me, Doctor. What is it you're asking me to risk my life for?"

"Get us out of this windstorm, Mr. Grunden. When you need to know, I'll tell you everything. But for now, get me inside. I'm choking on this devilish sand."

With Slogar wheezing audibly now, Grunden could sense the fear rising within his charge even though the darkness shielded his face.

"Okay, Doctor," Grunden said. "We're almost there. Just a couple more steps. Here. Now if I can just jimmy this door."

Mara heard someone trying to break in. She held her breath and flattened herself inside the bedroom closet. She wanted to get a look at whoever it was before she barricaded herself in her hiding place. She heard someone at the back door and a second later it opened with such force it slammed into the wall. As the men made their way inside, Mara noticed one of them was struggling to breathe. They were talking, but she couldn't make out what they were saying.

One of them is sick. Oh, Lord! What if it's an epidemic victim being brought here for isolation? The place must look deserted. She was on the verge of panic.

Suddenly, one of them entered her bedroom. Though his lamplight was dim, she let out a sigh of relief when she saw the Reglon Empire Guard emblem on his uniform: the indigo letters *REG* written across seven golden circles overlapping into one. Mara burst from the closet so abruptly that Grunden pulled his weapon and took aim, ready to shoot.

"Halt. I'm with the Reglon Empire Guard and I will drop you where you stand." When he detected that the enemy had halted, he approached with his lamp in one hand, his weapon still at the ready in the other.

"Don't shoot! I'm unarmed. This is my home you've broken into, and I've never been so glad for anything in my life. Please put your weapon down. I need help finding my husband. They took him and I don't know where to look for him. They're all gone. Everyone I love has been destroyed on this world. I wish I'd never heard of it." Mara had reached a near hysterical pitch, but the reality of what she just said sucked the breath from her.

She felt the room spinning as she lost consciousness.

Grunden reacted in a split second, dropped the lamp, and swept the woman up just before she hit the floor, saving her from cracking her head like a melon on the rough stone.

"Doctor, I need you in here, now," he called over his shoulder.

Slogar had by this time regained his breath. He went as quickly as his lumbering body could manage.

The sight of this small, blonde woman surprised him. *Why is she here alone? It's obviously a very dangerous location, so isolated on this forgotten plateau.*

"Well, Mr. Grunden. Who have we here? Surely, this little slip of a girl is no threat to a fearless soldier like you. Put that weapon down. You'll scare her to death when she comes to."

Grunden holstered his side arm but kept his hand close to it. He knew that women were warriors, too. He'd learned that from one of his first skirmishes as a young soldier.

Slogar approached Mara and patted her hand gently to revive her. She woke with a jolt, startled to see these two strange men leaning over her.

"My name is Simon Slogar, my dear. I am a physician. This rather brusque gentleman is my assistant, Mr. Grunden. We are with the Reglon Empire Guard's Special Research Team. And we've come to try to stop the epidemic that is plaguing Creedor. I am terribly sorry if we frightened you."

Slogar's patient, fatherly manner seemed to put the woman at ease. He patted her hand again and said, "Now, Miss, please tell us why you're living here all alone."

***

When Ram woke up, he found himself lying on a hot, stone floor. Though dimly lit, he could make out the forms of other creatures nearby. Like Ram, all were in shackles. At the mouth of the cave were two well-armed guards. From the look of them, they were from the asteroid colony Trotin. They were two-headed, so they were probably from Talea in the Translavan region. He wondered what they were doing on Creedor. Yes, he was sure he was still there. He just didn't know where.

Maybe it had something to do with the news blip about a ship from a neighboring world straying into Creedorian airspace. But Jarlod had knee-jerked and instead of negotiating, he declared sanctions against the Q'Aron Empire that prohibited any Q'Aron citizen, military or civilian, from setting foot on Creedor. He further made it illegal for any Creedorian to communicate with any Q'Aron. The penalty for breaking this law was death by space implosion, a brutal but instant demise.

Jarlod had assumed that his actions had preserved what he deemed as his. He refused to listen to any of his advisors who warned him that this win had been far too easy. And while Jarlod basked in what he considered a victory, the Q'Arons smiled at how easily they had planted some of their brightest engineers within the existing Reglon mine and lasered their way from there to the massive trizactl deposit several miles away.

But Jarlod was unaware this deposit existed. He'd have to acknowledge that their current supply would someday be exhausted before he could even consider looking for other deposits or alternative sources of energy. This error in judgment was no surprise to anyone.

Ram and the others had no knowledge of the politics involved in their predicament. It wouldn't have mattered if they had. They were living to survive, one hour at a time. Ram was a little disoriented at first. Thankfully, except for a few cuts and bruises, he was unharmed. Aside from being held prisoner, his biggest discomfort was the pounding headache. He licked his parched lips that were cracked and bleeding from thirst. As he squinted into his dim surroundings, he became aware that the others had stiffened and all but one had ceased making any sounds.

From the far corner the same raspy breathing that must have been there all the time finally caught his attention. He found that he could move about, though the chains on his wrists and ankles made getting on his feet difficult. Once he was upright, he tried to get a sense of his surroundings. The moaning in the corner was weaker now. Ram felt the tension among his fellow prisoners as he moved closer to the sound. No one spoke. Just as he almost reached his destination, a hand as rough as emery cloth seized his wrist. Startled, Ram jerked around to face whoever held him in such an iron grip.

"Leave him alone," the man whispered hoarsely in Ram's ear. "He can't help us anymore. He tried, but he was no match for them. Now we have to watch him die in this God-forsaken place." The man's hot, stale breath assaulted Ram's nostrils.

He leaned close to the stranger's ear and whispered, "Who are you, and why are you here? And how could…,"

"Quiet. You don't know what happens to us here. If they catch us talking, they'll send us to Lars to use for his amusement. Shhhh. Get in line. They're coming." The man pulled Ram into the ranks beside him.

"Well, let's see what we have in this cave. The others have been no sport at all." The voice was soft, feminine. "What filthy beasts! Too bad they can't be disinfected and deodorized before I have to make my selection. I think I'll tell Daddy to do that, or I positively refuse to choose from them. I don't know why I can't have one of the soldiers anyway.

They are younger and smell nicer. You wouldn't mind that, would you, Lt. T'Aron?" The woman was apparently speaking to the tall man walking beside her as they entered the cave.

Ram made note of the four as they approached. They were led by an old man, who appeared quite feeble, followed by T'Aron, and the young woman whose petulance was evident in her voice. A heavily armed guard brought up the rear. As the woman approached, Ram could smell her scent and hear the rustle of silk. Though the cave was dimly lit, the light of the old man's torch illuminated his weathered face and hands. On his gnarled right index finger rested a ring with a large fiery stone flanked by two sapphires set in serpentine gold. The light shifted when the old man held the torch higher. The woman's face was framed by raven black hair so shiny it reflected the glow of the torch. Her eyes glittered like huge dark pearls beneath what he thought were fake eyelashes. Ram had never seen a woman like this before.

The memory of Mara's pale beauty flashed across his mind as if to enunciate the stark difference between the two women. A pang of guilt and sorrow struck him deeply and swiftly. He'd left Mara in the hiding place and didn't know if they'd found her and silently praying that they had not. He wished now he had listened to her when she tried to talk him into going into hiding with her.

A hand on his bare chest snapped Ram back to reality. He became instantly rigid, fearful that he was to be taken to Lars, whoever that was. The tall woman stared at him full in the face.

"Hmm, this one is young and strong. Just feel these muscles, T'Aron."

Ram felt a harsher touch. He held his breath. "I'll take this one. What's that horrid sound? Slafe, bring the torch."

The old man followed the woman. An ancient-looking man lay crumpled in a heap on the floor in the cave's corner.

Ram gasped. It was his friend Stadar, whom he'd assumed was dead when he disappeared during the first intruder invasion. Stadar looked like a poor old grandfather, though Ram knew he was only a few years older than he. *What in God's name happened to him?*

He moved toward Stadar, only to be yanked back in line by his unknown comrade. T'Aron took one long stride and was standing in front of Ram, weapon in hand. Ram stood stock still, hoping that he had not perceived his recognition of his old friend, for instinct told him that this knowledge would mean more bad news.

Just at that moment, the woman told the guard to raise the old man to his feet. Ram silently breathed his relief as the soldier stepped aside to allow the guard to go to the woman.

Once on his feet, Stadar was closely scrutinized by the woman. It was almost as if she were trying to see into his mind, to read his thoughts. Ram could see the beads of sweat pouring profusely from underneath Stadar's shaggy hair, down his deeply lined, grimy face into his filthy beard. He could see why the others thought that Stadar was old. If he hadn't recognized the distinct shamrock shaped birthmark on Stadar's right cheek, Ram would not have known him either.

"Well, well. The old one seems to have nothing on his mind except his friend Humpty Dumpty. I will make you a promise, Old Man. Humpty won't be the only one that can't be put back together again if you try anything else." She continued to study him. "Have you lost your wits in the service of His Majesty's Master Slaver? Or perhaps you don't want anyone to know what is truly on your mind. Soon you won't matter – if you're still alive."

Then she addressed her party. "We'll keep him here just to be sure that he doesn't get more bright ideas like the insurrection he tried to start when he first arrived."

She turned back to Stadar and said, "My, my, how I hated to watch Lars turn you into the decrepit old man you are today. You were such a strong, stubborn man – quite the specimen. Did you know that the whip actually fell from Lars' grip he was so tired from his session with you? And now to find you a babbling fool. Lars will be pleased to know his work was not in vain. Release him. I don't think he'll be planning any more escapes." The woman stepped back, rubbing her nose to block the stench.

Stadar fell heavily to the floor. When his breathing momentarily ceased, Ram feared him dead but had no time to worry about his friend.

Lt. T'Aron jerked him forward by his chained wrists. Then he shoved him down a long, dark hall until they were outside the cave.

For the first time, Ram saw his surroundings. Spread out before him was an immense underground fortress. All around its perimeter were guard towers equipped with nucleo cannons. He estimated that each one had the ability to destroy a small village with one volley. He wondered what the Q'Arons intended to do with this installation. He knew whatever it was, it spelled catastrophe for the Empire. He also wondered how they were able to build such a place without someone high up in the Empire having knowledge of its existence. These thoughts led him to some very unsettling conclusions that he would have been better not to think about, at least not so close to the woman who was obviously clairvoyant. He recognized her scent, so he knew she was close. In an instant she sidled up to him. She spoke to him in a voice that sounded like a contented cat purring.

"It is easy to read your discontent. It is also easy to read your past connections with Stadar, innocent though they may have been. If you are wise, and I do hope you will be wiser than he was, you will forget him, and you will stop wondering about this place."

She paused as if considering something, and then she said, "Since there is no escape from here other than through death, I shall tell you where you are. The rest you will learn when you have performed to my standards and have earned the privilege of asking questions. Until then, ask none. Do you understand me?"

When Ram nodded affirmatively, she continued. "I am Li'Let, daughter of His Majesty's Master Slaver, Thurl. You are, as you so rightly suppose, in the Creedorian mine though not exactly as you envisioned it. This is Q'Door Hold. Its purpose is none of your concern. I am your only concern. Your life depends on how well you play my game. Many have tried, some have succeeded. Your friend Stadar could have been very good but could not put aside his futile notion that he could escape and take the other slaves with him. He was a foolish man, very foolish, indeed. He had a privileged life that he could have kept until I tired of him, which would not have happened for quite some time had he played by the rules. But Stadar doesn't matter anymore. Remember, your survival depends on me. Lt. T'Aron, take Ram. That is your name, isn't it? Yes, Ram. Take Ram to the spa. I want him in my chamber tonight. Slafe, please escort me back so that I can begin my preparations."

Ram didn't know if what she had in mind was what it sounded like. And he sincerely hoped that it was not. He had been faithful to Mara since the first time he saw her, even before they had made a commitment to each other. She was in his heart always. But now that he knew Li'Let could read minds, he would have to mask his thoughts. The ancient nursery rhyme that Stadar used had stymied her. Ram knew he would have to find something equally banal to protect his thoughts. He figured Li'Let hadn't been trying to read his mind earlier when his thoughts wandered to Mara. At least he hoped she hadn't. But he was certain of one thing. He had to protect Mara from this twisted woman because, in spite of her beautiful exterior, there was something about Li'Let that made his blood run cold.

A sharp poke in the ribs hastened Ram on. Cool, fresh air engulfed him as he entered the room which, as best he could reckon, was located in the northernmost turret. As he looked around him, he saw that the room glowed with a soft blue light. Then Lt. T'Aron shoved him into a side chamber equipped with a shower that was already running warm water.

"When I unshackle you, be smart. You can't escape so save us all some time and pain."

T'Aron ordered him to disrobe and step into the shower. Seeing no future in disobeying his captor, Ram did as he was told. The water smelled of disinfectant, spraying from the nozzles in huge ropes of foam. Eyes closed against the stringent liquid, Ram couldn't see who – or what – was roughly scrubbing him from head to foot.

As quickly as the unseen assistance came, it disappeared. The water was now light and cool, the disinfectant replaced with aromatic essential oils. When the water finally stopped, he took the huge towel offered him by an attendant, a rather large man whose eyes were oddly out of place.

"You look to be one she'll keep for quite some time, Creedorian – if you are lucky. Otherwise, you could end up like me, or dead."

Ram knew from the man's high-pitched voice that he was a eunuch – not a fate he wished for himself. Death would be preferable. He was going to ask the eunuch about Li'Let when Lt. T'Aron re-entered and tossed him a navy-blue uniform of a light weight, silken fabric that Ram had never seen before. Lt. T'Aron ordered him to put it on. He didn't much like the thought of wearing something so flimsy, but with his own clothes gone, he had no choice. He figured anything to cover his nakedness would do. He was a little relieved when he realized that the uniform was far more substantial than he thought.

"She's waiting for you. Be sure you play the game well, or we will all suffer – you most of all."

That was the second time T'Aron had hinted that everyone was punished when Li'Let was not pleased. He wanted to ask about the game, but the look on T'Aron's face stopped him. He'd find out soon enough. But he couldn't get past the feeling there was something distinctly odd about Li'Let.

T'Aron escorted Ram to her chamber which was just below the pinnacle of the turret and tapped on the door. From within came Li'Let's velvet invitation to enter.

"I bring the slave, Mistress. Will you need anything else this evening?"

"No."

T'Aron left. Ram could see the sheer anguish in his eyes. Perhaps he could turn that to his advantage later. Right now, he was faced with his own situation that demanded his full attention to remain alive, and masculine, for Mara.

"You know I can read your mind, don't you? Try to keep your thoughts on me. I do not like to compete with memories. Do you think you can do this?" Li'Let had slowly made her way from her huge, bone-shaped bed and stood some six feet away from Ram. Now she was wearing a black velvet body suit. Though it was warm in her room, the weird energy that spanned the gap between them sent chills down his spine. He tensed and stepped back. Her laugh, low and sinister, let Ram know he was not the first to try to resist her game. With two long strides, she stood before him. She reached up as if to gently touch his cheek. But instead, he felt a sharp pain.

Astonished, Ram rubbed his face. Drawing his hand away, he realized she had scratched him so deeply with her claw-like nails that she'd drawn blood. He noticed she was licking her lips. Ram stepped back, trying to reassess the situation. He had so feared she wanted intimacy. He knew now that was absolutely not what was on her mind.

This is crazy! What does she want from me? Ram couldn't stop this thought from forming.

"This is what I want, Creedorian."

Just then, the wall behind Li'Let dissolved revealing a huge, stone maze. He knew that he had no choice and took off running into the maze. She stretched like a lazy cat, and then bounded behind him.

The maze was both a blessing and a curse, as Li'Let seemed to have supernatural senses. Each turn brought him within a whisper of her. About two-thirds of the way in, Ram saw a small chink in the wall. He tried to squeeze his way in, but he was too big.

"Oh Lord, help me," he whispered the prayer. He felt himself slide through the opening. He expected to be on the other side of the wall but found that he was in a small cavern within it. He stood still, hardly breathing. Someone was coming. He was certain it was Li'Let and that she would find him. But then he heard something sniffing and snuffling followed by a blood-curdling growl. Whatever it was raced away. He listened for such a long time that he slid down to the floor and drifted into fitful sleep. When he woke up, he was back in the cell with the rest of the slaves. He was worn out both physically and mentally, and not a little confused.

After a short rest, he was returned to Li'Let's chamber. He wasn't sure what had happened, but he knew that this woman, if she was a woman, was not entirely human. What she was, he couldn't say, but she had a sadistic idea of play. What he had experienced was filled with sheer terror and physical endurance. His faith was still strong, though for the life of him he couldn't figure out why this was happening.

So, this is the game – try to make it through the maze without being caught. But she must be superhuman. How?

He knew that God had answered his prayer for help and that without His intervention, he could not have survived. Ram just had to believe that his fate would not be irrevocably sealed by death or emasculation. He knew there was something to learn here, so he'd learn it and to do that, he had to survive.

First, he had to find a better way to mask his thoughts, to sublimate his innermost fears. He had to be able to endure, to be more challenging prey for Li'Let. Then perhaps she would allow him to ask questions and maybe she would slip some information that could help him get out of here. He knew he had to try.

He heard her soft tread across the deeply plush floor as she returned. His thoughts became a litany of how exciting the game had been and how much he enjoyed it. The smile on her face let him know that she had read his mind. The look in her eyes told him recess was over. The wall disappeared again, and the game was on.

***

The heat from the steaming mug seemed to calm Mara. She paused from time to time in telling Slogar and Grunden her story. The thistle tea was strong and conquered the chill.

"I have to find my husband. The intruders will kill him, if they haven't already. I don't know where he is, but I know there's only one thing on this planet any Empire would find worth fighting over and that's trizactl. Ram told me that he thinks they're stealing it – and that they're kidnapping our people to do the work. If he's alive, that's probably where he is. Ram is young and strong, perfect for working the mine. Well, almost perfect. He is also intelligent, with enough courage to do the right thing or die trying. That's what really worries me. He may do something that gets him killed."

She paused before continuing. "I don't think I could take it if anything happened to him. I've lost everyone else in my life – my child, my friends, my horse. I won't let them take him, too. Not without a fight, anyway. If he's alive, I'm going to find him. Please help me. I can't do this alone." Mara's voice was steady despite the tears that streaked her face.

Grunden felt an immense surge of admiration for this little woman. She had indeed lost everything, but instead of steeping in self-pity, she was making plans to either get back what was hers or get even.

Slogar spoke first. "Mara, we can't help you right now; our mission can't wait. But if you'll stay here until we're done, we'll ask Commander Camdus for some help; if he agrees, we'll launch an all-out search for your husband."

Mara carefully placed the mug on the table, leaned back in her chair and looked Slogar directly in the eye.

"I hear what you're saying. Now you need to understand me. If he's alive, then there's no telling what horror he's facing at this very moment. I can't wait. I'm leaving as soon as I pack; I'll be heading for the far side of the dunes. Ram told me that's the most likely place for the rogue trizactl mine. If he's there, I'll find him. If he's no more, then nothing they do to me can cause me any greater pain. Good luck on your mission, gentlemen. Now, if you'll excuse me, I have to pack. Then I'm going to find my husband," Mara said. She stood up to leave the room.

Grunden caught her arm. "Mrs. Tonlin, wait. Let me contact the Commander. Maybe he'll give me permission to go with you. Sounds to me like finding your husband may actually help us in our mission. It'll take only a few minutes. Will you wait?"

Slogar witnessed this exchange with a mixture of amusement and annoyance but said nothing.

Mara slowly sat back down, willing to have Grunden's company if possible. Who knew what lay before her? Grunden looked like a soldier who had seen many battles. She felt a faint glimmer of hope that together they could rescue Ram.

She watched as he opened his communicator and contacted the Commander. After several exchanges between the two men, Camdus agreed to send some of his Special Forces as escorts for Dr. Slogar. Grunden would accompany Mara, with the strict proviso that he was to check in every four hours using the encrypted code devised especially for this mission. Mara breathed a silent *thank you*. For all her bravado, she was scared of what lay ahead, especially if she had to go it alone.

Mara shook Slogar's hand. "God be with you, Sir," she said softly.

"And you also," he replied. He watched through the tiny window in the door as they set out against the swirling sand and disappeared into the growing dusk.

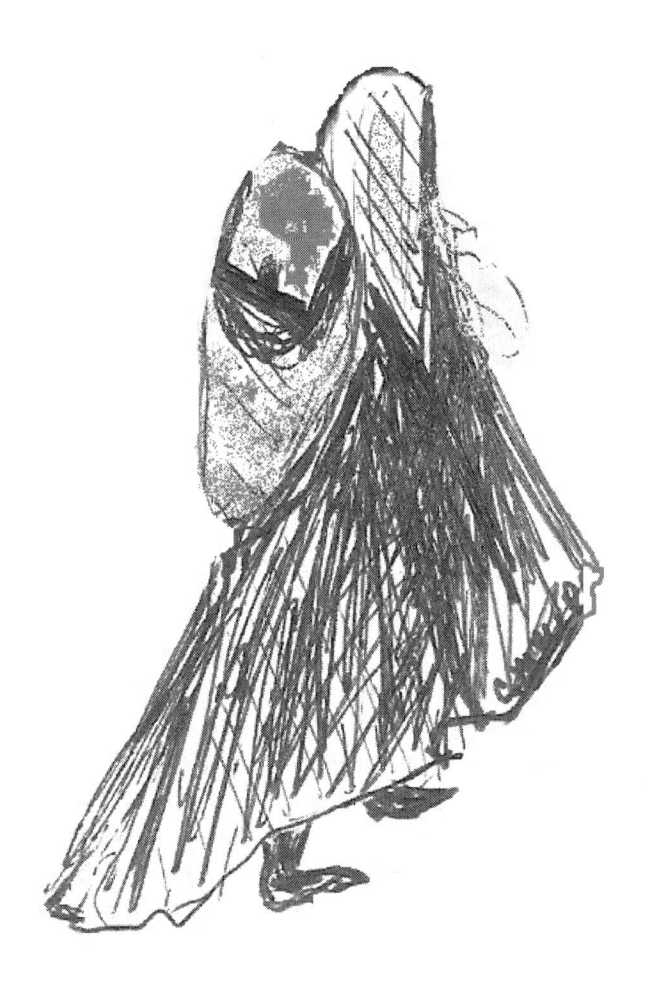

THE RIDERS

Rax stood beneath the skiabar tree once more. This time his son Kel stood by his side. Almost grown now, Kel asked his father a question.

"When?"

"Not yet, but soon," Rax replied, not taking his eyes off the horizon. In the distance they could hear the thunder and see the jagged lightning as the storm approached their world.

Did my riding bring this to us? Rax silently wondered.

Kel, revealing that he too shared his father's talent for knowing the thoughts of others, said "No, Father. You didn't. It was only a matter of time."

Rax raised an eyebrow and smiled, pleased that Kel would follow in his footsteps.

"Still," Rax said without further acknowledgement of Kel's growing talent, "it couldn't have helped." The ever-calm Rider then said flatly, "This subspace particle band is now corrupt. We have to find a new one. Until then, it's the local slipstreams for us."

Kel nodded. With a last look at the darkening sky, they linked arms and snagged the inner slipstream home.

***

With the storm now past and the slipstream repaired, Rax and Kel waited beside the gently flowing Alvion. They were watching for the next buffalo fish to surface.

"There," sharp-eyed Kel said to his father, pointing to a whirlpool distinctly out of place.

Rax smiled. "He's all yours, Kel."

The boy grinned and stepped in up to his knees. He stood perfectly still, waiting for the right moment. Then, in a flash, he plunged his long arms into the murky water.

"Ha, ha! I got a big one, Dad."

Realizing the fish was wriggling hard to get away, Rax waded in and took hold of its hairy tail.

"Watch out for the horns, Son," he cautioned.

It was at that moment that Rax received the call.

"Sorry, Kel. I have to go back to work. Take care of your mother and Zil. I'll be back as soon as I can."

His father's soft pop out of their world left the disappointed young Rider alone with the angry fish as it desperately tried to get free.

When Walls Talk

Rax was the subspace particle Rider charged with guarding the Reglon Empire. As such, he was frequently pulled away from his own domain to take care of various tasks that only a Rider could handle.

But today, he was home. He sat contentedly watching his family. At times like these, he weighed the possibility of leaving the Guardians. Rax was a new breed of Rider. Unlike his ancestors, he did not relish the job. No, he just wished he could stay home and fish, one of the few pleasures of his otherwise stressful life.

I shouldn't question my fate. I was born a Rider; I'll die a Rider.

He was prone to conduct internal conversations, a practice he'd fallen into when riding among the Ordinaries. Most of them ignored him, maybe because they didn't really think of him as a sentient being. Rax didn't mind because they discussed virtually everything in front of him – some of it inappropriate. But Rax did have thoughts and feelings.

In his service to the Reglon Empire, Rax had learned its history. He understood it perhaps better than their historians. He was intrigued by the Ordinaries' past. He knew that Creedor and Vartuch had been the first true worlds to be settled by the refugees from Earth that had been virtually destroyed by ecological ignorance and endless wars. The settlers had been astounded by the beauty of their new homes.

Creedor's lush valleys and mountain ranges skirted the seemingly endless deserts. Pristine oceans and lakes also graced the small planet, much to the delight of the men and women who settled there. The land in and around the valleys was perfect for farming. Pretty soon the settlers had built a handful of towns in the shadows of the Creedorian Mountains.

The first time Rax had been called to Creedor, he was pleasantly surprised at how similar it was to his own world. The Riders' domain existed in the space between the vast universes, safe from the pollution and wars of mankind.

As much as he'd enjoyed Creedor, he hadn't cared for Vartuch. Its temperatures overall ran just cold enough that the skinny Rider was extremely uncomfortable there. Even so, the people who settled on Vartuch adjusted to having only two seasons – fall and spring. There was no real winter or summer, only the unpredictable blast of snow. Summer temperatures rarely rose above seventy degrees Fahrenheit. But when they did, the Vartuchians stayed inside their bermed houses until their perceived heat wave passed.

The worst thing for the Rider was having to listen to the palace walls recount Jarlod's heinous deeds; they wanted him to know the truth and to help. But as a Guardian, he could only observe and follow orders. He understood why so many people longed for the days when Emperor Borm reigned. Though the Reglon Empire was technically a monarchy, Borm had made sure the citizens enjoyed more freedoms than they ever had before. Borm had encouraged them to establish an economy that gave every citizen willing to put in the effort an opportunity to succeed. They had to pay a modest percentage of their income for Empire taxes and an even smaller percentage in local world taxes. These revenues ensured that the military and schools were maintained, and infrastructures were safe and reliable. No one questioned that.

But taxes also paid the overhead for the Emperor and all government employees. When Jarlod took over, the once reasonable taxes had crept up so much that many could no longer pay. Civil disobedience gurgled among the struggling middle class, only to be met with imprisonment or worse. Rax had witnessed countless pleas from citizens for Jarlod to forgive their taxes or at least give them some kind of relief. But Jarlod had responded to their pleas harshly. Many families had been left to grieve their loss as a result.

Though Rax did not interact well or often with the Reglons, his heart ached from the travesty that was Jarlod's reign. He knew that if Emperor Borm had not trusted Jarlod enough to appoint him to the position of Commander of the Reglon Empire Guard, things would be different now. The Rider didn't understand why Borm ignored his Council of Elders when they questioned this choice. But he had chosen him, and no one had been able to convince him that Jarlod was not what he appeared to be. They knew the man was narcissistic and lacking book smarts yet infinitely cunning and ultimately dangerous.

The Council's frustration and Jarlod's wicked deeds soaked into the walls that cried out to Rax every time he came near. *I wish these walls would stop talking to me. I do not need to know these things, yet I do, and they plague my dreams,* Rax thought.

He tried unsuccessfully to forget these troubling whispers, but the walls had continued to cry out to him in excruciating detail what Jarlod had done to Borm. Their sorrow assaulted his senses causing him to cringe in pain as the story unfolded. When all was silent again, Rax knew the Empire was in even more danger than he'd suspected. Though he was the Guardian, he could not stop what was coming.

JARLOD MAKES LEMONADE

During the intervening years, Jarlod had taken a young girl as his primary wife. Princess Alora, daughter of Eldreth, the King of Lucernia, had tried desperately to get out of this marriage, but there was no hope for it. Her father had brokered the deal and his say was final.

Alora had borne Jarlod a child, not the son he wanted but a beautiful, healthy baby girl. Her mother named her Amielle.

Though she was his flesh and blood, Jarlod saw no value in her. He was disappointed that he had no son to carry on his name, so he distanced himself from the child and her mother. He allowed Amielle to grow up with him in her life only when it benefited him.

But the day came when he found a way to make this bratty lemon into lemonade

Years before Amielle was born, he'd established a harem of young women. As appealing as they were, he couldn't stop thinking about adding one of Elder Weilz' daughters to his collection. He'd first seen Weilz' oldest girl some years before, but he hadn't been able to get to her and now she was too old for his liking. But the youngest, the one her father called *Lulu,* filled his dreams. Because of Weilz' position on the Council, Jarlod knew he couldn't just take her. *So how?* he'd wondered. Then one day a light went on in his shadowy brain. He knew how he could get what he wanted. *She's the same age as Amielle. Perhaps they could become friends; sleepovers would be nice....* He didn't care what others thought; he'd made up his mind and he would have her. And that day came, followed by the night he'd dreamed of.

But even this diversion didn't stop his paranoia sparked by whispered doubts about his claim on the Empire. So Jarlod rewrote this part of Reglon history, giving it a noble tone. With Vandalen all but forgotten, Jarlod's rule had led to discontented subjects and broken trade relations with nearby empires. Jarlod considered handling these matters beneath him. His Council of Elders had to deal with the fallout. His pitcher of lemonade had grown bigger, but with the Empire facing an epidemic on Creedor and the possibility of a bloody war, it finally had lost its appeal. He discarded the broken girl as if she were nothing. Her anguished parents were left to deal with the wreckage of this gentle child.

Without even a thought of what he'd done, Jarlod turned his attention for once to matters of the Empire. He couldn't ignore the situation any longer, but he still didn't understand why his Council advised him to proceed with caution. No, what he saw was a challenge to his claim that he'd ended all diseases throughout the Empire. After all, he had ordered the elimination of all practice and study of medicine to emphasize his claim. He'd also had all medical personnel rounded up and reprogrammed for other professions. Those who did not fit in were taken to Andalla, a fairly prosperous true world graced with oceans, sandy beaches, lakes, deserts, plains, forests, and mountains. Like Ashtar, it too had a growing population of Less-Thans that affluent mothers warned their children to stay away from.

However, Jarlod didn't send the doctors to the affluent region of Andalla. Nor did he send them to live among the Less-Thans. Instead, he sent them to Andalla's most desolate area – the plains of Silden – hopefully to die. There they were put out of the transpods with nothing but the clothes on their backs. Those who ran after the pods were vaporized. A few of them survived. But no one knew for sure as none of them had been heard from again.

Seelah, known simply as the Elder Woman, had been one of those doctors. She had managed to survive the purification with her intellect and her health intact. She eventually built a secret facility beneath Silden's barren plains.

Jarlod had no idea any of them had survived. If he had, it would not have gone well for them. To him, his plan had been flawless.

"We have no need of physicians because I, the greatest of all the Reglon Emperors, have eliminated the need for them. I have decreed it; it is so."

He took every opportunity to remind everyone that he was their great and powerful leader. He spouted his own praises so much that he believed them. If he'd guessed what even his supporters had begun to think of him, he'd have dispensed with them, too.

He rode this wave of stolen fame quite contentedly until reports of people getting sick started coming in. With each report, a unit was dispatched to take care of the issue – along with the unfortunate people who had gotten sick.

But now with the unknown ailment decimating the Creedorians by the thousands, Jarlod had been forced to face the fact that he couldn't make this one go away. He called his Council together to get their feedback – and to have someone else to blame should this mess blow up in his face. Though they knew this issue with Creedor was dire, they were cautious. They'd learned long ago not to rely on Jarlod's understanding of any situation. They wanted to know more before advising any action.

King Eldreth, Jarlod's father-in-law and ruler of Lucernia, had suggested that Jarlod get his head out of the sand and see if he could find any of the doctors who had been banished. He reminded the tempestuous Emperor that he'd advised him against taking such rash action in the first place. He knew Jarlod feared him. Otherwise, he would have banished him, too – father-in-law or not. Now King Eldreth sat listening to Jarlod complain at the Council meeting. He remembered the rogue doctor that Jarlod had imprisoned for practicing medicine against his decree. He also recalled that Jarlod had bragged about it.

"I suggest you find that doctor, you know the one – what was his name?"

"Simon Slogar," Jarlod answered. "But he's not a doctor; he's a hack."

"Hmm. That's not how I remember it. At any rate, I think you should release him and enlist his services. According to your own reports to this Council, he was the only physician who wasn't purified because you said he wasn't a threat. Still, you had him imprisoned."

Jarlod didn't like hearing this, especially from his meddling father-in-law. But he had to admit he had no choice. *Damn it, Slogar. Now you're making me look like a fool in front of my Council – and by my father-in-law at that! I should have had you eliminated!* Jarlod was too savvy to say this out loud, but he couldn't help thinking it.

Never one to go into battle himself when he could send someone else, Jarlod called on Commander Camdus who now oversaw the troops from Entellés Base Camp on Reglon Minor.

Camdus set up his headquarters there, though Jarlod had opposed it at first. But he convinced Jarlod that he could keep a better eye on the prison colony on Vuthral, Reglon Minor's moon that maintained a ragged orbit around the planet.

Jarlod typically rejected anything Camdus pitched, but the more he thought about it the more he liked the idea – but for a different reason. He thought it wise to keep the Commander of the military well away from him. He himself had held that position when he killed Borm. He didn't want to give Camdus the opportunity to murder him.

***

It saddened Camdus that once beautiful Creedor was now suffering ecologically as badly as the Earth had when their ancestors made their exit. But unlike the ancients who left while they were still fairly strong and healthy, it took a catastrophic illness for Creedorians to seek more hospitable worlds. Even so, many of them stayed, thinking the illness would run its course.

Then when people started disappearing, local law officers sent reports to Elder Weilz who was in charge of the governance of Creedor, but he never responded. It was as if all the fates had joined forces to destroy the Creedorian people. This is the world that Jarlod sent the REG to without warships or reinforcements.

Camdus didn't like it, but he was the consummate soldier.

Jarlod, I know this mess is your fault. If you'd get your mind off yourself for a minute and think about the state of the Empire....

He shook his head in disgust.

SLOGAR SEARCHES FOR ANSWERS

Camdus had found Slogar, gotten him sober, and then sent him to Creedor to begin his work. The doctor was not pleased when they landed on a desolate plateau a number of miles from City of Clandil.

Simon Slogar was stuck here in this seemingly God-forsaken place. This smallest world of the Reglon Empire had been a leader in food production at one time but not anymore.

"Well, if I had to be stranded, this is about as good a place as any," he said to himself. Alone now that Lieutenant Grunden and Mara Tonlin had already struck out into the demon winds to find her husband, Slogar rubbed his grumbling tummy. He reasoned there had to be at least some stale bread to eat.

Though Creedor's surface was covered with fine brown sand, there were underground rivers that in places rose close to the surface producing valleys so lush and green that farming flourished. He smacked his lips at the thought of what he might find in the pantry of this farmer's cottage.

"With any luck, I might even find some slabs of tredon side meat salted away in there, too."

With his mouth watering at the thought, he rummaged around in the cupboard.

"Oh yes, here we are," he said, pulling a slab of cured meat from the corner. He backed his great bulk out of the tight space and placed the salty meat in a pan of water to soak.

"I see that Grunden was quite right in his assessment of this place," he said as he continued his conversation with himself.

Though his charge was a handful, the well-trained soldier had taken in every detail of their surroundings. With Slogar in tow, he'd examined the exterior of the property. There they found the remains of a small tredon herd. Their quick inspection of the barn revealed more slaughter. The front hooves of a dead horse were covered in thick, rancid smelling yellow goo. Its neck had been ripped open and chunks of flesh missing from its flanks. Unseeing eyes stared hauntingly as if frozen in the horror of its death.

Slogar had been on the verge of vomiting when Grunden grabbed his arm and steered him back out into the winds to the cottage.

He shook these thoughts from his mind so he wouldn't spoil his appetite.

"Thank goodness this cottage belonged to tredon farmers, but it's too bad their herd is gone. Milk would've gone nicely in my tea. Oh, well."

With only the roar of the winds pounding the cottage, Slogar tried to remember all he could about this bleak planet. He knew in addition to hosting small tredon farmers, Creedor was known for several large operations on the windswept plateaus where the animals were bred for commercial use. Tredons were among the few animals that could survive without shelter on the plains. In fact, the beasts were almost impervious to the elements. They thrived on desert vegetation, soaking up heat from the sunbaked sand, effectively curing the hides while the animals still wore them. Clothing manufacturers practically fought over the best products the farmers had to offer. The large operators sold the hides at a premium, but only after the tredon had lived on the plateaus at least four seasons. It took that long for the sun and wind-driven sand to cure the hides, and then etch the intricate patterns that were so prized among leather wrights.

The military managed their own herds there. They wanted to make sure that the hides of their animals were allowed to reach their maximum strength so that they could be used to make battle gear. Through trial and error, they'd learned that this didn't happen unless the hides were harvested after the tredons' tenth season. By then they were tempered like the finest metal making them virtually impenetrable. Even though the hides were expensive, tredon meat was the most inexpensive of any to be had in the Empire. It was always tender and most seasons there was plenty of it because only a few were selected at birth for the hide herds. The rest of the young tredons were shipped to farms in the valleys to be raised for meat or placed in the dairy stock. Almost all of the tredon could be used for something, so there was little waste, an attribute that Jarlod didn't understand. But this season was not a good one for any of the tredon farmers. Only the military herds still thrived.

"Hmm, let me check that side meat. It might be a little salty still, but maybe not so much," he reasoned then stuck his finger in the water and tasted it.

"Yep," he said and poured the water off. After rinsing it three times, he covered it again with fresh water and placed it on the stove this time.

Then he sat down to rest his aching feet. He had taken on the mission because he'd been ordered to, not out of a sense of duty to the Emperor who had imprisoned him. But now that he was in it, a piece of him that he thought was long dead awoke.

And though he'd tried to remain aloof, he felt compassion for Mara Tonlin. Her story tugged at his heartstrings.

He got up again to check on the meat which had just begun to boil. After turning it down to a simmer, he walked to the window; Grunden and Mara were just barely visible. Relieved when he spotted them, he stood there watching as they fought the demon winds in the growing nightfall. He couldn't help smiling at Mara Tonlin's bravado.

"Feisty little woman, she is. Hope they find her husband."

He squinted into the growing darkness trying to follow the two specks on the horizon. When they were out of sight, the realization that he was alone and unarmed hit him hard. He barred the door and brewed more thistle tea to calm his jangling nerves.

Once he was settled in a tattered but sturdy chair, his heart resumed its normal pace. He took a long draw of the hot tea and placed it on the wooden table beside him.

"There's work to be done," he said to the empty room.

Pulling his equipment case to him, he snapped it open. A device the size of a small typewriter from Earth's twentieth century popped into place.

He began swiftly querying and rejecting answers at such a rapid pace he almost missed the link he'd been looking for. The file he'd just accessed was a seemingly unimportant Boldoonian document from the twenty-third century. Many of the terms were archaic, but thanks to his insatiable curiosity during his early university years, he was familiar with most of them.

According to the article, an ailment suspiciously similar to the one decimating Creedor made its first appearance after the Q'Aron Empire's invasion of Boldoon some seven hundred years ago. Even though the Q'Arons were their strongest rivals, the Reglon Emperor at the time had laughed at this paltry attempt when only one ship of invaders arrived. It wasn't long, however, before he realized he'd underestimated the Q'Aron threat.

Within a shockingly short time, the Boldoonians began dying excruciating deaths – but not before viciously attacking anyone or anything that got in their way.

The Emperor had been reluctant to believe the Q'Arons were behind the Creedorian problems until his advisors presented him with a timeline and several surveillance tapes that revealed some disturbing events. Much to his chagrin, he finally had to admit what he'd dismissed as a ship accidentally veering off course was, in fact, behind the epidemic.

"Hmmm. That's odd," Slogar said as the information sunk in.

The more he researched, the more convinced he was that the Q'Arons had used either chemical or biological warfare against Boldoonians. These practices had been outlawed in the two empires' peace treaty centuries ago.

Yet, here he sat tonight with the knowledge that the Empire was dealing with nearly the same circumstances. Some of the reports he'd found indicated that chemical weapons had been neutralized many years before the bio-weapons had been destroyed. He had found declassified documents that verified that report. No matter how hard he searched for documentation that the bio-weapons had been destroyed, all he found were sworn statements of Q'Aron government officials. Slogar couldn't believe what he was reading.

"I'd bet a case of ale the Q'Arons are at it again."

Feeling the excitement that comes just before a breakthrough, he kept digging. He had to find what the Empire had done to eradicate that ailment.

"Now where is that passage on treatment and prevention?" He scrolled through more files.

"Ah, here it is," he said as he stopped his search abruptly. "Let me see. It says the first remedy came from the discovery that the disease was actually caused by a virus. They quarantined everyone who'd contracted the illness in an abandoned prison on the asteroid Killund until they agreed on the best solution. Hmmm." He began reading the article aloud.

"'Researchers theorized the virus could not survive in extreme temperatures. To test the theory, they placed a number of victims inside a sauna and a comparable number inside a large freezer....' Well, I'll be! Grandpa was telling the truth. I thought he was fooling us with a tall tale – either that or getting a little senile. But I remember his stories about people who'd been permanently scarred from blistering and others who lost fingers and toes during the Great Epidemic on Boldoon. Who in their right mind would believe our government would subject our own people to such cruel treatment? Okay, but that doesn't help me now. What I really need to know is what kind of disease would take such brutal treatment to cure. And why they didn't look for a solution that didn't result in the victims becoming disfigured or losing body parts. Surely, they must have known about the post-exposure prophylaxis treatment. If only we could find some infected victims. If only…," he continued talking to himself.

"Dr. Slogar, are you in there?" The soldier broke through Slogar's intense study by shouting and banging on the door loud enough to wake the dead.

"Open the door. The Commander sent us to take you the rest of the way."

Slogar hoisted himself up after putting his computer away.

"Give me a minute, will you? I'm not as young as I used to be." He peered through the tiny window at the top of the door. Then he slid away the heavy bar to let the guards in. He saw that Camdus had sent four soldiers – twice as many as he was expecting. The increased number punctuated how vital his part in this mission really was. It also reminded him that they were all in danger out here on this unprotected plain.

He led the men into the kitchen and motioned for them to take a seat at the rustic table. They ignored him and continued to search the cottage. When they were satisfied that they and Slogar were the only occupants, they returned to the kitchen.

One of them asked, "Who were you talking to?"

Slogar turned from the cabinet where he was at the moment pulling out well-used mugs. He didn't understand why the soldier thought he'd been talking to somebody else until he remembered what he'd been doing.

"Oh, that. Well, no one actually. I have a habit of talking to myself. Sorry," he said, embarrassed that he'd misled them, but even more because they'd caught him.

He could see they were not too happy to have been put on alert for nothing. To appease them he said, "Here now, gentlemen, I'm brewing you some tea before we set out. Who knows when we'll get such nice accommodations again?"

The guards double checked to see that all of the doors and windows were locked. When they returned to the kitchen this time, they found a plate of steaming side meat on the table and Dr. Slogar whistling along with the tea kettle.

THE SEARCH FOR RAM TONLIN

Once Mara and Grunden stepped out into the howling winds, she felt a fleeting moment of panic. *No, no, no! Get a grip okay?* She chided herself and managed to regain enough gumption to go on. She looked back only briefly at her home. Tears shimmered on her eyelids when she thought of the life she'd shared with Ram and Astril. A tiny wisp of smoke escaping the chimney caught her attention. The little cottage looked sad as it bravely took the wind's endless assault.

I feel like I'm trapped in some incredibly sick nightmare that I can't wake up from. She wiped the tears with her freezing hands. *No! I will not be sad, and I will not panic.* She knew she had to focus on the task at hand. Spitting and coughing, she remembered to pull down her protective face shield – but not before the sand had painfully assaulted the tender skin of her face.

By this time Grunden was already several strides ahead of her. Realizing it would soon be dark, her resolve returned. She raced against the wicked, swirling sand and the icy wind to catch him.

For more than an hour they trudged through the shifting terrain, pushing harder against the demon winds. When they got close enough, Grunden could see that the dark spot they'd been heading for was the opening to a cave. He stopped, pulling Mara close so she could hear his shout above the roar. "We don't have much time left. It'll soon be too cold and dark to travel. Do you think you can make it?"

Mara thought he was chastising her because she had not been traveling as fast as he would have liked. *But, I'm much smaller than he is, and my pack is really, really heavy.* Her unspoken excuses seemed thin. *This was my bright idea, not his.*

Despite her intense desire to collapse on the spot if only for a moment, she thrust herself forward – bruised pride and all – without answering. She would not let him hear the despair she was sure would resonate in her voice.

Grunden had not intended to fuss at her, but he was a soldier and he was used to marching with other soldiers. *Maybe I should have given more thought to joining Mrs. Tonlin. She is definitely not up to this; probably won't make it – not without some help.* Though she had started this mission, he realized that he would have to take the leadership role. But that was nothing new for him. Grunden was above all else a soldier.

He hadn't just grown up and decided to join the military. That was ingrained in him from his childhood, whether he knew it or not. Jacar Grunden had been brought up in Fort Bogue, one of Boldoon's ten military installations. His father Maximus Grunden had earned the rank of Admiral and was given his pick of bases. Though they'd been reassigned to other bases, Bogue was their favorite. Maximus and Louisa had always planned to retire there. They loved this area on the northern end of Boldoon's largest peninsula that jutted out into the Rapong Sea.

During the years his father had served as Fort Bogue commander, the five Grunden children – all boys – had been immersed in the military life. Jacar was what they considered their bonus baby because he was born years after his four brothers had grown up and moved away. Though his parents had not imagined they'd be blessed with another child at their age, they had embraced parenthood again and joyfully welcomed him. It amused his mother and pleased his father immensely that Jacar, or Jack as they called him, traipsed along behind his father, trying to walk just like him.

Little Jack had quickly become a favorite on base and was the unofficial mascot of Fort Bogue. It was here that he had developed his love of the military and his desire to become one of them someday.

It was also at Fort Bogue that he learned to distrust Emperor Jarlod. With no explanation, his father had been relieved of duty and sent into early retirement far away from their beloved ocean home in Bogue to the impoverished village of Naan in the rugged Tarshenian mountain range.

Grunden set these dark thoughts aside and let his professionalism take over, once again keenly aware of his current predicament. He understood Mrs. Tonlin's problem. He saw her struggling with the heavy pack, but she rebuffed his help, so he let her find out for herself that they had to work together.

Now he grabbed the pack and pulled it from her back, shouldering it beside his. Mara's feeble smile was lost as he picked up his pace, head low against the hateful wind. They continued their beeline for shelter.

When at last they reached the cave, they were relieved it was empty. It was fairly small but would give them protection from the harsh weather outside. At least it would once they figured out how to close off the opening.

"Here, Mr. Grunden. Let me help you unpack," Mara said as she reached up and pulled her pack from his shoulder. "Ooof," she grunted with the weight of it. Unable to hold on, she let it drop to the cave floor. "It has my cooking utensils and our provisions in it." She rummaged around until she found what she was hunting. "Oh good, now I can make a proper meal and some hot tea. Well, I'll try to, anyway. I'm not a fancy cook, you understand, but hopefully it'll be edible." She paused and then continued. "You have been so kind, Mr. Grunden, and I have, well, I haven't been easy to get on with today."

He didn't know what to say to her, so he turned around and went back outside. The broken top of a dead tree sticking up out of the sand caught his eye. He grabbed it and backed up to the opening holding it in front of him. Once the makeshift cover was in place, he braced it at its trunk with three big rocks.

"There, maybe that'll hold."

Mara didn't know why he ignored her, but that was the least of her worries. She busied herself setting up her micro-stove. Two of the pre-packaged home-cooked meals warmed on the stove's large burners. Thistle tea was left to steep on the small, pull-out eye.

Grunden stood just inside the cave and stretched his aching shoulder blades. He had been struggling with his pack, too, but couldn't let her know it. As the muscles began to relax, he realized that he'd been pretty hard on her.

You big dummy, she was just trying to help. You know she didn't deserve that. He took a deep breath and stepped closer to her.

"I'm sorry I was so short with you, Mrs. Tonlin. I guess you're not used to traveling like this, but there is something about this place that makes me uneasy especially when we're out in the open. I can't shake the feeling that somebody's watching us, just waiting...."

Mara gasped. She hadn't thought about how much danger they might be in. She was too focused on finding Ram.

"Mr. Grunden, I am so sorry! I've been incredibly foolish today. But I'll try to do better tomorrow, I promise I will." She stopped and then asked, "Do you think the wind will die down tonight? I dread the thought of going back out into it again tomorrow."

"I don't know, but I hope it calms down at least a little. Let's not worry about that now, okay?" He hoped this would ease the fear he'd unintentionally planted in her.

"Okay," she said, trying to sound brave.

He watched as she turned back to the food she was preparing and decided to say what he had wanted to say since they got here.

"And if we're going to be traveling together, we've got to stop apologizing for everything. Oh, and one more thing – please stop calling me Mr. Grunden. My name is Jacar, but my friends call me Jack. Since we have to travel together so intim… closely, I hope you'll consider me a friend. So please call me Jack."

Mara blushed, but smiled timidly and said, "Okay … Jack, but you have to call me Mara."

"Done. Now, I'm starved. Is that grub ready yet?" he said to steer away from anything mushy. He hated that.

"It is," she said, this time smiling shyly as she pulled their meals from the stove. She carefully opened them to avoid getting burned by the steam. The aroma was mouth-watering which made them even hungrier. After they each took one of the plates, they ate voraciously without speaking.

When he was full, he sat back from the inverted miner's crate they were using as a table and sighed loudly.

"Now that's what I call food. Where'd you learn to cook like that?"

She smiled at the memory. "Ram taught me how to cook. When we got married, I couldn't even boil water without burning the pot. And even after he was satisfied that I would not starve to death if he died before…." The thought that he could be dead was unbearable.

There I go again. Grunden mentally kicked himself. Seemed like every time he opened his mouth, it was only to change feet.

"Mara, I'm sorry. I didn't mean to upset you." He reached out to touch her arm but thought better of it and hid the gesture by picking up a stone that lay at her foot instead. *Damn it all! There I go apologizing again. But, I ....* He realized that grousing was a waste of time and abruptly sat down.

Mara didn't notice his discomfort. She lay down near the tiny heater he'd set up while she cooked their supper. Burying her face in her arms, she tried unsuccessfully to muffle her sobs.

He sat watching her, waiting for her to drift off to sleep. When she finally did, he too lay down and was soon out like a light. But he hadn't been asleep long when the ghost of his old friend Zander came to him again.

"Something's lurking about, old buddy. Wake up."

But Grunden was exhausted. Instead, he grumbled in his sleep and rolled over without waking.

The last time Zander had come to him, the ghost had saved Grunden's bacon with Commander Camdus. That was Zander's first foray back into the land of the living. He'd not asked to go. No, he was resting peacefully with the others in Soldier Field, when he was roused and sent to help his old friend. As quickly as he'd been sent, he was called back after he'd completed his task. And now, the same had happened again, only this time he found his friend and a companion in a frigid cave on Creedor.

Zander didn't know why they kept sending him. Maybe it was because he and Grunden had become friends when they wound up assigned to the same battalion.

The serious-minded Grunden at first had not liked Zander, who was always scheming to pull another prank on his buddies. To Zander nothing was funnier. If Grunden hadn't intervened, he would have been beaten to a pulp by one of his mates when the fellow discovered Zander had broken into the package his wife had sent him. The soldier would have laughed it off if Zander hadn't opened the personal letter she'd written and begun reading it out loud to the other guys in the barracks. From that day on, Grunden had taken the jokester under his wing, but not until Zander apologized and promised to knock it off. He still pulled one occasionally, though he never again went into any of his buddies' personal belongings.

It was Zander's inability to resist this foolish compulsion to pull one more prank that got him killed. It all started with Cookie, the battalion chef. Zander kept criticizing his biscuits, so Cookie made sure that Zander got the smallest portions and the worst cuts of meat he could find.

Zander just smiled and laughed, all the while plotting his revenge prank. One night the mischievous soldier decided it was time. He slipped out of his barracks and headed to the mess hall with a bucket of axle grease. He intended to plop it down inside the shortening tin. He didn't even see the grenade lobbed over the barrier. It exploded where it landed – smack dab in the middle of the bucket Zander was carrying. He died instantly, sending his spirit to Soldier Field to spend eternity. That is, until he was assigned this job of watching out for the soldier who had looked out for him.

Is this what I have to look forward to forever? Well, so be it. Let's get this over with.

"Wake up, Jack." Zander tried to poke him, but he found that he had arrived here on Creedor without any substance to back it up. His finger went right through Grunden unnoticed. "Dang it," the ghost groused, forcing his body to materialize.

Now, let's try this again. He poked him. Grunden didn't move. Then he picked up a stick and poked him once more. Grunden swatted it away.

"Why did you send me if I can't help?" he said in frustration and then disappeared. He reappeared outside. "Thanks heaps," he said sarcastically. "Why don't I just sit here and keep watch for him. Wooo oooo woo ooooo." He tried to make scary sounds. "I need more practice, but maybe I can look scary enough to run off anyone who tries to go in."

He dissolved down to his skeleton to keep watch at the cave's entrance while Grunden and Mara slept on, each tossing uncomfortably on the rocky cavern floor.

Sometime in the middle of the night, Grunden finally awoke. Not long after, Mara sat up and yawned, stretching to ease her sore muscles.

Neither spoke. They didn't know what to say, so they just sat there quietly studying the heat waves still radiating from the small stove.

A loud rattle outside broke the silence. Startled, Grunden jumped up and went to the mouth of the cave to investigate. The tree top door he'd put in front of the entrance had blown over. Strong gusts of bitter wind rushed in, adding to the chill clinging like icicles to their bones. When he stepped outside to put the door back up, Zander greeted him.

Even though he recognized the voice, Grunden jumped at the macabre sight of the animated skeleton.

Zander realized what he'd done and fully materialized.

"You shouldn't be out here, Jack," he warned.

"I don't appreciate your stupid sense of humor. Tearing down our door is not funny."

"It wasn't me."

"Then who?"

"That's for me to know and you to find out," Zander said, unable to control himself. The fact was, he didn't know but loved taunting Grunden.

"Don't you have someone else to bother, Zander? We'll freeze if I don't get this cover back up."

"I'm telling you, Jack, you need to go back inside."

"Bug off, Zander. I don't have time for your stupid games."

Grunden turned back to his work.

"That's a fine way to thank the one who saved your sorry hide. But, that's okay. Whatever you say," Zander said and disappeared.

Though working outside was an annoyance, he welcomed the escape. He didn't know how to comfort this grieving woman, or for that matter if he should try. He had always felt a little uneasy around good looking women.

Jack, old buddy, put those thoughts out of your mind. The woman is here looking for her husband.

He looked for something to brace the cover. *Maybe a tredon bone from this old carcass will do.*

As he reached for it, he saw a quicksilver movement followed by a vapor trail. His soldier instinct told him he had to get Mara out of there fast. He knew doing that without being seen would be impossible. Drawing his weapon, he slipped silently back into the cave only to find it empty.

"Damn it, Zander. You could've told me straight out what was up! Everything's got to be some stupid joke to you," he shouted.

Zander's bitter laugh echoed through the cave.

How could she have gotten out without my seeing her?

Grunden turned his focus to the task at hand. On close examination of the rear of the cave, he discovered a dark alcove he'd not seen before. By holding his lamp high above his head and peering over the pile of boulders stacked around it, he could see the entrance to a tunnel. Without looking back, he climbed over the obstacle and squeezed his shoulders through the opening.

When he first entered the tunnel, he realized that it wasn't just dark, it was pitch dark. He didn't want to use the lamp, so he pulled his nucleo and flipped it to the glow setting. With only this faint light he headed off down the low tunnel, banging his head occasionally when the ceiling dipped too low.

After he had gone perhaps a quarter of a mile, he heard a noise ahead of him. He quickly doused the light and quietly inched forward. Hugging the tunnel wall, he moved toward the tiny dot that glowed soft blue far ahead of him. As he started to step into the center of the tunnel from his position along the wall, a rasping voice warned him back. Looking into the darkness he saw nothing but could feel a presence within striking distance. Hand to weapon, he turned, ready to defend himself.

"Stow your weapon, mate. You'll get no fight from me. I've come to help you, Jack Grunden."

He wondered how this man could see him in the dim glow and how he knew his name. Things were getting stranger by the second – and as those seconds passed, he was painfully aware Mara was slipping farther and farther away.

The man hadn't tried to attack, even though Grunden knew he could have. *But why didn't he?* There was no time to question him. He had to press on. Turning on his heel, he swiftly stepped once more into the center of the tunnel. He was relieved to find that the ceiling was now high enough for him to stand and move easier, with only the occasional need to duck.

Risking attack from the rear, he raced ahead. He came upon an open chamber bathed in blue light so quickly he had to take a huge step back. *Oh, so this is where the light's coming from. But what exactly is making the light?* He studied what he saw from the shadows at the mouth of the tunnel. Though still on alert, he was relieved that the air coming from the chamber was warm and gently moving like a caress over his tired, bruised body.

The chamber itself was perhaps a hundred feet across, roughly round in shape. He could see openings to five more tunnels, evenly spaced around the perimeter. In the center was an elevated pedestal that looked like it had been crudely carved from one of the boulders littering the cavern floor. A delicate hand and slender arm hung limply over the pedestal's side. He recognized the thin gold band on that hand. Mara Tonlin was lying there so still, too still. Just as he was about to enter the chamber to retrieve her, he heard a cry so bloodcurdling he feared he'd stumbled into the gate to hell, with one of its demons preparing to claim a sacrificial offering.

As Grunden crouched in the tunnel, he knew once again he was not alone. A rough hand grabbed him and pulled him so close he could smell the tredon leather of the man's clothes. He hoped this was one of the Creedorian rebels, in spite of them having been outlawed by Jarlod. The truth was almost everyone else viewed them as heroes. Their only crime had been trying to remain free so they could keep Creedor's unique culture safe from the Empire Compliance Officers. Emperor Jarlod had sent them to live on the planet's nearly lifeless plains.

To ensure they would give him no more trouble, he had placed a substantial bounty on their heads. Even the law enforcers began to hunt down and exterminate them. All they had to do was present the left ear to get paid. Grunden speculated that non-rebel ears also were being added to the mix. He shuddered at these thoughts. But he knew in spite of Jarlod's harsh treatment, some of them had survived by hiding in the ragged bushes and icy caves, using stray tredons for food and clothing.

He shook these disturbing thoughts away. Right now, Grunden didn't know if this man was a rebel, a bounty hunter, or maybe an escaped slave. It didn't matter to him at this point. Gut instinct told him the man was probably the least of his worries. But just in case, he took a warrior's stance and prepared to fight.

***

If Slogar had known Clandil was so far from the comforts of the Tonlin's cozy cottage, he would have stayed there. But he was here now and armed with this new knowledge, he was ready to begin solid scientific experiments with samples from some of the mid-stage epidemic victims. The REG soldiers who had been dispatched to the plains to see if they could find any survivors had brought back only five. They hurriedly took them back to the facility, leaving the dead to be buried by the shifting sand dunes.

Slogar stood outside the isolation ward and peered at his test subjects through the large observation window. He could see that they all lay quietly in their hospital beds still fairly docile. But he knew that wouldn't last long. As pleased as he was to find the lab at Clandil had been preserved in such good condition, he was hesitant to begin the testing.

Why did it have to be me? Why couldn't somebody else do this? He knew the answer. *Suck it up and get in there.* He put on a hazmat suit and went in.

The broken humanity lying there before him touched his heart. He spoke kindly to each of them and asked if there was anything he could get them. Only one of them asked for water. He knew this was a sign of the disease getting worse.

"Here," he said, handing a tall bottle of purified water to the man who looked to be about thirty years old.

"Thank you," he rasped.

"Do you mind if I draw a little blood?"

"No, do whatever you need to. I won't be around much longer anyway."

Slogar knew that was probably true, but the man didn't have to suffer. He drew the blood and then injected him with a strong sedative placing him in a drug-induced coma.

Once he'd gotten all the samples he needed, he gave a generic antiviral drug to the ones who looked like they still had a chance. He didn't know if it would help because he didn't know for sure which disease he was fighting. But he had to try something, anything to ease their pain.

He left the ward, discarded the hazmat suit, and went to the showers where he thoroughly cleansed himself with a strong antiseptic soap. After he rinsed and dried off, he dressed in a clean uni and lab coat. He purged all thoughts of the five victims from his mind so he could concentrate on the work at hand objectively.

Slogar surveyed the lab again. "Well, at least it's maintained better than any of the other labs I've been in – except Seelah's. I guess I have Camdus to thank for making sure this one is clean and ready to use. Oh, for goodness sakes, here I go talking to myself again!"

He squared his shoulders. "This inventory isn't going to take itself," he said and started making a list of what he had to work with. Pretty soon he realized the lab was sufficient for many of his experiments. However, it seemed to have been designed primarily for diagnostic research, not for mass producing vaccines.

"I know I can get some of the items I need from Boldoon. But we're probably going to have to go to Seelah's lab for the answers." He took off his readers and closed his notebook.

Then he called his young assistant to him. "Waldo, please contact Commander Camdus. Tell him I need to speak to him at once."

Waldo had been listening patiently to Slogar's ramblings. He was pleased that he finally had something to do.

"Yes, sir, right away," Waldo said as he opened a secure channel.

When the young man called REG headquarters, he learned that Commander Camdus was still on the mother ship so he should be easy to reach. He didn't know his new boss Dr. Slogar yet and wanted to impress him with his efficiency.

Camdus was in his quarters trying to catch a few winks when the call came in. He snatched the communicator from his bedside table.

"Camdus, here."

"Commander, it's me, Waldo. Dr. Slogar wishes to speak with you."

Camdus waited to hear Slogar's voice before shouting, "Where in the hell are you and where is Grunden? Why haven't you called before now? Did you want me to send a search party to look for you? That's just what I need in the middle of this mess on Creedor," he added.

Slogar wheezed as he responded. "I know, Cam, I know and I'm sorry I didn't call in earlier. Even little things are easier said than done down here on Creedor – where you sent us remember," he snapped back at Camdus, but immediately regretted it.

He caught his breath and continued more calmly. "We're at the Clandil Museum lab. I appreciate your arranging for me to use it, but there are some things I still need before I can get anything significant done. I want to send Waldo to Boldoon to pick up supplies, though I can make do without most of them if I have to. But I cannot do without the proper equipment for analyzing the blood samples I just collected. They won't keep long. Seelah has everything I need in her lab in Silden. Can you get me there as soon as possible so I can get to work?"

"Sure, but could you be a little more specific? Then maybe … wait a minute! What the…? You haven't answered my question. Where is Lt. Grunden? He hasn't called in either."

Slogar spoke in a strained voice. "What do you mean, where is he? You're the one who let him to go. Why don't you know?"

It was then that the severity of the situation hit Slogar.

"Oh man! I have no idea, Cam. Grunden and the woman were supposed to have contacted you hours ago. I thought you'd have heard from them by now. Arrrgh, I need a drink – bad," he rasped. All thought of preserving the samples dissolved in his intense craving.

Camdus was irritated by this turn of events. If Slogar fell into his old habit again, Creedor would surely perish.

I cannot let this happen. When we're done with this mission, he can do whatever the hell he wants – but not now.

He knew Slogar didn't handle stress well and would give in to his craving if he got half a chance.

Camdus had one sure way to keep him from hitting bottom again, so he silently summoned Rax. The Rider popped in, skidding to a disheveled halt in front of the commander, a few crumbs stubbornly clinging to his tunic.

Camdus sent Rax a one-word apology before he gave him his new assignment.

With a nod of understanding, the Rider popped out.

"Listen, Slogar. You are well aware that I know how tough it can be sometimes. But I conquered my demons and you can conquer yours, too. Look, the bottom line is we don't have time for you to do anything foolish. You've got to stay sober whether you like it or not. What I need you to do right now is tell me everything you know about Grunden and the woman's plan. When I talked to him, he said he didn't know exactly where they were going, but as soon as he reached a safe haven, he was supposed to check in. For whatever reason, he hasn't. Now what did he tell you? Do you have any idea where they were heading? And when was he supposed to rejoin you, anyway?"

Before he could answer any of the Commander's questions, Rax suddenly popped in and stood beside Slogar.

"Hell's bells, Camdus! You could've given me a heart attack. Next time, give me some warning before you send the Rider, all right?"

He took the transcaps from Rax, who was standing just to Slogar's right side within inches of him. But Slogar needed the pills so badly he didn't even ask how Camdus had managed to send the Rider without speaking. All he wanted to do was calm this unbearable craving.

Then, after the brief wait it always took for the pills to work, he tried to answer Camdus' questions but couldn't concentrate.

"Do you mind?" he said to Rax who was still standing too close for Slogar's liking.

"Not at all," Rax said and continued to hover.

"No, no. Would you please find somewhere else to be?" Slogar said, thoroughly exasperated.

Without another word, Rax popped out

"Now then, back to your questions, Commander. You know as much as I do. Mara Tonlin is determined to find her husband who she is certain was taken by intruders. I thought her story was pretty unbelievable, but we checked the outbuildings on our way in. What we found there convinced us she was probably right. And Grunden told me he thinks whoever we're dealing with down here should be taken seriously. He thinks when they find her husband, they'll most likely get to the bottom of what's really going on."

Slogar was quiet for a moment then added, "In hindsight, it looks like his request for permission to travel with the woman may not have been wise. I'm sorry, Cam, but it looks like they're lost."

Just when Camdus thought he was through, Slogar started talking again, rehashing his defense.

"But Cam, how could he have told me when he would meet back up with me if he didn't know where he was going? Anyway, I thought he cleared his plan with you. It's just another bump in the road, right?" he said hopefully.

Camdus grimly accepted this new problem. Now he had no choice but to follow up with an armed unit – he only hoped it wasn't too late. He could not have anticipated the need for yet another mission. But here it was.

This is just great – another bump in an already bumpy road. But Grunden is a soldier of the Reglon Empire Guard under my command. It's my duty to try to find him with or without that fool-hearted woman.

"Stay put, Slogar. I'll get back with you as soon as I can, then we'll see about getting you what you need for your research."

Camdus dreaded having to deal with the blowhards who now populated the REG Command.

May as well get it over with. He took a deep breath and opened a secure channel to REG Command.

After making his report and getting the expected grief about the delays in their mission, he decided he should lead the unit himself.

Captain Slag could stay with the ship. *I don't like the way this is shaping up, but without an alternative we better get ready for a fight.*

When he'd completed a few more calls, he leaned back and took a deep breath. Alone in his quarters, he said a silent prayer that God would watch over him and his men. They had the strength and courage, but they could always use the Almighty's help.

Then he holstered his custom-made weapon, picked up his battle helmet and hurried to the pod launch to brief his hand-picked unit – Taw Johnson, Sy Worth, and Axel Monz.

When he entered the launch area, the men stepped into line and saluted. "At ease."

As he scanned their faces, he saw what he expected to see. These men were wary but not afraid. They were skilled warriors he could trust with his life and had more times than he cared to remember during the years they had spent together in the Emperor's service. And he'd met all three of them – with the exception of Axel – during his years in the Academy.

Taw had been his roommate for the first year. Though Camdus stood a decent height at a little over six feet tall, Taw towered over him. But he wasn't just tall. Taw loved to work out even after a day of physical training. The result was nothing short of amazing. In that first year alone, he turned his lanky frame reminiscent of Ichabod Crane into a powerful physique more like that of a world class body builder.

When Camdus had first met him, he figured he was probably of moderate intelligence. He quickly discovered he was mistaken. Taw turned out to be a solid student who excelled in mathematics and military history. He'd used his vast knowledge to design some brilliant military tactics that his team employed to shame the opposition during intramural war games.

But there was another side to Taw, too. When his buddies found out that he loved to bake, they teased him unmercifully until they got a taste of one of his specialty cakes. After that, they stopped teasing him and started helping. And every time he was given access to the galley, he came out with excellent desserts the rest of the guys devoured. His most popular dessert was what he called *My Blue Heaven Cake* which he made using Andallan wheat flour, horok eggs, tredon milk and lots of butter and honey. He slathered a rich creamy skiabar nut frosting between the three tall layers.

Though he didn't mind telling what was in the cake, he never gave away the actual recipe. Taw intended to protect his future which he was convinced included him opening a successful bakery in Capitol City.

Camdus stood enjoying these memories before he inspected the unit. Since Taw had been on his mind, he stopped in front of him. *He's pretty complicated, but I can count on him.*

Standing ramrod straight, Taw's determination to rescue one of their own showed plainly on his face.

"Ready?"

"Ready, Sir!"

He moved to Sy Worth. Barely five and a half feet tall and slender, he was the exact opposite of Taw physically.

During their second year, Camdus and Taw had met Sy when he'd been assigned to their barracks. At first glance, they both thought this guy would wash out before Christmas. That was before they got to know him. Though Sy was slight of build and not that tall, God had seen fit to give him incredible strength, speed, and agility.

Camdus remembered the last day Taw had teased Sy. The teasing was nothing new, but that day Sy had had enough. To his credit, he tried to ignore Taw by walking away, but Taw wouldn't let up and followed him outside. After a few minutes of taking even nastier teasing than usual, Sy turned around and in two bounds went up one side of Taw and down the other pelting him with steely blows the whole way. Taw was lucky a squad had been doing drills in the yard that day. It had taken four of them to pull him off. Taw had toppled over in the assault.

Sy just stood there, fed up and defiant. "Are you done?"

"Yeah, I'm done," Taw said through swollen lips, still in shock at what just happened.

"Good. Remember that." Sy turned and walked away. This time no one followed him.

Camdus smiled slightly as he now stood before Sy, who no doubt knew the reason for the smile. He nodded. "Ready?"

"Ready, Sir!"

Finally, he moved to Axel Monz. Axel hadn't gone to the Academy. In fact, they'd met him after they'd graduated. As young soldiers are sometimes prone to do when they're on leave, they got into a scuffle over a girl in a bar on Boldoon. Axel didn't start it, but he helped finish it. Everything was fine until a loud mouthed local who'd had way too many grabbed the pretty redheaded server and tried to kiss her. She jerked her arm away and told him to buzz off. As Camdus vividly recalled, the drunk became more aggressive and tried to overpower the girl. Camdus pulled him away from her, giving her time to make a hasty retreat into the office. But it hadn't ended there. About thirty more civilians jumped into the fray. Even though the three of them were not afraid to fight, they were just about to get their lights put out. It looked like a war zone with the REG soldiers on the losing side. That's when the man sitting in the corner booth nursing his ale jumped up and shouted, "That's enough!" They kept fighting. "Oh, you don't want to listen to me? Well, how about this?" He pulled out his vintage .357 Magnum and began firing above their heads. That got their attention, albeit with most of them on the floor covering their heads – everyone except the REG soldiers. They were too stunned to move. That night, Axel left with Camdus and his buddies and quickly joined the circle of friends.

Camdus had soon learned that Axel was a noncom assigned to the quadrant through the REG Military Police. And though he was off duty, he stood his ground and assisted his fellow soldiers. Camdus stayed in touch with Axel and when he'd risen to the rank of Commander, he'd had him transferred into his unit.

"Ready?"

"Damn straight! I mean, ready, Sir!"

Camdus then led them into the conference room to brief them on the rescue mission.

Once the meeting was over, the small band boarded their mini-pods with Commander Camdus and Taw in the lead pod, followed closely by the second mini flown by Sy and Axel. He looked gravely over the brown planet on which they soon would be tested one more time. According to the map, the trizactl deposits were northwest of the plateau where Dr. Slogar and Lieutenant Grunden had come upon the woman. By air it was not a bad trip even with the wind, but over land it must have been nearly impossible. Camdus couldn't help wondering if Grunden and the woman had found a safe haven or if they'd fallen victim to the ravenous sands – or worse.

He landed his pod on a hidden lea not far from what the map showed as the likely site for the rogue mine. Using the halogen array lights of his pod, Camdus marked the landing of the other pod until it was safely down. Quickly they engaged the automatic camouflage feature on each pod and silently prepared to enter the mine.

***

Rax popped home to check on his family and was at the moment resting peacefully outside his modest cottage.

He enjoyed sitting in the shade of the skiabar tree that grew beside the Alvion Stream. As he sat, he watched his children Kel and Zil struggling to bring in the morning catch.

Evy stood at the kitchen window watching as Rax supervised the whole affair. She smiled at the children's frustration. It looked to her like they were more irritated with their dad than with the fish.

"There, grab him by his hind legs. No, no. I said his legs, not his tail. You're just making him mad," Rax shouted above the bellowing buffalo fish and the squabbling teens.

"All right then, Dad. You bring him in," Kel said, letting his end go which left Zil with a handful of fighting fish. Rax got up from the chair he'd made from green tree branches, stepped into the stream to help his slender daughter bring in the fish. Kel had already gotten out of the water and was drying off on the bank.

"No fair," he pouted.

Rax looked into the deep blue eyes of the fish – a huge mistake. He saw its life story in that look. It was a female with young. Zil knew it at the same time as her father. She released her grip on the fish.

"Let her go, Dad. Her family needs her," Zil pleaded.

Rax knew she was right. He let go and watched her slip ungracefully back into the water and disappear downstream.

In a few moments, they saw bubbles rising around the base of the old cypress tree that grew in the stream close to the opposite bank. Sharing a sigh of relief, they smiled at the knowledge that she'd made it back to her babies. They saw the frantic swirling around their mother and knew they'd done the right thing.

Kel was furious. "You let him go!" he shouted.

Rax and Zil quietly sat down on the grassy bank, still smiling.

"Yes. We did," Rax said simply.

"It's a mama fish, you big bully!" Zil shouted, jumped up, and stormed back inside.

Rax stood up, patted Kel on the head, and went into the cottage to change. He found Evy still puttering about in the kitchen and leaned down, giving her a gentle kiss on top of her head. She handed him the huge sandwich she'd just made. He took it gladly, scarfed it down, and gave her a hug.

"You did the right thing, husband," she said as she wiped the crumbs from his chin.

"I know, but Kel doesn't understand. How can I make him...." He stopped in midsentence.

"I have to go. The Commander needs me." He dusted the crumbs from his hands and his tunic, chugged a quart of milk, and wiped his mouth with his sleeve.

Evy shook her head and gave him one last hug. Then she pulled her tall husband down to her level for a proper kiss and watched him pop out. A little piece of her heart felt the tiniest jab. *Such is the life of a Rider's wife.* The old saying ran through her mind but gave her no comfort. She'd learned that being the wife of a subspace particle Rider was not the glamorous adventure that she'd imagined as a young girl. *But I love him, so it is what it is.*

She returned her attention to the children, who'd gone outside again and were in the middle of yet another argument. This time they were bickering over who was the best Rider. They were about five limbs up the twisted trunk of a gigantic skiabar tree that stood near the portal to their secluded world.

By the time she got out there, they had made it to the seventh limb which was about twenty feet above the ground.

"Get down from there! Both of you! You know you are not allowed to ride without your father."

The youngsters carefully climbed down, scratched and bruised from the unyielding limbs.

"Sorry, Mother," Zil said earnestly. Her brother echoed the apology, but Evy wasn't sure if Kel was sorry for breaking the rules or for getting caught. But she was as glad they were safe as she was mad they disobeyed. She did not want her family to join the host of others who had lost their young Riders to the branches of that unforgiving tree.

The children sheepishly went inside and were soon deep in animated conversation. Evy was relieved to see them contentedly spending the afternoon talking, laughing, and drawing.

Thank you, Father. She breathed a sigh of relief and turned back to her household chores, at peace with her world once again.

THE TUNNEL

When Camdus and his men first set out to find Grunden, they had no way of knowing that their search would lead them to an escaped slave named Stadar.

Even though Stadar was grossly outnumbered, he was free now and would not let them take him again. As long as he had strength, he intended to work to save his beloved Creedor – even if he got killed in the process.

Bracing against the Q'Arons that he was convinced were after him, he thought, *Bring it on. You won't take me again. You may kill me, but I'm not going back to your filthy dungeon.*

He remembered the tales the village elders had told of how incredibly beautiful Creedor was when their ancestors settled in its tropics. They'd come from the Slavic region of Earth and were accustomed to a harsh climate. They welcomed the warmth and beauty of their new home.

However, it wasn't long before unscrupulous timber harvesters began destroying the virgin rainforests. By the time the people realized that this over-harvesting was devastating the entire planet, it was too late. They couldn't just stop and expect everything to go back to normal. No, recovery would take far longer than the destruction. As a result, many Creedorians once again packed up and left for a healthier world. Stadar's family was determined not to leave, so they stayed and eventually adapted. They moved to one of the few remaining valleys and partnering with their neighbors, managed to carve out an oasis amidst the ruin.

There Stadar had grown up under the strict home schooling of his mother. She made sure he understood if he wanted to succeed, he had to work hard. But it was his father, a retired soldier, who instilled in him duty to the Empire. It didn't surprise them when he joined in the REG and spent 20 years active duty on several of the worlds before retiring as a relatively young man. It was during his tenure in the REG that he met Ram Tonlin. They had become friends and stayed in touch after they mustered out of the service. Ram went back to Vartuch and Stadar returned to his own home on Creedor.

When Ram got home, he landed a job at Vartuch Interplanetary Minerals, Incorporated. That's where he met Mara Siptor. Her striking beauty was only part of the attraction. He found out pretty quick that Mara was a first-class researcher and could hold her own in most any setting. The first time he asked her out, she said no. The second time he asked her, she said no again. But the third time, she agreed to a lunch date with him.

Over their bowl of soup with hot bread coated with warm butter, he had asked, "Why did you turn me down the first two times I asked you out?"

Mara laughed easily, finished the spoonful of the comforting soup, and answered him with just the hint of a twinkle in her eye.

"I needed to know that you were really interested in me. I've always done that, no matter who asked me. My mother told me that if a fellow really wanted to get to know me, he'd keep asking me until I said yes or told him to go away."

He didn't know quite what to make of that but took it as a good sign.

They had been dating for about a year when he asked her to marry him, half expecting her to say *no* twice before she said *yes*. But she didn't. Her answer was *yes* the first time. They settled in and did fine until the atmosphere became so toxic they had to leave. They looked for jobs on nearby worlds. Mara landed one on Creedor, but there wasn't one for Ram. He took the opportunity to become a tredon rancher.

Their life there was idyllic especially after their daughter Astril was born. But they eventually recognized the signs that Creedor was becoming sick just like Vartuch. But they decided to stay. They had no way of knowing what that would mean for their family.

***

RAM'S NIGHTMARE

His beautiful captor, Li'Let, seldom slept, Ram observed. Too many nights he awoke to find her staring at him.

Maybe that explains some of the weird dreams I've been having lately. But how can she survive with so little sleep? And when does she eat? He usually did a better job of hiding his thoughts. She had no trouble reading them, and if they weren't about her then he could wind up dead.

"It's none of your business where I go or what I eat." She paused for emphasis then added, "Be careful, Ram. Your nightmare hasn't even started yet. Who knows? Maybe I eat …," She lightly bit his arm, then laughed like a maniac and flounced out of the room.

He was too tired to worry about her threats. That's how she controlled her victims. Ram was tired. Just getting up and getting dressed each day was hard. But the thought of that flimsy blue uniform she'd made him wear when he first got there made him laugh. *I must have looked like a flaming idiot prancing around in that thing.*

But now she was letting him wear his own clothes again, though he wondered why they had taken them in the first place. He suspected she had used them to give his scent to the animal that hunted him in the maze. So far, he'd managed to outplay it. *One more day, Lord, give me one more day.* He said this prayer every morning for he knew that each day he woke up was a day closer to getting out of here and home to Mara.

Suddenly he heard his captor coming back and replaced what he'd been thinking with praise for her striking beauty. That was easy to do because it was the truth. Even after all he'd been through, he still marveled at her. She was like a rare jewel or one of the fine marble statues that lined the Great Hall in Jarlod's palace.

She stretched out on her chaise lounge, watching him again. She was pleased by his thoughts and smiled.

"That's more like it. Are you ready?"

"You know I am."

The maze appeared and the game was on.

***

As the days passed, he had become increasingly wary of her. In spite of her beauty, it didn't take long for his anxiety to turn into hatred. He knew hating was wrong, but he just couldn't help it. Occasionally, when he was sure she was nowhere around, he plotted ways to get away. He knew she had no intention of letting him go so his only hope was to escape. He had to fight the urge to try to strangle her. But wisdom took over when he realized she was not an ordinary woman and would probably best him in hand-to-hand combat. *Think happy thoughts, be a good boy, live to fight another day.* These thoughts kept him going.

He took her abuse fairly well for some time. But then one night, in the wee hours he woke up with the sure knowledge that he couldn't stay with Li'Let. She was stripping away his humanity one taunt at a time. *I'm her plaything. She's enjoying this cat and mouse game way too much.* And he was convinced Li'Let would dispose of him when he no longer amused her. *The cat always kills the mouse, but not until it's too weak to run anymore. I need to find a way out of here, away from that witch.*

He caught himself before he let these thoughts creep to the forefront of his mind, especially right at this moment. At least he hoped he had.

She was standing far too close to his bed in the dimly lit room. Her sleek, well-groomed eyebrow arched as if a question mark. "Oh, what's the matter with my boy? What's all this jumbling around in your brain? Don't you like Li'Let anymore? If you prefer, I could send you to the mine or better yet, I could let Lars play with you awhile. He's a bit heavy handed, but you're a strong man. You wouldn't get hurt – well not much anyway." She broke off with a bizarrely high-pitched cackle that sent a chill down his spine. He began saying the *Mary had a little lamb* nursery rhyme over and over in his head.

"Oh. I see how it is. Daddy said there's a new supply for me to play with anyway. I think I'll send you to Lars."

Leveling his eyes to hers, he forced a smile and said, "Let's play," and jumped up off his cot. The maze appeared. She forgot about Lars – at least for the moment. The maze was different this time. It was distinctly darker and filled with strange animal sculptures. He recognized the tall, thin jyrabung and the heavy set, longnecked hippograff, but the others were too bizarre to even try to identify. He heard her coming, laughing insanely.

"Where are you? Come out, come out. No, no, no. You can't hide from me this time. My friends are with me tonight. Tonight's the night! Ah, ha ha, ha ha."

He ran as quietly as he could away from the direction of the taunts. He found the chink in the wall, but it was blocked behind a statue. This one looked like some kind of wizard. He tried desperately to squeeze in behind it, but the space was too small. Hearing the pounding footsteps getting closer prodded him to move on. Fear gripped him so hard that he couldn't look back. Then he heard a loud boom and was temporarily blinded by a flash of silver light. The howling that came next sent another shiver down his spine. Whoever was in the maze with him ran away, howling as they went. Soon the maze was silent. He went back to the wizard's statue to get a closer look. It was gone, but the chink in the wall was there. He slid in and fell asleep. When he woke up, he was back in his small room on his cot. Li'Let was nowhere to be found. He assumed that she'd gone back to her private chamber to lick her wounds, for he was sure she'd been hurt at least superficially.

Ram assessed his situation. Li'Let had lied to him about answering his questions – she'd never intended to tell him anything else. He should have known. He was painfully aware that his time was running short, and he'd have to find out the secrets of Q'Door Hold by himself. Hopefully, he'd find a way to escape in the process. The opening he had been waiting for was finally here, but he had to be careful.

It hadn't taken him long to learn that the only time Li'Let couldn't read his thoughts was when she was sleeping or not near him. In the beginning, she had stayed with him almost constantly.

But now, he sensed something was different. They hadn't played in the maze since the night she was injured. But she didn't leave him alone. No, if she couldn't punish him physically, it looked like she was determined to increase his mental torment. She relished making him feel small and powerless with her insults and threats. So far, he'd held strong, unflinching, which infuriated her. But no matter how hard he tried to protect his most private thoughts from her, she still managed to learn his greatest weakness and used it to deliver her cruelest blow.

"You think I can't find your pretty little wife? Really? Not only can I find her, I will. And when I do, I'll flay her soft skin, fillet her tender body, and serve her up on a platter. Yum, yum." Then she shoved him hard and taunted, "Think about that for a while." When she left him, he crumpled on the floor, sobbing uncontrollably.

The next two weeks had been the hardest for him to survive.

Li'Let had inflicted in him a level of pain that surprised even her, but she hadn't completely broken him. He became more mechanical in his response and proved time and again she couldn't beat him in the maze. Her interest was clearly waning, but she just couldn't release him to Lars or the mine. That would be admitting defeat and her ego would not let her do that.

After he'd been beaten down almost to the point of hopelessness, she started leaving him alone for long periods of time. At least she stopped taunting him, and she didn't hunt him anymore. But she still kept him in his nook in her chamber. At times, she came and stood in front of him without a word. Then she'd leave. Eventually, the hours she was away turned into days where he didn't see her at all. He had no idea what she did after she left him, but he used this time to continue his secret exploration of the prison.

Then one day he woke up to the sound of silence. After a quick look around, he realized that Li'Let was nowhere in sight. He crept through the apartment and then cautiously checked to see who was guarding him. He was surprised to find no one on duty outside his room.

Carefully opening the chamber door all the way, he stepped into the eerily quiet, dark hall. Once he got his bearings, he headed back to the holding cells to see if he could find Stadar. Hugging the wall, Ram swiftly covered the distance from his chamber to the jail.

"Stadar," he whispered. He fought the foreboding that covered his spirit like a shroud. "Stadar, are you in there?" Only silence answered him.

He pulled on the locked door, then stood back to regroup.

What if he's not there and I get caught out here? Then I'll have hell to pay for nothing. Maybe I should go back.

He shook the doubt away and turned his eyes to Heaven as if searching for an answer. That's when he saw the key hanging at the top of the left door jamb.

What's this? A trap? Well, so be it. I'll just have to risk it.

Ram held his breath and quietly took the key and opened the cell door. He slipped inside, closing the door behind him. He stuffed the key into his pocket and moved deeper inside the cell. The farther in he got, the more he was convinced this was a mistake.

Oh man, just my luck. They're all gone and I'm not where I'm supposed to be. She'll hand me over for sure.

But as his eyes adjusted to the almost pitch dark, he saw the large pile of rags in the corner. He carefully nudged the mass. A barely audible moan caught his ear as he leaned closer. "Stadar," he whispered again.

"Get out of here. They're coming back for me. They'll get you, too, Ram."

His voice was raspy from thirst and the last beating he'd endured. He tried to sit up but was too weak.

"Go on, get out of here! It's too late for me." Stadar curled over on his side, once again silent.

Ram knew two things: he had to find a way out and Stadar was going with him whether he wanted to go or not. He checked out the far wall where a thin piece of wood leaned, distinctly out of place. When he pushed it aside, he found what he was looking for.

This must be where Stadar and the others tried to escape.

He went back to Stadar, carefully lifted him, and stepped through the opening into the vicious demon winds. He hadn't given Stadar a chance to argue. He just took him.

"I've lost too much already. If I can save you, by God, I will!"

Once they were outside, he half ran half stumbled in the shifting sand with Stadar slung over his shoulder. They needed to find shelter against the storm. Just ahead he saw a clump of rugged miracle bushes, which seemed to be about the only shrub that could endure this climate. Ram knew getting to the center of the clump would be painful because the bushes were full of hateful little thorns, but it was their only hope.

The miracle bushes had been transported here with some of their ancestors from Earth's eastern shores during the Great Exodus of 2320. The ancients thought these plants had mystical powers. The refugees had eventually transplanted miracle bushes onto each planet in the Reglon cluster. However, over time most of them died out everywhere except Creedor. There they thrived in the sandy soil and harsh weather.

With no apparent alternative, Ram decided to see if what he'd heard about the bushes was true. If it was, then he and Stadar would be granted absolute protection – if they were deemed worthy enough to enter. He ignored what he knew about the fate of the unworthy who tried to get in. *Okay, then.*

With a deep breath and a prayer, he plunged into the thorny bushes. He saw stray bones on the way in – maybe animal, maybe human. But he couldn't let himself dwell on it because there was nowhere else to go. With his brute strength and determination, he pushed their way through to the inner circle. He was relieved to find a cozy interior that totally blocked the vicious wind and sand. Ram carefully placed Stadar against a large trunk of one of the bushes. Then he prepared a bed of leaves over surprisingly warm sand and moved Stadar to it. As he sat there trying to figure out what to do next, he noticed that Stadar was losing his haggard look and beginning to return to his former vigor.

Wow, this really is a miracle bush! Thank you, God!

Platters of food and flasks of water appeared in the center of the circle. Stadar sat up and reached for an apple. "Mmmm, this is so good!" he said to his friend. "But how...?"

Ram shrugged. "No idea, but I'm not going to question it. Let's eat."

They ate their fill and then sat quietly trying to assess their new circumstances. As much as he needed to rest, Ram knew he had to get back and find out where everyone else had gone. Something major must have happened, and he intended to find out what.

"Stay here. I'll be back in about an hour," Ram whispered.

"The hell you say! I'm coming with you. You're gonna need me. How did you get out from under that witch's thumb anyway?"

Ram briefly filled him in on the changes he noticed in recent days.

When he got to the part about the last time he was in the maze, Stadar said, "It was just a maze when I was in there. But I didn't run, so she sent me to Lars. I shoulda run, Ram, I shoulda run."

"You did what you thought was right, just like I did. No sense rehashing it now. We can't stay here; we've got to find out what they're up to."

Stadar knew Ram was right. Something big was in the works. And as much as he did not want to go back inside, he knew they had to. The part of him that wanted to stay in the miracle bush lost out to his soldier instinct. "I'm going with you," he said with such conviction that Ram took him at his word and led him out of their haven and back into the hellish wind.

They headed straight to the cell's opening and slipped inside as quietly as they had left. Stadar, now fully rejuvenated, returned to the pile of rags in the corner to wait until Ram needed him.

Ram fished the cell door key out of his pocket and handed it to him. Then he crept back to his chamber as softly as he could. He slipped into the room, allowing his eyes to adjust to the soft lighting again.

Just as he was heading for his cot, he heard someone in the inner chamber, or as he chose to think of it, the beast's lair. He was busy reciting the nursery rhyme when he realized it was Lt. T'Aron who approached. Though surprised, he was at the same time relieved.

T'Aron barked, "Where have you been?"

Ram thought he'd made a mistake coming back here. He was painfully aware that he was unarmed facing a Q'Aron warrior. He figured that if he remained calm, he might find out what the Q'Arons were up to. Ram gauged T'Aron's demeanor and decided that if he had wanted to neutralize him, he would've already done it. He stepped out on faith.

"I wanted to stretch my legs, so I walked to the perimeter and back."

T'Aron didn't speak, studying Ram intently. Finally, he asked, "Where is Mistress Li'Let? What have you done with her?"

Ram was surprised. "What do you mean, what have I done with her? I haven't seen her since day before yesterday. I'm her prisoner. You know I don't have a weapon, and you also know trying to keep up with her has left me weak," he lied again. The miracle bush had restored him both mentally and physically. Then he added, "And even if that weren't the case, you could say I like life too much to risk making her mad."

He noticed a slight easing of T'Aron's stance and decided to take a risk. "We – the prisoners, that is – are just substitutes for you. Come on, you gotta know that. These sick little games she plays are nothing more than her venting frustration. Unless her father changes his mind and lets her be with you, she'll always be the way she is now. I mean, you can't tell me you don't know how she looks at you. You would be a much better player than any of us captives. Besides, you know her. You know how she thinks, how she moves. Who knows, the maze might just disappear for good if she ever found out what it's like to be happy."

"Watch your mouth. You have no right to speak of such things. I'll send you to the mine myself if you don't shut up." He took a step toward Ram.

T'Aron's words said one thing, but his body language said something else. Ram knew that his only hope was to get T'Aron to take a chance with Li'Let. With any luck, she'd risk breaking the law to follow her heart, assuming she had one. After all, she didn't seem terribly concerned about anything other than satisfying her own cruel whims anyway.

"Look, I know you care for her. So why don't you let me help? I mean, it may sound twisted, but I can plant some ideas for you, if you know what I mean."

T'Aron paused. "Go on."

"Well, she thinks she reads my mind far too well. But if I want to, I can put thoughts there that will give you a chance. But you wouldn't just be her plaything; maybe you'd be her partner. What do you say? I'll help you with her. You help me escape."

T'Aron considered Ram's offer but remained silent.

Before either could say anything else, Li'Let entered the chamber. She looked at them – one a prisoner, one a soldier. She'd overheard some of their conversation which just made her problem of not being able to think when T'Aron was around even worse.

What is this strangeness in my chest? Li'Let saw T'Aron's muscles ripple beneath his shirt as he moved to make room for her. For the slightest moment, they locked gazes. The tension between them was palpable.

Ram suddenly felt like an interloper into a private moment. He quickly moved to the door, bracing for the blast he was sure was coming. When nothing happened, he slipped out, breathing another quick prayer of thanks. He knew her habits and was confident that he had several hours to try to further explore Q'Door Hold.

As he snuck out, he could hear their voices, low and tentative. This time, he hoped Li'Let would finally face the feelings she had for T'Aron. If she did, then maybe, just maybe he'd have time to get the information he needed and then get him and Stadar out of there.

Ram headed back to the cell and found the door closed but still unlocked. He slipped inside. The others weren't back yet. He figured they'd most likely been taken to the mine. Stadar lay in the corner completely immobile. Ram knelt beside him, touching him on the shoulder. Stadar bolted up off the floor nearly knocking him down.

"Hey, it's me. We've got to get out of here – now."

Stadar squinted at him in the darkness. "What are you doing back so soon? What's happened?"

Ram grabbed his arm and propelled him down the hallway. "Not now. Let's go."

They raced toward the tunnels, disappearing into the nearest one. Once inside they stopped to catch their breath. "It's getting ready to hit the fan, Stad. T'Aron is with Li'Let, but I don't know for how long. Lately, she been gone a lot and didn't even leave a guard today. That's how I got away the first time. But it's hard to say how long we'll have."

Once they were far enough away from Li'Let's chamber, Ram stopped to get his bearings.

Stadar asked, "What was she like, Ram? Li'Let, I mean."

"You know, she's like no one I ever met before. Just being around her gives me a bad vibe – she's that weird. When she chases me through the maze, I swear she changes into some kind of animal. Part hound, part lion, and part … I have no idea, but something evil for sure. But I'm just guessing because I never saw her change. All I know is this – we need to check out the mine and stay away from her chamber because I am not going back."

As for Stadar, right now all he could think of was getting out of here and setting the other Creedorians free.

"Sounds like a plan. How do we get there?"

"I'm not sure, but let's see where this tunnel goes."

Quietly they edged forward hugging the cold wall. They heard someone coming and plastered their bodies to the rocky edge. Stadar recognized the man and tried to stop him, but the man pulled away and kept going.

They stepped out into the center of the tunnel and followed him. The air became warmer as they went. There was a blue glow coming from a large chamber up ahead. A loud rumbling at the beginning of the tunnel caused them to stop dead still. Without saying a word, they knew they had no time left. Ram thought the guards must have missed them and were now within striking distance. The only hiding places were crannies too small to stand up in, so they flattened themselves as best they could. When they felt safe, they took off after the man into the chamber.

Stadar, whose eyes quickly adapted to the dark, realized they had caught up with Jacar Grunden again.

Grunden still didn't recognize him, but he was fairly certain the man meant him no harm.

"Jack, don't you know me? We served together in the REG some years ago."

When Grunden didn't answer, Stadar stepped out and grabbed his arm, pulling him back into the darkness of the tunnel. Just at that moment, they heard the rumbling again, this time followed by a feral cry coming from one of the tunnels on the far side of the chamber ahead. They froze. By this time, Ram was standing beside Stadar. He had seen the REG emblem but didn't know the soldier. Before either of them could move, they saw a huge, ebony beast. It entered the chamber and circled the base of the pedestal where Mara lay.

Grunden had never seen such an animal. Its eyes glowed deep gold. Its razor-like teeth jutted so far out that its upper lip was curled into a permanent snarl. The beast had a shaggy, black mane and great paws like a lion but rear feet cloven like a goat. It took one step up onto the base of the pedestal and poised as if to spring, a low growl rumbling again in its chest.

The men held their breath and got ready. Before it could attack, the sound of a long, low whistle came from somewhere above. The animal stopped and listened, saliva dripping from its grotesque mouth. The whistle sounded again. The beast sprang back from its perch, roared its disappointment, and disappeared into the far tunnel.

Carefully, the three men led by Grunden entered the chamber. Though the beast could return at any time, he knew they had to free Mara.

Ram had seen that slender hand and had known without a doubt that it was his wife.

Mara. I've got to get to her.

Without speaking, Grunden handed them weapons. They carefully, but swiftly, covered the distance across the floor to the pedestal. Ram leaped to the top and stood on the edge above her. Mara was not bound but was barely breathing. He scooped her up and with another great jump landed roughly on the cavern floor.

As he raced back toward the tunnel, the beast returned. Grunden and Stadar both took aim and fired. The beast was stunned but did not go down. With an incredulous glance at each other, they took off behind Ram and Mara. Once in the safety of the tunnel, Grunden blasted the rock above the entrance causing it to collapse. They saw the furious beast extend its massive paw with its bared claws digging at the top of the rubble heap.

"Run!" Grunden ordered when he realized the beast was breaching the barricade.

Once outside the tunnel, Ram and Stadar led the way to the miracle bush. And for once, they were glad the demon winds were so fierce. The heavy dust cloud gave them the cover they needed to get to safety. Ram and Stadar had an easier time than Grunden, though Mara was allowed to enter unscathed.

Grunden was scraped and scratched but otherwise unharmed.

"Where are we?" he asked no one in particular.

"You wouldn't believe me if I told you. Tell us who you are and what you're doing here – with my wife," Ram demanded.

"Easy, Ram," Stadar said firmly. "This is Jack Grunden. He's all right. Trust me, I know him."

Then Stadar asked Grunden, "What *are* you doing here? This isn't your normal posting."

"Stadar! You've no idea what's going on outside. We came to find a cure for the epidemic. But this mess with Q'Door Hold is crazy. And we don't even know what's causing the epidemic, or if the intruders are domestic or foreign. We took shelter in what we thought was an abandoned house, but we found your wife inside. She filled us in on what's been going on down here."

Screams and snarls coming from just outside their sanctuary sent chills through them. They held their breath until the sounds stopped.

Grunden whispered, "That was close." Then he picked up where he left off before the interruption. "So, you must be Ram Tonlin. You have a very brave wife, Mr. Tonlin. She's also stubborn – stubborn enough to risk her life to find you."

Ram listened as he cradled Mara in his arms. He prayed that she too would be healed while they were inside the miracle bush. But Mara showed no signs of rousing. Her breathing was slow, and she was much too pale, even for her. He felt for a pulse just to reassure himself that she was still with him. She had one, faint though it was. He sent up yet another prayer. Overcome with emotion, he leaned down and tenderly kissed her forehead.

Her eyelashes fluttered, and then she opened her eyes. "You missed," she whispered to Ram.

He kissed her again, this time gently on the lips.

"That's better. I thought I'd never see you again. God is so good." She snuggled into his shoulder and fell into a deep sleep. He placed her on the same bed of dried leaves he made for Stadar.

Then he turned to Grunden and asked, "Now what? We can't stay here forever, but I think the miracle bush will protect us as long as we need it."

Stadar quietly listened. Now he spoke, "You're right, we can't stay here. There are several openings to Q'Door Hold. It's probably safe to assume they're all heavily guarded by now – they must know we've escaped. We just have to figure out how to get in without being noticed. That's going to be hard to do, especially for you, Jack. And then there's Mara. We can't just leave her here without anyone to help her. God only knows what hell she's gone through."

Ram clenched his teeth. He knew she was weak, but he had to help Grunden and Stadar. They needed another miracle, a really big one.

Grunden checked his communicator. It was working again. He opened a secure channel and contacted Commander Camdus. After the expected chewing out, Grunden explained what had happened, where they were, and what they needed.

The Commander scoffed, "You're where? What the hell is a miracle bush? Never mind. It's too dangerous to send the Rider into the storm, so just give me the coordinates and we'll get you out of there."

It took Camdus and his men about a half hour to get back to their pod. While they quickly prepared for launch, he locked in on the coordinates Grunden gave him. In a matter of moments, they landed beside the miracle bush which looked to Camdus like a huge tangle of small trees. Hearing the pod land, Grunden, Stadar, and Ram with Mara in his arms made their way from their safe haven.

Without a word, they all boarded and buckled in. Grunden and his companions collectively breathed the relief they felt as the pod took off straight up and out of the demon winds. The pod then zipped across the heavens to the mother cruiser. Once on board, Mara was taken to the ship's infirmary while the three men were debriefed in the Commander's quarters.

Camdus looked from his crewman to the two strangers.

"All right, Mr. Grunden, who are your companions?"

"This is Ram Tonlin, Mara Tonlin's husband. Dr. Slogar and I used their home for shelter when we landed on Creedor," he said motioning to the taller of the two men. Ram offered his hand to the Commander, who shook it firmly.

Grunden introduced Stadar. "I served with Stadar when I first joined the REG. He and Ram were kidnapped and taken into Creedor's belly to mine trizactl."

"I'd shake your hand, Commander, if it wasn't so dirty," Stadar said as he self-consciously scrubbed his grimy hands down his equally grimy trousers. Camdus grabbed his hand and shook it.

"Looks like you've been through hell."

Grunden continued by briefing Camdus on what had happened at the cottage and what factors led him to ask permission to accompany Mrs. Tonlin to find her husband. He wrapped up with, "They think the rest of their neighbors and friends were taken into slavery by the intruders."

Ram interrupted, "And I know who took them – and why. It's the Q'Arons. They've been kidnapping us to mine the trizactl they're stealing. You won't believe the huge underground complex they built in Creedor's belly right above the mine. They call it Q'Door Hold and it's nothing short of a heavily armed fortress. And then there's Li'Let who's the daughter of Thurl, the Q'Aron Master Slaver. She's a different kind of threat." He stopped to let Camdus take this in.

"Okay. What else can you tell me, Ram?" Camdus asked, worry outlined in his deeply furrowed brow.

"Well, I found out the hard way that Li'Let is not human – at least not like us, anyway. She looks, sounds, and sometimes acts like she's human, but you have to trust me when I say she is *not* human. She has this huge maze behind her chamber that appears and disappears at her whim. That's where she sets slaves loose so she can hunt them. She never caught me because I found a small cavern inside one of the walls. I'd run and then she'd come howling through the maze to find me. But she never found the opening. I'm telling you I thought I was going to die in there more than once. It was so cramped, and the air was so warm I went to sleep every time. Every day when I woke up, I was back in my prison – in the beginning anyway. Later I'd wake up inside her chamber. I think when the maze disappeared, I was exposed and all they had to do was come get me. But then there was one time it was so weird in there. The maze had a bunch of statues that hadn't been there before. The one that looked like a wizard disappeared after it ran Li'Let off. Up until that day I didn't get much rest. I knew if I wasn't enough sport for her, she would turn me over to her sadistic eunuch. I never had to deal with that, but Stadar did."

Now Stadar took over the telling of this incredible story.

"Yeah, that was Lars. He's huge. I think he resents any man who is still a man. He took every opportunity to show me that he was my master. Commander, that sadistic son of a jackal whipped me with barbs until I nearly bled to death. When I finally passed out, they patched me up and sent me back to the cell with the others. But that didn't end the beatings. When they found out that I led an escape attempt, the guards made sure I didn't have the strength to try again. If Ram hadn't found me and taken me to the miracle bush for healing, I know I'd be dead now."

Camdus remained silent for some time, trying to take this all in. He needed time to think and to contact Dr. Slogar. He also needed to call his dad. He knew his father had grown up with Elder Tomer Arking, who was still a member of the Emperor's Council. He also knew that Elder Arking was still working in the Defense Department and was privy to high level information. Maybe with their help, he could make sense of all this data to give them a leg up on the Q'Arons.

Their accounts reinforced his understanding of the Q'Arons.

They're ruthless and even worse they have weapons that we don't. And who or what are the beasts? What powers do they have? We have to understand them if we're going to defeat them.

He turned back to the men. "You two look like hell. Try to get some rest; we have some serious work to do tomorrow."

Stadar said, "Thanks, Commander. I can hardly wait to clean up, get a decent meal, and sack out for a few hours. Have you got a uniform for me?"

Camdus nodded and summoned Rax who escorted Stadar to his quarters.

Ram asked, "Commander, do you think I could see my wife before I turn in?"

Camdus felt a twinge of envy for this man who'd been given a second chance with the love of his life.

"Rax will be back in a few minutes," Camdus said. "He'll escort you to the infirmary. But first, do you know what kind of weapons they have?"

Ram thought about it, and then answered him. "They all carry side arms similar to ours. They never used one of them on me, so I can't say what it does. And then there's the perimeter of the Hold. It's heavily guarded and has the biggest cannons I've ever seen. But I think the woman is potentially more deadly than any of their weapons. I know she's a changeling, and there's probably a lot more. Even if these beasts are not their deadliest weapon, they are the most disgusting. I don't know if they can shift into different shapes, but that cat-beast in the tunnels must have been one of them. I wasn't able to find out which of their forms is normal – animal or human. Either way, we have to watch out for them."

Camdus asked, "Okay, but what about the trizactl? Are they still down there mining it?"

"Based on the Q'Arons' altered behavior for the past two weeks, I'd say they've taken about all they need. They're probably getting ready to ship it to their home planet within the next day or so. Even the guards are gone most of the time now. It's like they forgot that Stadar and I were still there, or maybe we didn't matter anymore, like the woman said. That and the whole place has been a few degrees cooler lately. When the drills are running, it's hot as Hades in there. Commander, they may be finished with the planet, but somehow I think they have only begun to mess with the Empire."

Just then, Rax returned and stood waiting for orders. Camdus instructed him to take Ram to his wife. Then he told Rax to escort both men to his quarters at eight o'clock sharp the following morning.

Rax led Ram down the quiet corridor to the infirmary. They stopped at the third compartment. Through the observation window, they could see Mara sleeping soundly, attached to the diagnostic computer. Rax touched the identity pad and ushered Ram in. He handed him a guest entry card. Ram thanked him and waited for him to pop out. At last he was alone with his wife.

The soft light fell on her pale face and hair. Ram stood quietly beside the bed, watching his beautiful Mara. She looked so peaceful, but he feared she had suffered unspeakable abuse. He sat down in the chair beside her bed and gently took her hand. Her sleep was so deep that she didn't respond to his touch. He leaned over, laying his head beside her. Ram prayed with his whole heart and drifted off to sleep.

When he awoke sometime later, Mara was stroking his head. She noticed he had some gray creeping into his once jet-black hair. Blinking away the sleep, he saw her smiling at him and knew his prayers had been answered. They were still talking an hour later when the infirmary attendant came in to check on her.

"Ah, so you must be Mr. Tonlin. Let me ease your mind. Your wife is going to be fine. Look at this read out. The CompuDoc indicates that she has no physical injuries, but she's suffering from exhaustion and dehydration. She will be released first thing tomorrow if her vitals stay normal. But tonight, looks like you both need sleep."

Ram had to ask just one question, but he wasn't sure how. "Could I see you outside a moment?" he asked.

Mara raised an eyebrow but said nothing. "Certainly."

When the two were outside, Ram asked, "Ah, um, was she? I mean, did they do anything to …? Umm." He stopped, dropping his hands to his sides in a helpless gesture. Just the thought of what might have happened made him sick.

The attendant understood and answered the unasked question. "No. Mr. Tonlin. They didn't. But she may have been severely traumatized. While she has no visible wounds, she could have others that are deeper. If she does, then those'll take time to heal, I'm afraid. Just be there for her."

Ram felt relieved and saddened at the same time. He nodded, thanked the attendant and went back inside. Mara's smile melted his heart. He leaned down and kissed her. Then he stepped out into the corridor once again.

Rax appeared as if from nowhere beside him. If he hadn't been so worn out, he might have been startled.

"Follow me, Mr. Tonlin."

Ram walked with the Rider to his quarters. He was pleased to see that there would be ample room for Mara.

"Thank you, Rax."

"Would you like me to bring your supper?"

"No thanks, Rax. I just want to shower and then rest. Goodnight."

Rax popped out and, for once, without asking, he went home to check on Evy and the children.

RESPITE

When Rax got home, he found that all was quiet in their little cottage on the Alvion. He could see that the heavy rains had caused the stream to overflow its banks, but their cottage was untouched. Rax slipped into the house unnoticed. Evy sat in her overstuffed chair, reading. Kel and Zil were crouched over their meager breakfast table and to his surprise, they were not arguing. No, they were playing one of the old board games that had been given to his grandfather, who had passed them down to his father, and now they were his. Someday Rax would pass the games along to Kel and Zil. He knew that breaking the paternal tradition would be displeasing to some, but in his heart, he knew that he had to treat his children equally regardless of gender or birth order. It was a simple matter for the practical Rider. *The games belong to me and as such I can do as I wish with them – and I will.*

He walked into the room. "I'm ho-ome!"

The teens jumped up so fast they knocked the game pieces willy-nilly on the board. "Dad! Hey, come look what we've built out back." Kel grabbed his father and tugged at his arm, pulling him toward the back door. Zil firmly attached herself to her dad's waist hugging the air out of him.

Evy stopped them cold. "Ahem. Didn't you forget something?" she asked, gesturing toward the game. When they let their father go, she stepped in to get her own hug and kiss, something she'd missed more often now that he was away so much of the time. Rax knew that look.

"Children, you go on out. I need to speak to your mother first." Seeing their sad faces, he added, "Go on, now. I'll be out there after a while. I promise it won't be long."

Though disappointed, Kel and Zil raced each other to the backyard to make sure their surprise was in tiptop shape. They were soon engrossed in checking to see if their contraption worked before their father looked at it. They wanted it to be perfect.

Evy smiled ever so slightly and took Rax's hand. She led him to their private chamber and closed the door, slipping the latch behind them. Her husband was home and she wanted time with him, too.

When he and Evy stepped out into the backyard sometime later, the children didn't notice their parents' flushed and smiling faces.

"Hey, Dad! What do you think of this?" Kel shouted as he pointed to the large wooden object that rose nearly to the bottom limb of the skiabar tree. It looked like a crude staircase.

This can't be good, Rax thought.

He saw the look of joy on the teens' faces. Evy had an entirely different look on hers. She opened her mouth to let them have a piece of her mind, but Rax stopped her.

"Well, well. What have we here? Do you intend to climb those stairs to make it easier to get to the first limb?"

"Oh no, Dad, it's way better than that. Go ahead, Zil, start 'er up!"

Zil untied the rope that held the counterweights. When the stairs began to move upwards, Kel jumped on board grinning from ear to ear. He got about a third of the way up when one of the roughly crafted steps jammed, tossing him backwards and down.

"You did it wrong, Zil!"

"I did not! You made it wrong."

"Now, now, stop arguing. At least you didn't get hurt, Kel. And you know you could have, don't you?" Rax asked the red-faced boy.

Evy had resisted the urge to run to him as she had when he was a little boy. She had to let him stand on his own two feet. But she couldn't resist chastising them at least a little.

"How in the world did you two manage to build this death trap without me knowing it?"

"We built it in the edge of the forest and rolled it here just a little while ago. We were going to tell you, Mother, honest we were," Kel said trying to look pitiful.

"Humph, only because you knew I'd see it and you'd have to tell me."

"But Mother...,"

"Don't you *but Mother* me, young man. And Zil, I cannot believe that you helped your brother in this harebrained scheme. I am disappointed in both of you. Now take that thing down and don't you ever do anything so foolish again!"

Rax watched his crestfallen children hurriedly begin dismantling their invention. Then he turned to Evy. "Well said, my love, well said."

When she looked up at him and saw the amusement on his face, she had to laugh.

"Oh, come here you," she said.

He stepped closer, but before he could give her a proper kiss, he got the call.

"I've been summoned again. It's okay, though. It looks like you have these youngsters pretty well in hand. I'll be back as soon as I can." With that, he popped out of the home he loved so much and back to see what assignment Commander Camdus had for him this time.

Emperor Jarlod

Camdus dreaded having to ask the Emperor for anything. Jarlod was still the spoiled brat he'd always been. But what did he expect? After all, Jarlod had grown up an only child of well-to-do parents in Capitol City. The pampered, spoiled boy went through a succession of governesses until he was too old to need one. His mother, accustomed to the privileges and adoration of those she considered not her equals had fired the last governess when she told his mother that Jarlod had tried to grope her. She absolutely refused to believe that her precious, angelic little boy was now a lusty teenager or that he would do such a thing. But then she didn't really know anything about him. She spent most of her days flitting from one social event to another. If she knew of the treks to the illicit houses of pleasure that her husband took the boy on, she never admitted it. And young Jarlod grew up to be just like his father, understanding that a wife was necessary to bear a legitimate heir and to be hostess to his dinner parties. His father had ingrained in him the twisted notion that pleasure came only from the upscale red-light district on the other side of town. He was taught that seeking pleasure with his wife was disrespectful and totally unacceptable for a man of his station.

In fact, his first intimate experience with a woman was his father's gift to him on his sixteenth birthday. He'd been allowed to pick any of the girls he wanted. He chose a pretty redhead some ten years older than he was. That first taste of what he thought was manhood was like the first drink to an alcoholic. He could not get enough of the lascivious lifestyle. But in their world, these establishments were accepted as part of the social structure. Local law enforcers actually protected them. Of course, many of the madams sweetened the deal by trading favors for protection, an arrangement pleasing to everyone including the wives who knew their place and also knew better than to object.

This upbringing shaped the adult that Jarlod had grown into. But after he stole the Empire from Borm, he realized he didn't have to frequent the red-light district anymore. He established a stable of concubines who would be in daily contact with the future Queen. But he had been in no hurry to take on a primary wife and the Queen of the Reglon Empire. He bartered with the kings and other nobles to get the best dowry.

Commander Camdus was disgusted by Jarlod's weaknesses but had long ago accepted that he had to answer to this shallow, disinterested leader so he'd better keep his opinions to himself.

Now Camdus had first-hand information about the pressing issue on Creedor. Camdus knew Jarlod didn't want to hear what he had to say, but he needed him to listen and respond accordingly. But so far, he hadn't been able to get him to understand that there were intruders on Creedor and that the REG Special Task Force needed backup. Camdus knew that he and his men were on their own.

These were the troubled thoughts going through Camdus mind as he stood on the deck of the mother ship. He stood looking out of the immense windshield at the shimmering stars and stray meteors as if to find an answer there. Rax quietly popped in beside him, waiting. He noticed the haggard look and bloodshot eyes of his commander but said nothing.

"Where have you been?"

"Home."

"You went home without permission?"

"I did."

Camdus was too tired to argue with him. Truth be told, that's where he'd go if he could. But still, he couldn't let it pass.

"Rax, in the future, make sure I know where you're going. I understand that you can pop in and out on a moment's notice, but I'm still your commanding officer and I feel responsible for you. Have you forgotten the Rider who was captured by one of the Q'Arons?"

"No, Sir. I have not."

"He was lucky to escape. You might not be that lucky. So, no more leaving without my permission, understood?"

"Yes, Sir."

"Good. I need you to go to Entellés Base Camp on Reglon Minor. I've had reports of unauthorized activity down there. See if you can find out who's up to what and report back to me. And this time, please don't bring me any surprises."

Rax nodded and popped out.

Camdus returned to his chambers, worn out and ready to call it a night. He showered, brushed his teeth, and collapsed on his bed exhausted. Just when he was about to doze off for some serious sleep, his communicator buzzed to life. The voice he heard belonged to one of his least favorite Elders which seriously irritated him.

"Commander Camdus."

"Speaking," he said sharply.

"Emperor Jarlod wants a progress report – now."

"Now? This couldn't wait 'til morning?"

"Now."

"Report what? I've already filed my report, Spetch," he said wearily.

"Yes, I know. But he thinks you skipped some of the details. He wants to know everything – as in what's really going on down there."

Camdus wasn't sure the Emperor could understand the complexity of the situation, so he kept it simple.

"As I said in my report, we've retrieved our REG team and the Tonlin family. The woman was captured by the Q'Arons. But Grunden got to her in time. I'm meeting in the morning with Ram Tonlin and Stadar, who were kidnapped by the Q'Arons. I'm also going to debrief the members of the rescue team to see what they can tell me." He stopped, too tired to expound on it. But he couldn't help asking one question.

"Why now, Spetch? If he cares so much why hasn't he sent me the warships and additional troops I asked for?"

Spetch chose not to answer. "I'll be in touch." He rang off without so much as a *good evening*, leaving Camdus too ticked off to sleep.

ENTELLéS

When Hellritch was certain the heavens over Reglon Minor had been made black, the Q'Aron Emperor gave the orders to his men.

Silently and swiftly they flew to Entellés, landing in the woods beyond the military base. They scoured the thick woods until they came upon a fair-sized clearing. The surrounding trees made good building material for them to construct three simple cabins. Each one was equipped with essential sleeping spaces, small kitchen area, and a fireplace to provide warmth should the mission last into the cold of winter.

When they were done, they contacted Hellritch for further orders. He called them back to Q'Arrel and sent the trollish Ravagers to guard their secret encampment. Then he waited.

Since no one inside the base camp left the grounds when the Commander was absent, they didn't notice the darkness. They just went about their duties as usual. They never knew when he would return. And they worked hard to make sure everything was up to his standards when he did.

Even when Emperor Borm had gotten sick during the last year of his life, he had been adamant that they finish building Entellés. The project had faced opposition from some members of his Council, but he knew it would be important for the Empire's security. He also thought it could be used to expand commercial opportunities. So, he'd ignored their objections. The facility was completed shortly before his death.

Over the years since then, Camdus had grown to appreciate more and more Borm's foresight and unyielding determination to see Entellés Base Camp become fully operational. Camdus always thought that Borm had fought his terminal illness as long as he did because he was waiting for confirmation that this highly advanced installation was complete. As it turned out, he hung on long enough for Jarlod to get the courage to murder him, but that was another story.

At the Commander's orders Rax now popped into the Entellés Base Camp's large hangar that housed the transport pods and the minis.

"Rax, old buddy! How're things going?" Ensign Williams asked the Rider.

"Well, they're going with nucleo fuel and flight-ready design."

"No, no. I mean, how are you? How are Evy and the kids?"

"Oh, yes, right." Rax laughed a little nervously remembering that the only Ordinaries who talked to him liked to chitchat. "I'm doing fine. Evy and the children are well. Thank you for asking."

"So, what are you doing here, anyway? I know you didn't come here for pleasure, right?"

"Right." Rax chose to ignore the first question since he wasn't sure who or what he was supposed to be looking into.

Ensign Williams just laughed it off. He had learned long ago that Rax was different and no amount of questioning would change that. *Nope, that's one tight-lipped Rider.* He just shook his head when, with no word of parting, Rax walked out of the hangar and into the main building.

Rax did not want to disappoint the Commander again, so he took several hours to watch the comings and goings of the workers and their families. He found nothing out of the ordinary there.

Perhaps what I'm looking for isn't inside at all.

When Rax stepped out of the kitchen where he'd just gorged himself, it was dusk. The Reglon Minor sky at twilight was one of the most impressive he'd ever seen. In fact, he'd couldn't remember a time here when the sky didn't have meteor showers or comets lighting up the night. That is, until tonight. The sky rapidly went from the deep bluish purple to pitch black in the blink of an eye. Not even the starlight made it through the black night.

The Commander is right; something is not right here. Why can't I see the stars? He pondered this for only a moment before popping back to report to Commander Camdus.

When Camdus realized Rax was standing beside his bed, he sat upright, puzzled by this second breach of protocol by the normally compliant Rider.

"What is it, Rax? What did you find?"

"Nothing."

"You entered my bedchamber in the middle of the night to tell me you found nothing? That makes no sense. You are one of the most sensible people I know. What's going on?"

"You asked me what I found, Sir. I found nothing. No stars, no wind, no meteors, no comets, no nothing, Sir."

He got it. "So, something is interfering with Reglon Minor's normal state of being. Were you able to determine what?"

"No, Sir. It was dark. I couldn't see. Once I was outside, everywhere I popped was so pitch dark I couldn't see anything. I listened until the silence pounded in my head. Inside everything's fine, but outside, not so much. I just thought you needed to know."

"Thank you, Rax. Before you go, let me tell you one more thing. Please don't enter my chamber again without permission. It's only God's grace and your good luck that I didn't blast you. Understand?"

"Yes, Sir." With that, the Rider popped into the barracks to grab some much-needed sleep.

DEBRIEFING

Ram woke early the next morning thinking of his wife. *I have to see her.* He quickly dressed, then he went to the infirmary. When he got to her door, he realized he'd left his entry pass on the table in his room. But he could see her through the observation window. She was still sleeping peacefully. He raced back to his quarters, grabbed the pass, and went back. He tried to smile but worry twisted his mouth into a lopsided frown.

Now fully awake, Mara found her husband's expression amusing. But she knew his face reflected his feelings, so she said in a light voice, "They tell me my vitals are holding at normal." She paused then said. "And the best news yet – they're letting me go today!"

He gave her a big hug and kissed her tenderly. Then he sat down and took her hand in his. But Ram knew despite her desire to ignore what she'd endured, he was duty-bound to redirect their conversation to Creedor. The thought of asking her to relive her ordeal hurt as disturbingly dark feelings rose in his chest.

"Mara, I hate to do this, but I have to ask you what happened to you."

"Do we really have to talk about it now?" she asked.

"We do."

She sighed, knowing he was right.

"I guess I should have waited for you in the cottage, but I was so afraid of losing you. And when Lieutenant Grunden offered to help me find you, I jumped at it. But by the time we left, it was already late in the day. The winds and the shifting sand made it hard for us to get to safety, but we finally made it to a little cave. We were famished so we ate supper, hoping the winds would die down. No such luck, so we decided to stay where we were for the night. That was probably for the best anyway, because we were worn out and needed to get some sleep. But, Ram, that cave was cold, and the ground was rocky. Sleeping was almost impossible. Still, sometime in the night, we drifted off. I remember waking up and seeing these awful glowing eyes glaring at me. A tall man wearing a black hood was standing over me. I'm telling you I thought my heart was going to jump out of my chest. I panicked and tried to scream, but he rubbed his finger over my lips, and I couldn't move them. Then he picked me up and took off through a tunnel. I tried to fight him, but he was too strong."

She held her arms out to show Ram her bruises. He clenched his jaw.

"That's the last thing I remember until I woke up with you inside the bushes."

Ram put his arms around her again and held her tight. The tears he'd been holding back spilled over, silently ran down his face, and dripped off his chin. He couldn't say anything, but she knew.

For her part, she was just thankful she had Ram back. Even so, she felt a pang of sadness when she realized that they may never get to go home again.

"I guess we can't go back to our little cottage. But really, what's there anymore, Ram? We left nothing but a shamble-down house and painful memories back there."

She gently wiped away his tears and traced the scar on his cheek, a permanent reminder of what he'd gone through in Q'Door Hold. She kissed his damp eyelids and then his lips ever so softly.

The eternally optimistic Mara took a breath and said, "Ram, this next chapter of our life will be a grand journey, just you wait and see." Then she gave him that beautiful smile that always made him smile, too.

She rambled on about all the places they could go to start over, laying out plans for a new tredon herd for him and maybe a horse or two for her.

"…and flowers, Ram. I want lots of flowers. So, we'll need to settle in one of the…," she prattled on, becoming more animated as she spoke.

Listening to her chatter comforted him a little, but he knew there were many other things they needed to know and do before they could pursue any of her dreams.

When Rax and Stadar arrived, Ram gave Mara a gentle hug, kissed her brow, and left her with a whispered something that made her blush.

Rax led the men to the mess hall where they ate their fill of food that was simple but good and hot. After this much-needed breakfast, Rax escorted them to their meeting with Commander Camdus.

"Good morning, gentlemen. Please come in and have a seat." Camdus showed them to the sofa opposite him. "I've spoken to some of my sources, but I still don't have the full picture. I need to know more about what happened to you around the time you were kidnapped. We must be missing something. Stadar, please go back to the beginning. How exactly did they capture you?"

Stadar had to think a minute. It seemed like a lifetime ago.

"I was getting ready to do some security consulting at the office of the Reglon mine. I clipped on my i.d. and stepped outside the house just like always."

Camdus waited for Stadar to speak again but he just sat there as if in deep thought, so he prodded, "Anything else?"

"No, nothing. That's the last thing I remember until I woke up with shackles on my wrists and ankles in a grungy prison cell." He struggled to remember how it happened, but nothing came to mind. It was as if his memory had been erased.

"Commander, I have no idea how they did it. One minute I was outside my house getting into my pod and the next I was waking up on the floor of what I now know is Q'Door Hold. I didn't see, hear, or feel anything out of the ordinary – at least not that I can remember."

Camdus didn't accept this answer. He knew there had to be something, no matter how small, that might give them a clue. So, he pressed Stadar.

"All right, Stadar. But I want you to tell me everything you do remember. Sometimes our subconscious mind captures things and tucks them away. Now please, try to remember. Go back to that morning. Start at the moment you stepped outside your door. Describe everything around you no matter how insignificant you think it is. Take your time."

"Okay. I'll try, Commander. Just don't blame me if I can't remember." He stopped a minute, deep in thought. Then he said, "Well, when I first stepped out of the house, the pod was where it always is, hovering just to the right of the door. I have a special permit to use it because the work I've been doing is high priority for my company. It's a zero emissions pod, mind you. I guess you already know that the company I work for is responsible for maintaining private security equipment to some of the world's most affluent citizens as well as many military installations. With my security clearance, I've been able to access locations that are off limits to many of my superiors. The Q'Arons seemed pretty interested in this, but I pretended I didn't know anything. I would die before I would betray the Empire."

Camdus listened impatiently but tried not to let it show. The only interesting part of Stadar's story was the enemy's clear intention to steal classified information. Camdus was relieved that Stadar had stood strong. At least he hoped that was true.

Stadar read people pretty well. He cleared his throat and continued. "As I said, everything was the same. Let's see. There was a light breeze. Traffic on the moving sidewalk had halted like it does sometimes when too many people are trying to ride it at the same time. People were standing around, some complaining about being late, others just talking to each other .... Wait a minute! A man stepped over the side. He actually got off the sidewalk. I was so busy thinking about the work I had to tackle I guess I just didn't pay it any attention at the time. But now, in looking back, that was definitely not normal. Hardly anyone gets off the sidewalk when it stalls, not even if it's stopped for an hour or more. But this guy did."

Camdus, now sitting on the edge of his seat, asked, "Stadar, what did the man look like?"

Now that his memory of that morning had returned, Stadar didn't have to think too hard. "He was a little taller than you and thin, but not skinny. He had on a black uni. I'm sorry, but if I saw his face, I don't remember it."

Camdus asked a couple more questions. "Did he have on a hat?"

Stadar closed his eyes, trying to remember. "No, he wasn't wearing a hat, but he had long, black hair. Why?"

Camdus inhaled sharply before answering, "If he's who I think he is, things are about to get a whole lot worse. It sounds like the man you saw is Serin. I don't know if you know this, but he's a mercenary. He offers a menu of services including the most heinous crimes – like your kidnapping, Stadar. He probably took your pod which is how he transported you. Unfortunately, that's also increased his mobility significantly. And Serin or whoever he is must be working for the Q'Arons."

Of course, Stadar had heard of Serin; virtually everyone had. But Stadar reacted to this piece of information stoically. He set his jaw and straightened his shoulders.

Assassin or not, I want a fair shot at that traitor. If Stadar got the chance, he was determined to repay Serin in kind.

Camdus was satisfied he'd learned all he could from Stadar. Now he turned to Ram. "I need to hear your story, Ram, since you spent most of your time there in direct contact with the enemy."

Ram welcomed his turn to speak. "Yeah, I guess I did. To the best of my recollection, I was soaking my chilled bones in a hot bath trying to get warm as much as to get the grit out of every crevice of my body. I must have halfway drifted off to sleep because it took me a few seconds to hear Mara yelling for me to come to the front room. I got dressed as fast as I could and ran to see what was up. She thought we were being rescued. I doubted that, so we secured the house and Mara went to the safe room. When I was certain she'd be okay, I grabbed my weapon and took off to the barn. From my hiding place in one of the empty stalls, I heard somebody kicking in the cottage door, but I held my position. I knew they'd never find Mara, so I waited. And it wasn't long before the door to the barn slammed open. The intruders were hooded and well-armed. They slaughtered the tredons. You have no idea. They were so strong that they literally ripped them apart and began feeding on them. The last animal down was Mara's horse. The mare reared up and slashed the one attacking her with her hooves. His yellow blood splashed up her stall walls. You'd think he'd have left her alone, but he didn't. He just went after her again, this time more aggressively. I could feel the anger rising in my chest as I watched Abalon fighting for her life."

Ram stopped at the painful memory, but then he went on. "The mare's eyes flared wide when the brute lit into her. She fought hard, but in the end she went down. Her attacker went down with her and ripped her throat out with his bare hands. I couldn't take it anymore. I stepped out of my hiding place, took aim, and blasted him. It didn't faze him. He went back to his meal. I blasted him again, drawing more of his hateful yellow blood. This time, he stood up and sneered at me. The next thing I knew, I was lying on the floor of a cell in Q'Door Hold. There were others there, besides me and Stadar. They were shackled, just like me. It wasn't long before Li'Let and company came to inspect us."

Camdus wanted to know more. "Who is Li'Let and who was her company?"

"She's the Master Slaver's daughter. She had an old man and some armed guards with her. She called one of them by name – Lt. T'Aron. I found out later he's her assistant and her bodyguard. He's pretty smart and seems to be afraid of nothing, except for her. It didn't take me long to figure out he has a thing for her. The last member of the party was an old man who held the torch. She called him Slafe. The only thing that stood out about him was the ring he wore."

Camdus said, "He had a ring? What kind of ring?"

"Well, it was big, with a large diamond in the center that was flanked by sapphires and the letter *E* embedded in the golden entwined serpents. I didn't have time at that moment to consider how odd it was that this old servant possessed such a valuable piece. But now, knowing what I do about the Q'Arons, it doesn't make sense."

There was no doubt in Camdus' mind as to who this was, and his name was not Slafe. This was Elsnor, Vandalen's contemporary.

Camdus wondered how he got into the Q'Arons' midst. *I have to find out why he aligned himself with the enemy. When I do, maybe I can get to the bottom of this mess.*

"You still haven't told me what she inspected you for," he prodded Ram for more information.

"She was looking for young, strong men to play her game with her."

"To do what? What kind of game?"

"I'm pretty sure it was some manifestation of her twisted mind. So, let's just call it cat and mouse for now, Sir."

Camdus sensed this memory was painful.

"Okay. We'll skip it for the time being. I know you don't want to talk about it, but we may have to come back to it at some point."

Ram nodded understanding, though the thought of reliving the humiliation was definitely not appealing.

Camdus dismissed them. He needed time alone to process this new information.

***

BACK IN THE SADDLE

Willem Camdus and his old friend Tomer Arking had grown up together, gone to school together and served in the military in the same unit. They were together so often they were sometimes mistaken for brothers. Even though they weren't, anyone could see they were as close as brothers, maybe closer. They talked to each other almost every day and after one of the especially harsh hailstorms years ago damaged their homes, they'd taken turns repairing them. That close contact was lost after Tomer's last promotion. He became too busy to see Willem often. He didn't like it, but he eventually accepted the fact he couldn't keep that relationship up and do his job, so he stopped trying. But that didn't mean that he didn't still care about his friend. It just meant that his sense of duty had taken precedence. He was delighted when Willem contacted him. The chance to reconnect with his old friend was just what he needed. Even more to his liking was the idea of teaming up to work undercover again. That they could recapture some of their youthful vigor was immensely appealing. and if he was truthful with himself, he found it exhilarating. He had come to a point in his life where his work in the Department had become routine to the point of boredom. *Willem and I can do this. It's just like driving a rod-pod.* Tomer's excitement grew when he agreed to meet at a small restaurant called *The Captain's Table* on the east side of the Jevishal, a rapid river that ran through the heart of Capitol City. Its waters were thought to have curative powers if drawn on the first night that both moons shown in the southern sky simultaneously, an event that happened once every five hundred years or so. As far as either of them knew, this magical water was nothing more than a myth. He stood watching the people gliding along the boardwalk on moving sidewalks.

I wonder what would happen if folks all of a sudden decided to walk. But then what would be the point of walking when we can ride? My, but everything looks so orderly, so peaceful tonight. Don't know how much longer it'll stay this way. He took one last moment to scan the heavens. *Look at that! Two moons in the southern sky. If the legend's true, then tonight's the night,* he thought.

With darkness already blanketing the banks of the Jevishal, he was not able to see beyond the area just below the pedestrian bridge. So, he didn't see the tall figure that limped out of the woods, knelt, and drew seven small vials of water. Once the task was finished, the shadowy being placed the vials inside a voluminous robe and disappeared into the night. With the evening sky now coal black velvet spattered with glimmering stars, Tomer continued his trek to the restaurant. He knew Willem was already there waiting for him.

When he arrived, he quickly spotted his old friend and walked swiftly to the booth in the corner.

"Lynwood, so glad you could join me this evening. Would you like some wine?" Willem played the sophisticate impeccably.

"Thank you, Zachary old boy," Tomer said with a twinkle in his eye.

Willem called the waiter, who took their order and disappeared. He returned rather quickly with a bottle of chardonnay. The house wine was mediocre at best, but neither commented. After the waiter served their supper of tredon steak and fresh salad, he closed the heavy, burgundy brocade curtains that were tied back to the twisted post that marked each corner of their booth.

Willem secured their conversation's privacy by activating the tiny device he wore as a signet ring on his right pinky finger. He'd used it decades ago during his service years. It was the kind of thing that was expendable in those days, so no one in the Service had to account for them. He was relieved to find this one still worked.

"What have you learned about Enright?" Willem asked as he leaned over and poured more wine. The fresh bread was so warm the tredon butter melted into it. He took a bite of steak, slowly chewing as he listened to Tomer.

"I assume you know his position was a political appointment. My former assistant, Dormax, came in one morning and tendered a two-week notice. I didn't think much of it; he said he was leaving to take care of his parents. Since your visit the other day, I've been looking into his departure. According to Dormax's mother, he was home for maybe a week before he and his dad went hunting, but they never returned. She reported their disappearance. But then she received a message that they'd gotten snowed in and wouldn't be back until after the lull next year. She didn't like it, but there was nothing she could do about it. I found out that there wasn't a cabin on the hunting grounds where his mother thought he would be. Anyway, there's no telling where they are now."

Willem took in this news, seeing clearly how this tied to Enright.

"So, someone wanted Dormax replaced with their agent to carry out whatever they wanted done. From what Michael told me, Enright withheld reports from you that would have revealed the intruder's activities. But who could it be? Who has that kind of pull?"

"I have no idea, Willem. But whoever it is must have a spy on the inside, not just a pawn like Enright – if he's involved. We just haven't been able to get the mole's identity yet."

Willem finally understood how Enright had managed to replace Dormax. And he was getting a vague notion of why someone went to those lengths.

I don't like how this is shaping up, he thought.

"Well," he said aloud, "that piece of the puzzle is at least on the table, but how does it fit? But the better question is, 'Who put it on the board in the first place?'"

Tomer didn't hesitate to speculate. "Ah, that's the question of the moment – who, indeed? If you're looking for the Elder who's greedy enough to sell us out to get what he wants, then I'd say Spetch. But he doesn't have nearly the pull that he'd need for that because Jarlod doesn't trust him. They're too much alike, I think. And I'm not sure even the Q'Arons would risk allegiance with him for the same reason. Then there's Elder Weilz, the Prime Minister. As odd as it may seem, it's quite likely he's behind it. It's rumored that he's next in line for the throne, so that makes him the one who stands to gain the most by Jarlod's fall. But that just raises more questions. How can such a seemingly affable, loyal man become a traitor to his empire? Why would he risk everything he already has to help the Q'Arons? And if it's true, then what else has he done? Was Enright his only accomplice?"

"Hold on, Tomer, we have to focus on one thread at a time. What information did Enright have access to?"

Tomer thought a moment. "Though he was my assistant, I didn't know him well, so I only gave him access to data concerning troop assignments. He had no knowledge of our newest weaponry, at least I don't think he did."

Willem listened intently, slowly digesting his meal and the new information.

"So, he knew where it would be easier to slip in and out without detection. But what was his reward? We need to know whether he was a traitor or a victim. Tomer, you have to get back to your office and see what you can find out. But be careful. Whoever's behind this is capable of anything."

Willem fell back into his old habit of resuming his false identity several minutes before he needed to. He said, "Contact me, Lynwood, as soon as you know. Mrs. Radfield and I would love to have you visit – soon. We'll arrange it as we did this time. How about dessert?"

Willem deactivated the privacy device and was reaching for the curtain when his communicator alerted him to a call from his son. He dropped his hand, re-secured their space, and answered.

"Michael, what a nice surprise," he said in a lowered voice and gave Tomer a cautionary look.

"Dad, have you found anything out yet?" Camdus asked his father.

Willem filled him in on Enright and the Prime Minister.

"Matthew Enright? I was in the academy with him. I dated his sister Rayalla for a while. When their father Major Christoff Enright was promoted, they were re-assigned to oversee Killund, where his father was put in command of REG Special Forces survival training. Matt seemed like a regular guy. Are you sure?"

Willem had forgotten his son and Rayalla Enright had dated. He wondered if that had anything to do with the selection of Matthew Enright to steal classified data. *Maybe, but unless I know for sure, I'm not saying one word about it to Michael.* Instead, he answered his son's question.

"We're quite sure. But we don't know if his assistance is voluntary or coerced. Tomer will try to find out when he gets back to his office tomorrow. What's going on at your end?"

Camdus gave his dad a thumbnail report, making sure to tell him about Elsnor before telling him goodnight.

Rayalla. For years, Camdus had forced thoughts of her from his mind. The first time they had met was at a wedding reception for some of their friends. At that meeting he had thought she was stuck up because she stood off from the crowd, nursing a single glass of wine. He started to ask her to dance, just to see if she'd turn him down. But before he got to her, a short, round bride's maid grabbed him and dragged him to the floor. When the dance ended, Rayalla was nowhere to be seen. He didn't think of her until he met her again, this time standing in line to get her pod permit renewed.

"Hey, don't I know you?" he asked.

She turned around and looked up at the handsome soldier. "Nope."

"No, I'm sure I've seen you somewhere before," he pursued.

"Is that your best line, Sir?" she asked with just the hint of a smile.

"Uh, no. I could say, 'You must be a thief because you stole my heart,' but that seems sort of lame since I don't even know your name."

Her easy laugh was infinitely pleasing to him. "Rayalla," she said and extended her slender hand.

"I'm Michael," he responded. "When we finish here, would you like to go for a cup of tea?"

"Well, I prefer coffee. But yes, I'd like that."

That was the beginning of their tender, magical relationship that tiptoed around commitment. He knew they could have been happy together. Their life would have been filled with one adventure after another. But before he could tell her how he felt, life happened, and they were forced to set each other free. At times in the early years after their separation, Camdus wondered if Rayalla had found the freedom to love again. He knew she still held his heart and without closure to that chapter of his life, he could never think seriously about anyone else. He'd tried, but he found himself comparing each one to her. None of them measured up. But he knew this wasn't the time to rehash the past. He had to focus on the issue at hand.

What about her brother? This just does not mesh with the Matt Enright I knew. We were in the same class; we even shared meals. Hell, we used to get drunk together. Something just doesn't add up.

His head began to thump so badly the pain drove out his ability to problem-solve. He touched on his classical music, adjusted the sound to a softer level and retired for the night. He needed to be on his game from here on in. This journey down memory lane had accomplished nothing. He couldn't afford to take that trip again.

The next day he met with Grunden to bring him up to speed on what he'd learned from his father about Dormax and how Matthew Enright may have gotten sucked into the treasonous plot.

SERIN

"The Creedorian was way too easy to capture. What sort of world is this that its people live in herds without the ability to think? It's a good thing for them I didn't come here for sport. Now to business – I have delivered the Creedorians to you, so I will be on my way at first light. I trust you've enhanced my account with the agreed-upon sum?" Serin lounged carelessly in a large chair by a stone hearth crackling with blue flame. His long hair was now drawn back in a low ponytail.

Elsnor stood staring into the fire. No longer dressed as the old manservant, he wore splendid royal blue robes with a large golden Q suspended from a heavy gold necklace. He stood soldier straight, silent as Serin spoke.

"Yes, Serin, we have made the transfer, even though the Creedorians gave us nothing. Unfortunately, we cannot let you leave just yet. I'm sure your accommodations are comfortable."

Serin did not care for his tone. "I hope you know you cannot keep me here against my will, Elsnor. Many have tried. None have succeeded."

Elsnor looked at Serin, the faintest smile teasing his mouth. "Is that so? Well, I was not among them."

The seasoned mercenary, occasional assassin felt a chill run the length of his spine. His survival mode kicked in. He sprang from the chair and lunged at Elsnor only to be flung hard into the far wall.

Elsnor had not moved from his place at the hearth but was now facing his stunned assailant. "As I said, Serin, I'm sure you will continue to find your accommodations quite comfortable."

Serin had underestimated his adversary. This was a mistake he prided himself in never making. But how had Elsnor repelled the attack? Serin was unable to move for several moments.

When he finally was able to sit upright, he realized that Elsnor was still standing by the hearth studying his every move.

"Why are you holding me? I have performed my contractual duties. It's not my fault the Creedorians didn't give you what you wanted. That wasn't in the contract, so why are you keeping me here against my will?"

Elsnor studied Serin as if watching a fly struggling to free itself from a web and then answered him. "It's simple, really. You are a mercenary. Until our mission is complete, I cannot allow you to leave. For all I know, you'd sell your services – and privileged information – to our enemies. The alternative to staying here as my guest is something you're better off not knowing. Of that, you may be sure."

Suddenly the golden *Q* hanging around Elsnor's neck vibrated loudly. A voice spoke from it.

"Our people are in place on Reglon Minor. You may return it to its normal state now."

"Done," Elsnor replied.

Serin didn't have any idea who Elsnor was talking to or what they were talking about. And he didn't care because it didn't concern him. The only thing that mattered to him was this kink in his plans. His pride was bruised, and he finally had to admit what had just happened to him. *For the first time in my career, I've been outmatched. And by an old man, at that!* He scratched his head and carefully rose from the floor. Once he was sure his legs were steady, he walked from the room with as much dignity as he could muster.

Back in his quarters, he knew he had to find a way out of this predicament. He lay back on his bed, arms folded under his head, trying to think through this change in his situation. He'd been around long enough to recognize the Trilvarian wizard ring on Elsnor's hand. The giant diamond resting between two entwined serpents was unmistakable, though the snakes' eyes were sapphires instead of rubies.

Everyone remembered the awesome powers that Vandalen used to have. But his powers had not been enough to keep him safe from Jarlod's henchmen. And while most people had been dismayed when the wizard was taken prisoner, Serin had secretly gloated, relishing the thought of the once well-respected, powerful Emperor's undisputed favorite rotting away in a dismal cell. The grudge he held against Vandalen was not out of envy. No, it was so deeply personal to Serin that he held it completely locked inside. He never let anyone into that private space, ever.

A fresh pain from his recent injury ran up his back striking him like a dagger in the base of the skull. He realized just how hard he'd hit that wall when he felt his back muscles spasm again, sending more pain raging through his body. Tired but unable to sleep from too much pain and too many memories, he got up and stared out into the boldly lit courtyard. Just the tiniest hint of longing for his childhood pricked his consciousness, but he dismissed it.

Those days are gone. I have to concentrate on this mess I'm in. That ring Elsnor is wearing must be super powerful or else the old man would never have gotten the best of me. Just my luck to face a wizard when I'm without any of my weapons.

His thoughts then turned to Vandalen.

People said that if he'd been wearing his ring, Jarlod's men could never have captured him. But they did, and I'm glad. Damn it all, why am I wasting my time thinking about him anyway? He doesn't matter to me now. I'm the one being held prisoner by Elsnor. An old man, damn it!

Serin forced these thoughts from his mind and made his way back to the bed. After several minutes of stretching and turning this way and that, Serin at last drifted into a troubled sleep filled with incomprehensible dreams.

The next morning, he was awakened by the sound of his door opening. He lay still waiting for someone to call out, but no one did. He knew the only weapons he had were his bare hands and his experience, but they had always been more than enough – well until the little incident with Elsnor. He listened but all was quiet. After a few more minutes, Serin's curiosity got the best of him. He slipped from his bed and silently walked to the sitting area, enduring a dull ache with each step. A beautiful woman sat, legs crossed, looking him directly in the eye.

"Good morning, Serin. I hope I haven't disturbed your sleep," the woman greeted him.

He had seen her before. No man could ever forget her porcelain skin and jet-black hair. She was dressed in a black uni, much like his own. He wasn't stupid. He knew pretty women had been used for centuries to take down men.

He let her know that he wasn't swayed by her looks or her velvety voice.

"Who the hell are you and why are you in my room?" he asked, irritated by her boldness.

The woman stood up, walked over to him, and stopped just short of being too close for comfort.

"Tsk, tsk. Shame on you for cursing in front of a lady. But to answer you, I am Li'Let. And I've been sent here to keep you occupied for a bit," she purred.

Serin didn't like the look in her coal black eyes. He couldn't see, really see, into them. It was as if she were a shell housing something eerily dark and infinitely unappealing.

"Ladies don't enter men's rooms uninvited," he threw back at her. "And I do not need to be occupied, as you put it. I can while away my imprisonment alone," he said bluntly.

Li'Let scowled and clicked her tongue at him. "Imprisonment is such a nasty word. Shall we just call this your extended stay?"

Serin was seriously ticked off now. "Call it whatever the hell you like. I call it imprisonment. All I want is to make sure my funds are intact and to be on my way. I have other obligations I have to meet in short order or forfeit my fees, not that you give a flying rat's ass."

"Mmmm. Flying rats sound delicious," Li'Let said with a low growl she tried to mask as a laugh.

The hairs on the back of his neck stood up, but he ignored the warning. His disgust was evident, and Li'Let made it clear to him she didn't like it. In one step she was on him, twisting his arm brutally behind him.

What the hell! How did I let this happen – again? First the old man, now a woman!

His manhood threatened, he counter-twisted and brought her down with a knee to her belly. "If you want to fight like a man, then by the gods, you better be ready to take it like a man," he shouted.

She screamed in agony, sprang back and came at him again, slashing his side with her long claw-like nails. He felt a sharp pain where the claws dug deep. His rage exploded with a scream. He grabbed her arm and slung her backwards into the steel door, not letting go of her wrist.

At that moment, the door opened to reveal a Q'Aron warrior with his weapon drawn. On instinct alone, Serin pulled the woman back and held her in front of him just in time to take the full blast. She instantly crumpled, lifeless, to the floor. The man knelt beside her. The look on his face was unmistakable. Serin knew in that second that his only chance was to grab the weapon before the grieving man regained his composure. Serin knocked it out of his hand, chased it across the floor, grabbed it, and fled through the open door.

As he raced down the long hallway, Serin heard a blood curdling scream. If he didn't find a way out soon, he was certain he'd be keeping his appointment with the Dark Master that he'd long ago accepted as his only fate. He heard the thudding of feet coming after him. When he got to the lower level, he frantically began trying doors. They were locked. Then he made his way to the prison wing. He found the door to the slaves' cell standing wide open. With the soldier still in pursuit, he dashed into the dark cell. Jagged rocks stuck out from its walls, ripping his uni and bruising him as he ran into one rock after another. Soon he felt a blast of air and heard the rushing wind coming from the back of the enclosure.

A way out, he thought and raced toward the opening, still unable to see.

Soon he realized that he no longer heard the sound of the soldier's thudding steps. Now he heard the roars of what he thought was a lion. The roars became louder and louder until he imagined he could feel its breath on the back of his neck. Once over the pile of rocks at the exit and out of the enclave, the demon winds lashed at him nearly as hard as the woman's claws.

Now what? He darted into the blinding sand. As he ran with the cat close on his trail, panic rose in his chest. Then just when he was ready to give up, the wind died for a moment. He tucked his face inside his jacket and took off again, only to fall into a prickly bush that clawed at him, gouging chunks of flesh from him. Screaming in agony and frustration, he literally tore himself away and took off once more into the storm. The winds swirled faster, sand abrading his badly torn body. Serin hadn't gone more than a few yards farther when he stumbled over a huge rock in his path and fell face first into the sand. The weapon flew from his hand and was lost in the storm. Unarmed now, he painfully rolled onto his back. The last things he saw before losing consciousness were the glowing eyes of the huge cat. His screams faded into the demon winds. Thinking its prey dead, the beast released him and headed back to Q'Door Hold, its anger finally spent.

INVASION

The time before the dawn of this day was filled with the business of getting ready for what they all sensed would be the most dangerous mission yet. They had almost made it to Q'Door Hold before, only to have to abort to save Lieutenant Grunden and Mara Tonlin. But this time they would finish what they started. Whoever or whatever was down there was their target. They would not be side-tracked again.

They boarded the pods just as the pink pearl ribbon of day began to stretch across the horizon. Fully aware that danger lay ahead, they flew in camo mode to avoid detection. Camdus knew he couldn't take any unnecessary risks with an enemy as technologically advanced as the Q'Arons. They possessed strange powers and incredible weapons. Their shields alone were trouble. No one knew where they had gone, undetected, utterly invisible. And the changelings presented yet another problem.

The one we know about is a formidable foe. If there are more like that one....

He shifted his attention to Creedor's surface, looking for the best location to put down. This time they landed on the plateau near the mouth of the north tunnel. The wind buffeted the pods, but their auxiliary stabilizers held. Slipping from the transports into the demon winds in their sand colored uniforms, they seemed to disappear. Camdus took the lead as they struck out for their prearranged destination. After about fifteen minutes of fighting headlong through the wind and sand, they gathered to the left and right of the tunnel. Camdus signaled Grunden to make sure his party was ready, and then they entered. Grunden, Stadar, and Ram were accompanied by heavily armed Taw Johnson and Sy Worth. They entered quietly behind Camdus, Rax, Slag and Axel Monz, who wore crisscrossed ammunition belts and carried one of his antique AK-47s in addition to his more modern mini-nucleo cannons.

***

The tall witch stuck her face closer to the dirty mirror. "Come here you," she said to the long, gray hair stubbornly clinging to her chin. Her ragged fingernails got in the way at every turn. "I'll fix you." She stuck her hand into the cage and pulled out the dark green grasshopper.

"Okay, Oliver, git to work."

The grasshopper gazed up at her from the palm of her hand.

"Do I have to?"

"If you ever want ter go home to yer wife and chil'ren again, you will. Now do it!" she ordered.

The poor insect's big green eyes pooled with tears that spilled into her hand. She mistook the action and cast him aside. "No, you didn't! I know you didn't jus' pee in my hand! I ought to squash ya wi' my bad foot is wha' I oughta do."

"No! Elga, please don't do that. It's just my allergies, I promise. I'd never disrespect such a great and beautiful witch as you," he said to pacify her.

She wiped her hand on her dusty green robe. "Well, that's awright then."

Oliver grabbed the iron hair in his pinchers and tugged. It didn't budge.

"Ouch! That hurts. Be gentle, please. Ya know how fragile I am."

Oliver rolled his great eyes ever so slightly and tried again, using all four of his back legs for leverage. This time the hair came out so fast he was jettisoned backwards and landed on the wall, the hair still firmly caught between his pinchers.

"All done, Elga," he said as he dropped the hair into her waiting palm.

She added it to the growing collection she kept in a large mason jar. She was sure that some of the other witches were jealous and would love to get their hands on her chin hair for a toad spell. She'd been a toad once for more years than she cared to remember. And now that she'd been freed by the touch of a little boy, she had no intention of ever being transformed again.

"You said I could go," Oliver reminded her.

"I did."

"Then I'll be on my way."

"Not so fast. I never said when," she said and laughed as she placed him back in his cage.

Then she turned to her collection. Some vials contained liquids. Others held what looked like vegetation of some sort. Still others held items that looked like small, living creatures.

Oliver watched silently.

"Ah ha! Here it is!" she said as she picked up her latest acquisition. She'd been visiting her gentleman friend who lived in the woods beside the Jevishal River when she realized that there were two moons riding in the southern sky. Though not the most polished of witches, she knew all the folk lore. Overjoyed with this stroke of luck, she'd reached into her cloak's inner pocket and withdrawn the vials she always carried with her just in case. Then she had knelt in the damp river moss not caring that she was getting mud and muck on her robe from the knees down. She'd filled seven vials one by one, her bizarre laughter echoing through the forest behind her.

Now as she looked at her treasures, she wondered how much she could get for them. If the legend was true, it would be a pretty penny for sure. She carefully put them back into the burled-wood cabinet and magically locked it.

With one more look at herself in the mirror, she was quite satisfied that without the stubborn chin hair, she was once again restored to her normal beauty.

I think it's about time to go see my sweetiekins again. He's gone be so tickled!

She went out into the night leaving Oliver perched above the ever-growing puddle of tears that fell to the bottom of his cage.

"She promised! Why won't she let me go? I'll die here, I know I will!" Oliver cried aloud.

"Stop it, Oliver!"

"Who said that?"

"Me."

"Me who? Where are you?"

"I'm Winnie and I'm down here, on the floor."

Oliver climbed to the top of his cage and peered down.

Sure enough, a little gray mouse sat on its haunches looking up at him.

"Miss Winnie, do you think you can help me get out of here?"

"I'm not a *miss,* but yes, I think I can. Just please don't cry anymore."

As Oliver watched, Winnie disappeared only to reappear beside the cage a few moments later. He examined the latch; then he quickly went to work.

"There you are!" he said as the door swung open.

"Thank you, oh thank you so much, Mr. Winnie!" Oliver said, tears welling up again.

"It's just plain Winnie – no miss, no mister. And for Pete's sake, stop crying! You're making it flood. Now get outta here before she comes back!"

"Who's Pete?"

"I don't know, but I know you better get on outta here. Your family's probably worried sick," Winnie said, exasperated with the silly grasshopper.

Oliver jumped out and headed for the door. He looked back expecting Winnie to be right behind him. He wasn't.

"You coming?"

"No, this is home. Me and my family live pretty well on the old witch's crumbs. She's not a bit tidy. But you know that, don't you?"

"Yes, I do. Hey, if you ever need anything, Winnie, just let me know. If it's something I can do, I will do it gladly. I owe you my life!"

"No, you don't. Now get out of here. Go on now. Go," Winnie said and scurried back down to the floor. He hurried away.

Oliver knew Winnie was right – he had to go while he still could. He walked under the crudely hung door to freedom – and began his journey home.

***

Camdus and his men had just entered the tunnel with Grunden and his crew following close behind. Much to their dismay they realized they couldn't easily navigate this passageway because it was way too narrow for them. Camdus was determined not to abort the mission so they moved on in single file. When Grunden realized what was happening, he sent his party ahead of him. He took on the duty of covering their backs. Nine men in any tunnel was bad enough, but nine men in a tunnel this small was ten times more dangerous. They made agonizingly slow progress in the cramped, stifling passageway. Eventually they felt a blast of too-warm air coming up from somewhere below. Though finding the extreme warmth underground somewhat disconcerting, the men welcomed a break from the bitter, cold wind outside and the clammy chill of the tunnel.

Progress continued to be slow but steady. They hadn't been in there long when they came upon a side passageway that branched off the main tunnel. Camdus decided to take Rax and Slag and explore it, leaving Taw and Sy to guard the entryway. Grunden saw where they were going and held up to see if the Commander would signal them to follow. Camdus gestured for Grunden to take his men on through the main tunnel. Silently the two parties moved apart, yet ever closer to the center of Q'Door Hold.

Grunden heard a low rumbling coming from somewhere beyond their position. *Strange, I don't remember the beast's growl being so deep. Must be a different one. That's not good.* He slowed his column down nearly to a halt. He had engaged one of these beasts before and wanted to avoid another encounter if at all possible.

Ram, Stadar, and Axel also heard the animal. A chill ran down Ram's spine at the thought of having to deal with another one of them. But then the image of the great beast crouching over Mara crossed his mind, swiftly replacing dread with anger. "Let's get the bastard!" he whispered.

Grunden edged along the tunnel, stopping short of the inner chamber which was just a widening of the tunnel. The beast's ferocious roars had receded. He hoped it would be safe to enter. But just in case, he motioned to the others to hang back a bit. The chamber was smaller than the one where Mara had been held, reminding him of an ant hill. It had tunnels and secondary chambers he guessed would lead to the main chamber where he was almost positive the Q'Arons had their headquarters. He noticed oddly colored layers of minerals running through the walls of the chamber.

Okay, near the cavern floor a layer of rust – that must be iron. And the black layer is probably coal. Then there's a layer of yellow sand about head high. But what's that shimmering cobalt blue layer at the top? Hmmm, interesting.

He stored this information away until he had time to analyze it. Right now, he was worried about the Commander. They still hadn't heard from him. When he tried to call him, he got nothing. He signaled the rest of his party to join him. Not knowing what might be waiting for them, they entered as cautiously as they could.

Grunden spoke barely above a whisper. "We've lost contact with the Commander. Either they've run into some pretty thick tunnel walls, or they've been taken. Whatever, we need to find them. You two were here," he said to Ram and Stadar. "Maybe you can remember something that'll help."

They exchanged a knowing look. What they remembered they had hoped to never have to think of again. But Grunden was right. They had to find the Commander.

Ram said in a low whisper, "We didn't spend too much time down here in the tunnels, at least I didn't, but there are places to hide in some of them. I think Commander Camdus is just being careful. He's probably close to the Q'Arons and their changelings so he's keeping radio silence."

"I wish that were true. The fact is the communicators still aren't working in here, so we just don't know," Grunden whispered back.

"Look, we don't have time to worry about the Commander. If he needed us, he'd send the Rider for us," Ram said, unwilling to entertain the thought that the others might have been captured.

"Yes, he would, but he hasn't. So, we'll just have to go on without them," Grunden said to put an end to this troubling conversation.

From the shadows of the tunnel, he studied the chamber. The center contained a huge tube of steel and glass. There was a double door at the floor level.

That has to be a transport tube. But transport to where, and if we get on, can we get off without being captured?

Making a quick decision, he whispered to his team, "I'm going in. If I'm not back in twenty minutes, go back to the Commander's tunnel and find him. He'll know what to do."

He noticed that the lights around the tube flashed on and off at regular intervals. He counted. The lights pulsed off, leaving the chamber dark for about fifteen seconds. Then back on for five more. Off. On. Off. On. He held his breath and counted. When he reached the end of the five-second cycle, the lights went off. He moved to the door and touched it. It didn't open. He tried to wedge his fingers between the door and jamb. Just then the light flickered on with Grunden plastered to the door. Dark again, he gave it a jolt from his nucleo. It opened. He breathed a prayer and stepped on. The door closed behind him. The tube then launched upwards, throwing Grunden to the floor. In an instant, it jerked to a halt and he jumped to his feet, weapon ready. The door opened onto a wide empty foyer. As soon as he stepped off, the tube swooshed on its journey to a level somewhere above him.

Quickly getting his bearings, Grunden took off down the corridor to his right. He hadn't gone far when he heard loud, angry voices. He peeked around the corner and saw a hulking Q'Aron officer growling something in Q'Aronese at the trembling soldier.

Grunden didn't know what was going on and ducked back around the corner to look for a place to hide. There was nothing but solid wall until he tripped a sensor. A panel slid open and he staggered sideways into a small dark room no bigger than a walk-in closet. He stood motionless, listening while his eyes adjusted to the darkened space. He was surprised to find that he was not alone. Three other people were in there, apparently asleep on their feet. Carefully, he approached them. The first one he didn't recognize at all. But he knew the next one immediately. It was Dormax, Elder Arking's former assistant. A slender woman stood to the left of Dormax.

Grunden knew he needed to find Commander Camdus fast, but first he had to revive Dormax and the others. He set his weapon to shock and delivered a jolt to Dormax's shoulder. Nothing happened. He shocked him again, this time on the left chest. The young man went limp and dropped to the floor. Grunden bent down to check for a pulse. Dormax opened his eyes and started to speak but Grunden shushed him, pointing to the REG emblem on his uniform.

Grunden whispered, "Dormax?"

The dazed man replied, "Yes. How did you know?"

Grunden grunted, "Lucky guess. Who's the woman?"

"I don't know much about her, except her name's Rayalla and she was already here when we got here," Dormax answered.

Ah. Enright's sister. That explains why Enright got involved in this treasonous affair.

Grunden returned his attention to Dormax and asked, "Who's *we*?"

"My dad and me." Then he asked, "Is it over?"

Grunden looked at the man harder, trying to discern his meaning. "Is what over?" he demanded.

Dormax fell silent.

Grunden shook him.

"Look, I didn't come here to be lied to or misdirected again. If you want out of here, you damn well better tell me what you know – now."

Dormax began, "You gotta know, I didn't want any part in this, but I was threatened. Prime Minister Weilz forced me to steal some classified documents regarding upcoming troop deployments to Creedor."

"There were no troop deployments to Creedor."

"Yeah, I know that now. He must have changed their orders to leave Creedor …,"

Grunden interrupted, "Vulnerable and ripe for invasion. Why didn't you tell Elder Arking?"

"Weilz said that if I told anyone, he'd kill my family. So, I didn't tell. But you gotta know I didn't have a choice," Dormax pleaded.

"You had a choice. Look where it got you," Grunden said gruffly, but he was not at all sure he wouldn't have done the same thing.

Dormax whispered, "I should have known he was lying. But he gave me a pod to go see my family to make sure they were all right. I planned to stay with them for a while then move on, you know, disappear. Dad and I went hunting. But after only a week, Weilz sent the mercenary Serin to find us. Dad and I tried to defend ourselves, but we were no match for him. We woke up here in Q'Door Hold." Dormax paused as if in thought. Then he continued. "They treated us pretty well until about a week ago when we were escorted to the old man's quarters. We didn't know what to expect, but he served us tea and made small talk. Then he just looked at us and smiled. That's the last thing I remember until just now when you woke me. Can you wake my father, too?"

Grunden shocked the old man back to consciousness.

Dormax grabbed his dad before he collapsed, helping him stand up.

"Where am I?" the old man rasped.

"I'll tell you later, Dad. We have to be really quiet, okay?" His father nodded understanding and remained silent.

Grunden stood watching them. Then he asked about the woman.

"I've told you all I know," Dormax replied with a slight edge to his voice. Grunden ignored it; everyone was on edge down here.

He left Dormax tending to his father and moved to the woman.

If I want to know more, she'll just have to tell me, he thought. He set his weapon to the lowest level possible because she was so slender. She woke instantly and stood blinking into the dark. He expected her to panic, but she didn't.

She reached out to him, felt his face, and then dropped her hand. "I thought you might be someone else," she whispered and fell silent again.

Just as Grunden was about to speak, he heard a soft popping sound. Rax appeared from nowhere.

"Commander Camdus needs your assistance, Mr. Grunden. He sent me to bring you to him."

Grunden looked at the nonplussed Rider. "Listen, Rax, you need to go back and tell him we've found Dormax, his father, and Enright's sister. I think he'll want to see them in here first. Can you do that?"

Rax nodded, and with another soft pop, disappeared.

Within a minute, Rax and Camdus both popped into the now crowded closet. Camdus did not speak but reached for the woman.

She stepped close to him and felt his face. She released a low sigh and fell into his arms. He held her to him, gently stroking her hair.

"Rayalla." He spoke her name softly.

Grunden cleared his throat. "Commander, we have a situation here. I'm not sure where we are, but we seem to be safe in here. How do we get them out of here without getting caught?"

Camdus instantly let go of the woman. "I can get them out. Rax, take them back to the ship. When they're safely aboard, return to me, wherever I am. Got it?"

Rax nodded, encircled all three of them in his long arms, and with a pop, transported them. Within half an hour, they were in the infirmary.

The Rider stopped by the galley and stuffed himself with leftovers before he went back. When he popped back in on Commander Camdus, Grunden and the others had moved to a storage area behind the transport tube.

". . . to get to whoever's running this place, Commander. I know you don't expect us to just free the captives and leave," Grunden was saying.

"I have no intention of leaving without finishing the job, Lieutenant Grunden. Even though our initial mission is to end the epidemic, we've got to handle this mess down here before we can even think about that."

He paused, then said, "Now we know how important this mission is. We don't know what we'll find, but no matter what, we have to win this one."

He studied the soldiers' expressions. He had to know he could still depend on each man to give one hundred percent.

They straightened in unison, saluting their Commander. Grunden spoke for them. "Yes, Sir."

Stadar and Ram knew they could walk away, and the Commander couldn't stop them, but once a soldier, always a soldier. So, they stood with the others, just as determined to win this fight or die trying.

Satisfied, he continued. "All right. We need to find their headquarters. I know we're near it, but I'm not exactly sure where it is. I've heard them and have seen two of their beasts." He mulled the problem of the changelings over in his mind. Then he said, "For the last few hours, one of them has been prowling around down here. But that's just one of them. I don't know where the other one is. Not knowing where that one's hiding is worse than knowing where this one is. If we had a clear idea of the layout, I think we'd have a better chance." Then he turned to Ram and Stadar. "What do you two know about this part of Q'Door Hold?"

Stadar knew nothing of it and said so, but Ram had been to the tower once when Li'Let left him alone for a while. The harrowing ride on the transport tube had taken at least a few years off his life, he was sure. From his hiding place in a seldom used stairwell, he had watched various people coming and going from two huge doors at the end of the hallway. Li'Let had been one of them.

Ram said, "I saw a tall man with long black hair dressed completely in black; probably Serin. Whether he was or not, he looked like somebody I want to stay away from. But the most interesting one I saw was an older gentleman dressed in royal blue. His bald head stuck strangely out of the thin fringe of snow-white hair that flowed halfway down his back. It was clear that he was the head honcho because others stepped aside whenever they saw him coming."

Grunden and Camdus exchanged a knowing glance.

Camdus didn't try to hide his concern. "So Elsnor's in charge. He probably has powers at least equal to Vandalen."

Then he addressed Grunden, "With Vandalen still locked up on Dartal, I'd be willing to bet that's who you saw talking to Slogar at the Boor's Nad Inn. He still hasn't told me who it was or what they were talking about. Well, that's about to end."

Without a word, Rax disappeared with his signature pop. "We'll get to the bottom of this when Slogar gets back. And, I think you're right. It's likely that Serin was the man dressed in black. We have to find out where he is. It's your good fortune that you didn't cross his path."

Ram felt a slight shiver run down his spine. *God is good.*

Before long, Rax popped back alone. "I'm sorry, Commander. The doctor is not able to join you," he said casually.

Camdus said, "I see. Well then, Rax, take me to him." With that, they were gone.

Grunden thought this was a good opportunity to check out this part of Q'Door Hold. He started to step out of their hiding place, but Ram pulled him back. "I know I'm not in the REG anymore, but I know more about Q'Door Hold than you do. And I know that halfway between dusk and dawn there's hardly anyone in the corridors I've been on. I don't know where they go or what they do, but they're not in the passageways; then again…."

Grunden interrupted, "Sounds like the safest time for us to move."

Ram nodded but registered his concern. "Yeah, I thought so too, but I found out that's when the big cats roam the hallways."

Grunden grunted and said, "Okay. What do you know about the cats?"

Ram replied, "Well, for one thing, the female can read minds when she's in human form. I don't think she can any other time, but I don't know for sure. At first, I thought she brought a beast in with her to hunt me. It took me a little while, but I figured it out. She's the beast. When she hunted me in the maze, she used animal instincts – and hers are keener than most. If she could read minds, then she should have been able to find me. She always snuffled and pawed sometimes so close I held my breath even in my hiding place. But she never found me which ticked her off royally." Ram shuddered. "I still have nightmares."

Grunden already knew about the beasts, and he was pretty sure that one of them had changed shapes. If that was so, then it just made matters worse because they didn't know what it had changed into.

Before they could explore this problem any deeper, Rax popped back in with Camdus. Then he popped out and back, this time with Slogar.

The Rider's face was purple from the strain of holding his cargo. Slogar had gained weight – again. Rax gratefully released him, sat down on the floor, and struggled to catch his breath.

Camdus had never seen Rax so exhausted. He leaned down and asked, "Are you all right?"

It took Rax a few seconds to answer. "Yes, Sir, I think so."

Camdus helped him to his feet, secretly amazed that the Rider had been able to transport Slogar at all. "Okay, Rax, report to the mess hall. I think you need a break."

Rax smiled broadly at the thought and popped out without a word.

Now Camdus gave the men an update. "The way things are going we may have to shift back to our original mission. The latest reports from Creedor are grim. The epidemic is getting progressively worse. And Slogar needs the Elder Woman of Silden to help him, but she can't come here. He'll have to go to her."

The disappointed soldiers took this all in without comment.

Then Camdus addressed Slogar directly. "Before I let you go, you have to explain to us what you were doing on Boldoon and who exactly it was you were meeting with at the Boor's Nad Inn."

Slogar was eager to be on his way, especially to see Elani again. But he knew that Camdus wasn't going to let him leave until he gave him what he wanted. It occurred to him that he might say something that'd get him in trouble. *So what, won't be the first time and probably won't be the last,* he thought.

The truth was Slogar would do anything to see Elani again – even if it meant facing Camdus and his men, and even if it meant having to ride the slipstream to get there. That in itself was like punishment for him because it made his insides feel like they were stuck on the end of a whirligig in a stiff wind.

Grunden got straight to the point. "Tell me, Doctor, who was the cloaked man you met with on Boldoon at the Boor's Nad Inn before the Commander contacted you?"

Slogar had known this day would come. Now he had no choice but to tell the truth no matter what.

"Oh, him. Well, that was Vandalen of Trilvar."

Camdus and Grunden looked at Slogar in disbelief. Then Camdus said emphatically, "Come off it, Slogar. That's not possible, and you know it. There's no way he could have escaped his cell in Dartal."

"No, Commander. You're wrong. Jarlod never knew the instrument of the wizard's power. Everyone assumed it was the ring. But it wasn't." Slogar began his history lesson.

"You see, the ring was one of twelve. Only members born into the ancient Fraternity of Benevolent Wizards have them. And it is true that with the rings, the wizards' powers are amplified. But the root of their power is within them. They need nothing to facilitate its use. Vandalen is well aware of this and though limited in what he can do without his ring, he's always been able to travel for short amounts of time. Of course, with the ring there is virtually nothing he can't do – good or bad. But he's a peaceful man. He served Emperor Borm because he was a good man and kindly leader. Unfortunately, Borm's kindness was mistaken as weakness by some people including those power-hungry serpents who had insinuated themselves into his inner circle. But Vandalen knew the kind of man Borm was and served him willingly. Of course, when Jarlod overthrew Borm, he knew the wizard would always be a threat because he couldn't get away with the wicked lifestyle he craved. No, Vandalen could see into the heart of this man and what he saw was pure evil. These two were so different there was no way …."

Camdus was growing tired of not having Grunden's question answered and interrupted. "So Vandalen and Jarlod didn't have the same values – I know that already. Answer the question. What were you two talking about that night at the Boor's Nad Inn?"

Slogar took a deep breath. "We were talking about a coup. There is and has been for quite some time a movement among certain groups to remove Jarlod from power before he completely destroys the Empire. He was trying to recruit me. He said that when the time came, there would be need for learned men who could not only teach, but also do. As I recall I laughed out loud at such a notion. It had been so long since anyone had taken me seriously or remembered me at all. I thought he was poking fun at me like the bullies at the Inn did. But after outlining how far he'd come already toward putting his plan in motion, I knew he wasn't playing. I listened but politely declined. You saw me, Cam. I was an ale junkie with no further ambition than to drink and eat myself sick. Hell, if you hadn't gotten me out of my funk when you did, I'd never have made it. When I was with Seelah and Elani, I got into pretty good shape physically, and my head was clear for the first time in years. They are not going to be happy to see the way I've let myself go."

Camdus stopped his ramblings again and asked, "So you know how to contact him?"

"I didn't contact him. He found me. But I know who can – his daughter, Elani."

"Wait a minute! You mean the same Elani you spent all that time with on Silden? That's Vandalen's daughter and you didn't think that was important enough to tell me? What is wrong with you?!" Camdus shouted. He could feel the anger rising and stepped closer to Slogar. He spoke in that low tone that every man who'd ever served under him knew. "I ought to have you…."

Grunden quickly assessed the situation. They didn't have time for this now. He stepped between the two men.

"Look, Commander, let's take a step back for a minute. Remember, the doctor is under the Emperor's protection."

Any other time Camdus would have disciplined Grunden for his insolence, but he needed every man. And to be honest with himself, he did need to cool down. He knew that decisions made in anger were seldom wise.

"One more question, Doctor. If Vandalen could think himself free, then why did he go back to Dartal?" Camdus expected a straight answer. He wasn't going to allow Slogar to get away with lying.

"First of all, he couldn't get out at all until the enchantment on his cell degraded. When he realized that it was virtually gone, he began to transport for brief periods. But to answer your question: He kept going back to save his wife and daughter. Jarlod threatened throw Nell in prison and add Elani to his harem. Though Vandalen's power without the ring allowed him to travel, it was not enough to protect them. Believe it or not, he gave up his freedom for nothing more than sentiment."

Camdus was still skeptical but figured this was not the time to question it.

Finally, they had concrete direction. They knew at least two things had to happen now – Slogar had to go back to the plains of Silden, and then he had to convince Elani to contact her father so she could get him to help them. Camdus instructed Grunden and the others to keep a low profile, but to gather as much information as possible. They would need more provisions; with the Rider in their midst that wouldn't be a problem.

Camdus realized for the first time in his career he was out of options. He remembered his father's gift and instinctively knew that now was the time to open the package. He'd placed the small tredon leather pouch around his neck and worn it as a talisman of sorts but had never felt the need to open it – until now.

Stepping away from the group as they continued to strategize, he opened the pouch. Inside he found a collection of small items. One was a ring. Camdus was dumbfounded as he stared at it. This ring was strikingly similar to the ones worn by the wizards he knew, though the huge diamond in this ring was flanked by deep purple amethysts. The letter *C* was embedded in the golden band. Like the rubies and sapphires in the rings of Vandalen and Elsnor respectively, the amethysts in his ring formed the serpents' eyes.

His curiosity got the better of him. He tentatively placed it on his right index finger. As soon as it was in place, he felt an intense sensation of power pulsing through his body. He snatched the ring off his finger.

What the hell is this?! The ring was supposed to hold no special powers, yet clearly this one did. He put it back on his finger. Again, he felt the pulsating sensation and intuited many things that were unknown to him. And now he had a whole lot of questions for his dad, not the least of which was where he got this ring. But his questions would have to wait. He took the ring off and put it back in the pouch. Next, he found a tiny button-like device. He had no idea what it was.

Okay, he reasoned as he pulled out the ring and placed it on his finger once again. Instantly he knew what the button was used for. It was a cloaking device that could help protect the group until he and Slogar returned, hopefully with Vandalen. As soon as he had the answer, he put the ring in the pouch. Then he stepped back into the midst of the men as they continued to brainstorm.

Camdus cleared his throat and said, "Lieutenant, a word please."

Grunden looked away from Stadar, who'd been describing the inhabitants of Q'Door Hold.

"Yes, Commander?"

Camdus indicated he wanted to speak to him in private, so they both stepped away. The others paid little attention, for each had something to offer to the discussion. He placed the button in Grunden's hand. "Just touch the back of this button and a perception baffle will be created to hide your location. To disengage, hold it ten seconds."

"Where did this come from, Commander? I've never even heard of anything like this."

Camdus replied honestly, "It was a gift. But now the doctor and I have to go. Take care of the men. We'll be back as soon as possible. I'll send Rax back after he delivers us to Silden."

Grunden stood at attention and saluted. "May God go with you, Commander."

"And you as well." With that said, Camdus summoned Rax, who took a deep breath and held on to both the Commander and Slogar. In a split second they were gone.

THE WIZARD

Rax brought them to the rotting porch of the old shack that sat on Silden's desolate plains. Commander Camdus thanked him and told him to go back to Q'Door Hold. Rax was sweating profusely, completely winded. As soon as he could stand up straight again, he nodded and was gone in an instant.

"All right, Doctor. Lead the way," Camdus said.

Slogar dreaded the wobbly steps but knew that Seelah and Elani were below. Without rails to hold onto, he leaned over and crab-walked up the steps.

Camdus saw Slogar struggling to stand up so he grabbed his elbow to steady him.

"Thanks," Slogar said. With Camdus' help, he finally stood upright.

The porch looked the same, with the rotted chair and half-hung door. He went inside. It too was as he remembered it, but this time Seelah was waiting for him by the hearth. She was dressed in her full regalia instead of the tattered clothes she'd worn when he first met her.

"Why, Simon! It's so good of you to come. And this must be Commander Camdus. Welcome."

Camdus didn't know how she knew his name but was not surprised. Slogar had told him about the time he'd spent here, so nothing much would surprise him.

"Thank you for having us, Elder Woman," Camdus said.

When she smiled, her pale eyes twinkled. He noticed that she was a tall woman who bore herself with a sense of knowing. He wondered how much she knew.

"Come along, gentlemen. Elani and I have been waiting."

"Seelah," Slogar asked, "you didn't will us here, did you?"

Now she laughed that rare, cathartic laugh that he had missed.

"Not this time. But your coming was made known to us. Let's go below where you can rest a while before supper." She laid one hand on the mantel and one on Slogar, who in turn laid his hand on Camdus' shoulder. Slogar was prepared for this particular mode of transport and the disinfectant mist.

"What the…?" Camdus sputtered after he found his legs again.

"Oh yeah, I forgot to tell you how we get from the surface to below. Sorry."

Camdus shot the doctor a look that made Slogar thankful that a lady was present. Both men were grateful for the ointment Seelah used to stop their eyes from burning.

Seelah called Elani, whose face brightened with fondness when she first saw Slogar. But that was followed by a look he'd never gotten from her before – disappointment.

"Elani, please take Simon to his room. I wish to speak to Commander Camdus a moment, and then I'll show him to his room myself."

Elani replied, "As you wish, Ma'am." She and Slogar went down the long hall to the guest rooms. She paused outside waiting for him to enter.

Slogar opened the door but didn't go in.

"Please stay," he said.

"I'm sorry, Simon. I don't think there's anything left for us to talk about."

"What do you mean?"

"You've given up."

"Given what up?"

She shook her head and walked away. There was no use trying to talk to him when she could see he'd fallen into his old ways again.

Slogar watched her retreat down the long corridor. *What did I do to put her off?* He closed the door and walked into the inner chamber. There a full-length mirror gave him the answer. *Ah, hell.* His reflection seemed to scoff at him. No wonder she didn't want to be around him. *But I can change this, I know I can.* He disrobed and entered the shower. He realized that he once again couldn't see his feet. *I will lose this gut and I will ....* His next thought was unexpected and not a little scary. But he smiled. *Yes, I will!*

***

Seelah invited Camdus to have a seat. A porcelain pot of thistle tea was on the table between them, steam pouring from its delicately curved spout. She leaned over and poured a cup and handed it to him. Then she poured one for herself. The warm tea steadied his dizzy head.

"Thank you, Elder Woman. But this is an official visit."

"Yes, I know. And please call me Seelah. I feel quite ancient when addressed by my title."

Camdus realized his mistake. "I'm sorry, Seelah. I didn't mean to offend. I guess I was just unsure of the proper…,"

Seelah interrupted. "No apology needed, Commander. We have more important issues at hand."

"Then thank you. Tell me. How much do you know about why we're here?"

"I know that you need Elani to help you get in touch with her father," Seelah said. "I also know you left some of your soldiers on Creedor and that they're in danger. Beyond that, I'm afraid I'm in the dark."

Camdus wondered if she was ever really in the dark.

"Seelah, we do need to contact Vandalen because Elsnor has joined forces with the Q'Arons. We know they've kidnapped Creedorian citizens and are using them as slaves in the trizactl mining operation they have on Creedor. We also know they are, whether they know it or not, part of a plot to overthrow Jarlod."

Seelah laughed. "Which one?"

Camdus realized she knew quite a bit more about what was going on.

"What do you mean, 'Which one?' How many are there?"

Seelah sat back sipping her tea. "Commander, you do know, of course, I only have knowledge of some things not everything." She waited for his nod of understanding before continuing.

"Well then, let's see. Elsnor wishes to become an Emperor himself. Then there's the group of Boldoonian rebels who want to take power but have no clear plan of who the Emperor should be, but they're reacting to the poor treatment they have endured. They too are without solid plan. I'm quite sure they assume that the proper leader will rise to the top. There are so many problems with that. But I digress. Then there's Elder Weilz, who seems to have hungered for the Emperor's power since he was appointed Prime Minister. He's behaving like an ungrateful dog, but I sense that there is a much deeper and more personal reason behind his desire to rid the Empire of Jarlod. His true motive is hidden too far within his heart for me to clearly discern. I suppose one could say that our Emperor has made many enemies and even those he thinks are his friends are of the fair-weather variety."

Camdus listened carefully. He knew she was right. He only hoped there were no others to contend with. "That's a pretty accurate assessment, Seelah. I have the Boldoonians under my control currently, so that's one less to worry about. But of the other two, which do you feel is the greater threat?"

Without a pause, Seelah answered, "Elsnor."

Elsnor had been born to wizarding and had been among the first twelve to complete their training in Trilvar. He had been somewhat smaller than the others with reddish blond hair and a pair of emerald green eyes so dark they almost looked black. He'd been proficient at his studies but liked to take shortcuts. It was this lack of thoroughness that troubled his peers the most.

But in Elsnor's mind he was the greatest, the smartest, and the most important of all the students. He became resentful and withdrawn when he regularly got the lowest marks on his papers. Some of the other wizarding students had tried to get him to realize that it wasn't that he couldn't do the work. No, the problem was that he didn't take time to learn any of his subjects well enough to understand what could happen if he misused his powers. But he'd managed to score well enough to become a full-fledged wizard, though the School Master had been reluctant to give him the title and all the privileges that went with it. It was Elsnor's disregard of his responsibilities as a wizard that worried the others.

Only after his carelessness had destroyed a village of Ordinaries did he briefly wish he'd paid more attention in school, but it was too late. He couldn't undo what he'd done. No one could bring back the dead. When the Council of Wizards realized what he'd done, they stripped him of his title. But their action was too late – he was long gone before they could reclaim his ring.

Camdus agreed with Seelah's assessment. "I think that also could explain why some of my men have seen him there in the Hold. According to their reports, though he's old now, he still has all of his powers. The men say the way everyone bows to him whenever he enters a room or steps aside for him in the corridors makes it seem like he's running the show. But I don't get it. How's it possible for him to get the Q'Arons, who're barbaric at best, to take orders from him? He must have enchanted them."

Seelah thought about this as she poured more tea for herself and offered more to Camdus, who declined.

Then she said thoughtfully, "I'm not so sure it's enchantment he uses. He was always adequate, but never the strongest wizard. He was the hungriest for power. My guess is he's using his powers to torture the Q'Arons. He never understood that true power is benevolent."

They sat quietly for a moment, the Elder Woman sipping her tea, while Camdus was deep in thought.

After a few minutes, Seelah put down her cup and said, "Come with me, Commander. I can see how tired you are. Your room is just down this hall."

Camdus realized he was bone weary and gratefully followed her. She stopped at a door with his name on it. The inside looked like the room from the happiest time of his life. He half expected to see his mother there tidying his things as she had done when he still lived at home.

"Seelah, I don't know how you've done this, but thank you," he said earnestly.

She smiled and said, "You're welcome, Commander. Elani will escort you to supper in an hour."

Though Seelah's extraordinary powers were evident, he didn't think that's what they needed for this particular fight. He turned to find that clean clothes had been laid out for him. He also noticed something here he hadn't had at his childhood home – a private bath and walk-in changing area. He gratefully stepped into the bathroom and warmed his weary muscles in the steaming shower. And too, it was such a relief to get the smell of disinfectant off his body. He dressed in a clean uniform made of the finest tredon leather. Then he sat down to read before Elani came to fetch him for supper.

He didn't have long to wait. She knocked on his door within a few minutes of his settling down with one of the magazines he remembered from his youth. He stepped out into the hall and greeted her. She smiled acknowledgment and went ahead of him.

"Elani, please, may I have a word with you?" Camdus asked.

She stopped and looked back at him, giving him a chance to catch up. When he was standing beside her she said, "Of course, Commander. What is it?"

Camdus had no idea how to broach the subject of her father, so he was direct. "Elani, you're Vandalen's daughter, right?"

She looked at him, cautious now, but nodded affirmatively.

"Can you contact him for me? I, uh, we need his help."

She was stunned and didn't know what to say.

He tried again. "Well, I guess it's me in particular that needs his help. You see, I have this project of the utmost importance to our mission and I can't finish it without his advice." He waited for her answer.

Elani still didn't speak. She was truly at a loss for words.

How long has it been since I've spoken to my father? He spent most of my brother's and my childhood away. When we were growing up, we thought his career was more important to him than we were. And what good did his work for Borm do him in the end? Not one bit – he wound up in prison.

Elani shook these thoughts from her mind. She had spent too many years brooding over what she'd long thought of as her father's careless abandonment and could not let the bitterness get a hold on her again. It had taken all of Seelah's skill and wisdom working with her, but at last Elani had forgiven him. Seelah helped her understand somewhat better the position Emperor Borm had placed him in. Seelah told her how Emperor Borm had touted her father as an almighty wizard, though he considered himself no more than a man with a gift who had learned to make science and physics work for him. And yes, he had mastered the techniques necessary to channel various types of energy and make it do his will. There was none greater than he, at least not in Seelah's telling of the story to Elani. And just as Seelah had hoped, Elani's anger had melted. In its place was a longing to see her father, to tell him what was in her heart. Up until this moment, she had thought that would never be possible. But now Commander Camdus was standing beside her, asking her to contact him.

She spoke quietly. "Commander, it has never occurred to me that I might be able to see my father again." But even as she spoke, her heart leapt with joy. It was common knowledge Commander Camdus had a Rider among his troops. Rax could surely transport her to her father.

"Elani, tell me you will ask your father to help us, and I'll have Rax here in a matter of moments."

She took a deep breath. "Yes, Commander, I will help you, but I must go with Rax if we are to have any hope of getting him to cooperate." She stopped, her heart pounding in her chest, and took a few deep breaths. When she could speak again, she said, "But right now the Elder Woman is waiting for us to join her for dinner. Doctor Slogar is already there. We can talk to her after dinner."

Camdus breathed a sigh of relief. Getting them into and out of the Dartal prison without detection would require planning. He would need a little time to gather some information before he allowed Elani and Rax to try it. That is, if Seelah approved.

But he knew one thing for sure – he was hungry and the smell of whatever was on the menu made his mouth water.

Conversation during the meal was light. Camdus felt that it would be rude to bring up the subject that needed to be addressed so he waited patiently. After a perfectly prepared meal of white fish with a lovely salad from Elani's garden, Seelah invited them to join her in the larger sitting room. The fireplace's flames, pink and gold this evening, gave warmth to the otherwise austere room. Once seated, she served tea with candied fruit compote for dessert.

Camdus sat back in his chair, savoring the wonderful flavors. "This is really good, Seelah," he said.

The Elder Woman, never one to take undue credit, made sure he knew that all meals were the result of Elani's talents.

"Then, Elani, thank you. I can't remember when I've eaten so well."

Elani smiled shyly and nodded her acceptance of his praise.

Camdus knew that Slogar had enjoyed the meal, but he thought perhaps he was enjoying seeing Elani even more.

Then Camdus spoke to Seelah. "I need Elani's help. I've asked her to talk to her father for us. I think she may be the only one who can. But," he went on, now looking directly at Elani, "she wants to go to Dartal with Rax to get him. How do you feel about that, Seelah?"

The calm expression of the seasoned hostess was ruffled for a split second and then returned to its normal, placid state.

"Commander, this sounds like an extremely dangerous job for her. Why can't she send a message by the Rider and wait here for Vandalen to join her?"

"She can. That's what I told her. In fact, that was my original request of her. But Elani thinks she has to go with Rax. I prefer that she stay here, but whatever it takes, so be it. I mean if that's what she thinks will get him to help, then it's worth the risk," Camdus said bluntly.

Seelah moved her gaze from Camdus to Elani. For the first time, she saw fire in her charge.

"Elani, my dear, are you quite aware of the danger you will be putting yourself in? You could be seriously injured – or worse. Is it worth risking your life to speak to your father again?"

Elani answered firmly and with no hesitation, "Yes, Ma'am. It is. I am well aware of the risks. But while I've been here with you, I have had time to consider the relationship with my father, and I've let the hurt heal. I need for him to know that I'm okay. He needs to know I love him unconditionally. I want to go, Seelah. I am asking your blessing, but I will go without it if I must."

The tears that shimmered on Elani's eyelashes touched Seelah's heart. She got up from her seat at the head of the table and went to Elani, who stood to face her without knowing what to expect.

Seelah enfolded her in a tender embrace, holding her for a moment. Then she let her go, stood back, and placed a hand on her head.

"Then God be with you. I trust we'll be together again soon."

Elani was elated. Feeling a bit lightheaded with relief, she turned to Camdus. "When do we leave, Commander?"

With one hurdle cleared, Camdus asked Seelah to help him with the logistics for Rax and Elani's mission. They excused themselves to Seelah's study, leaving Slogar and Elani alone in the dining room.

Throughout the evening, Slogar had been unusually quiet, but he finally spoke.

"Elani, I promise I'll get back in shape. I'll do whatever you say, just please don't go."

She placed a slender finger over his lips and said, "Simon, please don't. This is not about you or me or us. This is about doing what's in my heart."

The look on his face spoke to her spirit. "Oh, Simon. Yes, you too are in my heart, but this is different. I have a compelling need to find him and make things right with him again. For so long, I blamed him for everything bad in my life. Only after spending a number of years with Seelah did I see that my perception was not necessarily the way things really were. He *is* in prison, but it wasn't because of any wrong-doing or carelessness. He was blindsided by a bunch of cowards or they would never have captured him. I know that beyond all doubt. My father did not abandon us."

Slogar took her hand. "I have no reason to hope that you could ever consider me as a partner to travel with through this life, and yet I do. I am so much older than you and look at me. I'm not a catch, you might say. But Elani, you have stolen something that used to be mine. And I do not want it back."

He stopped talking, embarrassed at his schoolboy gushing.

Who is this idiot, anyway? he thought.

Slogar was still slamming himself when he realized that Elani was laughing softly at first, then out loud.

"Simon, you are so funny. You think you're older than I am? Do you have any idea how old I am?"

Slogar shook his head *no*.

"Let's just say I hope you like older women." His embrace and gentle kiss told her it didn't matter at all.

But stepping back he said, "Elani, all my life I hoped for someone to share my dreams. I can't abide the thought that now that I've found you, you may not return to me. Please don't go."

Elani knew how he felt for she felt it too. But she had made up her mind.

"Simon, pray for my safety. I will return to you. And when I do and all this is over, we're going to whip you into shape. We'll continue our evening walks and, oh yes, our fishing. You still have your destiny to fulfill, and I want you to be healthy enough to do it. What do you think of that?"

He was so taken aback by this whole revelation, he quietly said, "Sounds good to me."

Camdus and Seelah were working in the study when Slogar and Elani joined them.

"Well, what've you come up with, Commander?" Slogar asked as they entered the room. They looked up from the hologram that stood glimmering atop the table.

"This is the prison, and here …" Camdus indicated the far tower, "is where Vandalen is being kept. His night guards are not as diligent as those during the day. And even though Rax can pop in and out fairly quickly, he is not invincible. One good nucleo blast would be devastating to the cause."

Seelah raised a brow, "Hmmm. I'm fairly sure it would not be so good for Rax, either."

Camdus took the reprimand in stride. "Of course, Seelah; however, at this point, we never know when any one or all of us will be in harm's way. All we can do is try to make sure we execute each maneuver as precisely as possible."

Then he turned to Elani. "Are you quite sure I can't talk you out of this mission? You may have forgotten that Rax was once under your father's command. I believe he'll trust him enough to go with him. Rax can bring him back here in no time, so you don't have to go. I just need you to send him a message, that's all."

Elani listened respectfully but had that look on her face that only Slogar recognized. There was no backing out. There would be no more waiting. "I do remember, and I appreciate your concern, Commander, but I will go with Rax. When can we leave?"

Camdus knew he was fighting a losing battle, so he conceded with, "Tonight, around midnight seems to be the perfect time. I'll call Rax an hour before your departure. I want to make sure he is well-versed in all the details of this mission. And I want you to wear a tredon battle uniform and helmet. They offer pretty substantial protection. Do you have them?" Seelah assured him she would see to Elani's outfitting.

"Good. But do you have a weapon? You may need one of those, too, you know."

Elani had never needed a weapon before but trusted the Commander's judgment.

Seelah pulled a small nucleo from the folds of her robe and handed it to Camdus.

Surprised, but pleased, he said, "Perfect. Now, Elani, is there a place where I can teach you how to use this?"

Elani knew the perfect location. "Come with me, Commander." She led him from the room to a large empty space one level down.

Camdus marveled at the intricacies of this facility. After about half an hour, they returned to the others. Elani was relieved to have learned the fundamentals of firing the weapon. She was certain she could defend them if she had to.

At midnight, Elani and Rax stood silently together with his arms wrapped around her. Elani showed no emotion. After one last *God speed* from Seelah, they popped out.

DARTAL

The wizard was not asleep. He lay looking up at the tiny spider dangling from a silken thread attached to the ceiling above. He'd found dozens of ways to keep his mind alert, including trying to count the number of times the spider swung from left to right. *Three hundred and fourteen, three hundred and fifteen, three hundred and sixteen ....*

A soft pop in the darkest corner of his cell caught his attention. He was instantly on his feet, ready to fight. The sight of a woman threw him off a little. Then he noticed a tall man standing behind her.

Rax, but how? Oh yes, Elsnor's enchantment has grown too weak to keep him out. But…?

Now Vandalen questioned whether his mental exercises had backfired.

"Father," Elani whispered as she removed her helmet revealing her short black hair. She stepped toward him. He relaxed his stance only a little. How could this be? Was it possible that standing before him was the young girl he had left at home all those years ago? He was afraid this was another one of his captor's tricks. After looking at her for a long moment he knew that he was looking at his only daughter.

"Elani? Why are you here? Your mother, your brother, are they…?"

Elani touched her finger to her lips and stepped close to his ear.

"Father," she said softly, "we will have time to talk later. But right now, Rax and I need you to come with us."

Vandalen was trying to comprehend. He couldn't be sure this wasn't another example of Elsnor's sadistic humor.

"All right, Elani. I'll go with you, but where are we going?"

Elani spoke softer still, "Silden."

With that, she put her helmet back on and they stepped into the shadows with Rax. With his daughter safely beside him, he was finally free.

Seelah, Slogar, and Camdus sat silently in the parlor. The air was electric with anticipation.

Slogar was in the middle of what seemed like an endless prayer when the Rider and his charges popped back in.

215

Camdus was the first to greet them. He thanked Rax and told him to go back to Q'Door Hold.

But Seelah interrupted, "Please wait a moment, Rax."

He looked at Camdus for affirmation. Camdus nodded.

Seelah soon returned with a large package filled with provisions for Rax and the soldiers at Q'Door Hold.

"Thank you, Ma'am," Rax said. With the package securely wrapped in his long arms, he disappeared.

Next Camdus turned to Elani and Vandalen. The resemblance was striking.

Elani walked to Slogar and gently touched his arm. "Simon, will you join me for a walk? I'm sure that Father and Commander Camdus need to talk."

"Of course, my dear, but don't we need to eat first?" Elani blinked at him and placed her hands on her hips. He read the look in her clear blue eyes.

"Okay," Slogar said. "We'll be in the garden if you need us."

After they left, Camdus spoke to the wizard respectfully. "Sir, I thank you for agreeing to help us. We have a fight on our hands and if we're not careful, it'll be all out war."

Vandalen remained silent, wary of this new situation.

Seelah led them to her study where a hologram of Q'Door Hold hovered over the desk.

Vandalen looked from the image to Camdus. Then he spoke for the first time.

"I'm not sure I've agreed to anything yet. My daughter asked me to come with her, so I did. What do you want from me, Commander?" His distrust of anyone working for Jarlod was evident.

Seelah brought a platter of leftover tredon steaks and bread. She offered tea, which both men declined.

"Do you have anything stronger?" Vandalen asked.

She placed a carafe of red wine on the table and sat down beside them, pouring herself a cup of steaming thistle tea.

As Vandalen greedily laid into the food, he listened to Camdus.

"Elsnor has joined forces with our enemies."

"Which ones?"

"Th Q'Arons. They've kidnapped every able-bodied Creedorian they could get their hands on to work the rogue trizactl mine. They've been stealing as much of it as they can transport – right under our noses. And that's not all. They've released a deadly plague to eliminate any of the citizens left topside. They're keeping the ones they captured in deplorable conditions in a holding area right outside the mine itself. A few of them have been jailed in their fortified enclave they call Q'Door Hold. Jarlod refuses to pull his head out of his backside long enough to realize that we're in a hell of a mess. We need reinforcements, which he has yet to send." He saw the look of distaste on Seelah's face and immediately said, "Sorry if I've offended."

"You haven't offended me, Commander. I'm just as disgusted with Jarlod as you are, I dare say," she said, much to his surprise.

Vandalen was relieved to learn that Camdus and Seelah were not among Jarlod's cronies. When he finished stuffing himself at least for the moment, he drained a goblet of wine. Now quite full, he spoke again.

"Elsnor? That sorry excuse for a wizard. The Council expelled him for unethical use of his powers. We tried to retrieve the ring, but we couldn't find him."

Camdus took mention of the ring as the opening he needed to get to the real reason he wanted to talk to Vandalen. "Seelah, would you please excuse us? We need to have a word in private."

"Of course," she replied, got up and left.

Then Camdus said, "Please step over here to the light. I've something to show you." He pulled the pouch from his shirt, removed the ring his father had given him and held it glimmering under the bright light that hung from the center of the room. "Was Elsnor's ring anything like this one?"

Vandalen looked at the object in Camdus' hand.

"Yes, except for the letter and its serpents had blue sapphire eyes," he said and reached for Camdus' ring.

Since he did not yet fully trust the wizard, Camdus closed it in his fist and said, "First let me tell you what happens when I put the ring on."

When Camdus had finished, Vandalen was briefly speechless. Then he said, "Well, for one thing that looks like the genuine article. And you must be Willem Camdus' son for that is without a doubt Willem's ring. Only someone of his direct lineage could experience any of its power. I don't understand why he passed it along while he was still able to use it. But I can speculate. Willem was one of the best of us, until he met a certain young woman who had no idea that he was a wizard. He gave up his seat on our Council, but we asked him to keep his ring just in case a time came when we needed his help."

Vandalen realized from the look on Camdus' face that he had never been told any of this. "My apologies if I've spoken too boldly. I thought you knew at least some of it."

Camdus asked another question. "So, are you saying that my father is a wizard?"

"Yes."

"Does that mean I am, too?"

The Master Wizard nodded but followed with a warning. "You are new to wizarding, and you don't know how to use the ring yet. The ring is powerless unless worn by the wizard born to wear it – or his heir. When an old wizard dies without an heir, the ring loses its power and becomes nothing more than a pretty bauble. You also need to know that just because you have a talent or gift doesn't mean you're ready to use it. One last thing, for some wizards the thrill of power overcomes their self-control."

"Like Elsnor?" asked Camdus.

"Exactly like Elsnor," Vandalen replied.

Camdus set down his wine goblet, the new information about him and his father swirling in his brain.

"Then teach me," he said as he poured a cup of thistle tea. He didn't want fuzzy thinking to interfere with mastering this new tool.

Vandalen asked bluntly, "Why should I, Commander?"

Camdus looked squarely at him. "Your daughter is in just as much danger as the rest of us. Once they finish with Creedor, how long do you think it will be before the Q'Arons locate this facility?"

The truth of Camdus' words hit its mark. "Point taken, but do we have time for a short rest? Riding the slipstream always leaves me exhausted."

Camdus offered his room, but Seelah returned as if on cue. "Thank you, Commander, but I have prepared a room for him," she said. Then she turned to Vandalen. "Well then, if you'll follow me...."

Camdus should have known. The Elder Woman always had a room for her visitors

"Commander," Seelah said, "perhaps you should take advantage of this time to rest while you can. You will need all your strength and energy for what's to come."

He got the feeling that somehow Seelah had an idea of what that was, but he knew better than to ask. He was certain she would tell him what he needed to know when the time was right. He took one more sip of tea.

Then he headed back to his room and flopped down on the bed to try to get a few hours of much needed rest.

Seelah's knocking on his door woke Camdus after what seemed like only a few minutes.

"Commander, it will be daylight soon. Breakfast is ready."

Daylight? I should have been up and ready long before now. He rushed to cleanup and pack what he'd need for his journey. He made sure his father's pouch was hanging securely around his neck and well-hidden beneath his uniform. Then he took off down the long hallway back to the dining room.

When he got there, his first reaction was relief that he was not the last to arrive. That, however, was followed by a sense of disappointment that his tutor was not there yet.

"Vandalen?"

His one-word question was answered by Seelah. "He will be here momentarily. Oh, wait, here he is now. Good morning. I hope you slept well."

Vandalen said with a smile, "Quite well thank you. Nice to be in my old room, too." He wasn't surprised to find the room a replica of his own. He was familiar with her reputation.

Pity she's limited to Silden. Her skills might be useful in the days ahead, Vandalen thought.

Then he took his place at the table. He was pleased to see his daughter already seated.

"Elani, how have you been?" he asked, before reaching for a fresh biscuit. He pulled his hand back and asked Seelah, "Is it okay to eat now?"

She smiled. "Yes, we've returned thanks for the meal and asked God's blessing on it and us. Please go ahead."

Elani was pleased to get this glimpse of the man she'd vilified for so many years. She now knew beyond all doubt that Seelah had been right about her father. Her heart melted when she realized the last vestige of anger was long gone.

She answered her father's question. "I've had a good life here with Seelah. Before she took me in, not so much. But that's hardly fit conversation for the breakfast table. I'll be glad when this terrible business is finished. Then we will have all the time in the world to catch up." Smiling at him, she felt the tiniest sense of *home* slipping back into her spirit.

Vandalen returned the smile but took the answer in stride. He wanted to know more. He pressed her with the questions he'd tried to ask last evening.

"How is your mother? Jarlod told me she had forgotten me, but that she'd found his company pleasant." He stopped and shook his head.

"Jarlod is a liar," Elani said firmly. "Mother was furious, but not with you. At least I never saw it. And I know that after she helped Andria bury Emperor Borm, she made a point of staying out of Jarlod's way."

He felt relieved, but Elani still hadn't answered his question, so he asked again.

"That's good to know, but how is she doing now?"

Elani didn't want to be the one to tell him, but clearly it had fallen on her shoulders.

"Father, I'm so sorry, but Mother has passed on to the next realm. You know she loved you for all her life, but the loneliness was more than she could bear."

Vandalen felt as if a knife had been thrust into his heart but asked another question. "And your brother? How is Serin?"

Camdus nearly fell out of his chair. "Serin is your son?! Are you kidding me? Do you know what he's become? Soldier, assassin – whatever the hell anyone is willing to pay him to be!" He slammed his fist down on the table for emphasis, rattling the dishes.

Elani looked as if someone had slapped her. She was well aware of her brother's profession but had hoped to spare her father the pain she knew it would cause him.

"Commander! Please, let's not discuss this now. Perhaps later but not now." Seelah tried to intervene, but Camdus would not be stopped.

He roared, "No! By God we're going to deal with this here and now. He's at Q'Door Hold – working for Elsnor. What am I supposed to do – sit back and give him a pass because of his family? Hell no! He never cared about the families of the people he hurt, and…"

Seelah spoke again, this time in a low, menacing tone.

"Commander, I'm warning you. Do not continue this conversation. I said later, and I meant it. But now we have to find a way to rescue him."

"Rescue a murderer? Have you lost your mind, Seelah? Here I am, wondering how many of my men he's killed while you're feeling sorry for the sick son of …!" Camdus couldn't finish the sentence. The impact of this stunning revelation had finally left him speechless.

Seelah replied, "Commander, you don't know if that's true. And even if it is, it's not for us to judge. We are obligated to help him, no matter what you think. Now let's drop this and finish our meal."

Camdus had lost his appetite. He jumped up from the table, knocking his chair over, and stormed out of the room. *I can't believe it!* His thoughts raced. *Have I fallen into some parallel universe where everyone but me is insane?*

He had been aimlessly walking for a few minutes when he rounded a curve in the concourse revealing, of all things, a vast ocean with a beach far better than the shores he remembered from his youth. There was no one else there, much to his relief. He walked beside the water for some time before finding the perfect spot and sitting down to watch the waves roll in. His mind was still racing, though his heart had resumed its regular rate. *As if I didn't have enough to worry about – now this!* He lay back and soaked in the warmth of the sun on his face. The hot sand radiated through his uniform easing his clenched muscles. Right now, he wished he knew the power of the ring so that he could find out for himself if Seelah was right.

At that moment, a shadow fell across him, blocking the sun.

"Commander, it's time for your lesson." Vandalen had followed him, knowing that he had to save Serin no matter what. But he did not want to become ruthless to do it. Perhaps he could instruct Camdus in the tools associated with his heritage and together they could discover the truth about Serin. He knew as a seasoned wizard and soldier that even good men can turn. But he had hope that his son was ready to remember his birthright and mend his ways. Otherwise, well he just did not want to think about that – not unless he had to.

Calm now, Camdus got up and faced the wizard. "You're right. I know I have to trust Seelah's wisdom and your experience, at least for now. And for you and Elani, I pray Serin has changed."

Camdus led them back to the room where he taught Elani how to use the nucleo.

"Will this do?" Camdus asked.

"Yes, this'll work. Now may I hold your ring?"

Camdus pulled the ring out of the pouch and handed it to Vandalen, who held it for a moment in his hand. Of course, he felt none of its power because it wasn't crafted for him. He feared that it had been planted by Elsnor to trap them. But after he inspected it more closely, he was convinced that this was the real deal. Now the young Camdus could help him.

"First you have to learn how to calm the confusion you feel when the power courses through you when you wear it. If you don't, it will consume you. I can only tell you what works for me. Please understand that you might have to find a different technique."

Camdus nodded.

"All right then, the first thing I do is breathe deeply and evenly. I don't let the excitement of having this much power run away with my common sense. It's a matter of mental fortitude. Are you ready to try it?" He studied Camdus, hoping this session would go well. *If he can't handle it and I don't have my ring....*" He didn't want to think of the outcome.

Camdus had been ready, but now he hesitated.

"What will happen if I can't control it?"

Vandalen smiled. "You said you've worn the ring before?"

When the question registered through the doubts, he answered, "Yes, I have worn it a little."

"How did you feel when you put the ring on?"

"It was exhilarating but scary. I was afraid of what would happen, so I took it off every time I tried to wear it."

Vandalen listened carefully. "That's how it was with me too in the beginning." Then he asked, "But weren't you able to wear it a little longer each time you put it on?"

Camdus admitted that he had, adding, "But it got scarier every time because the power seemed to be getting stronger, more organized. But was it organizing itself, or was I? I need to know."

Vandalen was relieved to hear this. "The power of the ring knows no discipline. So, if it was organized, then you were in control of it. Now put the ring on. Please."

Camdus put it on. The familiar feeling flooded his body so strongly that he snatched it off.

"Put the ring back on, Commander. This time imagine a stream going where you want it to go. If it tries to go where it doesn't belong, build a mental dam to redirect it. Please, try again," Vandalen said patiently.

Camdus put the ring back on. The tsunami surge almost overwhelmed him, but he did as he was told. It took a river not a stream, but he was able to control it. He looked up when he realized what had happened.

"I think I have control. What now?" Camdus asked.

Vandalen replied without hesitation. "Summon my ring to come to me. It will come. No matter where it is, it will come."

"How do I summon it? Is there some kind of spell or special word or gesture or something like that?"

Vandalen smiled again, easier this time. "Just think of me, my ring, and me with my ring on my finger."

"That's all?" Camdus was stunned at the simplicity of it.

"Yes. That's all. Now, please get my ring. We'll need them both if we're to overcome Elsnor and the Q'Arons."

Doubt crept through Camdus' being. "Wait a minute. You just told me I'm a wizard. That's a lot to dump on me without telling me how this can be. I just don't understand how that's possible. But I know it's true. Still, am I ready? I mean, can I really do this?"

"You can and you will."

Camdus stepped away just a minute to calm his jangling nerves. He took a deep breath and did as he was asked. Within a few moments, he heard Vandalen inhale sharply.

Turning back around Camdus saw the ring, slimy with river moss, sitting on the wizard's right index finger. Camdus blinked in disbelief. He hadn't thought this would work, but now the possibilities were endless.

Vandalen looked up from his ring and recognized the expression on Camdus' face. "Listen to me, Commander. Don't let the ring take control. It's tempting, especially after your first success with it. But you are stronger. You are better. You have purpose. You're in control."

As he spoke, he saw the struggle Camdus was fighting with his newly tapped power, but Vandalen knew he had to fight this one alone.

After what seemed like an eternity but was less than a minute, beads of sweat were pouring down his temples. He said, "Now I understand what you've been telling me. Even though I never wanted this power, I have it and I know I can use it as long as I practice restraint. I've got this, I'm okay now. I won't let it control me again. All right then. Let's get back to Q'Door Hold. I think things are just about to get interesting."

Vandalen nodded agreement, though he would not have chosen the word *interesting*. He followed Camdus back to Seelah's sitting room where they found the others deep in conversation.

"Seelah," Camdus greeted their host. "It's time for us to be about our business. Thank you for your help. With luck, we'll see you again."

Seelah said resolutely, "May God be with you, Commander. We'll be praying for you, but please be careful."

Elani looked from her father to Slogar. No words were necessary. As always, her facial expression said it all.

Vandalen stepped forward and gave his daughter an unexpected hug.

"I'll be back in no time, Princess," he whispered in her ear.

The endearment sent both joy and sadness straight as an arrow piercing her heart. She clung to him a moment.

"I'll be waiting, Father."

Rax popped in. With a brief review of their strategy, Camdus asked Rax to take Vandalen and him back to Q'Door Hold.

Slogar spoke up. "What about me? I can help you. Don't you think I need to go, too?"

Camdus intended to leave Slogar here but maybe he was right.

"Okay. Rax after you've taken us to Q'Door Hold, please come back for the doctor."

Elani sighed deeply and bowed her head, her heart heavy.

The Rider silently complied. In a few minutes he popped back in to fetch the doctor.

Slogar knew that Rax had standing orders to find the Commander wherever he was, no matter what. But he hadn't given it much thought until the moment they popped back into Q'Door Hold.

Camdus and Vandalen were standing back to back, outnumbered three to one by gigantic, helmeted Q'Aron soldiers. The appearance of Rax and Slogar threw the Q'Arons off balance for a split second. That was all the wizards needed.

Vandalen yelled, "Now, Commander!"

Camdus knew what he had to do. He felt the power coursing through his body. The urge to let it run wild was strong, but he knew he couldn't let it. He didn't want to kill the Q'Arons, just disarm and disable them. Weapons flew from his combatants' hands as they writhed in agony and fell to the floor. Vandalen's foes fared no better.

Magically, Vandalen bound and gagged them. He shouted to Camdus, "You've got to get them out of here, Commander."

Seeing the logic behind this, Camdus hid the unconscious men.

"Rax, get the doctor to the rest of the group. Now!" Camdus shouted as the wizards turned to face another onslaught. Once the Q'Arons reached the center of the passageway, Camdus released the captives. The stunned enemy soldiers were slammed hard by their larger comrades who fell, bound and unconscious, from the ceiling. In the heat of battle that had been the only place Camdus could think of to hide them.

Vandalen was as impressed as he was amused.

"Nicely done, Commander. But now we need to get all of them out of here. If you put them back on the ceiling you can't keep them there long, and we don't want them getting loose and coming back at us. Any ideas?"

Rax popped in at that moment. "Where would you like me to take them, Commander?"

Vandalen was startled. He'd forgotten how quickly Rax traveled, but Camdus was used to the Rider showing up when he needed him.

"Take them to Dartal. Put them in Vandalen's old cell block." Several pops later, and they were all behind bars.

Camdus thanked Rax and told him to take a break. He was sure it had been way too long since Rax last ate. The Rider needed his strength now more than ever.

Rax gratefully popped out and joined the other soldiers.

Camdus and Vandalen were the only ones left in the passageway. They had to get to the others and bring them up to speed on their recent skirmish.

Normally Camdus summoned Rax when he was in a hurry, but he knew that would be unfair. So instead of calling the tired and hungry Rider, he led Vandalen to the end of the passageway and then down a level. He was relieved to see that all of his men were where he'd left them. Rax was there, too, sitting on the floor, propped against the wall. He was obviously enjoying the jerky and tredon milk Seelah had sent.

Camdus filled them in. Then he asked Grunden for an update.

"Thanks for the cloaking device, Commander. It works great. We were able to use it to conceal our location, but we also used it to send out scouts to see what else is here." He saw the disapproval registering on the Commander's face, so he followed this piece of information with an explanation. "I know, Commander, I know you told us to stay put. And yes, I knew it would be risky, but after we discussed our options, we decided our time would be better spent by scouting around. We couldn't just sit around and wait for your return. I hope you can understand that."

Camdus begrudgingly nodded.

Grunden continued. "Not long after you left, Ram and I took off to get a look at the upper level. We found a hidden stairway in the rear northern corner. Since most of the activity is to the south and east, we decided north would be our safest route. We didn't see anything interesting until we got to the top. The entire floor was dark with only an eerie, pale yellow glow to light our way. When we rounded a corner, we heard something. We knew we were cloaked but still solid, so we hugged the wall as close as we could. We saw a man carefully making his way along the hallway. He was so covered in blood and sand, he hardly looked human. We followed him. He wound his way back to where we'd just come from, but he took a left into a minor corridor that ended outside a door secured by two well-armed guards. They tried to stop him, but he attacked them. He dodged a blast from one of the men but was in the crosshairs of the other. I sent a stun blast to stop the Q'Aron. The injured man didn't see us but knew he'd had help. He looked around, then sprinted off down the corridor, and disappeared. The other guard struggled to lift his buddy all the while keeping his weapon pulled in no particular direction. I thought he was just about to get trigger happy, so I stunned him, too. We needed to see what was in that room, and we couldn't do it without both of them down. We also knew that we didn't have much time, so we approached the door and just barely opened it a crack. I squinted to get a look inside. Elsnor alone, sitting down with his back to us. We hadn't made any noise, not even a whisper but he called out to us. 'Who's there?' We closed the door and ran like the devil was behind us. We went in the same direction as the man we helped to try to find him, but he was gone. We've been back here ever since."

"So, you know where Elsnor is?"

"Yes, Commander, we do," Grunden answered. "But if he knew we were there while we were cloaked and not even in the room, I don't see how we're going to be able to take him. He may be old, but he's still pretty powerful."

Ram echoed this sentiment. "Elsnor can do stuff unlike anything we've ever seen before. He looks like he's just a weak old man, but all of the Q'Arons we've seen are afraid of him. And if my guess is right, the injured man was going to pay him a retribution visit."

Vandalen spoke up. "I know you said the man was covered in blood and dirt, but please try to describe him to me."

Ram tried to remember. "He was tall, with long hair that was either gray or looked gray because it was full of dirt – I couldn't tell. I think his uni was black, but it coulda been gray. I didn't see an emblem on it."

"Gentlemen," Vandalen said solemnly, "I believe that man is my son. We need to find him. He's going to need our help before it's too late – whether he knows it or not."

Camdus had no intention of helping the mercenary and said so.

"Look, Vandalen, we need your help, but not if it means we have to bring a killer into our midst. He's not the good son you remember."

Vandalen stood his ground. "Maybe so, but I am the good father I hope he will remember. If what you've told me about him is true, how could he have let himself get into this pitiful shape? If for no other reason, we need to find out who injured him and how he survived the attack. What we learn could help ...."

He was interrupted by angry, desperate cries of one of the beasts. They knew that it could smell them, even if it couldn't see them. The sound was getting closer by the second.

Camdus rallied his group with the ancient Irish battle cry of *Faugh a Ballagh*, which meant *clear the way*. The ferocity with which he roared those words made plain his intention to do just that.

Now with his men no longer cloaked and at the ready, he gave orders.

"Grunden, take your men to the service room to our left. Vandalen, go with them. The rest of you, come with me."

He sprinted down the far hallway with Taw, Sy, Axel, and a young soldier they'd nicknamed Satch close on his heels. Camdus hoped that they would be able to trap the beast between them and destroy it. But before they reached their assigned spot, the animal appeared. Its eyes glowed like burning coals. A mix of blood and saliva slopped out of its mouth.

Without warning, it sprang toward the last man in Grunden's party. Satch was now trapped beneath the great hulk. He blasted the beast with his nucleo. The great cat howled in pain but renewed its attack. With one great paw, the beast smashed Satch's skull, its contents spattering across the floor and up the wall. The beast then took the lifeless soldier in its vise-like jaws and slung him like he was nothing more than a ragdoll. It stood on its hind legs, pawing the air, challenging the men to battle.

Grunden had gotten to know Satch fairly well. He knew he was a fresh recruit with a wife and small baby at home. Rage as he'd never known before flowed through him. He stepped out, screaming at the beast.

"Come on, coward! What? You can only take men whose backs are turned? Try me, you sorry piece of...."

By now both Camdus and Vandalen had stepped into view, one slightly in front and to the left of the beast, the other directly to its right.

"Grunden, get down!" Camdus ordered.

Grunden instantly obeyed. The beast was hit by double jolts of lightning – one scarlet, the other purple. It tried to extract itself from the current flowing through its body but was no match. It fell, writhing on the floor. Camdus and Vandalen lowered their right hands, stopping the voltage. Before their astonished eyes, the beast began to change.

Ram stepped over and looked down at the man who now lay where the beast had been and said to no one in particular, "Lieutenant T'Aron. I should have known. Why else would he have been attracted to Li'Let. Well, look where that got him."

Camdus thought they'd contained the threat at least for the moment. But he had to operate as if more Q'Aron soldiers were on the way. He knew they had to find Elsnor before more enemy soldiers found them and engaged them in another fight. Besides, any more delay would give Elsnor the time he needed to escape.

"Take us to Elsnor, Mr. Grunden."

Grunden complied, activating the cloaking device as he took the lead.

Once on the top level, they followed Grunden to the double doors. Those closest could hear voices.

"… but not this time, old man. Now it's my turn. You're not so arrogant without your ring, are you, Wizard?"

Vandalen recognized the voice. "It's Serin," he whispered to Camdus. "Let me go in. We need Elsnor alive."

Camdus knew he was right, but he still didn't like the idea. "Go but be careful."

Vandalen slipped into the room unnoticed. He stepped over two Q'Aron guards lying on the floor just inside the door. Their yellow blood pooled around them. Serin was standing over Elsnor, his right hand on the old man's throat. He was pressing the primitive dagger he held in his left hand against Elsnor's chest.

Vandalen spoke evenly and calmly in a low voice, "Son, don't do this. This is not who you are."

Without taking his hands off Elsnor, Serin whipped his head around to see his father. "You don't know who I am. How could you? Just like you, isn't it? Always take the other man's side. You never fight for yourself or stand up for your own."

Elsnor's face was turning scarlet, the fight leaving him. "Serin, we need him. He has information we need. Let him up – please."

Elsnor felt the buzzing in his ears ease off and the pressure on his neck slacken. But he still felt the point of the knife firmly poised at his chest. He started to speak but thought better of it. He knew the slightest wrong word could be his death warrant.

"Son, please. We need you, too. I need you. I've found your sister. Actually, she found me, but she's safe." Vandalen wanted his son to respond through free will, not by force. He could see that the mention of Elani had struck a chord.

Serin stepped back, jerking Elsnor to his feet as he moved. Elsnor's eyes were so swollen now they were little more than slits.

Vandalen guessed that his son was venting his anger at him on Elsnor, at least in part.

Serin's hatred for his father had been a slow evolution fed by his failure to understand that his father's duty to the Empire had to, at least for a time, take precedence over his family. The fact that Serin had idolized him made it even worse. His desire to be like his dad was gradually replaced by hatred.

Though Serin probably would not believe it, Vandalen had regretted not spending more time with him. But he did the best he could, teaching him all of the martial arts. But the boy had been disappointed that he never got to go to Trilvar to learn the wizarding way. And he would never admit that the skills he learned from his father were what made him the most sought-after mercenary in both Empires.

As Emperor Borm's illness had become progressively worse, Vandalen had even less time to spend with his family. Young Serin's resentment of the job that took his father away grew making Serin more and more bitter every day. Nell had worried over her son's bouts of dark brooding but thought that when he and his sister went off to University, he'd mature enough to understand. She was disappointed as he became more and more distant. When Jarlod had become Emperor and then imprisoned Serin's father, the young man had felt a stinging moment of triumph. With his studies complete, he'd left home and sold the skills his father had taught him, as well as those he'd learned in back alleys, to the highest bidder.

He'd actually been away on a job for one of his most frequent clients when he heard the Emperor's version of his father's fate. By this time, Serin had reinvented himself leaving no shadow of a connection to Vandalen. His employer had no idea when he casually dropped the news about the great wizard's fate.

"... That's right. They said Jarlod's men caught him when he wasn't wearing his ring. Said the wizard was so scared he wet his pants. Ha ha hah! All because he was too careless to keep his ring with him. Stupid mistake, as it turned out. And according to my source, Jarlod couldn't wait to get his hands on it. But when he tried to use the ring, he found out it didn't have any power. They said Jarlod threw one of his famous tantrums and hurled the ring into the Jevishal River where it curves behind his palace. You know it runs directly under his great room window. Humph, I wonder what else he's thrown in there. I'm telling ya, I wish I could've seen that one. Someday I'm going to get in that river and find that ring. The diamond in it alone must be worth a fortune."

The older man had guffawed at the thought of Jarlod having one of his infamous fits. Serin had drained his cup, wiped his mouth, and joined in the laugh at the Emperor's expense. But he'd secretly delighted in his father's capture far more than anyone could possibly know. He had collected his fee and left for his next job, his employer none the wiser.

Now Serin was standing face to face with his father.

Father? How convenient. Where were you when I needed you? He thought this but didn't say it. No, this was not the time. Instead he said, "I assume you are not alone."

"Correct," Vandalen answered. "I believe the Commander will find this the perfect place for our headquarters." He went to the door and signaled the others, who entered the chamber quickly without making a sound.

Elsnor had yet to recognize Vandalen, who'd moved silently to one of the large windows. He stood with his back to the room staring at the nothingness outside.

Camdus posted guards at the doors. Then he turned his attention to their captive.

Through the slits of his swollen eyelids, Elsnor curiously looked at the ring Camdus wore.

Vandalen still stood staring out into the dusk's dim light, but he was keenly aware of what was going on in the room behind him.

Serin was not in the mood for ancient Geneva Convention civility. He shoved Elsnor back into the chair – hard – keeping his knife at the ready.

"Go ahead, old man. Just give me an excuse," he snarled. Then he pulled the bloody ring from his pocket and shoved it into the Commander's hand.

Camdus took it but looked at Serin sharply. He knew that if Serin had wanted Elsnor dead, he'd have already dispensed with him. He correctly assumed that Serin had no intention of putting the old man's lights out – at least not yet.

Camdus pulled a chair up directly in front of Elsnor, toying with the wizard's ring as he spoke. The old man's long white hair was bloody and disheveled. "You're going to tell us what we want to know, Elsnor. And you get to decide what happens to you afterwards. Cooperate and you'll have the pleasure of an Empire Tribunal where you have at least a shot at life. Or you can refuse, and your last words will be to tell us where to send your remains. Like I said, you decide. But know this – what little patience I had has been gone for a really long time. Now tell me, who are you working for?"

Elsnor tried to muster his arrogant smile, but his swollen, bloody, mouth and missing teeth made it impossible. He tried to let his bravado do the talking.

"Do your worst. You can't hurt me."

Camdus scoffed at this absurdity as he pocketed Elsnor's ring.

"Sure we can. We haven't even started yet. But if you're waiting for your beasts or your guards to rescue you, you can forget it. We've met them. They won't be back. Now, let's start again. Who are you working for?"

Elsnor sat silently, staring ahead, clearly trying to see a way to turn this situation to his advantage. Camdus sat patiently, absentmindedly stroking his own ring. He felt the power coursing through him and reminded himself of Vandalen's warnings. He channeled his thoughts with his mental river.

The Master Wizard turned now from the window and stepped in front of Elsnor.

At first, Elsnor didn't recognize him; his attention was on Camdus' ring. When he looked up, he was looking straight into Vandalen's dark blue-green eyes. There was no mistaking his identity. He realized that the Master Wizard was standing close to him with the ring he himself had seen Jarlod throw into the Jevishal, once again neatly seated on his right index finger. This knowledge helped bring Elsnor around to a more cooperative frame of mind.

"How did you....?"

The wizard interrupted him. "How did I get out of that hell hole Dartal – the one you and Jarlod made sure I was sent to? Elsnor, you'll never understand the power that freed me." His cool voice chilled the room.

Camdus was sitting there watching this exchange impatiently.

Vandalen knew that now was not the time for this indulgence. He took a deep breath before speaking.

"Commander, I believe our prisoner is ready to cooperate," he said as he stepped back, with a sweeping gesture of his hand, inviting Camdus to continue.

"Who are you working for?"

Elsnor knew there was no alternative. He said, "Weilz."

Camdus pressed. "Weilz? What, he couldn't wait for his turn to move up from second to first?"

Elsnor nodded, "It was not about power or wealth. It was revenge. Jarlod seduced Weilz' youngest daughter – I think her name was Lulu – before she had reached her seventh school year. He used his friendship with Weilz and his wife to get to the girl, and then began inviting her to visit his own daughter. His depravity sickens even me, though I admit to fancying younger women. But even I would never stoop into that cesspool. Jarlod offered Weilz his current position in the Empire to appease him. When Weilz accepted, Jarlod thought he'd struck a deal. He could now see himself as the kindly friend, not the perverted molester he truly was – and is. Jarlod never asked about the girl. He didn't want to know the wreckage of her gentle spirit and damaged mind he'd left her with."

Camdus needed to know more, so he asked, "What enticement did he use to get you to become a traitor?"

"He offered me my own world, complete with everything I could ever want or need," Elsnor said.

"Which world?" Camdus demanded.

"Boldoon."

Though Grunden was a soldier in the REG, his Boldoonian roots ran deep. He stepped forward, glowering down at their captive. "The demon winds on Creedor have a better chance of calming down forever than your chance at getting your filthy hands on my world, Elsnor. Not if I have anything to do with it."

Camdus spoke quietly to Grunden, "Stand down, soldier. Elsnor is full of – hot air. If he believes that Weilz would ever give him his own world, then he is way too easy to deceive."

To Elsnor he said, "Where are the Q'Aron leaders who've been in charge of Q'Door Hold?"

Elsnor managed a triumphant look despite his now discolored, swollen face. "There's no use looking for them; they're gone. And they have taken all the trizactl they need to complete the weapons they will use to finish you off."

He laughed bitterly, not for a Q'Aron victory, but at his own defeat.

Camdus was sick of Elsnor, so he stunned him into unconsciousness.

"That'll take care of him for a while," was all he said before addressing more pressing needs.

Camdus realized that he had two injured men to contend with – Serin and Elsnor. "Rax," he said aloud.

The soft pop was followed by the Rider who must have been eating again. The remnants of his meal clung to his chin.

"Yes, Commander?" Rax responded.

"Please bring Dr. Slogar to us. Tell him he has two patients waiting."

When Rax returned, Slogar had his small bag with him, eager to assist.

He surveyed the situation, and decided that Serin, though full of fight, had the more pressing wounds.

"You see, I told you you'd need me. Now, Mr. Serin, if I may...."

Serin had not realized the severity of his injuries – he must have been running on pure adrenaline. Seating himself at one end of the long conference table beside the doctor, he allowed Slogar to examine his wounds.

"What happened to you?" Slogar asked.

Serin snarled, "Does it matter? Just patch me up."

Slogar quickly responded, "It matters. If I know what made the wounds, then I can know better how to treat them."

Serin saw the logic. "These gouges here," he said, pointing to the gaping wound in his side and the minor gouges on his arms, "were made by the beast. The rest of them were made by some bush I tried to hide in." He showed Slogar his legs, shoulders and back. "Damn thing would have eaten me if I hadn't got away!"

Slogar cleansed the wounds and applied an antiseptic ointment. He then pulled a needle and a vial out of his bag to draw blood. Serin's objection was plain when the medical items skittered across the polished stone floor after he knocked them from Slogar's hand.

"Now, now, Mr. Serin, please. My supplies are limited. We can't go wasting them," Slogar scolded.

"You're not sticking me with a needle. I've been stabbed enough!" Serin was adamant.

But Slogar was just as insistent. "I have to know if you've been infected with a disease, specifically the one that's killing the Creedorians. Now will you allow me to do my job?" Slogar said impatiently.

Serin stuck his arm out and endured the blood drawing, which to him was no more than an insect sting – as long as he looked away.

Once Slogar had collected a large enough sample, he turned to Camdus and asked, "Can you get me back to Seelah? I need her to help me with this analysis."

Then he handed a small jar to the Commander and said, "Here's some ointment for your prisoner, too."

Camdus took the ointment, though he thought it would be a waste. He handed the small container to Rax and told him to leave it with the prisoner. Then he asked him to take Elsnor to Dartal to join his cronies.

Once Elsnor was squared away, Camdus gave the doctor permission to return to Seelah. In a few minutes, Rax and Slogar popped out.

During the interim, Grunden had begun to sort through all the data he'd collected since they first entered the tunnels. The memory of the chamber with layers of minerals kept pushing into his consciousness. He had recognized all except one and his gut told him they needed to identify it. And as much as he hated to go back into those narrow passages to get there, he knew they had to. He convinced Camdus to let Taw and Axel go with him to that chamber to collect some of the strangely shimmering blue strata.

Going was slow, especially for Taw. He banged his head and bruised his shoulders and arms along the way. When they got there, Axel stood guard while Taw lifted Grunden up high enough to run a test on it to make sure the substance was safe. Satisfied it was not hazardous, he filled the three expandable containers they brought with them. They slung the fabric handles over their shoulders and headed back.

When Rax popped back in, Camdus quickly sent him to the mother ship with their haul. They'd analyze it later. After the Rider popped in again, Camdus called all his men together to assess their strength and plan their strategy. He surveyed what was left of the group. Only Satch had died. Serin was banged up, but otherwise okay – if he didn't have the disease. Taw, Sy, and Axel were unharmed and ready for another go at the Q'Arons. Stadar, Grunden, and Ram had formed a team that worked pretty well together. Rax was fearless and completely loyal, as was his nature. Some of the enlisted men who'd joined him from the mother ship had minor injuries, but the rest of them were unharmed.

This left Vandalen and him. He knew their power could be used together to overcome some fierce opponents. He also figured that the combined power could be dangerous if they weren't careful. But at this stage of the battle, they had to go full out if they wanted to win.

"Gentlemen, please sit down," Camdus said, indicating the chairs around the conference table. He seated himself at the head. "When is the last time you saw any of the Q'Arons?"

Stadar said, "I haven't seen any since we overpowered Elsnor and his bodyguards. That's been a while ago."

"That's right, Commander," Ram added, "and I think that tells us we need to get to the mine now. We can't stay up here. Remember what Elsnor said? The Q'Arons already have what they need. They're probably still loading the ships."

"Yes, I know we can't stay here. But that's not what he said. What he said was they're already gone. Maybe so, maybe not. Knowing him, he lied to buy time for them to get away. Let's operate on the assumption that they're still here. I don't want to think about what a mess we'll have if they've already made off with our trizactl. But you're right – we've got to get to the mine either way," Camdus said thoughtfully.

"Commander," Grunden interjected, "have any ships responded to our mayday yet?"

Camdus didn't want to answer this particular question. He knew it would be disheartening. But he owed the men the truth.

"No, and I don't expect them to. I know we need reinforcements. But we can't waste time worrying about what we don't have. Besides, what we lack in numbers we make up for in skill and power. We've just got to breach the Hold's docking station. And we need to do it now. Who knows how to get into the mine?"

Stadar spoke up. "I do, Commander. When I first got here, I worked in the mine. The docking station is at the base level on the east side. I'm pretty sure I can find it again. The closer we get, the warmer it is. There's a shaft off the transport tube that goes directly into the heart of the mine, but it's out of the main traffic."

Vandalen had been listening quietly. Now he said, "That's fine, but what are we going to do when we get there?"

Camdus was surprised by the wizard's impatience because he was usually the most level-headed of them all. He answered him calmly.

"Like I said, we have to assume that Elsnor lied and they're still here. Grunden and Stadar, disable the transport pods. Rax, go with Taw and Ram. Help them neutralize the Hold's communication system. Sy and Axel, I want you to cover us when we breach the docking station. Serin, you're with me and Vandalen. The rest of you, secure the perimeter. Everyone be on your guard. If they get in your way, do whatever you have to do. But try to take them alive. We'll want to interrogate them later. All right, Stadar. Lead the way."

With that they left the relative safety of the conference room in the abandoned tower and headed down, down into the hot belly of the planet.

***

SEELAH SENDS FOR SERIN

Once back in the facility on Silden, Slogar had no time to settle in. He and Seelah went straight to her lab.

"Simon, please give me the sample," she said. She sat down on a tall stool in front of a small contraption that looked like an old compact disk player from Earth's 1990s. She gingerly opened the vial and extracted a tiny dot of Serin's blood. She then placed it in the machine. While it whirred softly as it processed the sample, Seelah took a moment to talk to the doctor.

"What happened on Creedor, Simon? You look like you've been through forty hells."

Slogar was a bit surprised by her language, but he answered her as best he could. "We captured Elsnor, but not without loss. A Q'Aron beast killed one of our men, but Vandalen and Camdus killed it. The thing turned out to be a changeling. Sounds crazy, I know, but it just got crazier from there. Serin was attacked by the beast, and according to him mind you, by a bush. That's why I brought his blood here for analysis. I want to see if he's got the disease that's killing the folks on Creedor. They've got their hands full down there."

Seelah didn't say anything for a bit, but then she asked, "A bush? Are you sure he said *a bush*, Simon? Bushes generally don't attack."

Slogar got the distinct impression that the Elder Woman was about to make light of what he told her, and frankly, he was not in the mood.

"I'm quite sure he said a bush tried to eat him. I know how that must sound, but Creedor is not your ordinary world. Really strange things are happening there, so if he said it was a bush, then I believe him."

Seelah started to say something, but the machine *beep beep beeped* indicating that the analysis of the blood sample was finished.

"Well, I have good news and bad news, as the saying goes. Serin has contracted a disease, but it's one that I think we can cure. The bad news is we don't have enough blood to culture a post-exposure prophylaxis."

Slogar asked, "Do you think Serin has the disease we've been looking for?"

"I do. And your guess was right. He has rabies, but it's a new strain. Do you know how long ago he was exposed to it?"

"Two days ago, I think. If he has rabies, we have to treat him soon or he'll die but probably not before infecting the men he's with."

He was quiet a moment, and then added, "Seelah, I think the strain is not a natural mutation. I think it's been engineered. Can you find a cure if that's the case?"

Her reply was not the one he wanted to hear. "Simon, I probably can, though without a huge stroke of luck, it's unlikely that it will be in time. But if we can get Serin here, then I think we'll at least have a chance. Please contact Commander Camdus and see if he can persuade Serin to come to Silden."

Slogar said, "I'll try but there's no guarantee. He's not under his command so he can't make him do anything. But maybe his father can."

"I don't think Vandalen can sway Serin to do anything either, Simon. Their relationship is too broken. But Elani could."

Slogar nearly roared, "No! I won't have Elani going to Q'Door Hold, Seelah. It's just too dangerous."

"What's too dangerous?" Elani asked. She had walked in on the tail-end of their conversation. Seelah and Slogar were facing each other, each ready to make a case for Elani either going or staying.

"Elani, we need to get your brother back here as quickly as possible. He's been infected with a serious disease. If he's to survive, I need him here so I can try to formulate a cure."

Elani spoke without hesitation, "Of course. Where is he? Can Rax take me to him?"

Slogar blurted out his objections. His genuine concern for her was evident in his every word.

"No, Elani. Please don't go. Your brother is at Q'Door Hold which is at the moment in the middle of a bloody battle. It's too dangerous for you right now." He knew he was wasting his breath this time just like when he tried to keep her out of Dartal.

Damn, this is one stubborn woman, he thought. Any other time, he'd find that quality somewhat endearing, but not this time. All he could do was pray for her safety. He knew no matter what, she would go to her brother, just like she had gone to her father.

"Simon," Elani said, "I will come back. And Serin will be with me. You and Seelah get everything ready. We'll be back before you know it."

Simon knew when he'd lost, so he contacted Camdus.

"Commander, Slogar here. Seelah needs Serin to come to Silden as soon as possible. He has rabies, possibly a genetically engineered strain. We have to get him here to run more tests and then to work up a cure. Elani wants to go to Q'Door Hold to fetch him. Can Rax bring him here?"

Camdus' voice over the communicator was barely audible there was so much static. "Rax is t - - d up right h- - - at the mome- - - dis - - ing commu- - -tors and - - -spods." The communication crackled one last time and then fell completely silent.

Slogar knew that things were far worse than they had been when he left. He hoped that Camdus had understood his request and would send Serin anyway.

Elani said nothing. She left the room, returning in a few moments with a tray of thistle tea. This time she'd spiked hers with mulled wine. Careful not to mix up the cups, she handed one to Seelah and then handed Slogar's to him. They gladly accepted the warm drink. The three of them sat on the sofa by the fireplace without speaking. The only sounds were the soft crackling of the flames and Slogar's occasional slurping. After a long wait, they heard a soft pop.

They jumped up and turned to see that Rax had popped in with Serin, who was wounded again. Rax carefully placed his unconscious charge on the sofa.

Seelah rushed to him to examine his wounds. She knew immediately that his injuries were life threatening. She asked Rax and Slogar to take him to her lab.

The unconscious Serin moaned in pain as they put him on the bed.

Then Rax addressed Slogar. "Doctor, the Commander wants you and the Elder Woman to be ready for more guests. Not all of them are human."

Simon asked, "What do you mean, not human? What else is down there?"

Rax calmly let him know what to expect. "They are changelings, Doctor. We found a nursery abandoned by the Q'Arons. In it, there are half a dozen infant changelings. Perhaps cute by your standards, but knowing what they grow into, not at all harmless. The Commander thinks we have to save them, even though they become beasts."

"You mean Camdus intends to send six of those beasts here, to Silden? Has this skirmish rattled his brains?" Slogar asked, unwilling to believe what he'd heard.

Rax nodded affirmatively, leaving Slogar to interpret which one of the questions he'd answered. He then departed as suddenly as he'd arrived.

THE Q'ARONS

Losing Serin was a serious blow to Camdus. He had to admit that he'd turned out to be a fearless warrior. *Can't dwell on what I don't have. We've got to go on.*

The heat from the mine was stifling, making it difficult for the men to breathe. Vandalen and Grunden were behind one of the disabled ships, battling a group of the hooded Q'Arons. Stadar and Ram were pinned behind the transport tube, unable to do anything but fend off the attacking beasts. Axel was at the moment firing his AK-47 at the latest onslaught of changelings. Though a few of them fell, too many escaped.

Taw and Sy, now separated from Axel, had their own problems. They had tried to make it back to Axel to help him, but they found themselves in hand-to-hand combat with the Q'Aron who outnumbered them five to one.

If Camdus had known what he was leading them into, he might have waited until he could convince Jarlod to send help.

Yeah, yeah. Hindsight's 20/20, he thought.

As for his own predicament, he had cornered two fairly inexperienced looking Q'Arons he was pretty sure he could subdue. But as soon as he blasted them, they changed into raging beasts. Now it was he who was cornered. He imagined a protective barrier around him, but the beasts attacked it again and again.

Camdus knew he couldn't keep the shield up much longer, and in his final moment of desperation, he reached into the pouch for his father's last gift. He pulled the small white feather out of the bag and stroked it three times.

The feather leapt from his hand, becoming a huge winged beast, part lizard, part bird. Its talons were the size of a man and razor sharp. The snowy creature rose above the battle and roared.

The changeling beasts, startled by the new threat, screamed and ran away, leaving their prey unharmed. The alarmed Q'Aron soldiers threw down their weapons and knelt in submission.

Vandalen and the rest of the unit walked across the body-littered battleground that the Hold had become. Camdus and what was left of his small band had come through this latest battle in much better shape than the enemy. The men who'd been assigned to the perimeter had been outnumbered but had held fast. They were surprised but relieved when the changelings rushed past them out into the storm. Inexplicably, their attackers had taken off behind the beasts which gave the REG troops the opportunity to regroup.

Breathing a silent prayer of thanks, Camdus walked over to the kneeling figure whose uniform had the most braid and medals. Though he was unfamiliar with Q'Aron military rank, he guessed this one might be an officer.

By now the Reglon beast had come to rest atop the largest of the transpods and sat quietly observing what was going on below. Camdus knew he would have no trouble as long as it was perched up there. The ring offered him no insights into how long that might be.

"Grunden, I want you to take Stadar, Ram, and the rest of the unit to secure the enemy. Bring them back to headquarters. Vandalen, please come with me."

Once the others were gone, Camdus spoke to the wizard, gesturing toward their fierce champion still looking down at them. "What do you know about that?"

Vandalen was as surprised as Camdus. "How would I know? You're the one who brought it here. How did you do that anyway?"

Camdus knew he needed his father's help. "I don't know, but I'm going to find out. You go ahead and help with the prisoners. I'll be up shortly."

Vandalen gave Camdus a quizzical look, but with one glance up at the birdlike creature, he hurried off.

Camdus leaned against the wall and touched his communicator. He was relieved to see that he finally had a secure channel that worked.

He quickly contacted his father, all the while watching his companion who was now preening its feathers.

When Willem answered, Camdus got straight to the point. "Dad, you know the pouch you gave me before I left for the Academy? I've found the first two items quite helpful. By the way, we need to talk about this wizard thing. But the feather, I'm not sure what to do with the animal or bird or lizard or whatever it is that it turned into."

Willem laughed heartily, "You must mean Sorbeau, my old friend and protector." Willem sobered instantly, "So this means you found yourself with no other options. Son, are you all right?"

Camdus quickly filled his father in on what happened since they last spoke. Then he asked, "Dad, do you think you and Tomer can join us here in Q'Door Hold to help interrogate the prisoners? I know both of you have more experience with the Q'Aron language and customs than any of us down here. I also need your help with Sorbeau, if you please."

Willem laughed but agreed to contact Tomer.

Within an hour, Camdus got a call back from Willem. He let Camdus know that he and Tomer were ready. Camdus gladly dispatched Rax to bring them to the Hold.

Lost and Found

When Serin opened his eyes, he saw his sister sitting beside him. Having her here with him melted his heart. He'd missed being able to talk to her – and taunt her. It looked to him like she was napping, so he couldn't help himself.

"Well, Sis, I guess I know how much you're worried about me. Sleeping like a baby, and right here by my sick bed no less."

Though he was teasing her, Elani responded seriously.

"I was praying, Brother, not napping." Elani then softened her voice, and said to Serin, "Slogar and Seelah gave up hope for your recovery. But I knew with all my being that you would wake up. And I'm thankful I was right, even if you did wake up only to aggravate me."

Duly chastened, Serin asked, "How long have I been here? The last thing I remember is one of the beasts dragging me by my ankle. It felt like my leg was about to be ripped off, the pain was so bad."

Elani knew she had to tell him but was unsure how. She started by saying, "Not too long. But Serin, Slogar and Seelah tried… I mean to say they really did everything they could to …, but everything was so mangled, they couldn't."

Thoroughly confused, Serin asked his sister, "What are you saying? Just say it, Elani. They tried to do what?" But before she could answer, he looked down and realized his left leg was missing just below the knee. He let out a roar of anguish. Elani burst into tears, her sorrow for her brother flooding down her face.

Seelah and Slogar heard the commotion and hurried into Serin's room.

He glared at them. "What have you done to me? What in God's name have you done?"

Seelah was prepared for this, but it wasn't easy. "Serin, to save your life, we took your leg. A good trade, we thought, though it's plain you do not agree."

"You took my leg. You took my leg! How could you? I didn't even get a say in it. What did you expect me to say? 'Thanks for saving my life, and it's okay that I'm crippled.' Well, I can't be that magnanimous. You didn't save my life, you took it. How am I supposed to live now?"

Seelah waited until he was finished, then she said, "Do you remember being attacked by a bush?"

Serin was in no mood to play what he considered stupid guessing games.

"Hell yes, I remember being attacked by a bush. What's that got to do with anything?"

Slogar took over. "Everything, Serin. The bush you were attacked by is known as a *miracle bush*. It left its DNA in your blood, and from it we have formulated a cure for the disease that is ravaging Creedor. Not only that, if our theory is correct, it is possible that your missing leg may – *may*, not will, for we can't be sure – regenerate in time. You'll just have to wait and see."

Serin lay back exhausted by trying to digest all this information at once. He understood his blood had been instrumental in formulating the cure for the disease killing Creedorians. And his leg might grow back! That's where it became too much. He looked at the three standing by his bedside, closed his eyes, and for the first time since he was a young boy, began to pray. He drifted off to sleep, not knowing what the rest of his life would be but knowing one thing for sure – it would not be the same as it had been.

Seelah checked to make sure Serin's vital signs were strong.

Then she left Slogar with Elani, who showed no signs of leaving her brother's side.

"Elani," Slogar began gently, "you've been here since yesterday. You need to eat and to rest. Please come with me. I'll cook you something to eat, simple but nourishing all the same. Serin is going to be fine. He just needs time. And while he's resting, I think you should, too."

Elani looked into Simon's eyes and read his concern for her.

I've been so selfish, she thought.

"All right, Simon, but let me help you. We make a pretty good team at catching supper, so we should make a good team preparing it. Besides I find cooking most cathartic." She leaned over and gave her brother a kiss on his forehead.

Then she turned to leave. Slogar held out his hand to her, which she took gladly. They went to Elani's garden to gather a few fresh vegetables and herbs before heading to the kitchen. Simon could see that her spirit was lifting.

As she bent to pick fresh dill, he said so softly she almost didn't hear him. "Elani, marry me."

She dropped the dill and turned to face him. "You know that we would never have children, Simon."

"That doesn't matter. What matters is I want to spend what's left of my life with you, if you'll have me. I'm too set in my ways for children anyway, though if we did by some miracle have them that would be fine – as long as they take after you."

Elani picked up the dill, stood up straight, and gave him the answer he'd longed to hear.

Slogar could not believe his good fortune but intended to make every day with Elani as full as possible. With God's help, he would be the husband she deserved.

***

Rax popped back into the conference room at the Hold with two complete strangers. Camdus was taken aback but knew that Rax seldom made mistakes. He almost always brought back who or what he'd been sent to retrieve. He just have to trust that these men were sent by his father.

Perhaps they'd been sent by his dad. Still baffled, he decided not to let the others know his doubts.

"Allow me to introduce myself – Zachary Radfield at your service. And my colleague is Lynwood Styles. How may we be of assistance?"

Camdus recognized his father's voice, if not his appearance. Relieved, he welcomed them with a brief handshake, followed by his request, "Mr. Radfield, I understand that you speak fluent Q'Aronese and are familiar with their customs. Is that correct?"

"Quite right, Commander. Lynwood and I are both experts in these areas. You are fortunate that he was available. He's a very busy man, very busy indeed. But his knowledge of the Q'Arons by far surpasses mine."

Camdus found this whole cloak and dagger routine disturbing but knew his father had his reasons.

"Well, then, gentlemen. We should get started. I need to find out everything about this facility, its purpose, and how much of their mission they managed to accomplish before we got here."

Then he said to Stadar, "Please bring in the Q'Aron."

In a few minutes, Zachary and Lynwood were conversing with the Q'Aron officer.

Though he spoke some Q'Aronese, Camdus would have to rely on his father and Tomer to get to the truth, if that was possible.

Willem addressed the man first, and then Tomer took over for a while.

The interrogation seemed to be going nowhere until Willem took a small item from his pocket. It was a seven-pointed star carved from an unusual pulsing, orange substance.

As soon as the officer who identified himself as T'Engler saw the object, sweat began to bead on his forehead; his words became calmer and flowed more easily. After another fifteen minutes, T'Engler's eyes rolled back in his head and he slumped in his chair, passed out cold.

Alarmed, Camdus stepped into the room.

"What happened to him? Please tell me he isn't dead." His heart felt like it was being squeezed in a huge fist.

"No, he just couldn't take any more exposure to the Q'Aron Sacred Star. They are physically unable to lie in its presence. I tried to get him to talk without it because prolonged exposure can be lethal, but he wouldn't budge. However, I think we've learned much of what you need to know. Thankfully your prisoner has a strong constitution. He'll be out for a while, but he will revive."

"That's a relief. Now tell me what he said," Camdus pressed.

"The Q'Arons have been here for about two years, though the facility itself was finished only a few months ago. Their mine is directly below Q'Door Hold, which is why the lower levels get so hot. Trizactl mining generates incredible amounts of energy that manifests as heat. They were sent here by the Q'Aron Emperor Hellritch himself to steal what they needed to complete their power plants first and then to build a store of massive weapons. Just one of them can tear a chunk out of a planet large enough to knock it out of orbit, effectively destroying all life on it. But the destruction won't be sudden, which would be kind, if destruction can ever be described as such. As the planet moves farther and farther from its sols, its inhabitants will begin to die from hunger, exposure, insanity."

When Willem paused, Tomer took up the story.

"They have taken twenty thousand tons of trizactl from this mine – give or take a few. The last shipment – half of their take – is currently on its way back to the Q'Aron Empire. If it gets there, then I think it's safe to assume that it's only a matter of time before our Empire will be destroyed, one planet at a time."

"But why," Camdus asked, "why destroy us? Though our leaders hate each other's guts, we've managed to co-exist for centuries. Why now? What can they possibly expect to gain from our demise?"

Tomer said, "As to why, it's because they can. You see, to the Q'Arons nothing outside their realm is sacred. They are barbaric by our standards, yet they have a religion. They worship the Sacred Star. Its seven points, they believe, represent their victory over seven empires. Ours is to be the first, primarily because it has seven worlds. At least that's what T'Engler told us, and I believe him. There would have been no need to steal our trizactl if they already had the weapons they needed. Unfortunately, that's not the only reason they built this facility."

Camdus could think of nothing worse but asked anyway.

"What other reason?"

"They have been breeding changelings. Their plan for them was to set them loose in their own world to keep their populace in check. Population control, maybe. Keeping the citizens powerless, for sure."

"You said their plan *was* to set the changelings loose. What happened to the plan? Did they succeed?" Camdus asked. He knew that at least some had been used in Q'Door Hold to torment prisoners. He also had just survived a battle that the changelings may have helped win had it not been for Sorbeau.

Willem set his mind at ease. "The plan failed miserably. Most of the changelings were too hard to control, so they aborted that part of the mission."

"That explains the nursery," Camdus said. "Infant changelings have been left on one of the upper levels, probably to die. I plan to take them to Seelah to see if she can help them."

Up until this point, Ram had stood in one corner, quietly taking in every detail. But now he spoke up.

"Commander, you can't mean that. Have you forgotten what these things are capable of when they are fully mature? I say we destroy them here and now."

Vandalen stood by Camdus. "No, we can't kill the young changelings. They will grow into whatever they're raised to be. Here they were brought up to be vicious beasts. With a different environment and kinder handling, they can become gentle beings who may at some point in time return our kindness."

Ram shook his head and walked out of the room. He had no choice but to acquiesce to Commander Camdus, but he didn't have to like it. The best thing for him to do now would be to get back to Mara and try to regain some sense of sanity in his life.

Camdus followed him out, "Ram, wait a minute. Listen, we're going to need someone to help with the supervision of Q'Door Hold. How would you feel about taking on that task?"

Ram turned, astonished that the Commander would make such an offer, especially now. "No, Sir. I want to start over with a new tredon herd, maybe in one of the valleys this time. I think Mara would like that better. Besides, I'm not a soldier anymore. I'm a farmer now. There are far more qualified men who might like a posting here."

Camdus had expected as much. "All right, I respect that. But if you change your mind, let me know."

He figured that Grunden and Stadar could handle it. They were both smart and resourceful. They could be instrumental in strengthening the REG presence on Creedor. Of course, he'd have to convince Jarlod of the wisdom of this. But then there was the matter of Weilz, who to Camdus was a changeling of a different kind and far more dangerous. With the evidence Camdus had of Weilz' treachery against the Empire, he was fairly sure that Jarlod would handle him as harshly as Weilz had handled those who got in his way. Camdus could understand why Weilz wanted to hurt Jarlod, but he didn't have to become a traitor to do it. His selfish quest for revenge had jeopardized the entire Reglon Empire. And Camdus was also keenly aware that he would have to deal with Jarlod's wickedness sooner or later. He didn't know when or where, but it was inevitable. However, for the time being, he had to tread carefully around the volatile Emperor.

His communicator buzzed to life. A message was coming in from a

Reglon warship that Jarlod finally sent to help round up the intruders.

Camdus shook his head and let the ship's captain know what happened and what he needed to wrap up the operation here.

Soon there were Reglon soldiers fanning out to search the Hold. Thankfully, Willem had given his son a crash course in handling Sorbeau. Once he was comfortable with his newest protector, Camdus sent him after the beasts that had escaped when the Reglon guardian first appeared.

But the young changelings were still babies and he simply could not allow them to be harmed. He knew that it would be some time before their alternate shapes were known. So, for now, they were taken to Seelah. She'd make sure they were treated kindly. He prayed he was right to save them.

Bone weary as he was, Camdus made sure the Q'Aron prisoners were taken to await military trial on cold, rocky, and foreboding Vuthral. Prisoners there had to adjust to the short days, which consisted of four hours of daylight, twelve hours of darkness, and eight hours of twilight. They also were affected by the heavy cloud cover that perpetually shadowed the asteroid's surface. All in all, Vuthral was the perfect location for holding military prisoners. Some didn't survive the gloom, but the ones who were successfully reprogrammed became valuable members of the REG Counterintelligence Corps.

Finally, with Q'Door Hold secured, Camdus and his troops along with his father and Tomer were transported back to his ship.

At the first opportunity, Camdus sent a holographic report to Jarlod, who finally understood the severity of the situation.

The arrogant Emperor reluctantly re-commissioned the Medic Corps to handle the health issues on Creedor much to the relief of the Creedorians. The antiviral for the disease had been dispensed by a small army of medics trained on the fly by Slogar and Waldo. The Creedorians saw an almost immediate drop in the death rate. They once again had hope.

Camdus made sure the families that had been separated for so long were reunited. He personally arranged for the release and relocation of the first family Slogar had helped all those years ago – without asking Jarlod's permission. The parents had grown older and their asthmatic son had grown up while locked away in that nearly forgotten tower. He made sure Slogar had their new address so he could visit them. Camdus was pretty sure the doctor still blamed himself for their incarceration all these years and that at least in part, had driven his cravings. Now he could let go of that guilt.

Alone and totally exhausted, Camdus went back to his quarters and washed the filth of battle from his body. That was a lot easier than washing it from his mind, but he knew he had to let it go. He was just settling into his chair for some long overdue rest when he was alerted to a visitor requesting entry.

When the door swooshed closed behind her, Rayalla Enright stood there unsure of what to say or if she'd made a huge mistake in coming here. Her heart was thudding in her chest. With all the courage she could muster, she whispered his name half hoping he'd send her away. But his own heart was racing. The only woman he'd ever cared for was standing right here in front of him. He stood up and embraced her. They talked until she read the tiredness in his eyes.

After she left, his fell asleep and dreamed about life with Rayalla.

But sometime later, in the wee hours of the morning, Camdus awoke with the knowledge that the fight wasn't over. He had to stop the Q'Arons from completing their weapons. And he knew just who he was going to tap to go with him.

He dressed quickly, raced to his office, and called his team together. When they were all there, he told them what they already suspected.

"Men, we have a mission."

THE CALL

Rax sat languidly on the bank of the stream behind his home. He cherished this time away from battle, away from riding. He watched as Evy and their children splashed each other in the shallow water.

The massive meal Evy had prepared for them was just settling when he sensed the call.

He waded into the water, fully clothed, and hugged his wife. She looked up at her husband. He didn't have to say a word – she knew.

He gently kissed Zil on the cheek and playfully shoulder-punched Kel. With a soft pop, Rax left his home for yet another adventure in the Reglon Empire.

About the Author

Gail Morgan McRae is the author of the Reglon Empire Series. Creedor is the first part, followed by Hellritch, and then Dunmyrr rounding out the trilogy. But she's pretty sure that there will be more.

She lives in a small southeastern North Carolina town with her husband Philip, their rescue dog Louise, and their fearless cat Tammy. The author enjoys writing, painting, and singing. She and her family attend the little church down the road, where she is a member of the choir.

She has been a jack-of-all-trades including truck driver (10-wheel, not 18!), English teacher, candy counter clerk, mediator, project director, and property manager. She hopes to continue producing the stories that spring from her own rich experiences and her vivid imagination.

Made in the USA
Columbia, SC
03 March 2020